# Unforgettable Novels of the West by

# JACK BALLAS

## THE HARD LAND

Though Jess Sanford left Simon Bauman for dead, the man is still alive. And there's one thing more relentless than the law: a shamed son with all the wealth of the Bauman family behind him . . .

## IRON HORSE WARRIOR

Hunting for his brother's killer, Chance Tenery takes a job on the Union Pacific Railroad and begins a long fight for his honor, his life, and the woman he comes to love . . .

## ANGEL FIRE

When Kurt Buckner agrees to escort a woman to the Colorado Territory, he finds that hostile Indians are no danger—compared to the three men who want her dead . . .

## POWDER RIVER

Case Gentry is no longer a Texas Ranger. But the night a two-bit gunhand rides up to his cabin, he has to bring back every instinct to survive . . .

## GUN BOSS

Raised by an Apache tribe, Trace Gundy never forgot their lessons in survival. Now, to avenge the loss of his beloved wife, he must call upon the fighting spirit he learned as a boy . . .

# BANDIDO CABALLERO

## JACK BALLAS

BERKLEY BOOKS, NEW YORK

BANDIDO CABALLERO

A Berkley Book / published by arrangement with
the author

PRINTING HISTORY
Berkley edition / July 1997

The Putnam Berkley World Wide Web site address is
http://www.berkley.com

ISBN: 0-425-15956-6

PRINTED IN THE UNITED STATES OF AMERICA

10  9  8  7  6  5  4  3  2  1

*In memory of Robert Sanchez,*
*my best WWII combat buddy, a man who stood*
*and fought, and my friend until his last long ride.*
*I love you, Bob.*

# BANDIDO CABALLERO

# CHAPTER

## 1

LYING ON HIS BUNK, SWEATING, TRYING NOT TO THINK, Tom Fallon stared at the small barred window far above his head, waiting. At any moment Union soldiers would escort him to the brick wall, blindfold him, and fire bullets into his body. That's what they did to Confederate spies.

They'd not taught courses at the Virginia Military Institute on how to die. Maybe if they had he'd not have graduated with honors. But now, after attempting two escapes, and getting shot in the leg once for his efforts, he resigned himself to feeling bullets tear through him. His only consolation? The feeling would last but a fleeting moment. Then nothing.

He looked at his filthy clothing with revulsion. He'd not had a bath since they captured him a month before Lee surrendered. That had been two months ago. Body lice crawled over every inch of him. He'd not bathed, shaved, or had a change of clothes in that time. And the stench—human excrement, vomit, dirty bodies, and garbage, much of it in his cell—combined to make him want to stop breathing. The stench of this Union prison, not many miles outside of Washington, D.C., would foul the air for miles around. And, worse yet, he'd never smell the clean air of Texas again.

A rhythmic clomp of boots sounded in the dark corridor outside his cell. The metallic grating of a key clinked in the lock only two feet away. The door squealed on rusty hinges and swung open. A hard-bitten old sergeant came in and jerked him to his feet.

Fallon stared from the sergeant to the squad of soldiers standing outside his world of two months. His stomach churned; his throat muscles tightened, choking him; brassy fear flowed under his tongue. So this was how it all ended.

He straightened, squared his shoulders, and looked the noncom in the eye. He was damned if he'd give them the satisfaction of showing fear. Despite his determination, he tried three times to swallow the lump in his throat. It stayed there.

Lapsing into his West Texas drawl, he said, "Well, y'all finally got round to it, huh, Sarge. You already let most of the Rebs go home." He shot the sergeant an insolent grin. "But I ain't goin' home, am I? You gonna shoot me in a few minutes. Well, damn you. Have a good time of it."

The sergeant only stared at him and pushed him out the door, and the troops fell in on each side.

When they opened the gates to the outside world, Fallon blinked several times and squinted against the sudden brightness. He'd not seen sunshine since prison doors slammed behind him.

*The wall* stood only twenty or so feet away, with bullet pocks and splatterings of flesh and blood gouged deep into its brick surface. Automatically he turned toward it.

"You ain't headed for that wall, Reb—yet. Come with us." The sergeant ordered the men to a barracks close by. Inside, they stripped him, deloused him, cut his hair, and gave him a razor with which to shave. Through the whole operation he wondered what the hell difference it made whether he died clean or filthy, but he was glad for the chance to experience once again the feel of warm water and soap.

Finished with the scrub down, they took him to another room and tossed him clean garments, including a Confederate uniform befitting his rank of major. At least he wouldn't die a hypocrite.

Fallon dressed and, feeling like a human being, followed the sergeant outside, where they loaded him into a wagon of solid iron walls with a small window at the top. The Union non-com locked the door and ordered his men to mount, and they drove off.

After hours of sweating in the iron oven of a vehicle, bumping and clanking over rutted roads, dust boiling through cracks in the wagon bottom, Fallon guessed they entered some sort of city. The bumps got regular, like perhaps they traveled over cobblestones. Finally the wagon stopped. The noise ceased. The door opened. A wide expanse of green lawn and beautiful shade trees spread before him. Not more than ten yards to his right—the White House.

"Git out. The President wants to see you."

Fallon could only stare. What would the President of the United States want with him? Then it hit home. Maybe he wasn't going to face a firing squad after all. Or perhaps Andrew Johnson would have him driven through the streets in chains to show the people what a spy looked like, or, or . . .

"Git out, Reb. Ain't gonna keep the President waitin'. Brush your uniform, git some of the dust outta it."

Fallon slapped with his hat at his trousers and the shoulders of his tunic, then looked to the sergeant. He thought to make a run for it, but there were too many rifles loaded and ready for just such an act. Instead of running, he said, "Let's go."

They escorted him to the President's office, where marines stood guard, one at each side of the double doors. One of them went in, apparently to announce the prisoner.

President Johnson came to the door, looked at the sergeant, and dismissed him. "Come in, Major. Meet Secretary of State Seward."

Fallon stood at rigid attention and saluted them both.

"Relax, Major Fallon. Have a seat. I have a proposition for you, if your loyalties rest in the right place."

Fallon now decided to use grammar like his mother taught him, and what he'd learned while attending VMI. "Mr. President, I'm afraid I don't fully understand, so I'll set you straight, then there'll be no doubt. If you mean my loyalties to my state and to my country, my first loyalty is to Texas, and my second is to my country."

Seward and Johnson exchanged glances. Seward smiled. "And, Major, to which country do you refer?"

"My country, Mr. Secretary, before we lost the war was the Confederate States of America. Today, my country is the United States of America, and I've loved it all my life. I fought for the Confederacy because my home is there. My parents and my friends are there. It was a hard decision I made, but I just flat couldn't turn against home folks; I never would. That may be hard for you to understand, sir, but that's the way it is."

His face set into a stubborn look even though he tried to show no emotion. "Reckon under the same circumstances I'd make the same choice today."

Seward frowned. "You mean, if we went to war today, you'd again fight for the Confederacy?"

Fallon cast him a hard look. "Mr. Secretary, that's exactly what I mean, 'less my folks moved north of the Mason Dixon line, and that's not likely."

The President smiled. "Son, that's not as hard for me to understand as you might think." He cleared his throat and glanced at Seward, then back to Fallon. "Major, I have an assignment I need a good man to undertake. It came down to you because I'm told you are very good with both rifle and revolver, you speak Spanish fluently," he smiled, "and your English grammar is excellent when you choose to make it so, although I understand you prefer to 'talk Texan.' "

Fallon, sitting stiffly on the edge of his chair, grinned.

"That's right, Mr. President. Reckon they ain't nothing sweeter to the tongue than talkin' with a bunch o' good ole boys down yonder."

Johnson and Seward laughed. "Relax, son. We won't bite you." The President waited until Fallon made himself comfortable, then continued. "You were a Confederate spy during the war, and I don't mind saying you gave us fits with your ability to infiltrate our lines, get what you wanted, be it information or supplies, and return to your troops. I've heard it said you had to be part Indian, and the rest ghost, to do the things you did."

"Sir, I come from Apache country. A man learns to get around kinda quiet like if he figures to keep his hair."

Seward picked up a small silver bell, glanced at Johnson, who nodded, then shook it. In only a moment a servant rolled a coffee service into the room, served them, and withdrew as quietly as he'd entered.

The President sipped his coffee, and blew between pursed lips. "Whew, that's hot." He settled himself in his chair. "Now, Major, here's my proposition. You don't have to do as I ask, but it would be a great service to your country if you would."

He looked Fallon straight in the eye. "Your answer will have nothing to do with your freedom. I intend to turn you loose regardless. The only reason we detained you as long as we did was to investigate your background." He smiled. "And, of course, we found you to be even better than reported."

The President stared at him a moment, then, like a master salesman, began to maneuver him into an answer before he stated the proposal. "I'm prepared to offer you a commission of colonel in whatever Army outfit you choose, and if you desire, I'll make it a permanent commission on completion of your assignment."

Fallon allowed a slight smile to crinkle the corners of his lips. "You ain't said what I gotta do for that, Mr. President."

Johnson studied the grounds in the bottom of his cup a moment, wondering how much he should tell Fallon, then decided with all that was at stake he had no choice but to tell him as much as he knew. He pinned Fallon with a spearlike gaze. "All right, here it is." He leaned forward in his chair. "I'm taking your word as to your loyalty, and I can't impress on you enough the importance of keeping secret what I'm about to tell you." He took another swallow of his coffee, again leaned back in his chair, and continued. "Napoleon's forces are spread quite thin, and his money is getting even thinner. Prussian forces are pushing Austria, France's ally, to the wall. I believe that to support his effort in Austria Napoleon will be forced to pull many of his troops from Mexico—and the support of Maximilian, who he installed as emperor down there—but I don't expect that to happen soon enough to do the United States any good.

"Our people are tired of war, tired of seeing their young men come home maimed, sick, missing arms and legs—or not coming home at all. And, Major Fallon, if by chance Napoleon manages to keep his troops on Mexican soil, despite violation of the Monroe Doctrine, we'll have no choice but to go to war against them."

Johnson let his last words hang between them a moment, then pinned Fallon with a hard, unbending stare. "This is where you come in, Major. It is a plan I believe will work or I would not ask it of you. I want you to support Benito Juárez in any way you can. Primarily, you're to ferret out information on gold shipments from Napoleon to Maximilian, hold up those shipments on Mexican soil, and see that Juárez gets the gold. Our intelligence tells me France is even lower on funds than we previously believed. Any loss will hurt them desperately."

He sat forward, shuffled a stack of papers in front of him, and again looked at Fallon. His voice soft, he said, "The catch is, you'll be alone. You'll dress as a civilian. If you're caught, we'll deny having ever heard of you. Even if it is the United States law that catches you and wishes to hang you, we'll do nothing."

He took another swallow of coffee, and smiled. "If

that's not hard enough, Juárez knows nothing of this, and is to remain ignorant of U.S. participation in his war. So, Major, you must find some way to meet him without getting shot in the process.''

Fallon's gut tightened, putting the lie to the grin he showed the President. ''Damn, sir, why you bein' so nice to me? Sending one man to defeat Maximilian.'' He frowned, and slipped back into good grammar. ''Another thing that puzzles me, sir, what is the connection between Napoleon and Maximilian?''

The President frowned, obviously sorting his knowledge of history, then nodded. ''Maximilian, Archduke of Austria, was a way for Napoleon to get a foothold in the Americas. He had two reasons for wanting to do that; he wanted to further his own imperialistic desires, and to collect a war debt owed France by Mexico.

''Conservative Mexicans, and the Catholic Church, conspired with Napoleon to seat Maximilian as emperor, and Major Fallon, he did just that, but went even further, when he seated Maximilian, he did it with French troops—they've been there ever since.''

Johnson ignored Fallon's sarcasm as to why he was being so good to him. ''After you get the French off of Mexican soil, you'll be free to accept the permanent commission and further serve your country.'' He frowned. ''You seem uncomfortable. What's the matter?''

In his thickest Texanese, Fallon said, '' 'Side from wantin' to smoke my pipe, usin' some o' your tobacco of course—ain't had none of my own since y'all insisted I be your guest—don't know as anythin' much is the matter, less'n o' course the thought of a brand new rope around my neck gives me a slight bit of discomfort. But heck, maybe I'm overly squeamish. Cain't understand why a li'l ole thing like gettin' hanged would make me uncomfortable.''

Johnson and Seward laughed. The President pushed his humidor of tobacco across the desk. ''Smoke, then give me your answer.''

Fallon took his time packing and lighting his pipe,

while thinking of Johnson's offer, then squinted through a cloud of smoke and nodded. "Mr. President, I b'lieve you done said it fair an' square, but I got a few things I want settled before I say yes.

"First off, I want one o' them Colt revolvers, three spare cylinders for it, a belt an' holster, not of Army issue, a Henry rifle, and the best unbranded black horse you can find in this part of the country." He squirmed, ashamed to ask for his next item. "An', Sir, I'm gonna need some pocket change to travel on if you reckon you could round up a few dollars."

He frowned, then grinned. "Reckon 'fore I leave here I oughtta change to jeans along with a civilian shirt. Ain't gonna look too good for a Confederate officer to come strollin' outta your office.

"Too, reckon I want you to be the one to swear me in. I'll look for you to create a service file you could forward to my folks if anything happens to me. They ain't gonna understand me just up an' leavin' the ranch without sayin' nothin'. After me bein' gone so long durin' the war, they're gonna be mighty hurt. My service folder would give them a right warm feelin', knowin' I served the United States."

A few hours later, all of his wishes granted, Fallon was walked to the door by Johnson. "Best of luck, son. You're going to need it—and thanks. You have no idea how much this means to your country. If it works, you can rest peacefully knowing you've saved more American lives than we could count, despite the hard, often savage things you may have to do."

Fallon stepped toward the door, stopped, and asked, "Sir, where is Juárez supposed to be?"

Johnson looked at his calendar. "June 15, 1865. Last I heard, he was still in Chihuahua, but he moves every time Maximilian's troops get close."

Fallon nodded. "Thank you, sir. I'll do the best job I know how. Good-bye, Mr. President, and you, Mr. Secretary."

One of the marines outside the President's office escorted him down the stairs and on to the outside entrance. The marine grinned and said, "Good luck, *Colonel,* sir." He pointed at a saddled black Morgan horse standing under the porte cochere at the main entrance.

Fallon wondered how often luxurious carriages had pulled under the shelter to discharge the President's distinguished guests. He also wondered, since the marine knew the President had made him a colonel, how much the honor guards standing outside the oval office heard during any normal day.

Fallon stood by his horse, loaded his weapons, toed the stirrup, and left.

The first few hours after leaving the White House he rode across familiar country, country he'd crossed many times wearing the Confederate gray, or sneaking between Union lines to garner information.

Not until that night, as he sat by his fire to the west of Alexandria, Virginia, did it sink in that he'd not stand in front of a stone wall and feel the bite of bullets pierce his body. It was a strange feeling. He'd become so accustomed to the thought of his future as no more than a few minutes, that being able to think of next week, or next month, tended to confuse him.

Finally, he accepted being able to slow things down and do them at his leisure, not having to live each moment as though it were his last. It was a good feeling.

Fallon took it easy. He had half the continent to cross, and wanted to get to El Paso del Norte in good physical shape. Two months as a prisoner of war, short rations, and no exercise had left him in poor shape. Too, he didn't want to ride the big black Morgan horse into the ground. It was one of the best horses he'd ever ridden. He stopped early every night to let the black graze, and the infrequent times he came on a settlement, he fed the horse grain.

While traveling, he studied on the best way to find when and how the French sent gold to Maximilian. He decided, before heading for El Paso del Norte, to go to the nearest seaport and watch cargo vessels, see if he might pick up information in that manner.

In St. Louis he had the feeling for the first time since going off to war that he was back in the West. Looking at the town, teeming with riverboatmen, frontiersmen, cattlemen, and pioneers ready to trek into the unknown wilderness, gave him a greater sense of freedom than he'd known in years. It also gave him a hard knot between his shoulder blades—a feeling of danger.

Men, dirty, hard-looking, gave the black horse he rode looks of greed, envy, looks that caused him to slip the leather thong off the hammer of his Colt.

That night, he studied on whether to stay in a hotel or sleep in the livery with his horse. The livery won.

After sitting in a cafe where he could watch the black while eating his supper, he went directly to the livery and bedded down in the stall where his horse was stabled. He'd had a long day in the saddle and soon slept.

Fallon came awake, his senses searching for what had wakened him. He didn't move, but his ears searched for noise. Something stirred outside the stall. A soft, stealthy step brushed through loose hay; cloth rubbed against boards. Then, on silent hinges, the stall gate swung outward.

His holstered .44 lay by his head. He eased his hand to the walnut grips, pulled the Colt from its holster, and waited. The intruder slipped a hackamore over the black's head, and pulled him toward the entrance to the stall. "Turn loose that horse, an' grab a handful o' sky."

At Fallon's words, the horse thief spun toward his voice, his hand sweeping for his side gun. Fallon thumbed off a shot. The intruder stumbled back, and, his revolver now in hand, he fired toward Fallon's voice. The slug buried itself in the boards alongside his head. Fallon fired again. The thief dropped his weapon, stumbled back another step, and fell to the side. Fallon put on his hat, stood, and walked in stockinged feet toward the stretched-out gunman.

"Y'all through shootin'?" The voice came from the back of the stable.

Fallon glanced toward the man who'd spoken. "Yeah,

light a lantern. Somebody tried to steal my horse. I shot 'im.''

A match flared at the back of the stable, then a lamp threw out its weak light. The liveryman walked to stand over the thief, turned his head to look at Fallon, and said, ''Drilled dead center one shot, the other'n got 'im in the belly. Reckon I better get the law.'' While walking toward the doorway, he said over his shoulder, ''You ain't got nothin' to worry 'bout, young'un. I've had trouble with this one before.''

The marshal came, told Fallon he'd saved him some trouble, and let him go. Within minutes, although it was only three o'clock in the morning, Fallon saddled, packed his gear, and rode out.

ALMOST A MONTH LATER, FALLON CROSSED THE BORDER into Mexico at Matamoros, which, although not a seaport, was close to the Gulf of Mexico, where he watched each ship come in from New Orleans, or direct from France. If they off-loaded cargo to freight wagons, some of it in obviously small, heavy bags, he logged that shipment down as one he'd hold up on the chance that what he'd seen was gold.

He stationed himself along the trail to Monterrey, and, his face bandanna-covered, he held up the wagons. After two of these holdups, he frowned. He was getting practice at banditry, but his take was minimal. Juárez could have bought few arms and supplies with what Fallon had been able to get.

Finally, about late June, Fallon knew he had to see Juárez, see if he had an intelligence organization across the border in the United States, an organization that could feed him information about gold shipments worth sticking his neck out for, one which would benefit *El Presidente*. He saddled the black and headed toward El Paso del Norte.

In Laredo, he had a blacksmith forge him a huge Bowie knife. Now all he lacked to feel fully armed was a throwing knife. He figured to find what he wanted in El Paso

del Norte; he'd bought one there before the war and liked
its heft.

In El Paso he found out that Juárez was still in Chihuahua, and he also heard that Johnson and Seward were
getting more irritated with French troops being in Mexico.

Seward issued pointed statements for the Frenchies to
go home. Rumors had it that one of the United States'
famed war generals would be sent to the border with many
troops. Fallon filled three canteens and set out for Chihuahua.

He rode into town about a week and a half later. He
went to Juárez's headquarters and asked to see *El Presidente*. The single trooper at the door to the headquarters
building refused him permission.

Fallon made as though to leave and, while turning,
pulled his Bowie knife, twisted, and held it to the guard's
throat. "Reckon you didn't get it straight, soldier. I'm
tellin' you I'm gonna see *El Presidente*. I don't mean
tomorrow; I'm talkin' 'bout right now.'' The Bowie at his
throat convinced the guard that Juárez waited anxiously
to meet *Señor* Fallon.

In the room, Fallon walked toward Juárez's desk, leaving the guard standing at the door. Juárez glanced at the
sentry. "Stay until I determine what this man wants. Keep
your rifle on him, and shoot if he makes a suspicious
move.''

Fallon studied Juárez while walking to his desk. He was
a man of less than medium height, dark, with definite
Indian features, and a large scar across his face. Fallon
had heard the man was a full-blood Zapotec; now he believed it.

Juárez's desk, a chair pulled up to a box, was the only
place Fallon saw where he could place the contents of his
pockets. He dropped several small bags to the top of the
box.

Juárez looked from the bags to Fallon and, speaking
Spanish, asked, "What is this, *señor*?'' He searched Fallon's face. "I don't believe I know you.''

Fallon, knowing his Spanish was as good as any Spaniard's, and for now wanting to leave the impression he was Mexican, said, "No, *Señor Presidente,* you do not know me, but I hope in the future you will know me well. Those bags hold a small token—gold. I have taken them from Imperialists. I'm sorry they don't hold more, but I must now determine when the French are shipping an amount of substantial value, then I propose to relieve them of it and deliver the prize to you."

Juárez studied him a moment, cocked an eyebrow, and smiled, obviously not believing him. "And, *señor,* why would you do this thing? What will you gain from such acts?"

Fallon smiled, but his gut was tight as a bowstring. From all he'd heard, he knew the little Zapotec would have him shot in an instant. He had to make his reason strong enough that *El Presidente* would believe him. He spread his hands at his side. "I will gain only my poor worthless life, *Señor Presidente.* There are those, friendly to you, who will have me killed if I do not do as they order. I would not be safe anywhere in the world. I am not at liberty to tell you who they are until you rid our country of the hated French Imperialists; then I'll be free to tell you all. I can only say for now, *señor,* you have very powerful friends."

Juárez cleared his throat, looked at the bags, and almost in a whisper said, "It is time I found powerful friends somewhere." He looked from the gold to Fallon. "Where is your home, *señor?*"

Fallon shook his head. "I am not free to tell you even that much, *Señor Presidente.* This much I can tell you if you will trust me. I will deliver the gold I collect directly to you. I will not ever again show my face to your troops; there are some who might recognize me, so I'll ask you to give them the word when a man wearing a bandanna comes into camp that he be brought to you with his face covered. I ask this because I must associate with Imperialists to find out when and where they'll have shipments."

Juárez picked up a quill pen, put it down, shuffled papers on his desk—obviously wanting to believe Fallon, but too cagey to buy his story out of hand. Finally, he sat straight, stiff, and looked into Fallon's eyes. "I do not know why I should believe you, except now I will not, cannot, turn aside a hand offered in friendship. I'll tell you when and where gold will be shipped this one time. I can't send my own men to take it. I need them here."

He then told Fallon about the shipment. Fallon knew all the while he was being tested. Juárez was too smart a man to trust anyone, especially one he had reason to believe was of the Spanish gentry, judging by his use of the language, and the black hair and green eyes often associated with those of pure Spanish blood, although some Spaniards had red or blond hair.

When Fallon left *El Presidente,* he had all the information he needed to pull his first big-time holdup.

He pulled it off, and delivered the gold, not a great amount, but every bit helped. Juárez needed money. His troops were in rags, and needed weapons and ammunition.

From Fallon's own intelligence, he heard about three more shipments, and delivered that gold to Juárez also. By now, *El Presidente* had begun to trust him, and he'd not once had to show his face before being escorted to see Juárez.

Then he heard of a shipment he'd try for in his next holdup, one which would enrich the Republic's coffers far more than the ones he'd pulled thus far.

# CHAPTER

2

TOM FALLON HELD HIS HORSE'S NOSE AND SQUINTED against the brassy white glare of the northern Mexico sun. The air had a faint smell of dust, dust that settled over clothes, in hair, and the back of one's throat.

More than a mile down the trail, a cloud boiled toward the sky. At its leading edge lumbered a large, luxurious coach. Fallon counted eight riders, four on each side of the vehicle. He checked his weapons.

A glance at his surroundings showed large boulders nested close to the road. The trail curved around a couple of the larger rocks, and straightened coming out of the last curve. Fallon took his position where the coach would have to slow for the first curve. He had chosen well.

During the fifteen-minute wait for the coach to approach, he breathed deeply, trying to relax his taut nerves. Still, a touch of fear, bolstered by excitement, quickened his heartbeat and caused hot saliva to flow under his tongue. If the coach's escort chose to fight, eight to one made for poor odds, and he didn't know how many men might be inside the bouncing, tossing vehicle. He tried to shrug it off, thinking that if anyone was worth putting himself in jeopardy for, the small, caring man for whom he committed this act would stand at the head of the line.

When the coach drew within about seventy-five feet, Fallon pushed the roiling fear to the back of his mind, pulled his bandanna up over his nose, and stepped into the trail, revolver leveled.

The driver sawed on the straps, slowing the team and stopping the coach. "Hands high," Fallon yelled in Spanish, swallowing the fear trying to choke him. "Be wary, men," he called, as though he had men hidden in the rocks. "Keep your rifles trained, one on each man."

Standing close enough to the nearest boulder so he could dive out of harm's way, he motioned to the escort with his saddle gun. "All eight of you come to this side of the coach."

A glance showed each of them, eyes riveted on the rocks, searching for men who might be there while they edged their horses around the coach and drew up in front of it. Fallon let out a pent-up breath. So far, so good.

Then, still talking to his imaginary band of bandits, he yelled, "If a gun pokes from the window of the coach, riddle the whole thing with shots." He again trained his orders toward the escort. "Now, using only the tips of your fingers, pull your saddle guns and drop them to the ground, then drop your *pistolas* alongside 'em." He watched while they did as they'd been told, but he couldn't watch them all. As he was about to turn his attention to the coach, a flash of movement within the group of horsemen pulled his eyes and his six-shooter's aim in that direction.

Two shots sounding almost as one punctured the still air. Before Fallon could swing his eyes to look at the other riders, two black holes opened in one rider's chest, knocking him from the saddle. Fallon had fired only once.

Every muscle in his back knotted painfully. The second shot had come from the rocks behind him. He'd thought until now he was alone, but he hadn't searched the boulders when he took his stand. If he lived, this would be another lesson in how to prepare for a holdup.

He stood still, waiting for a shot to tear through his

back, open a huge hole in his chest, and take his life as though snuffing a candle. It didn't come. Instead, a voice, with only a slight Spanish accent, sounded from the boulders.

"Ah. Do not worry, *señor*. You 'ave start this job, now finish it. I, and our men, will hold these *hombres* from shooting you."

Fallon wanted to look over his shoulder, see if he could spot the man who'd horned in on his game, but didn't dare. If he drew the stranger's attention, and the guards saw that they weren't being watched closely, they would bring whatever weapons they'd not gotten rid of into play, and once the firing started—he would be the target of the guards and perhaps the intruder. He'd play the hand like the stranger called it.

Fallon motioned with his six-shooter for the escort to move away from their weapons. "Sit your horses quietly and you won't get hurt." He stepped farther into the trail and walked to the coach, stopping short of the windows. "If any in there has a gun, throw it out. My men will kill any who tries a shot."

"I alone am in here, *señor*, and I have no *pistola*. What is it you wish of me?" The voice was that of a woman, a young woman. He heard no trace of fear.

Fallon felt a tinge of admiration for the woman, but not enough to let his guard down. Knowing the passenger's attention was focused on the side where he stood, and hoping his accomplice would keep things under control there, he ducked under the coach and came up on the opposite side. He eased his head above the edge of the window and peered in.

The woman had spoken the truth. She was alone, and sat with her back toward him, facing the side from which he'd first spoken. "*Señorita*, it is well you speak the truth. I do not wish to hurt you."

She twisted to look at him, and Fallon gazed into the bluest eyes he'd seen, and, contrasting with the black mantilla she wore, her hair shone like burnished copper. Her mouth opened slightly to form an O. Fallon smiled behind his bandanna. "*Señorita,* permit me to say you are the most beautiful woman I've ever met, and of course I would not hurt you. All I want is the gold you are carrying—gold for Maximilian's coffers."

"But, *señor,* we carry no gold, only my meager funds for food and lodging during this trip."

"*Señorita,* it is not my habit to doubt the words of a beautiful woman, but I've been told there are some who twist the truth a mite. Even so, perhaps you were not told what your coach is carrying. Please step to the ground while I search your vehicle." Fallon opened the door and helped her step down, aware that she searched what she could see of his face. Her eyes seemed to penetrate the bandanna pulled high on his nose.

Standing straight, her head tilted to look into his eyes, and still devoid of fear, she said, "*Señor,* you are not the usual run of border trash I would expect to be performing such a low act. Why do you do this thing to me?"

She stood only a couple of inches over five feet by Fallon's guess, a full foot shorter than him, but she somehow made it seem she was of equal size and height.

"*Señorita?* Or should I say *mam'selle*? I do nothing to you—only to your gold." He took her reticule from her arm, hefted it, reached inside, and removed a small-caliber revolver. He allowed himself a slight smile, then his voice hardened. "Now, stand aside, *por favor;* I must get out of here before your French troops arrive."

She stepped aside. Fallon watched her wilt. Some of her bravado had left her when he removed her gun. He entered the coach. Under the cushions, he found two heavy bags. He shook them. They clinked. He nodded, and again let a smile crease his lips. After ensuring he'd found all the inside of the coach had to offer, he climbed to the top and searched the front and rear boots, finding two more sacks, of weight equaling those he'd found inside.

"You—you are a scoundrel. You dress like a gentleman, speak like a gentleman, but you have the heart of a villain. Who else would take gold from a poor defenseless woman?''

Fallon smiled under his bandanna. Somehow he couldn't imagine this woman as defenseless under any circumstance. ''Ah, but, *señorita,* I take your gold not for myself but for one who needs it more than either of us, so of course you will pardon me.'' His voice hardened, ''Now, get in the coach.''

Fallon walked to the other side of the coach. When there, he swept her mounted guard with a glance. ''Stay on your horses. Leave your weapons where they are, and . . .'' A thought broke into his words. He needed an extra horse for the gold and weapons. ''Which of you men is in charge?''

A tall man, with black hair and a mustache, nodded. ''I, *Cápitan* Phillipe Escobar am in charge, *señor,* and unless you kill me, I'll hunt you down with many troops.''

''*If* you get anywhere to find troops, Captain. Now, dismount. You'll ride in the coach with the *señorita.* I need your horse.''

Reluctantly, and mouthing threats all the while, Escobar dismounted and entered the coach. Fallon waved his handgun toward the coachman. ''Move out. And *muchas gracias* for the gift, *señorita.*''

Standing in the middle of the hot, dusty trail, Fallon watched the heavy coach gain momentum, stirring a cloud of dust. He stood with his back to the boulders, a hard knot drawing his back muscles tight. ''All right, *señor,* I have finished the job, now what do we do?''

''Why, *Señor Bandido Caballero,* I know of you from our *presidente,* and I know you have no intention of keeping that gold for yourself. Turn around. I mean you no harm.''

Fallon turned slowly. The man facing him, slender, tall, only a couple of inches less than his own six-feet-two, stood relaxed, but not enough so he couldn't fire the handgun in his right hand.

''You mean me no harm, yet you hold a gun on me?''

The man wore no bandanna about his face. He smiled.

"*Sí, caballero,* I hold thees gun to make certain you do not shoot *me.* You see, knowing who you are, I also know you can get that six-shooter of yours in action *mucho rapido,* and I hear you do not miss." He shrugged, then dropped his gun into its holster. "But I will trust you not to shoot me." His eyes shifted to the coach growing small in the distance. "If we are to keep others from shooting us, we must leave pronto."

Fallon reached to pull the bandanna from his face. "No, *señor,* do not uncover your face. It is best I know you only as the *Bandido Caballero,* or as you *Americanos* would say, the gentleman bandit. If we should meet in more polite company, and that is not entirely unlikely considering we're both what most would call 'of the gentry,' I will be unable to give away who you are."

"How do you know I'm an *Americano*?"

The stranger shrugged. "Only a guess, *señor,* but I imagine a pretty good one."

Fallon led the captain's horse, with the bags of gold and the soldiers' weapons firmly attached to the saddle, to his own big black horse. He toed the stirrup, climbed to the saddle, and looked at the man who'd horned in on his act. "*Como se llama?*"

"Juan Valdez, *señor,* one of *El Presidente's* most trusted men. He has told me about you."

Fallon's gut tightened. His hand dropped close to his six-gun. "You're with Benito Juárez? If you're one of the Valdez family who owns half of the state to the west of us, I'm surprised."

Valdez folded his hands on his saddle horn. "I hope not surprised enough to draw that weapon and kill me, *señor.*" He kneed his horse around to ride at Fallon's side. "You see, the only way my family could keep our lands was to *appear* to sympathize with Maximilian's cause. We do not, *señor. Mi papa* and *El Presidente* are good friends. They went to school together. It serves Juárez best if none know our true loyalty. We attend French functions without suspicion." He grinned. "We learn much that way. And I suspect you learn about these gold and silver shipments in a like manner.''

They spoke in Spanish. Fallon frowned, then asked, "You speak English?"

Valdez nodded. "As well as you speak my language, *señor*."

Fallon relaxed enough to lapse into his west Texas vernacular. "If you figure I get information the same way you do, keep it to yourself. You'd purely spoil all my fun, not to mention you'd most likely get me killed."

While they rode, Fallon studied Valdez from the corners of his eyes. He liked the man, with his nonchalant attitude and the way he thought fast and adapted to a situation. He pondered asking him to join him in his life of banditry. After giving it hard thought, he shook his head. President Johnson had inferred he was to act alone. He had accepted the conditions laid down by his president. He was a man of his word.

Fallon kept his horse to rocky terrain, trying to leave as little sign as possible. If the captain came back with troops, they would no doubt have a Yaqui scout with them, and a Yaqui could track wind across glass.

He looked at Valdez. "We'd better split up, and you'd do best to head somewhere away from your father's hacienda. I'm gonna do some trail smudgin' to keep from leading them toward Juárez's camp."

"You know where *El Presidente* is?"

Fallon grinned. "Does anybody ever know where he is? Naw, I don't know—but I got a good idea. I'll find 'im. I always do."

Valdez reined his horse to the side. "Good luck, *amigo. Vaya con Dios*. Perhaps we'll meet again."

Fallon had not accepted all Valdez told him. He didn't turn his back until the slim Mexican disappeared from sight over a ground rise.

Fallon wanted to put the gold he'd taken into Juárez's hands. The small Zapotec had put up a valiant fight against Maximilian's forces. Often forced to run after losing a battle, he carried the nation's constitution and his

few belongings in a small black carriage to the next place
he'd set up government, thus keeping Mexico a free republic. Fallon intended to keep the little president, and his
bankrupt government, in business as long as gold would
do the trick.

By Fallon's best guess, Juárez had left Chihuahua and
was again running, this time toward El Paso del Norte on
the south bank of the Rio Grande, where he would again
set up his mobile government.

Fallon thought to go home to his father's ranch along
the north banks of the river and wait for Juárez to come
closer. He shook his head. Too dangerous. He'd have to
swim the river twice with a packhorse loaded with gold.
American, Mexican, and the Emperor's troops all pa-
trolled the Rio Grande in hopes of catching gun runners.
"They'd catch a prize worth a helluva lot more than a
load of old rusted out rifles," Fallon muttered, then decided to find a place to hole up until things quieted down.

He swept the landscape with a look that missed little.
He stared at the horizon and searched back toward where
he sat his saddle then, inch by inch, scanned back out to
the skyline. The third time he did this, he saw a thin dust
cloud. His gaze locked on the disturbance, hoping it was
a dust devil.

After a while, frowning, he shook his head. Didn't take
Captain Escobar long to find troops, he thought, and at
the same time figured they had not yet seen him. He kneed
his black down the rock-strewn banks of a dry arroyo.

He kept his horse to a slow walk, not wanting to raise
dust. Every fifteen minutes or so, Fallon crawled to the
lip of the ravine and studied Escobar's progress. The third
time he figured the troop's progress as being only a mite
faster than his own.

He nodded, knowing they were already depending on
their Yaqui tracker. He figured to stay ahead of them until
dark, then he'd open the distance. He had no idea how
many men rode with Escobar.

Staying to low ground, he picked up his pace. His
horse's hooves kicked up only small handfuls of the al-

kali, which fell to the ground with hardly a sign of disturbance.

Sweat stained Fallon's shirt. He rubbed the side of his face. A two-day-old beard stubble and an accumulation of grime scoured his hand. A shave and bath would feel good, but that would have to wait. A glance at the sky showed about two hours of daylight left.

# CHAPTER

# 3

FALLON MOVED METHODICALLY. HE CIRCLED BACK TO shorten the distance between him and Escobar. Then, with the sun leaving less than a half hour of daylight, he pulled his long glass from its case and crawled to the top of a land swell. A glance at the sun told him there was little chance the glass would cast a reflection.

A moment and he had the scope focused. He counted. Sixteen troops. If his plan didn't work, he was dead.

He slid down the bank to his horse, climbed aboard, and headed northwest. While riding, he pushed the telescoping parts of his long glass together and stashed it in its leather case.

If Juárez left Chihuahua, and headed toward El Paso del Norte, Fallon figured to find him by the sign his entourage left; horse droppings, trash, tracks. He hoped he could find the little president before Maximilian's troops found *him*. Juárez's escort could easily handle sixteen men, and by his calculation the little Zapotec and his men should be close.

ESCOBAR KEPT HIS MEN IN RIGID FORMATION, WEAVING their way around giant yucca. He rode at their head. The

Yaqui scout rode far in front. They had seen where the two bandits separated, and Escobar agreed with the scout the man to follow was the one leading the packhorse. There they would find the gold.

He glanced worriedly at the sinking sun. If they didn't come on their prey by sundown, they'd have to make camp, and he had not a doubt the one they followed would ride long into the night.

Escobar silently cursed the country, the prickly pear cactus, the yucca, the ocotillo, the creosote bush, and the ever present heat and dust. If not for this assignment, and a burning desire to get the bandit who had made a fool of him under his revolver sights, he would sooner have been in Mexico City with a cool drink and a warm *señorita*. He couldn't believe two men had pulled the whole thing off, bluffing him and his men into thinking they were a gang. His anger mixed with admiration. His only consolation was that the Emperor's forces again had Benito Juárez on the run.

He pulled his handkerchief, mopped sweat from his brow, and sucked in a breath of air that felt like it came from a blast furnace. He cursed again.

They rode until the Yaqui returned. "Make camp. Follow trail again when sun come up out of the great waters."

Escobar gazed at the Indian, then at the ground. His temper got ahold of him and he clamped his jaws tight, then an idea blossomed. He looked at the Yaqui. "Could you follow his tracks by torchlight?"

The scout shrugged, then nodded. "Maybe."

Escobar twisted in his saddle. "*Vamanos,* we ride by torchlight." He thought he heard muffled groans from his men. "When it gets full night, strip down some of this creosote bush and twist it into torches. We stop when we find the *bandido.*"

JUST AS ESCOBAR HAD THOUGHT, FALLON DID RIDE LONG into the night. Finally, the sun painted the eastern sky with a pale blue rim, and washed night's velvety black to shades of gray, gradually snuffing out the stars.

Fallon, his shoulders sagging with weariness, decided to stop. He found a dry wash to his liking, a place deep enough that the horses could not be seen from the surrounding area. He would sleep for an hour, boil a bit of coffee with what water he had, then get back to looking for Juárez.

Hurting in every joint and muscle, he slid from his horse, wrapped the reins about his wrist, looped the reins of the other animal over his Morgan horse's saddle horn, and stretched out on the bare ground. He slept as soon as he lay down.

In an hour, almost to the minute, his eyes opened. He groaned inwardly, rolled over, and squatted. A tug on the reins and his horse stood over him. He pulled the cork from his canteen, poured a swallow of water into his hand, and held it for the black, then he did the same for the captain's horse. He wet his hand again, wiped his eyes, took a couple of swallows, then poured the less than a cup of water from his canteen into his coffeepot, thinking he'd soon find Juárez and replenish his water supply.

He made a small fire of greasewood and not long after sat sipping coffee.

Fallon felt safe, thinking his pursuers would have camped as soon as daylight dimmed. He finished his coffee, threw out the grounds, and flexed his back muscles. They didn't loosen. They were the kind of tight he always got when there was danger close by. He frowned, thinking it impossible Escobar had stayed on his trail in the dark. Gripping the handle of the pot to scoop sand over the fire, he glanced at his horse. The animal stood facing the southeast, ears peaked.

Fallon grunted, put his cup and the pot on the ground by the fire, and crawled to the lip of the dry wash. He didn't have to search. His neck hair tingled as though sticking straight out. Escobar's soldiers rode less than a mile away, headed directly toward him. It was the last time he'd undrestimate the Spaniard.

He rolled down the bank, grabbed the coffeepot, threw sand on the fire, and toed the stirrup. He kept to the ravine until the sides slanted off such as to form no cover, then he looked for a place to defend. Neither of the two horses could stand a chase; they'd been ridden hard and long without feed or water—but so had the soldiers' horses.

About a quarter of a mile away a small jumble of boulders lay on the side of a brush-studded hill. He headed toward them, pulling his Henry model 1860 rifle from its scabbard. While riding, he checked the rifle's tubular magazine. It held fifteen .44 blunt-nosed rimfire cartridges. The magazine was full. Fallon thanked every deity he'd heard of for each cartridge. Those, with the six shells in his handgun, and the six in the spare cylinder he carried in his pocket, could help even the odds.

He'd not cleared the ravine but a few seconds when shots sounded. He glanced over his shoulder. They were too far away for any chance of hitting him, unless very lucky. The big black horse needed no urging. He'd been in these situations before and somehow sensed the danger. The Morgan, despite being tired, found the heart to run. The captain's horse stayed with the black.

Drawing up to the rocks, Fallon left the saddle and pulled both horses with him into the cluster of boulders. Fear, if any, left him. Now he experienced only the strange exhilaration he felt when in combat. His mind worked clearer. His heart beat faster. He came alive. The feeling prompted a savage desire to kill, and keep on killing until all danger was gone. Fear—and perhaps shakes—would come later.

He centered a fine bead on the lead rider. Fallon hoped it was the captain when he squeezed the trigger. The heavy slug knocked the rider back over his horse's rump. Quick, but smooth, Fallon moved his sights to another rider and fired. That soldier fell to the side, his foot caught in the stirrup. His horse stopped.

Bullets ricocheted off the rocks around Fallon. He flinched each time the sharp whine of a slug tore into the loud report of rifle fire. Some of the bullets carved great creases into the boulders, spraying his face and eyes with sand and dirt.

By the time the soldiers were within a hundred yards, they had six empty saddles in their midst. Fallon wiped sweat and grainy dirt from his face and eyes. "Damn! Y'all gonna ride right down my rifle barrel?"

The words were no more than out of his mouth when the troops pulled rein and withdrew. While they were getting out of range, Fallon emptied two more saddles. A couple of Escobar's men dragged themselves toward a clump of yucca. He sighted on the front one, shook his head, and eased the hammer down. He had never killed senselessly.

A glance at the area in front showed no immediate danger of another charge. He looked to his back. The captain's horse lay on his side, breathing hard, nostrils quivering. He'd been shot through the neck. Fallon took careful aim and shot him in the head, feeling worse about killing the horse than he did those soldiers lying on the desert floor.

A quick check showed his black horse to be all right. He pulled him flat behind the boulder, then gave the area in front his attention.

Out of range, Escobar gathered his troops around him. Fallon stared hard. They were trying to figure the best way to get at him. They would not give up. He reloaded his rifle. His handgun still had a full cylinder. They'd not gotten close enough for him to use it. He hoped they wouldn't.

The rocks in which he crouched caged the desert's heat, not allowing even a vagrant breeze to brush him. He pushed his hat back and wiped his forehead, then tilted his hat back to his eyebrows. He pushed fear to the back of his mind. Time for that later—if there would be a later.

Escobar's troops stayed bunched out of range, but one rider detached himself from the cluster and rode toward Fallon. He carried a white flag. Fallon thought on it a moment. It was not in him to violate a flag of truce. He waited.

The rider drew closer. Fallon recognized him. Escobar. "Why the flag of truce, *Capitán*?" Fallon spoke Spanish.

Escobar pulled his horse in and stared toward him. "I 'ave come to offer you a way to keep from getting keeled, *señor.*"

Fallon smiled grimly behind the bandanna he had again pulled to his eyes. "It appears to me, the worry about that should all be on your side, *Capitán*. You've lost several men. I do not have a scratch." Then, his words dripping sarcasm, he said, "However, your concern touches me."

Escobar's lips drew down in a straight line. His jaw muscles tightened. He made an obvious effort to get his temper under control, then said, "*Señor,* let us quit fencing. You are outnumbered, and I'm willing to sacrifice every man I have to get back what rightly belongs to my emperor. You give me the gold and you can ride off unharmed."

Fallon chuckled. "Like hell, Captain. I'd be dead before my horse cleared these rocks." Even if he believed Escobar, Fallon had no give in his makeup. "You get back to your men, Captain, and turn your wolf loose. I'll take as many of you with me as I can. We'll see how many you're willing to lose."

Escobar jerked on his reins. Fallon cringed at the pain the cruel Spanish bit must have caused the horse as the magnificent animal reared, turned on his hind legs, then galloped back toward the troops.

When he reached his soldiers, Escobar, apparently still furious, drew his sword and motioned for a charge. This time Fallon knew which one to draw a bead on. He sighted on the center of Escobar's chest and waited until the Mexican came within range. He squeezed off his shot, but at the last moment the captain's horse stumbled. Escobar grabbed his shoulder and reined to the side. His men pulled rein. One of them grabbed the reins of Escobar's horse, then they turned tail and retreated. Fallon watched until they grew dim in the distance.

"Close, too damned close," he breathed, but thought

they wouldn't be back. Their leader was wounded. Fallon transferred the bags of gold and the bundle of rifles to the black and, leading the horse, continued toward the north-west.

The sun lifted higher in the heavens, and with each passing hour sucked life-giving moisture from his already depleted body. He shook his canteen, then tilted it to let only a few drops trickle to his palm. He wiped the black's lips with his wet palm.

By noon, when he thought all the heat in hell had cen-tered itself on him, it got hotter. About two miles ahead, in an upthrust of granite, he remembered there being a sump that usually held enough water for his horse and him. Narrowing his lids, he squinted toward the strange rock formation that held the basin, but between him and the upthrust finger of granite, grotesque heat waves danced, shimmered, and stretched from the parched desert floor, blocking his view of anything over a few hundred yards.

See it or not, he knew the water was there. A small spring fed little more water to the hollowed-out rock than the sun could evaporate in a day's time. Fallon stumbled, straightened, and put one foot in front of the other.

Another hour and he occasionally caught glimpses of the sharp granite finger pushing its way from the earth's crust before heat waves again closed off his vision. He stopped, pushed his hat back, and rubbed his eyes, then stared toward where the rocks were supposed to be. Noth-ing. He squeezed his lids tight and looked again. Yes, it stood there, brown, streaked with black in the afternoon sun. He gauged the distance, wondering if he could carry one of the bags of gold that far, then looked at his horse. The black was about done in.

Fallon figured he had no choice. He untied one of the heavy bags and, holding it by its tie cords, trudged on. If his horse died, so would he.

Where was Juárez? He'd thought to meet him before now, if the small Zapotec had left Chihuahua as he'd heard. Fallon had planned his raid based on the time he thought it would take to intersect the little Indian's trail. Juárez couldn't be far, but if Fallon didn't get to that water sump soon it would make no difference.

When the heat waves thinned before making another assault on his vision, he tried to guess how far he had yet to go. It was no use. Just when he thought the spring would be only a few yards away, the granite finger again seemed to withdraw, mocking him, driving him mad bit by bit.

Fallon stumbled, fell, climbed slowly to his feet, staggered a few more feet, and fell again. His whole world became fall, struggle upright, go a few feet, and fall again.

The time came when he could only push to his knees. He'd sink to the ground, push himself to his torn, bleeding knees, and will himself to crawl another few feet.

After what seemed hours, he again pushed himself up, only to see a worn, heel-less pair of boots in his bleary eyesight. His gaze followed the boots to a pair of ragged trousers and on up to a tattered shirt with crisscrossed bandoliers of bullets across a massive chest.

The man he saw through his blurred vision was certainly not a Maximilian soldier. He could be a bandit, but whatever he was, Fallon thought he might have water. "Water. Then *El Presidente*. Bring horse and this bag."

The man stooped and scooped Fallon into his arms as though Fallon's two hundred and twenty pounds were no more than a rifle. He reached to pull the bandanna down, shook his head, and left it tight across Fallon's face. He muttered, "Maybe theez eez the hombre *El Presidente* wants no one to know."

He walked effortlessly to the side of a black buggy. "*Mi Presidente,* this hombre wants to see you. I brought his horse and this heavy bag. Shall I look inside?"

Juárez glanced at the horse with the three bags tied to his saddle, along with the weapons. "Place the hombre in the buggy with me. Leave his horse and that bag here." He looked to the other side of his carriage. "Colonel, we make camp here. When my tent is ready, place this man inside. Leave his face covered and bring a canteen of water."

Only a few minutes passed before Juárez's tent was ready. He lifted the flap, ducked through the opening, and squatted at Fallon's side. Tenderly, as though handling a baby, he pulled the bandanna down, lifted Fallon's head, and trickled water into his mouth, crooning, "Ah, *mi amigo*, what things you do to yourself to help my cause." He dripped a little more water into Fallon's mouth.

Fallon, aware of all that went on around him, wanted just to lie still and let his friend take care of him. He opened his eyes and tried to talk, but no words passed his lips.

During the hours he lay there, feeling his body heal, he wondered that he put himself through thirst, hunger, and pain for another man's cause, when only a few miles away his father's ranch waited to give him more luxury than most men would know in a lifetime. Despite all the reasons he gave himself to quit the assignment President Johnson had given him, he always came up with two reasons to continue: He'd given his word to Johnson, and he'd not ever broken his word; and he'd made a friend in the small Indian who only wanted to help his people. Loyalty to a friend might get him killed, but he'd stick with Juárez until the end, even though it might be his end.

His thoughts went to the woman in the coach. He couldn't remember ever meeting a woman with more spunk. Other women he'd known would have been in hysterics in a like situation, but not that little lady. She'd stared him in the eye, even showed a touch of temper when he took the gold. Bundled up in her petite body was a streak of iron. To top that she was beautiful. Someday he would again find her and see if she drew on him then as now.

He lay in Juárez's tent two days, while the *presidente* administered to him personally, making sure he drank every time he awakened. Juárez fed him broth made from beef jerky, and ensured that no one looked upon Fallon's face. The morning of the third day, the *bandido* again tried to talk.

"*Señor Presidente*, good to see you." His voice came out hoarse, scratchy, in a whisper. "Better let me have a little more of that water, then I'll give you my report. It's still best no one sees my face."

Juárez nodded. "*Sí*, my friend, that is so. Not even the man who found you uncovered your face. I think I am the only one who knows you."

Fallon smiled. "Someday, *Señor Presidente,* we'll meet openly, as friends, but first you must rid your mother soil of the French."

With the water—although Juárez was careful to give him only a small amount at first, to make sure he didn't vomit it all—his strength soon returned. He felt he would live, and after he dined with Juárez in his tent, he gave a full report on the holdup and the subsequent gunfight with Escobar. "Don't know how much gold's in those bags, but it'll hold you till I find more. Those weapons I brought in should be welcomed by a few of your troops."

A heavy frown creased the little Indian's brow. "We need many things, *amigo*. My armies are in rags. Our weapons are worn out, and ammunition is low. Yes. What you have brought will help much."

Fallon smiled. "*Amigo*, I have news of something surely more valuable than the gold I brought."

Juárez cast him a doubtful glance. "*Señor*, I somehow doubt you could have anything more important to me than money to buy food, clothing, and arms. What is the news you've brought?"

Fallon took a small swallow of the hot coffee he and the president shared. "I'll not tell you how I know this, but trust me, it's the truth. I don't know exactly when, but as soon as the U.S. Army can get things organized, and right now they're in disarray, they'll begin stacking arms, ammunition, even limited amounts of clothing, food, and blankets, along the banks of the Rio Grande, on the American side of the river.

"Have your men take it all. There won't be guards

there to stop you. Every night do the same thing till they stop putting 'em there.'' Fallon shook his head. "I wish I could tell you exactly when—it might even be six months, but it'll happen.''

"What do you mean, take it all, *amigo*?''

Fallon emptied his cup and poured another, wondering how much to tell his friend. Of course he trusted him, but he might let something slip when in the wrong company. He decided to tell him as much as would help him. "*Señor Presidente,* now that we Americans have quit fightin' each other, we have supplies we either gotta destroy, sell, or find some use for. Now, seems like Andrew Johnson's gonna continue Lincoln's policy. His aim, and Secretary of State Seward's, is to get the French out of your country. Fact is we don't want nobody this side of the ocean who don't belong here. The Monroe Doctrine pretty well said it like it is. If you don't b'long here, get gone.'' He laughed. "We gonna help ourselves by helpin' you get rid of the French. They're too close to our border.''

Fallon stopped, studied Juárez a moment, took another swallow of coffee, and continued. "Seward said it so's the whole world would hear when he said, 'Frenchie, go home.' All he an' President Johnson get from the French is a bunch o' double-talk.

"General Sheridan, with a hundred thousand troops, has been ordered to the border. Figure we're ready if the French push us even a little bit.''

He sighed and looked Juárez in the eye. "Most o' us are tired of war.'' He hesitated, staring into his cup. "Yeah, I know a whole bunch has joined up to fight for you, and probably as many more, Rebs and Yanks alike, joined Maximilian but, *mi amigo,* there ain't any work in my country, and our soldiers from both sides need food and clothing.'' He speared Juárez with a penetrating look. "The stuff I told you 'bout will be 'longside the river. It might be a few weeks, maybe even a few months, but when they get there I'll let you know. Take them. They's an old sayin' in my country, 'Don't never look a gift horse in the mouth.' ''

The Zapotec returned Fallon's stare. "I believe you, *amigo,* but I wish I knew how you find out so much. My own spies know nothing of this."

Fallon nodded and grinned. "Yeah, lots o' people would like to know those things, as well as who I am. But, sir, while tryin' to find out about gold shipments, I hear other things. That's all I'm gonna tell you—for my good as well as your own."

They were sitting on the ground inside Juárez's tent, by a small fire on which sat the coffeepot. Fallon looked toward his blankets. "Now, sir, if you'll excuse me, I'm 'bout ready to fall asleep drinking your good coffee. When you wake in the mornin', I'll be gone. I'll find you next time I got somethin' for you."

# CHAPTER

THE SETTING SUN PAINTED THE SKY WITH SHADES OF pink, lavender, purple, and aquamarine the next evening, when Fallon drew rein on the banks of the Rio Grande. Juárez and his little carriage were miles behind, and his father's ranch, Falcon Nest, the Flying F, lay across the river about twenty miles downstream.

Before fording the river, Fallon glanced back. In the distance, a small group of riders lined the ridge above the river. Those riders were the squad of soldiers Juárez had sent to protect him, even though he was supposed to be unaware they shadowed him. His friend intended no harm to come to him.

Satisfied his backtrail was safe, Fallon studied the American side and saw nothing that spelled danger. He kneed his horse into the muddy water, looked longingly toward the ranch, and turned his horse upstream. If he was to keep his lawless activities secret, he must go to Las Cruces, where he could leave the black Morgan horse, and once again dress the part of the rancher's son, then he would go home and suffer the questioning, hurt looks in his father's and mother's eyes.

Since his release from the Yankee prison camp and return home, he'd seemingly taken no interest in the ranch, although when he'd gone off to war he'd been as good as any top hand—working cattle, roping, branding, trail driving, and riding anything with hair on it.

He'd heard his parents talking, his mother insisting that his father let the internal wounds of war heal, and his father saying hard work would heal anything.

Until Juárez had his country back, Fallon didn't want his parents to suspect what he was doing. He'd tell them someday, but the telling had to wait.

He again looked toward the ranch that spelled a bath and clean clothes, then a glance at the sun told him to make camp before it got too dark to find firewood.

By the time a velvety black settled on the land, Fallon had his fire going, coffee sitting close to the coals, and six thick strips of bacon frying. He mixed flour with water, rolled it into a ball, and tossed it in the frying pan along with the bacon. Although he'd drawn skimpy provisions from Juárez's supply, the meal looked like a feast. His stomach felt it would take anything he offered.

Only a couple bites into his meal, his horse's ears peaked. Fallon grabbed his Henry and faded into the darkness.

He'd hardly settled behind a giant yucca when eight riders showed in the dim firelight. "Hello the fire. We're friendly. How 'bout us ridin' in?"

"What you want?"

"We're Army, checkin' those who mighta crossed the border."

Fallon grimaced. He didn't want to be seen by anyone until he could resume his role as the rancher's son, but he could hardly turn them away without arousing suspicion. Besides, he had a week's growth of beard, and that many days' accumulation of dust in it and in his hair. He didn't think he'd be recognized. "Ride to the fire an' let me look at you."

They eased their horses closer to the light, hands held away from weapons. Their uniforms were those of Yankee soldiers. Fallon walked to the fire. "Sorry I ain't got

enough victuals to feed y'all. Climb down an' set a spell.''
Strange, he thought, how quickly he shed precise, correct
grammar. Just by crossing the river, getting back in his
native Texas, and switching from Spanish to English—or
switching to Texan as he chose to look at it—he became
a different person—in speech, dress, and mannerisms.

The cavalrymen slid to the ground. The sergeant in
charge raked Fallon with a glance that went from head to
toe. Fallon saw a look of distaste in the non-com's eyes.
''You ain't been around water lately judging by your
looks.''

Fallon's face stiffened. Blood rushed to his head. ''Mister, I didn't invite you to stop here. You can get on yore
horse—put some distance 'tween us if you don't like my
looks.''

The sergeant backed up a step. ''Aw hell, mister, I
didn't mean nothin'. What you doin' out here all alone?
You might run into bandits, or Mescalero. Either one's
gonna be right unfriendly to a man alone.''

Fallon decided to play along with the sergeant. ''Ain't
got much choice, Sergeant. I'm lookin' for work. Ain't
been able to hook up with a outfit since they let me outta
the Army.''

''What side you fight on?''

Fallon's face hardened. ''Don't make any difference.
The war's s'posed to be over.''

The Army man studied Fallon a moment. ''Mister, it's
over for most, but there's some who'll never figure it that
way. Don't matter whether they wore the gray or the blue,
some still got a chip on their shoulder.''

Fallon returned the sergeant's gaze. ''Yeah, you're
right, but they's a many o' them crossin' the border and
fightin' for Juárez—some even hookin' up with Maximilian.'' He shuffled his feet and looked at the ground a
moment, then eyed the sergeant. ''Mister, I ain't one o'
them. I done had enough war—win, lose, or draw.''

The sergeant looked at Fallon's coffeepot. He licked
his lips.

Fallon took the hint. "Ain't got much, but I'll share what I got."

The sergeant smiled. "Naw. 'Preciate it but we better get goin'. 'Sides there wouldn't be more'n a swallow apiece." He looked at his men. "Mount up. We got a bunch o' miles to cover." Then he apologized to Fallon for interrupting his supper.

After they faded into the darkness, Fallon finished eating and moved camp, not liking the idea of camping anywhere known to others.

Before again making camp, he pondered the couple of extra hours it would take to reach Las Cruces, shrugged, flexed the tired muscles in his shoulders and back, shrugged again, and decided to ride on to Sanchez's livery stable.

True to his estimate, Fallon rode to the back of the stable almost two hours later. A glance at the Big Dipper told him the time—midnight.

He had put the black in a stall, forked hay, poured a bucket of oats for him, and pulled the bars across the front of the opening when a quiet, refined voice broke his thoughts. "Ah, *señor,* you have returned. I was worried for you."

" 'Twas nothin' to worry 'bout, *amigo.*"

Sanchez chuckled. "I'll wager our friend below the border worried more than either of us." He frowned. "You think anyone saw you come in here?"

Fallon shook his head. "I took great care as always." He sighed. "Reckon it's too late for a bath and change of clothes."

"But no, *señor. Mi esposa* said only this afternoon, 'The *señor* will be coming tonight. I know he will.' She told me to stop worrying about you. Come. We go to my *casa.* As always, Carmella will have hot water waiting for you. I'll go first and make sure the streets are empty, then you come." He grinned. "*Amigo,* there is no one in the territory would recognize you. That beard, those rags, that dirt. You do not look the handsome, dashing *caballero* of the Flying F ranch."

• • •

TWO HOURS LATER, SHAVED, BATHED, AND DRESSED IN A
black bolero jacket, black trousers belled around shiny
black boots, and a snowy white shirt with black string tie,
Fallon not only looked like a different person—he felt like
one. Much of his tiredness disappeared when he sat to eat
the meal *Señora* Sanchez prepared for him. He knew she
had cleaned and brushed his clothing herself, not trusting
a servant to do so in that the servant might get too curious,
or talk to others of the strange visitor in the Sanchez
house.

She pinned him with a look. "Tomas, why do you put
yourself in such danger for us time and time again? You
have no ties to the Republic of Mexico."

Fallon smiled. "Carmella, as you well know, my
mother is pure Castilian Spanish—it's from her I get my
black hair and green eyes—and my father has been in
Tejas so long I think maybe not even he knows from
whom he descended, and me, *señora,* I have friends on
both sides of the border. If I was not doing what I'm
doing, I would join Juárez's forces and fight alongside
them."

She continued to stare into his eyes, then said softly,
"*Muchas gracias, mi amigo.*"

Embarrassed by her candor, Fallon looked at Sanchez.
"My cantankerous line backed dun ready to go?"

"*Sí,* Tomas. He is ready and frisky as a young colt.
Now you get some sleep. I'll have him saddled when you
waken, and the next time you need that black animal you
ride, he'll be ready to go. Be careful when you leave my
house." He grinned. "Once away from it no one will
know but what the rich rancher's son has had another
night with a beautiful *señorita.* Now, finish your supper
and get to bed. You've had a hard few days."

They watched Fallon walk toward the room they kept
for only him, a room where he had a complete wardrobe
of clothes. Carmella Sanchez looked from Fallon to her
husband. "*Mi amor,* if I'd not seen you first, that man

could have taken my heart. He is so handsome, so big, so strong, and not afraid of anything.''

Sanchez grinned. ''You trying to make me jealous, Carmella?''

She gazed at her husband, thinking that here under her roof were perhaps the two most handsome, most dangerous men in the New Mexico Territory. A pang of both fear and pride swelled her throat. ''No, Roberto, I know you are secure in my love for you—and yes, I love Tomas, but in a different way. Probably in the same way you love him.''

Roberto nodded. ''Of course you're right, *mi amor*. We and our people are fortunate to have a friend such as he.''

BEFORE SUNRISE, FALLON SLIPPED FROM SANCHEZ'S house and made his way back to the livery stable. When he walked through the stable door, he smelled bacon frying, mingled with the tangy aroma of fresh brewed coffee. He walked directly to Sanchez's office.

Sanchez looked up and grinned when Fallon pulled the door shut behind him.

''Morning, Tom. You don't look much the worse for wear.''

Fallon grimaced. ''Looks can be deceiving, my friend. I slipped out knowing Carmella would have the servants fix breakfast; now damned if you haven't done it.''

Still grinning, Sanchez said, ''Got eggs, tortillas, and really hot salsa. You're gonna eat a good breakfast before you head for home.''

After eating, Fallon cleaned and oiled his weapons, honed his big Bowie knife, and checked the throwing knife he hung from a leather thong at the back of his neck. Sanchez gazed at him. ''Damn, Tomas, if I didn't know you so well, I'd figure you were expecting a war.''

Fallon grunted. ''Yeah, knowing me so well you know danged well I always expect war.'' He held out his cup for Sanchez to pour, then said, ''Roberto, you hear of any big fiesta where you might finagle me an invite?''

Sanchez frowned into his cup, then a slow grin broke through the frown. "*Sí, señor,* I know of such a thing, but I think you could go without an invitation."

"You know danged well I wouldn't invite myself to somebody's fandango." Fallon grinned. " 'Less, o' course *you* were throwing it."

Deadpan, Sanchez shook his head. "Even better than me having one, Fallon. Your mother is having a big party at the end of this week."

Fallon frowned into his coffee cup, took a swallow, then looked at Sanchez. "Sounds good. She'll probably invite people from both sides of the border. Ought to be a helluva chance to gather information. You goin'?"

Sanchez nodded. "*Sí, mi esposa* received the invitation only yesterday. We'll be there. Three sets of ears will be better than one. If there is another shipment of gold or silver headed south, we'll know."

Fallon's stomach churned. "Try and find out how strong the gold shipment escort will be. I'm right fond of livin' "

They talked awhile longer, then seeing the rising sun slice vertical streaks of silvery light between the rough boards of the stable, Fallon stood. "Thanks, *amigo,* and thank Carmella for taking care of me. Reckon I better head out. Figure to get home by mid-afternoon."

By ten o'clock, Fallon had been on the trail three hours. He let the dun, who knew the way home, set his own pace.

Fallon's eyes never rested. He searched the long, crooked, dusty trail for signs of other humans: Mescalero, Mexican, or white. His searching gaze scoured the grease-wood and cactus flats on both sides. The idea of strangers being friendly—or honest—didn't fit the times.

White men, many of whom had only recently been turned loose from the Confederate and U.S armies, were broke, hungry, and in rags. Many had turned outlaw in order to survive. The Apache were always on the prowl and would kill for the pure hell of it. Most Mexicans were as bad off as the veterans of the War Between the States.

Fallon rode with the thong off the hammer of his Colt, and his Henry riding easy in its saddle scabbard.

He looked for strangely shaped prickly pear clumps, or bumps in the yucca where no bump should be, and he searched the ground around the scrubby creosote bushes. Outlaws bent on robbery would have long since taken their places of concealment, so Fallon didn't look for dust kicked up by their horses.

His gaze passed over a clump of greasewood—then came back to it. The bushes looked thicker, darker, than they should. His breathing thinned down, his neck hair tingled. He stopped his horse to pack his pipe. His look swung to the opposite side of the trail. He found what he expected—another man. This one he saw plainly; although his head and shoulders fit well behind the brush, his rear end stuck out in the open.

Fallon lighted his pipe and kneed his horse off the trail so as to keep both men on the same side of him. He slipped his Colt from its holster and held it under his horse's mane, hoping there were only the two he had sighted. More than two he didn't think he could keep tabs on.

He'd not ridden more than twenty yards when the men stood, guns pointed at him. There were only the two he'd seen from the trail. He rode a little closer to make sure he was in easy handgun range.

The dirty, round little man across the road said, "Drop your hardware, cowboy. We don't want to hurt you less'n we have to."

The bony, ragged man closest to Fallon, who looked as though he hadn't eaten in a week, eared back the hammer of his side gun. "My partner done said it like it is, mister. We ain't gonna hurt you if'n you give us what food you got."

Fallon grinned at the two. Strangely, he felt no sense of danger. Even though these men had guns in their hands, they didn't seem ready to use them. "Damned if y'all ain't the scraggliest, sorriest lookin' outlaws I ever did see. Too, you ain't very smart. If you'll look a little closer, look at my hand that's covered by my horse's mane, you're gonna see I got a gun on you, an' the first one I shoot's gonna be you, slim, 'cause you're closest, an' even skinny as you are, an' makin' a mighty thin target, I can't miss. Course, fatty, you might get me, but your partner's gonna be dead.''

The fat bandit looked dumbfounded. He slanted his partner a questioning glance, then his look came back to Fallon. His face hardened. He again glanced at his partner. ''Aw hell, Slim, I told you we ain't cut out to be outlaws.'' His gun hand dropped to his side. ''Mister, whoever the hell you are, all we wuz gonna do wuz take some o' your grub off'n you. We ain't et in some time.''

Slim holstered his handgun. ''Toby's done said it, mister. All we want is something to eat.''

Fallon eyed them a moment, then asked, ''Why didn't you just sit your horses in the middle of the trail until I reached you, and tell me you were hungry? I'da give you somethin' to eat.''

Slim looked close-lidded at Fallon, his face hard. '' 'Cause, mister, ain't neither one o' us used to beggin'. I figger stealin' ain't near as low as beggin'. 'Sides all that, we ain't got no horses.''

Fallon chuckled. ''Yeah, you might be right, but stealin'll get you killed. There's a right nice-sized ranch back down the trail behind you. Why didn't you see if there mighta been a job there for you?''

Toby spread his hands at his sides as though to say, ''Look at me,'' then dropped his hands to his sides. ''Mister, ain't neither one of us ever been outta the hills of West Virginia till we joined up to fight with the Union. We don't know nothin' 'bout cowboyin'.''

''Toby, most men out here nursing cows never knew anything about them till they came this side of the Mississippi. Go back there and tell the foreman that Tom Fallon said to give you something to do to earn your keep. He'll fix you up. But first I'd recommend you take a bath and shave in the nearest water you can find.'' Fallon pulled the knot on a bag behind his saddle and opened it.

Carmella had fixed him sandwiches, more than he could eat. He took two from the bag. "Here. I'll share these with you." He handed them each a sandwich, and kneed his horse toward the ranch. "I'll see you at the Flyin' W, an' you better be workin'."

"Mister," Slim cut in, "it's gonna take us a mite o' time to get back there. We gotta walk, remember."

Fallon eyed them a moment, nodded jerkily, and said, "All right. Those sandwiches'll just about hold you till you get there, then Cook'll feed you—if you're clean." He nodded toward his right. "The river's right over yonder." He urged his dun toward home.

Walking his horse, he wondered why he'd taken a chance with the two men, wondered why he'd offered them jobs. The country was full of men like them—homeless, hungry, no qualifications for work of any kind. He shrugged and marked it down as a gamble—they might be able to make his father a couple of hands, although he knew he'd have helped them anyway. Right now he sure didn't have many on the American side of the border he could count on for help. He kneed his dun toward the ranch.

BRAD FALLON SAW HIS SON APPROACHING FROM A DIStance, and studied him while he rode toward the ranch, studied him as though he'd never seen him before. The tall, black-haired, green-eyed man sat the saddle like he'd been born to it, which he had been. Fallon's throat tightened. Even considering his son's attitude since returning from the war, he admitted to himself that Tom was still his greatest source of pride. He refused to believe his only son spent his time in saloons and bedding whores—his physical condition denied such evaluation.

Brad met his son at the bunkhouse. "Have a good time doin' whatever the hell it is you do when you disappear like this?" His voice came out harsh to hide his relief at seeing Tom alive and safe. While talking he looked harder at his boy. "Damned if I see how you stay so tan, an' your hands all calloused like you been workin'. If you got

that way in some bar, either the glasses you been drinkin'
outta, or the skin you been carressin', is rougher'n a cob.
You need to change saloons or find softer women." He
cocked his head and looked at Tom squint-eyed. "You
hire on with 'nother outfit?"

Tom chuckled. "No, Pa. I ain't hired on with any cow
outfit. Figure you got the best spread around, an' I ain't
been hangin' around any saloons." He lowered his lids
over his eyes, shutting out any chance Brad could read
them. "Reckon I just been spendin' a lot o' time ridin'
around the country, tryin' to get my head clear as to what
I oughtta be doin'. Why? You 'bout to run me off?"

Brad slowly shook his head. "Son, I don't know of
anything could make me do that. When you get ready to
get back to cowboyin', I'm gonna be right here dishin'
out chores for you." Brad locked eyes with his son.
"Cain't say I understand. I know that prison camp you
were in must have been pure hell, an' I ain't never fit no
war, so I don't know what it'll do to a man's insides.
Whatever the problem, son, take your time gettin'
straightened out." He glanced toward the sprawling ranch
house. "Take care of your horse, then go see your ma.
She's been worried sick 'bout you."

A sharp pang of guilt pierced Tom's chest. Keeping his
parents in the dark about his activities was not of his
choosing, but it was the safest way. The American law
was not seeking him, so far, but the Mexicans were.

# CHAPTER

5

PULLING OPEN THE MASSIVE OAK DOOR, TOM BRACED himself for the hurt look in his mother's eyes. He never had a chance to see it. She threw herself into his arms, hugging him and kissing his cheek.

He drew back and, holding her shoulders, looked down at her. He was always surprised at her beauty: auburn hair, green eyes, not much over five feet tall, and a perfect figure. "Ma," he said, "if I ever find me a woman like you, I figure I'll marry her."

A slight frown creased her forehead. "And, my handsome son, I'll warn her of your wayward ways before you can make her as miserably worried as you do me."

He stepped back. "Look at me, Ma, I'm healthy, no signs of carousing. You have nothing to worry about."

She held him with a piercing look. "Tom, in this day and time, carousing is not all I have to worry me. There are many bad and dangerous men out there who would do you harm."

Tom grinned. "Well, I hope I'm not bad, and I'm probably not dangerous, but I'm here to tell you, Ma, there ain't many men I can't handle."

"I wish you wouldn't say 'ain't.' I've told you that

since you were a small boy, and it hasn't done one bit of good.''

Tom threw back his head and laughed. "Now I know I'm home. Ma, you raised me a Texan. Reckon that's the way I'm gonna talk. It's sort o' easy on the tongue.''

She sighed. "I never win that argument, do I? Well, I'm having a fiesta Saturday. Have Maria see that you have the proper things to wear. If you don't, I fear you might show up in jeans.'' She stepped toward the kitchen and said over her shoulder, "And try to use proper grammar when talking with my guests.''

Shaking his head, Tom headed for his room. He needed a bath and shave.

FRIDAY MORNING, CARRIAGES, COACHES, BUGGIES, AND buckboards began to arrive. From the bunkhouse doorway, Tom checked the guests. There were some among them, both French and Spanish, all of the aristocracy, who gave their allegiance to the Catholic-backed Maximilian regime. He wanted to make certain he talked with most of them. They might drop a hint as to valuable shipments leaving Texas for Maximilian's stronghold in Mexico City.

The only ones Fallon could consider allies were Roberto and Carmella Sanchez. The Sanchez family, dating back to the 1600s, was one of the oldest in the New Mexico Territory, and one of the first Spanish families to receive a land grant. Many crooked American politicians, lawyers, and land promoters tried by fair means or foul to strip them of their land, and in addition to the livery, the Sanchezes owned several businesses and one of the largest ranches in the Las Cruces area, all of which would be quite a plum for some crook.

The afternoon shadows grew long before Fallon recognized the Sanchez coach, a heavy black Concord, luxuriously appointed for comfort. He stepped from the doorway and went to greet them.

When he helped Carmella from the coach, she looked from his run-over, scuffed-up boots to his faded jeans.

"Tomas..." She always called him Tomas when she was serious. "If you don't dress soon, you'll give Juanita the vapors."

Tom laughed. "Ah, *mi amiga,* I think I already got a good start on causing Ma troubles. She worries as much about how I dress as how I talk. Anyway, your usual room is waiting for you. I'll help with your bags."

"How many will be here?" Carmella asked.

While shaking Roberto's hand, Tom answered. " 'Bout a hundred, I reckon." He cast a glance around the area to make certain no one stood in hearing distance. "Should be a few here with information we need, and some might have loose tongues."

"Tomas, you just got back from one dangerous trip. Why don't you take a little time before the next one?"

Fallon frowned. "Don't dare, little one. Our friend down south needs everything I can channel his way. You and Roberto keep your ears open."

A couple of ranch hands walked up to help with the Sanchez luggage. Tom grabbed a valise and a heavy suitcase.

After showing Roberto and Carmella to their rooms, he went to his room to dress for dinner.

When he walked into the dining room, his breath caught in his throat. The first person he saw was the copper-haired girl from the holdup. He had often thought of her since then, but never expected to see her in his own home. He sucked in his breath. She must have canceled going on to Mexico City after his surprise visit with her on the trail.

From across the room, her gaze locked with his. At Fallon's nod, she acknowledged it with a slight one of her own, but he could discern no recognition in her eyes. He let his pent-up breath escape and walked toward her.

When within a couple of feet, he said, "Don't reckon I've had the pleasure of making your acquaintance, ma'am. I'm Tom Fallon."

Her eyes reflected interest. She held out her hand. "I'm

Joan Boniol." She cocked her head to the side. "Fallon? Are you related to Nita and Brad Fallon?"

Tom let a slight smile show at the corners of his lips. "There are times, ma'am, they deny anything more than a distant relationship, but yes'm, I reckon they have to claim me. I'm their only son."

"But of course, your mother's spoken of you many times." She frowned. "I wonder why we've never met— yet there's something vaguely familiar about you."

While she talked, Fallon grew more tense. Perspiration trickled between his shoulder blades. He swallowed a lump in his throat. She might, with her next words, denounce him as a common outlaw.

She shook her head. "No, it must be that your mother has described you in such detail I feel I *do* know you."

Tom sucked in a deep breath. He smiled and relaxed just a bit. "Well, ma'am, it's my misfortune we aren't old friends with this meeting. Perhaps you'll let me make up for lost time? Are you from hereabouts? I'd like to see you again."

"No. I came out here several years ago from New Orleans—one of the original French families there. I make my home in El Paso del Norte." She smiled. "And, yes, I see no reason, now that we've met, why we shouldn't become fast friends."

Fallon glanced about the room. "I'd like to talk with you more later, but right now I'd better roam around and talk with some of my folks' friends or Ma will surely disown me."

After greeting several of the family friends, Fallon wended his way through the laughing crowd to Roberto. Standing alongside him, trying to appear to be looking only at the people gathered there, Fallon said out of the corner of his mouth, "The beautiful, auburn-haired woman, Roberto, the one I just talked with, you see her?"

"*Sí,* she is a good friend of your mother. Carmella and I know her well."

Fallon swept the room with a glance to see if any might be close enough to hear. He stepped closer. "*Amigo,* she is the one who was on the coach I briefly detained down south of here the other day. Just now, while I spoke with her, she toyed with the idea she had met me somewhere. I don't dare be around her too much. My voice, my eyes, anything, might give me away even though I had my face covered during the holdup." He took his pipe from his pocket, packed it, and lighted it. "You and Carmella go talk with her, hint that you feel sorry for the way Maximilian is having to fight this war—you know, make like you sympathize with his cause. She may let something slip."

Roberto nodded and moved out into the throng, many of whom were from Franklin, the small settlement on the American side of the border, and only now beginning to be called El Paso. There was talk of changing El Paso del Norte's name to Ciudad Juárez in honor of their president.

Sanchez, so as not to make his intentions conspicuous, stopped and passed the time of day with several couples, but kept aware of Joan Boniol's location in the crowd. After only a few moments he stood beside her. "Ah, *señorita*, I wondered if you would find it in your heart to let the poor men from hereabouts look upon your beauty."

She smiled up at him. "Roberto, there is not a woman here more beautiful than your Carmella, but thank you for the compliment. Why haven't I seen you lately?"

"Been stayin' close to home, Joan. With trouble surrounding us, I keep Carmella close to me in Las Cruces. I don't dare let her stay at the ranchero. Many there are loyal to Benito Juárez and they, knowing we are of the old families, might cause her harm." He looked around as though wanting only her to hear him. "It's a shame Maximilian doesn't get this war ended soon."

He didn't expect her to offer anything right then, but wanted to plant the idea that he sympathized with the emperor. She might come to him with information later.

At his words, he thought he saw more than a flicker of interest, then she changed the subject. "You seem to be acquainted with Nita's son. Where has she been keeping him?''

Carmella walked up in time to hear Joan's question. She laughed. ''He *is* a handsome devil, isn't he, but to answer your question, Tomas has just returned from the war. They held him in a Union prison camp until most were released and on their way home. He seems to be having a hard time adjusting to the life he had before going off to fight for the South.'' She leaned closer. ''It's rumored he spends some of his time with the Mescalero.'' She laughed. ''I wouldn't put it past him; he's always been a reckless, devil-may-care sort. But he worries poor Nita to distraction.''

Joan frowned. ''He must be totally lacking in compassion. He is poor Nita's whole life, and yet he must not care that he worries her.''

Carmella moved closer. ''Joan, Tomas is a very caring man, but also a most dangerous one; surely you have heard of the gunfights he's had in your town of El Paso del Norte. If the stories are true, and I were a man, I'd not care to cross him.'' She stepped back and studied the petite copper-haired woman. ''Heavens, why are we standing here discussing Tomas?'' She smiled. ''Unless, of course, you really want to know more about him. If I were not married to a most wonderful man already, I *know* I'd like to know him very well.''

Joan blushed. She looked from Roberto to Carmella, then frowned. ''I could deny being interested, but you know me too well to swallow that. Yes, he intrigues me. The fact is, I've already promised to see more of him, but I honestly, somewhere in the back of my mind seem to think we've already met. I can't imagine when or where.''

Carmella pierced Joan with a knowing look. ''Tell me honestly, Joan, if you had met him before, would you be likely to forget him?''

Joan's face flamed. She laughed. ''You're awful nosey, my friend.''

Carmella didn't join her in the laugh; instead she held her gaze on her friend. ''No, Joan, I'm not nosey.'' She forced a mocking smile. "But, my dear, your face answered my question."

Her expression now serious, Joan asked, "Before we leave here, would you tell me more about him? I *am* interested. I want to know everything you know about him."

Before moving out into the group of people again, Carmella agreed to tell Joan what little she knew. She looked across the room. Tomas stood talking to one of the French officials who had recently moved his delegation to Franklin when word came that Juárez was headed to El Paso del Norte.

Fallon listened intently to the suave Frenchman, Charles Lebeau, who talked in detail about his emperor and his goals for the people of Mexico. Lebeau was saying, ". . . and, *monsieur,* the Spaniards are not to be trusted. Many of them change their support more often than they do their underwear, depending on who won the last battle."

Tom shook his head sympathetically. "A shame, sir, a terrible shame. A man should always know who his friends are. Our emperor . . ." He paused, letting his use of the word "our" sink in, hoping the Frenchman would assume his loyalties rested with Maximilian. "Our emperor," he continued, "needs to know his friends now more than ever. The war's going against him, and it's rumored Prussia will soon defeat Austria. If that happens, it's possible Napoleon will call his troops home." He shook his head. "It is sad, sir, but I'm afraid that'll be the end for our emperor."

The Frenchman took the bait. "*Non, m'sieur,* the most important thing now is gold. People are greedy, and loyalty can be bought. We must see that he gets the money to win this miserable war."

Fallon, careful to keep the surge of elation from showing in his face, and not wanting Lebeau to see his interest, thought it best if he left the man with a hint that he could be depended on if needed. "*M'sieur,* if you think of anything I can do, let me know and I'll do my best to see that our emperor gets the support he deserves. I can always be found either here or across the border." He smiled, and added, "The *señoritas* are most cooperative over there." He winked. "And I'm yet a young man." He nodded and again moved into the crowd.

Yeah, he thought, I'll be happy to see that that old boy down yonder gets the support he *deserves*. He chuckled to himself.

The rest of the evening, Tom avoided being left in Joan's company for more than a few moments. Every time he glimpsed her through the crowd, he wanted to go to her, get better acquainted, but fought the impulse. That petite woman could ruin everything.

Mentally, he scrubbed down every way one person might recognize another, and again the only two things he came up with were that she might recognize his eyes or his voice. He couldn't change his eyes, and to try to change his voice might be readily discerned. Then it occurred to him that he'd spoken only Spanish during the holdup. He thought on that for a moment, then nodded. When with her, he'd speak Texan. It, when played against good Spanish grammar, should keep her off balance—and it could open the door for him to see her again.

He admitted to himself that since the holdup, seeing her had become a need, not just a wish, even though there would be risk of discovery. Satisfied he had solved his problem as much as he could, he shrugged, glanced over the crowd, and went to his room. He didn't want to start the next day tired. A look at his watch showed it to be after midnight. It was already the "next day."

FALLON AWOKE TO SOUNDS OF MARIACHI MUSIC. HE groaned, pushed down the covers, shaved, bathed, and went to breakfast. Joan Boniol sat about halfway along the huge table, an empty chair beside her. Fallon considered going to the bunkhouse to eat with the crew, but discarded the idea. Cookie would get madder'n hell if he went in there this time of day and wanted breakfast. Too, Joan was looking right into his eyes. It would be a definite snub if he turned and walked away. He headed for the chair next to her.

He pulled out a chair. "Mornin', ma'am. Sleep well?"

"Quite well, thank you, but I didn't get to bed until long after you disappeared."

Tom wanted to smile—she had noticed his absence— but instead he said, "Ma'am, I knew today would be long, and I didn't want to miss a chance to dance with you."

She looked straight into his eyes and said, "Sir, all you have to do—anytime—is ask." She blushed. "That was rather bold of me, wasn't it?"

Fallon shook his head and allowed a slight smile to crinkle his lips. "Not at all, ma'am. Way I figure it, we've already lost a lot o' time. I'll have to speak to my mother 'bout not introducin' us sooner."

After their meal, they talked a few moments over coffee. At one point in the conversation, Joan frowned, and asked, "Do you not speak Spanish, Tom?" They were now on a first name basis.

He nodded, and felt his gut tighten. Was she probing, searching for where she might have met him? He toyed with a fork a moment, then said, "Yes'm. Not well, but a sort of border Spanish. I understand their language a lot better'n I speak it." With his lie, he hoped his mother wouldn't let the truth be known.

They talked awhile longer before he excused himself, saying he had to see the boys in the bunkhouse. She looked at him straight on. "Don't forget, you promised to dance with me."

"Ain't a chance I'll forget that, ma'am." He headed for the bunkhouse with mixed feelings—elated at the progress he'd made with her, and worried she'd figure out where they'd met.

LATE AFTERNOON, AND FALLON HAD MANAGED TO stay away from Joan. He helped the ranch hands barbecue the sides of two beeves, sat in on a small-stakes poker game in the bunkhouse, and had decided to mingle with the company when Sanchez caught up with him by the corral.

In little more than a whisper, Roberto said, "Tomas. The Frenchies're planning to kill Juárez. They haven't found a killer yet, but that won't be much trouble."

Fallon looked a moment at his friend, then squinted into the sunset. "Where'd you hear this, *amigo*?"

"I escaped to your father's library to get away from people for a while, an' was almost asleep in one of those deep leather chairs when three of them slipped just inside and closed the door behind them. I reckon they didn't see me, because they made no effort to talk in less than normal tones. *El Presidente* is not yet in El Paso del Norte, but when he gets there they plan to be ready."

"Did you get a glimpse of the three?"

Sanchez nodded. "Only briefly, *mi amigo*. When they were going out the door, I twisted in the chair enough to glance back. When I turned on that rawhide, I almost swallowed my cud. It squealed under me like a new saddle. Anyway, they apparently didn't hear. They were all three in those fancy uniforms they wear."

Fallon studied his boot toe a moment, then looked straight on at Sanchez. "Reckon you an' me better get back to Mama's guests and see who we're dealin' with." He clapped Roberto on the shoulder and headed toward the ranch house.

Back in the big room, it took the two of them only a moment to spot the Frenchmen huddled together, as they always seemed to be, perhaps sensing they had few friends here. Fallon stood against the wall and studied them. He remembered their names from being introduced earlier. Their every feature came under his scrutiny: Henri Bienville, tall, dark, with a mole at the corner of his left eyebrow; Charles Lebeau, medium height, square-shouldered, big nose; Anton Belin and Francois Berne, short, thin, hatchet-faced, with eyes set close together.

He and Sanchez could watch two of them if they split up when back in Franklin, but who else could he get to help? He thought on that a moment. The old Mescalero, Two Buffalo, who refused to cowboy but hunted, scouted to keep the ranch aware of anyone in the area—including other Mescalero—and performed special tasks for which he was uniquely fitted. He was well qualified for what Fallon wanted, and he wouldn't have to explain to his father about needing the Indian's services, because Two Buffalo came and went as he pleased.

Fallon circled the room toward Roberto's position at the far end. On the way he stopped to pass the time with Brad Mason, a Big Bend rancher; his wife; two young sons, Cole and Clay; and a hellion Mason had raised by the name of Quint Cantrell. He wished he dared take the Mason boys and Cantrell with him, but they were too young and wild. He didn't stop when he came abreast of Sanchez, but said out of the corner of his mouth, "Got a plan, find Two Buffalo and come to the stable."

• • •

FALLON STOOD IN THE COOLNESS OF THE STABLE, SAVOR-
ing the smells and the aloneness. In only a short while
Sanchez and the old Indian showed up. When he explained his plan, Two Buffalo grunted and said, "Want
dead?"

Fallon and Sanchez both laughed and Tom went on to
explain that he only wanted to know the identity of every
man the Frenchmen talked with the first day they were
back in Franklin. Two Buffalo grunted, "Better dead."

That night, Fallon had danced only two dances with
Joan when he saw the four uniformed men offering their
thanks for their invitation to his mother and father. They
were about to leave.

Fallon caught Sanchez's eye, leaned his head in the
direction of the four, then went to his room and changed
into jeans, work boots, heavy chambray shirt, and his old
floppy-brimmed black hat. Last, he checked his weapons
and buckled his gunbelt. His rifle was in its saddle boot
in the stable, and so were the extra cylinders for his handgun. He looked around his room, wondering what he
might have forgotten, then went to his chest of drawers,
took a sheaf of paper money, shoved it in his pocket,
opened a window, and slipped across the sill into the darkness.

He was still working at saddling his line-backed dun
when Roberto came in dressed much as Fallon was. Two
Buffalo came right behind the handsome Mexican. Looking at Sanchez, Fallon asked, "You say anything to Carmella?"

Roberto nodded. "She'll offer some excuse to your
folks about us leaving."

Fallon pulled the cinches tight, waited a few moments
for Roberto to finish, and looked at Two Buffalo, who
had already thrown a blanket across his horse and sat
waiting.

Speaking softly, Fallon said, "The Frenchmen left five
minutes ago. We'll stay about that far behind. Let's ride."

They'd been on the trail only a short time when it occurred to him that Sanchez had said there were three

Frenchmen in the library. He shrugged. It made no difference, they'd probably fill the other one in on their plans later.

FRANKLIN, A SQUALID LITTLE TOWN, HUDDLED CLOSE TO the north bank of the Rio Grande. Saloons there far outnumbered businesses, such as the hotel, bank, general store, feed and seed store, blacksmith shop, and livery stable.

Before coming into town, Fallon led his companions around the Frenchmen's path and posted them one each at the hotel and a lawyer's office the French had rented when they moved across the border. "We'll make sure they bed down before we sleep. Might be best if we stay at the livery stable. They would wonder how the hell we got here so soon, maybe even why we left the party almost when they did."

Fallon stood in the shadows at the corner of the hotel when the four stabled their horses and walked to the door. Before they entered the hostelry doorway, Bienville said, "We'll sleep late. Meet you at the cafe about nine—then we have work to do. We need to find the right man, one that can't be traced to us. All right, let's get some sleep." They spoke French, and although Fallon's French fell short of his knowledge of Spanish, he understood what they said.

After Bienville and his cohorts disappeared into the hotel, Fallon signaled Roberto and Two Buffalo. They met him in the barn. "They gonna eat 'bout nine. We'll eat 'bout seven an' be gone before they get there. Okay, let's hit the hay." He had to smile to himself at the truth of his words: Hay was exactly what they'd sleep on, which wasn't unusual for any of them.

AT SEVEN, AFTER WASHING UP IN THE HORSE TROUGH, Fallon and his companions crossed the road, already cluttered with wagons, horses, mules, stray dogs, and pedestrians. They stepped onto the boardwalk and Fallon had reached for the cafe door when words cut into his act.

"You ain't goin' in there an' eat with white folks, Indian."

Fallon dropped his hand from the door handle and faced a bearded, mean-looking giant of a man. He smelled as though he'd spent the night in a saloon, but a look at his clothes said he'd slept in the shovelings from one of the stable stalls.

"Suppose I told you I'm an Indian, you gonna try to keep me from eatin'?"

With a sneer, the big man swept Fallon with a gaze from foot to head. "Reckon with you, I ain't gonna need to be told nothin'. First, I'll knock your teeth down yore throat, then I'll stomp you till you cain't hold nothin' to eat for a month."

Fallon smiled, then nodded. "Well, reckon you just explained it so's I understand." He twisted to his right as though to turn away, then with work-hardened fingers held straight and stiff, he whipped back to his left, and jammed his fingers into the man's Adam's apple.

The huge hulk choked and struggled for air, face purpled, eyes bulged. He clutched at his throat and chest, fighting for air that would never again pass through his crushed windpipe.

Fallon, holding his face devoid of expression, stared at the man, now on the ground kicking his feet into the inches-thick dust. After a couple of minutes, the man's kicking became feeble, then stopped.

Fallon, his face feeling stiff as dried leather, looked at Roberto. "Now, that just goes to show you, if a man don't keep his mouth shut an' tend to his own business, he can spoil his whole day." He again reached for the door. The scene had happened so quickly only a few people gathered to stare at the corpse. Many of them asked the person standing at their side, "What happened?" Before pulling the door open, Fallon heard one man say, "Reckon it don't hardly pay to mess with Tom Fallon 'fore he's done et his breakfast."

When he was only about halfway through his breakfast of six eggs, a thick slice of ham, ham gravy, and biscuits, the town marshal edged up to the long table made of unfinished lumber.

"What happened, Fallon?"

Tom finished chewing the bite he had in his mouth, swallowed, and eyed the marshal. "Man out yonder figured to keep me from breakfast. Didn't mean to kill 'im, but he brought it to me."

The marshal shook his head. "Tom, I've known you since we were kids. You were never this mean 'fore you went off to war."

Around another bite of food, Fallon said, "Ain't mean now, Jess, just learned that sometimes it don't serve a man to put off what cain't be avoided." He chewed a moment, washed the food down with a swallow of coffee, and asked, "You gonna arrest me?"

Jess Minter shook his head. "Nope. Just wondered what could bring a man to kill another before breakfast. You told it pretty much like those men outside did." He took an exaggerated sniff of air. "Mmmm, smell of ham, bacon, an' eggs always did make me hungry. Ain't et yet. Mind if I sit with you?"

"Nope, but we're gonna be leavin' pretty soon."

All during breakfast Fallon felt the marshal's eyes studying him. He kept his face as devoid of expression as he could, not wanting to show how much he regretted killing the man. His breakfast sat in a lump in the middle of his stomach.

They finished their meal, and on the way out, Two Buffalo asked, "Why you fight my fight, Tom? I could kill 'im."

Fallon looked at the old man who he'd known since he was a small boy. "Two Buffalo, under the circumstances, if I kill 'im I ain't in no trouble—you kill 'im an' you're in a heap o' trouble. It ain't right, but that's the way it is."

After breakfast Fallon stationed Sanchez at the cafe, Two Buffalo at the hotel, and he took the lawyer's office, but he took his position across the street so he could see the front door as well as one side of the building. "Pull your hats down over your faces much as possible so's you can still see. I don't believe they'll recognize any of us anyway. They ain't ever seen you or me in work clothes before, Roberto, an' you, Two Buffalo, they got no reason to know you.''

The Frenchmen came out of the hotel a few minutes before nine and crossed the street to the cafe. Fallon waited. After a half hour or forty-five minutes, they came out and went directly to their rented office.

He felt a pang of relief that the office was only a one-story building. Maybe he could get close enough to a window to hear what they said, and he hoped they would speak in English. Although he could understand quite a bit of French, he didn't consider himself fluent enough to chance knowing all they said. He again crossed the street, and stood at the corner of the building, then, even though it was daylight, he took a chance no one would get curious as to why he squatted under one of the side windows. He pushed his hat back, wiped sweat, and pulled his hat down over his face again. Inside the building a voice he thought to be that of Henri Bienville said in French, "*M'sieurs,* it will do us no good to go blindly into the saloons looking for the kind of man we need, and I know of nowhere else to look." A short silence followed before Bienville continued, "Any ideas, *m'sieurs*?" Relief flooded Fallon. He had understood almost every word.

A voice he didn't recognize came to him outside the window. "Henri, I have a friend of French extraction who might help us find a man for the job. If it was an American we wanted killed, he'd never turn on his adopted country, but the Mexicans mean nothing to him. I believe it's worth a try."

Then a third voice, this time Fallon thought he recognized it as the whiny voice of Francois Berne: "We will see if your friend can help us, Charles. If he can't, I'll do it myself. However, I'd rather stay clear of it."

Then Henri spoke again. "Yes, Francois, I want us directly involved only as a last resort. Who is your friend, Charles?"

"The man who owns the apothecary shop about four stores south of here. Raoul Martine."

Henri's voice sounded doubtful. "Killing a man, even a Juárista, is a serious thing. What makes you think he might help us?"

"You said the key word, Henri. American, or Spaniard, it wouldn't work, but a Juárista would trigger Raoul's remaining patriotism for his mother country."

A long silence followed. Fallon figured they were thinking over Charles's suggestion, then Henri, apparently the leader, said, "I think your idea might work, Charles. We'll try it. See if your friend will meet us here after dinner, perhaps about eight o'clock."

Charles agreed. "In the meantime, we have work to do for our country right here in our office. I'll see Martine during the noon hour."

Fallon had heard enough. Tonight, he would place a man at the windows on both sides of the building. Two Buffalo would understand what they said only if they spoke English, and there was slight chance they would, so Fallon decided to keep the old Indian with him.

He looked toward the street and the rear of the building to see if anyone might be interested in what he was doing, then headed for his two friends.

In the street, he looked toward each and motioned toward the Red Dog Saloon, the one nearest to him.

Inside, he told them they had time for a beer or two. "Fact is, we got time for several, but we're gonna only have two."

Two Buffalo grunted, a sound of disgust making its way into his voice. "No make dead, no drink much, no fun. Damn, Tomas, you ain't no fun no more."

The bartender edged over to where Fallon stood. "Fallon, you know we ain't s'posed to serve no Indians in here."

Fallon locked gazes with him. "You gonna serve Two Buffalo, no matter what you s'posed to do."

The bartender drew three beers.

# CHAPTER

# 7

T HE THREE OF THEM SAT DRINKING THEIR BEER, THEN
Fallon ordered a second, all the time feeling the ugly puss
of hate aimed at him from around the room, aimed at him
because they feared him, and aimed at his companions,
one for being an Indian, and at both the Indian and the
Mexican for being his friends.

He scanned the room. Many there were ex–Yankee soldiers, men who'd fought for the negro's freedom, yet
would kill or enslave the Indian. He grunted in disgust.
Trying to figure the human sense of values, of right and
wrong, was futile.

Fallon explained what he'd heard, keeping his voice
low. "Tonight I want you, Roberto, at the windows on
the south side of that shyster's office. I'll take the north
side with Two Buffalo. We need to know the name of the
man Raoul Martine gives them, then I want you to go
home. I'll take it from there. Don't want either of you
mixed up in what I'll have to do. If something happens
to me, our friend down south will still need someone up
here to help him." He looked at Two Buffalo, took a
swallow of beer, and grinned. "Two Buffalo, I know you
don't know what the hell's going on, an' I also know that

the fact is you don't give a damn; all you want outta this is the fun of raising seven different kinds of hell. I promise you, the next time I need help, I'll send for you.''

The old Indian studied him a moment and said, ''Lot better make all dead. No more bother you. No more trouble.''

Straight-faced, Fallon said, ''We kill 'em, they make no more trouble, then I won't need you to help me make big fight. How you want it?''

Two Buffalo's grin widened. ''Wait for big fight.''

They finished their beers and went to the livery stable to while away the afternoon and evening hours. Mostly they got comfortable in the haymow and slept. Between naps, Fallon thought of Joan Boniol. How was she mixed up in this? Would she voluntarily be a part of killing Juárez? Even though of French extraction, would she feel any loyalty to France? The more he thought on it, the more confused he got. Finally he shrugged, lay back, and dozed again.

That night, crouched under the windows, they got the information Fallon needed. Martine told the Frenchmen of a gunman they could get for one hundred dollars, a man by the name of Darrel Dennis, a deserter from the Confederate Army who came west, joined the Union Army, deserted it, and had since made a name for himself as a gunman—one who preferred a back shoot rather than a stand-up, head-on gunfight.

Back at the stable, before heading home, Roberto asked Fallon, ''What you intend to do, *amigo*? You might need someone to watch your back.''

Fallon slowly shook his head. ''No. I figure to find 'im, follow 'im to El Paso del Norte, an' once on that side of the border find a way to take care of him without causing a ruckus with the law.'' He packed his pipe, put fire to it, and inhaled a lungful of the rich aroma before saying, ''You men go on home, and, *amigo*, if one of these mornin's my big black horse is gone from your stable, look for me to show up three or four days after. We didn't come up with information on 'nother shipment this time, but there'll be another.''

Two Buffalo grunted and said, ''Sleep now, go home later.''

EARLY THE NEXT MORNING, FALLON SAT SLUMPED against the wall of the general store across the street from the lawyer's office, hat pulled low on his forehead. He didn't know Darrel Dennis, but he figured to find the name of anyone entering the Frenchmen's headquarters. He went to the livery, saddled the dun, left the cinch straps loose, then went back to the store.

The morning sun, hot and dry, brought sweat trickling between his shoulder blades, and perspiration soaked his hat's sweatband. He sat there through the morning and into the afternoon watching the shadows grow long. About four o'clock, a nondescript, tall, slim, bearded man walked to the front of the lawyer's office, looked both directions, settled his crossed gunbelts more comfortably around his hips, and pushed through the doorway. Fallon smiled, his breath shortened. He would bet every cent he'd ever have that was his man. He stood, walked across the street, and slouched against the wall beside the door.

Close to an hour later, the man came out of the building holding a sheaf of bills. He folded the money, tucked it in his shirt pocket, and walked toward the nearest saloon to the south. Fallon followed.

In the saloon the bartender confirmed his suspicion the man was Dennis. Fallon bought a beer, went to the back wall, pulled a table close to it, and sat looking into the room.

He nursed his beer until it grew warm, ordered another, and had finished about half of it when Dennis stood and pushed through the batwing door. When the panels swung open, Fallon saw that night had set in. He went out not far behind the gunman, who went to a hitchrack in front of a different saloon, tightened the cinch straps on his horse, mounted, and headed toward El Paso del Norte.

Fallon hurried to the livery stable, tightened the straps

on his Texas rig, mounted, and took the same route. He wanted Dennis in sight by the time they crossed the river. A man could disappear right sudden in the maze of streets in that north Mexican town.

While riding, Fallon pondered what to do. He didn't know whether Juárez had yet reached El Paso, and hoped he hadn't. He had no idea what Dennis planned, but from what he'd heard of the man, he'd pick a spot, shoot from the dark, and make his getaway—nothing complicated. Fallon figured to stop the assassin before he could get his plan in motion, and the only way he could figure to do it was to pick a fight, and kill him.

He'd never set out to deliberately kill a man and didn't like the idea, but weighing the two men, Dennis against Juárez, Fallon could think of no alternative. Dennis was the loser.

If he succeeded in eliminating Dennis, then he would have to deal with Francois Berne, who said he'd take care of the job himself, and who Fallon guessed to be much more intelligent and, as a result, more dangerous, than Dennis.

Stopping the Frenchman would be tricky. Berne had a personal interest in ridding his country of Juárez. Where the gunman would shoot and run, Fallon figured the Frenchman would carefully plan every move.

He caught sight of Dennis before he reached the river and closed the distance between them. On reaching the main street, Fallon figured Juárez had not yet gotten to the town, but the people anticipated his arrival. They were even now, at night, decorating the storefronts for the arrival of their *presidente*.

He followed Dennis the length of the street and turned back when he did. The gunman pulled rein in front of a *cantina* about midway along the street and went in. Fallon, only a few steps behind, shadowed him.

The aroma of chili peppers, fried meat, tortillas, and frijoles made his mouth water, a reminder he hadn't eaten since breakfast.

Dennis elbowed a place to the bar, getting curses from

those standing there. Fallon figured there wouldn't be many close by who would give a damn what happened to the gringo. He pulled up short, only a step behind the hired gun.

Shallow, quick breaths filled his lungs. His throat tightened. His heart beat faster and harder, like a trip-hammer against his rib cage. Fallon settled his Colt against his side and said, "Pushin' people around like that, you must figure you're pretty good with them guns you got tied down to yore legs. Course from what I've seen, most two gunmen ain't worth a damn with either one."

Dennis whirled to face Fallon, his eyes slitted. "Some o' yore business, cowboy?"

A dead calm invaded Fallon. "Reckon I'm makin' it my business. Don't like to see people pushed around by a gutless bully. An' for your information, them two guns don't scare me even a little bit."

Now there was plenty of space at the bar. The crowded, cursing men drew to each side and still pushed for more room. Dennis crouched, his fingers curved, his arms hanging tense at his sides. "You sayin' I'm gutless?"

Fallon stared into the gunman's eyes, waited a long moment, then in almost a whisper said, "Reckon yore hearin's mighty good."

Dennis's hands slapped his gun butts. Fallon's right hand, in a smooth, flawless motion, drew his Bowie knife and pushed it into the gunman's gut.

Dennis, his eyes wide with fright, and pain, grabbed for the knife with his right hand, his other hand groping, trying to draw his left-hand revolver. Fallon held onto his knife handle with his left hand, and swung his right to clutch the handle of the gunman's six-shooter to keep it in its holster. He stepped in close to Dennis, and so low no one around him could hear, he said, "Juárez lives." Then before the gunman could draw his last breath, Fallon pulled Dennis's handgun, dropped it to the sawdust-covered floor, reached to the slim man's shirt pocket, and withdrew the sheaf of bills the Frenchmen had paid him.

"These gentlemen thank you for the drinks you're about to buy."

Only then did he draw his knife from the gunman's gut and let him slide to the floor. He looked across the bar and handed the bartender the money. "*Señor,* serve these *hombres* drinks till the money is gone. I'll take this poor gringo back to Norte Americano, and leave him with some of his friends." He shook his head. "Shame he fell against my knife while I cleaned my fingernails."

He looked at the man next to him. "He rode a bay horse with a Texas rig. It's out at the hitchrack. Take 'im out and tie 'im across his saddle, *por favor.*"

The Mexican grinned. "*Sí, señor,* eef only they weel save me some of theze free drinks."

Fallon pulled a cartwheel from his pocket. "*Amigo,* they don't save some, this'll get you a few *cervesas.*"

Soon, satisfied Dennis was securely draped and tied across the animal, Fallon led the would-be assassin's horse from the *cantina* and headed for the river upstream of the bridge.

After fording the shallow stream, he rode to the shyster's office, hitched Dennis's horse to the rail in front, found a piece of paper, and scribbled on it, "Do your own killing." He pinned the note to the gunman's back, looked at his handiwork, toed the stirrup, and headed for the livery.

He wondered if anyone who knew him had noticed his activities of the evening. The entire thing in the *cantina* lasted only a few minutes. He'd had his hat pulled low, needed a shave, and was dirty from trail dust. He doubted anyone on the Mexican side could come close to describing him. Any one of a hundred gringos would fit his description.

Fallon thought on why he'd used his knife instead of his Colt, then decided a bullet from his six-shooter would not have killed the gunman quick enough to prevent him triggering several shots into Fallon's chest. He'd seen dying men empty a six-shooter while sinking to the ground. With the knife, Dennis had been kept awful busy trying to pull it out with one hand and get his six-shooter into action with the other. Fallon had been right. Cold steel is a mighty hard thing to ignore.

When he rode into the livery stable, he looked at his watch. The time, not yet ten o'clock, caused Fallon to muse on how much could happen in a short time. While caring for his horse, he decided to sleep under a roof, and headed for the hotel.

Long after lying down, he thought of Francois Berne, and wondered how the Frenchman would try to kill Juárez. Would he get together several men to carry out the deed? Would he try it alone? Would he use a rifle, or poison, or, or, or . . . ?

Fallon gave up on trying to figure what another man would do. The only thing he could do was stick to Berne like a cocklebur and, when he made his move, nail him.

Before sleeping, he thought of the petite, copper-haired girl who in an instant could label him an outlaw—a tag he could not deny, but one he was willing to risk having pinned on him if that was the price for seeing her again. But seeing her would have to wait. Berne stood between them.

Finally he slept.

FALLON OPENED HIS EYES TO FIND A NEW DAY HAD dawned—hot, muggy, with a light drizzle. His watch told him it was almost seven o'clock. A look at the clothes he'd worn for more than two days caused him to sniff, wrinkle his nose, and crawl from bed. He went to the window and looked across the street to the general store. The front door stood wide.

He put on his dirty clothes and went downstairs to the desk, where he told the clerk to have hot water taken to his room, he'd be back in a few minutes.

In the store, he bought everything to clothe him from the skin out, then went back to his room, wishing he could wash the stiffness from the clothes he'd bought. Bathwater arrived about the time he opened his packages.

After his bath, the barbershop was next on his agenda.

He'd not feel ready to meet the world until he got a shave. His razor was back at the ranch.

Feeling like a new man, Fallon went to the cafe for breakfast. He sat at the table closest to the front window, where he had a clear view of the Frenchmen's headquarters. A crowd stood around the horse he'd left in front of the shyster's office the night before. A man went inside and came out with Bienville, who took the note from the gunman's body, read it, wadded it in his fist, and threw it to the ground. He reached in his pocket and took out what was obviously a coin of some size, waved to the corpse, and pointed toward boothill. After that, several men, all tough-looking customers, went in and out of the small building, causing Fallon to wonder why so many Americans would find business with the French. He studied on that while watching.

French sympathizers, with the move of Juárez to occupy El Paso del Norte, had probably traveled to Franklin. Then it occurred to Fallon: In all probability the plans for gold shipments to Maximilian were made in that small building right across the street. Why had he not thought of that before? The idea chased a chill up his spine. How could he protect Juárez, uncover plots for gold shipments, and hold up the vehicles hauling the gold? A man could be in only one place at a time.

Sitting there, taking his time drinking coffee, the problems took him back a few months, to when he'd been dragged from the Yankee prison. Despite Johnson saying he intended to turn him loose whether or not he agreed to take on his special mission, Fallon figured if he hadn't agreed he'd have stood by that brick wall and been shot to rags. He'd been closer to death many times, but never when he couldn't defend himself.

Fallon's thoughts returned to the present, and still looking across the street at the French headquarters, he worried at how naturally he'd taken to being an outlaw. He'd done things, ruthless things. He'd hurt his mother and father because telling them would jeopardize national diplomacy, and probably national security. But he'd done all those things because it was in the best interests of doing the job to which he was assigned, in the best interests of his country. Abruptly his gaze sharpened.

A figure he'd recognize among a million others had just entered the shyster's office: Joan Boniol.

# CHAPTER

8

FALLON STARED AT THE DOORWAY THROUGH WHICH Joan had disappeared, realizing for the first time that *she was a French agent, his enemy*. He had known all along she was helping the French, but had only now realized how coolly she operated right under the nose of her own country. Of course, she had to know there was little the United States could do openly to oppose Maximilian. Slightly above a whisper, he said, "Little one, I have you at a disadvantage. I know you, know who you work for, and so far, you don't suspect who I am, and don't suspect the United States of being involved."

Fallon paid for his breakfast, went outside, and sat on the boardwalk, using the cafe wall to support his back. He pondered whether to send for Roberto and Two Buffalo, or to try to handle it alone. He could let the gold shipment go through and concentrate his efforts on stopping Francois Berne, or he could send for his friends and trust them to stop Berne.

Letting the gold go through troubled him. If it was a large shipment, it might be enough to tip the scales in Maximilian's favor again. If he called in help to stop the gold from going through, Joan might get hurt—even

killed. He couldn't stand the thought of that. And if he
trusted Roberto and Two Buffalo to stop Berne, he might
get them killed. He wouldn't consider such.

He sighed. That put him right back where he'd started.
Somehow he had to stop the gold *and* foil Berne. Right
now, it seemed that the sensible thing was to try and find
how much gold would be going south. He didn't think
Berne would set any plan in motion without first giving
it a lot of thought and then studying the area in which
he'd try to kill Juárez. Too, Juárez was not yet in El Paso
del Norte. That might give Fallon time to locate the gold
and determine how it would be transported.

His attention sharpened, focused on the door across the
street. Joan and Bienville came out. Bienville had on a
cloak to protect against the rain, and Joan had a shawl
over her head and shoulders. Fallon's back muscles stiffened. A surge of anger shot through him at the way Joan
held the Frenchman's arm. He forced himself to relax.
Hell, he had no claim on her, and besides, that was the
way any lady would be escorted down a busy street by a
gentleman. And, he admitted ruefully, Bienville was a
gentleman, despite being on the wrong side.

Fallon let them get far enough down the street, then
followed.

They walked to the edge of town, then walked the rutted, muddy trail another quarter of a mile, to a large barn
sitting in the middle of a cleared field. Fallon stopped at
the corner of the last building on the street. To go farther
would put him in the open.

He hunkered at the side of the weathered, grayed, un-
painted wall, now black with moisture, and watched. They
walked directly to the barn, stood there a moment, until
someone inside opened the smaller door, beside the one
used for pulling wagons and such into the dark maw of
the stable.

When the door closed behind them, Fallon squinted into
the misty, miserably hot morning, thinking he'd give all
hell and half of Georgia to know what they were doing
in there. They came out over a half hour later. He stood,

went around the corner of the building, and waited. They passed only a few feet from him.

He watched their backs until they turned into the French headquarters. Again he glanced toward the large barn. What was in there? What would draw the attention of Joan Boniol *and* the French? He could come to only one conclusion; they were readying another gold shipment.

If his suspicions were correct, he'd find a large coach or freight wagon parked there, along with animals to pull it, and it would be heavily guarded.

He studied the sturdy but weathered building. Like most stables, at ground level it had no windows, only one large door at each end, and the smaller one through which Bienville and Joan had entered.

To make matters worse, there wasn't a cactus, or yucca, or even a scraggly creosote bush, within a hundred yards of the stable on any side. They had made sure they had an excellent field of fire. The thought of trying to get to the barn, and then get inside, made chills run up and down Fallon's spine.

His chest tightened with the thought that regardless of how well guarded, or how clear, the grounds were, he had to get inside the building. Then from the haymow door, above the big door on the ground level, came a reflection of dull light on metal. That had to come from a rifle barrel. Fallon's neck hair felt as though it stood straight out. One thing for sure, he wasn't about to try to approach the stable during daylight.

He walked slowly to the hotel, in such deep thought he bumped into a couple of cowhands on the way, and when they growled at him to watch where the hell he was going, he absentmindedly offered an apology and walked on.

He'd been told if you gave any problem your entire attention, you could solve it. He pushed his hat to the back of his head, mopped sweat, and pushed it forward again. He was about to test that theory to the hilt. He hoped it didn't get him killed.

Fallon again mopped his brow, glanced at the hotel,

and grimaced, knowing the tiny room he'd rented would be even hotter than where he stood. A glance toward the nearest saloon turned his footsteps in that direction. A cold beer would taste good.

While he drank, it came to him he still had time to find what the stable held before Berne put any plan he might have into action.

He pondered the problem awhile longer. He thought of setting the barn on fire, or using dynamite, but that wouldn't do anything but expose the French for hoarding gold. That wouldn't get the gold to Juárez. Too, he'd kill the animals he knew must be in the stable. He couldn't do that. He drank the rest of his beer and stood. He'd do it the hard way, the only way, since there was no easy way.

He waited until night, then let the early hours of dark pass before he headed for the outskirts of the scrubby little town. At the same building from which he'd watched Bienville and Joan, he turned sharply to the right and went into the desert, until he was on the far side of the barn. Now the hard part.

From behind a giant yucca, he stared at the bare ground between him and the stable, hoping most of the guards' attention was focused on the town side, then, his heart in his throat, he dropped to his stomach in the gooey mud and, a few feet at a time, slithered toward the barn.

Every so often he stopped to listen. When satisfied he wasn't close to a sentry, he moved another few feet.

If guards were stationed outside, they probably would be hugging the lee side of the barn, out of the wind and rain. In Fallon's favor, he was on the windward side.

Now, about ten feet or so from the wall, he congratulated himself on getting there unseen. Then, a match flared only a few feet away. Fallon froze. His breath caught in his throat. He lay still for what seemed like an hour, but only a few moments passed, because in that time the guard took only three drags from his smoke.

The sentry would be blinded from the match flare, and then like most smokers in the dark, he'd watch the glow at the end of his cigarette when he took a drag. That would be in Fallon's favor. But if he managed to kill the man, what would he do with him? If he left him for his friends to find, they'd be alerted that their scheme was known.

Maybe after he found what he wanted he could drag the man away, out into the desert, where perhaps he'd not be found. Drag him far enough that the buzzards and coyotes would soon make his corpse unrecognizable.

Fallon sucked in a deep breath, waited for the sentry to turn his back, and stood. His joints cracked from the long, tedious crawl across the open space and then lying still. To his ears, the noise sounded like a rifle shot, but apparently it didn't make a noise outside his own head. The sentry stepped toward the stable doorway.

Making no more noise than a slight squish when he pulled his feet from the sucking mud, Fallon, glided to the back of the man, wrapped his arm around his neck, covered his mouth with his hand, and pulled his Bowie across the man's throat. Only a small gurgle came to his ears when the sentry tried to cough, stiffened, and went limp.

Holding him for a moment longer, Fallon eased him to the ground, hoping the man was not due to be relieved before Fallon had a chance to do what he'd come to do and escape.

He stood without moving for a moment, breathing slowly, trying to settle his nerves. To attempt entering the barn was foolhardy, so he cast that idea aside. Maybe he could find a knothole, or a crack between the boards through which he could see, and hopefully hear, what was going on.

He slipped along the side of the building and peered through several cracks as he went. At every crack or knothole, stalls stood in his line of sight.

Fallon eyed the door at the end of the building. To find a place there from which he was certain he'd be able to see down the stable runway would leave him hung out to dry if someone opened the door. He studied on it a moment, tried to relax, then figured to hell with it, he never figured to grow old anyway.

Placing each foot with care, he searched the width of the door before he found what he wanted—a chest-high knothole about the size of a silver dollar.

He bent and put his eye to the hole. Inside, he counted seven men working on a large, heavy coach, about the size of the one Joan Boniol had been in during Fallon's previous holdup. The workers had the floorboards torn out and were now working on the sides.

One of the men straightened and looked at the one who must have been in charge. He opened his mouth to say something and Fallon shifted from looking to hearing. He hated to do it, because he wanted to see what went on, but he placed his ear against the hole. "Boss, when we gotta have this finished, an' ready to replace the flooring an' sides?"

The man in charge hesitated, obviously to think on his answer, then said, "We ain't the ones who's gonna finish it. Soon's we get the insides stripped we're through. If someone's gonna rebuild the inside, they'll do it after we're gone. The Frenchie said we had five days to get through so's not to mess up the boards we took out. They gonna try to use the same stuff to rebuild with after they get it loaded. That leaves us four days to get the job done."

Fallon found he could hear even when his eye was at the knothole. He looked again.

The workman who had questioned the boss scratched his head and eyed the coach. "Somethin's gonna be hauled in this contraption what ain't none o' our business."

The boss gave him a fish-eyed stare. "You're right, so don't worry yore head 'bout it. Get back to work. We don't get paid to ask questions."

Fallon knew all he needed to know for now. He moved from the door, looked toward each corner of the building, went to the man he'd killed, shouldered him, and, bent under his heavy load, headed for the chaparral. He didn't draw a normal breath until he'd put several yards between him and the edge of the clearing.

His pace didn't slow until the desert brush and cactus closed off the silhouette of the stable. He walked another half mile into the desert before he looked for a place to drop the body.

His eyes, accustomed to the dark, soon found a dry wash. He dropped the body into the ditch, now running almost half-full with runoff. When he took a last glance at the lifeless hulk, a pang of pity stabbed him. The poor bastard had only tried to earn a living. Fallon shook his head, hating that he'd had to kill once again. He glanced at the tracks he'd left, then turned his face to the heavens, hoping the rain continued and washed out his sign. He headed back to town.

In the lamplight cast from a window at the back of the hotel, Fallon looked down at his clothes. Mud plastered him from boots to high on his shirt, but what bothered him most was the blood from the sentry's throat that soaked his left shirtsleeve. That would cause questions. He needed a bath, and a way to dispose of his clothes after he changed.

He climbed the outside stairs to the second floor, then scraped mud from his boots and peered down the empty hall. He pulled the squeaky screen door open, went in, and cat-footed to his room.

Stripped, and using water from the white porcelain pitcher, he washed up; then he changed clothes, wrapped his muddy clothes in a bundle, and stretched out on his bed to think.

He had four days before the crew had the coach torn down for loading, then those who would load it and put the boards and siding back in place would take another few days. This gave him time to find Juárez before he entered El Paso del Norte. Maybe he *could* protect the *presidente* and take the gold shipment. He swung his legs off the bed, buckled his gunbelt about him, checked his weapons, and left the room carrying the package of clothes, which he'd discard on the Mexican side.

•   •   •

IN EL PASO DEL NORTE, FALLON HAD TO FIGHT HIMSELF
not to go see Joan Boniol. He told himself he had plenty
of time—but duty came first. He satisfied his yearning by
seeking out her house and riding by it in the dark.

The rain slackened to a steady drizzle. Fallon pulled his
neck deeper into his slicker and headed northwest out of
town.

Dreary, chilly daylight pushed weakly against the sod-
den darkness before Fallon topped a ridge above the La-
guna de Guzman, now running bank full, and looked upon
a sprinkling of campfires along the near bank. Those fires
had to be Juárez's camp. He pulled his bandanna up over
his nose and rode cautiously down the slope.

Drawing closer, he soon was able to see the outlines of
the *presidente*'s little black carriage silhouetted against a
fire larger than the others. Only a second after he had
identifyied the carriage, a voice sounded to his side.
"*Alto,* or I shoot. Why do you ride into our camp at this
hour?"

Fallon, irritated he'd gotten this close only to be chal-
lenged now, growled, "Why the hell did you wait so long
to stop me?" Then, not waiting for an answer, he said,
"It is important I see *El Presidente*. I am a friend of the
Republic."

The guttural Mexican voice commanded him to ride
closer. He did as told, then in the murky light the sentry
peered at him. "Ah, ees the *Bandido Caballero*. Come. I
ride behind. You ride in front. I take you to heem."

Inside Juárez's tent, Fallon closed the entrance flap and
pulled the bandanna from his face. "I come empty-handed
*Señor Presidente*. I come to warn you, and to ask a favor."

"Ah, *amigo,* ask your favor. If possible, I'll grant it."

A warm feeling flooded Fallon's chest. Juárez put the
favor he would ask ahead of a warning. He smiled. "I
reckon they're really one and the same." He accepted the
steaming cup of coffee Juárez handed him, and continued.
"There's a man, a Frenchman, who is planning to kill

you once you get to El Paso del Norte. I want you to delay entering the town until I come to you and tell you I know his plan and can protect you.''

Juárez looked at him over the rim of his cup. ''Tell me who he is and I'll have him taken care of.''

Fallon shook his head. ''Can't work that way. He'll stay on American soil until he figures to carry out his plan. I don't want him killed up there. He's a French official, and killing him on American soil'll bring on even more strained relations with France. I want to wait until he's in Mexico, but I also want to be sure you have many troops about you so he can't easily get close to you. Don't worry, I'll take care of him.'' He smiled. ''And now, I'll tell you something to warm your heart, the main reason I want you to delay your entrance. I know of a gold shipment—a very large shipment I want to bring to you.''

Juárez shivered. ''It's cold and damp, *amigo*. Let me warm your drink with a little brandy.'' Without waiting for Fallon's consent, he reached to his cot and pulled a bottle from under it, then proceeded to sweeten Fallon's coffee. He slanted Fallon a questioning look. ''You say this is a large shipment? Surely you don't hope to commit the holdup alone.''

Fallon shook his head. ''That's where you come in, *señor*. I want you to put at least fifty troops, a hundred would be better, under my command. I want them to meet me in that arroyo south of town, and, *Señor Presidente,* I don't want even one shot fired at the coach. There'll be a woman in the coach who I want unharmed. I want you to tell your troops, and I'll repeat your orders before we attack and take the coach for you.''

''Ahhh, do I detect a romance here, *mi amigo*?''

Fallon studied the bottom of his cup a moment, then grinned at Juárez. ''Sir, she doesn't know it yet, but I figure to make that young lady a very close friend, maybe even closer than that. She doesn't know I am *your* friend. When she learns my sentiments, she'll probably end our friendship.'' He frowned. ''I'll figure something. I sure don't figure to lose her very easy.''

Juárez held the brandy bottle to the lamp, frowning as he studied the amber color. After a bit, he turned his attention back to Fallon. "It will be as you say, *mi amigo,* but how am I to know when to send my troops?"

"Been wonderin' about that myself. Do you have a man you could send with me, stay with me until I know for sure when the shipment will leave Franklin, a man you would trust with your life?" He took a swallow of coffee. "This man will be one I have to trust also, because he'll learn my identity soon after we leave here. I'll send him to you as soon as I'm sure of my information."

"I have such a man. Then, too, I must also know when you want me to enter El Paso del Norte."

Fallon nodded. "That's the easy part. After we take the coach, your troops will bring it to you. I'll go back to Franklin as soon as I see the coach firmly in the hands of your troops. When the vehicle gets to you, break camp and go on in to town." He hesitated. "And, *Señor Presidente,* the girl will stay with the coach until you reach town, then I want her escorted to her *casa,* safely."

Juárez nodded. "She'll be safe, *amigo.* Now, get some sleep. When you awaken, I'll have a good breakfast awaiting you, *juevos rancheros,* and some good hot coffee." Obviously thinking, he looked at a calendar, counted some days, then looked at Fallon. "Whatever happens, I must be in El Paso del Norte August fifth."

"All right. Let's hope everything is done by then. I'm going to Franklin soon's you have the man brought to me."

Juárez called for an orderly, and Fallon pulled his bandanna up to his eyes.

Juárez spoke in rapid Spanish, telling the orderly whom he wished brought to him. Fallon wasn't surprised at the name he heard.

In only a few moments, the tent flap lifted and Juan Valdez came in. He apparently wasn't surprised either. "Ah, my bandit friend, we meet again."

Fallon lapsed into his south Texas drawl. "Yep, my friend, reckon I figured our paths would cross again."

They shook hands while Juárez told Valdez his assignment.

Daylight dawned a dreary, misty gray. An hour later, well beyond sentries circling the Juárez camp, Fallon pulled the bandanna from his face. Valdez studied him a moment. "Yes, Señor Fallon, I have seen you many times, but never thought of you as the *Bandido Caballero*. What brought you to help *El Presidente*?"

"Valdez, that's a question I'm not at liberty to answer. Don't mean to be rude," he shrugged, "but reckon it's that way."

"Ah, my friend, no offense taken. We'll forget I asked."

# CHAPTER

FALLON AND VALDEZ RODE INTO TOWN TOGETHER, then decided to split, thinking it would be wise for them not to be seen together. Valdez's access to the Maximilian court and the Spanish aristocracy was important for finding troop movements and other information Juárez might need.

"You go ahead and get a room, Valdez. I'll follow in a few minutes, but first, I'm gonna get me about three fingers in a washtub of the strongest bourbon I can find. Maybe it'll knock the chill outta my bones."

Valdez raised an eyebrow, grinned, and said, "We might not drink together, but I'll tell you right now, I'll be in one of your American *cantinas* doing the same as you."

Fallon looked down the deserted, soggy street. "Might be a good idea for you to renew acquaintances with the French. They could drop something of use. 'Til then, I'll be watching the stable pretty close. *Vaya con Dios, amigo.*" He kneed his horse toward the center of town, and a tall glass of bourbon.

Before walking to the bar, Fallon shrugged out of his

slicker, shivered, and swept the large room with a glance. He saw no one he knew.

He looked at the crusty old man pouring drinks. "Gimme a water glass full o' the best bourbon you got."

The old man topped off his drink, and when he reached for it a puncher down the bar from him said loud enough for all at the bar to hear, "Gonna kill you, *hombre*. You knifed my partner."

Curious, Fallon, his drink still sitting on the bar, looked to see who had spoken and to whom the stranger talked.

A tall, slim, bearded man looked him right in the eye, and said, "Yeah, you, knife-fighter. Gonna see can you use that six-shooter good's you use a knife."

Quicker'n scat, not a man stood between them. Fallon studied the man a moment. "You ain't got it straight, cowboy. I never seen you before."

"You right, but I seen you down yonder in El Paso del Norte. They wuz too many Mexes around for me to call you then, but you ain't bought no friends up here with free drinks. If you can use that there sixgun, you better pull iron or I'm gonna shoot you anyway."

A man standing off to the side said, "Don't know you, cowboy, but I'm here to tell you, Tom Fallon can use that iron on his hip good's any I ever seen. Fact is, he's as good or better with it than he is with a knife. Get smart an' leave 'im alone."

Fallon had gone quiet inside, a cold alertness gripping him. The tall man hesitated, the spectator's words apparently worrying him.

Fallon didn't want another killing. "Cowboy, leave it be. I'll buy you a drink and we can forget it."

Fallon knew instantly he'd taken the wrong fork in the trail. The thin man took his words for fear, and where he'd apparently had a moment's caution, Fallon's words gave him the confidence he wanted. "Done told you, drag iron, or I shoot you anyway."

Fallon stood relaxed, the fingers of his right hand barely brushing the walnut grip of his .44. "Ain't pullin' first, cowboy, but I'm tellin' you, if you touch that handgun you're wearin' you gonna make a mighty smelly corpse."

The man hesitated, opened his mouth to say something, then his hand dived for his six-shooter. Fallon waited until the gun almost cleared leather, then drew, thumbed off a shot, and watched it dimple the gunman's shirt at his right shoulder. The heavy slug knocked the gunny back a step. He regained his balance and his left hand reached for a belt gun. Fallon, lazy-like, thumbed a shot into the man's other shoulder. The would-be hardcase stared at Fallon a moment, the holes in his shoulders only now beginning to show blood, then he fell on his face.

The big Colt .44, still emitting a string of wispy smoke, disappeared into Fallon's holster. He swept the men surrounding him with a glance. "If he's got any friends here, drag iron, or better yet take 'im to the doc's office down the street. He ain't dead—but will be if he don't get those holes plugged right soon."

He picked up his drink, took a mouthful, swallowed, and gasped for breath. Looking the bartender in the eye, he stuck his hand out far enough to clear the other side of the bar and turned the glass upside down. "If that rotgut's your best, I'll find me another saloon."

Fallon's words didn't faze the old man, he grinned, glanced at the spilled whiskey, and said, "Reckon you done 'splained it to me pretty good." He reached under the bar and pulled out a bottle with a seal on it. "This one's on the house."

Fallon's lips quivered, and when he couldn't hold it back, he laughed outright. This time when he reached for his drink they were carrying the unconscious cowboy through the batwing doors.

He sipped his whiskey, let it sit on his tongue a moment tasting it, and nodded at the old timer. "You got it right this time." He found himself a table against the wall at the back of the saloon.

Valdez came in, ordered himself a drink, took a swallow, coughed, put the glass back on the bar and walked out. Neither he nor Fallon acknowledged each other, although it was all Fallon could do to keep from laughing when Valdez took the one swallow.

Finishing his drink, Fallon went to his room, bathed and went to bed. It had been a long day. Tired as he was, he lay thinking, wishing he had brought a change of dress clothes from home, because while pondering what to do the next day he decided that sitting around wishing to see the girl with copper-colored hair wasn't getting him anywhere, so on the morrow he'd ride across the river and call on her.

At two o'clock the next afternoon, dressed in range clothes, Fallon banged the knocker on the door of Joan's casa. A servant answered the door. Fallon removed his hat and said, "Please tell Miss Boniol, Tom Fallon would like to see her."

Only a moment and a rustle of taffeta told him she was near. His heartbeat quickened.

"Why, Tom, what a delightful surprise, come in."

"You'll have to pardon me, ma'am, both for the intrusion and for my dress. I brought a few head of cows over this morning and thought to make good on my promise to see you."

She took his hand and led him toward another room. "Come, I was about to have a cup of coffee. Would you like a cup?"

He smiled. "Ma'am, if it's like what they serve in New Orleans, I surely would. Seems like after one gets used to it, all other coffee lacks character. Fact is, if it ain't thick enough to chew I don't care for it."

She laughed. "I didn't know you'd spent time in my home town. When?"

"During the war, ma'am. I was there about six months."

She led him to the drawing room where a maid served coffee and some sort of little cookies. Fallon thought they were delicious. He felt Joan studying him.

"Something the matter, ma'am?"

She frowned. "No, but I'm more certain now than ever we've met before."

Fallon's neck and shoulder muscles tightened. "I been thinkin' on that a bit myself. Best I can figure, it was during the war. There were several dinners and dances held for us by the kind people of your town."

Frowning, she nodded. "Perhaps, but my hazy memory doesn't bring into focus a uniform—or dress clothes."

Damn, Fallon, your idea of coming here like this wasn't very smart. She's getting too close. He tried to lead her in a different direction. "Perhaps if you visited the wounded you saw me in a hospital." He smiled. "I was in neither a uniform nor dress clothes then."

She shrugged. "Of course. That might be it. But enough of that. How long will you be in town?"

"Gotta get back to the ranch. Soon's I leave here I'm headin' out. Just couldn't seem to leave El Paso del Norte without stoppin'. If you'll see me again, I promise to bring dress clothes with me. We'll have dinner and maybe see a play if there's a good one in town."

She looked him right in the eye. "Tom, I don't care what you wear. Come see me. I'll have dinner prepared and we'll dine here, that way we'll get to visit more. Oh, and please stop the ma'am. Surely we don't have to be that formal."

They talked a while longer, and it was then Fallon made up his mind as much as he wanted to see her often, he'd have to put that desire on the back of the fire. She was too close to remembering where she'd seen him. She settled that question when she let him out the door.

"Tom, I'll be gone for about three weeks. The Empress Carlota has invited me for a visit. I'm not certain when I'll leave for Ciudad de Mejico, but it'll be in the next few days."

He studied her a moment. "Joan, that's a dangerous trip; bandits, Juáristas, and I hear Juárez is right close. I hope you'll be safe."

She laughed, and put her hand on his arm. "I'll be safe, Tom. The Emperor is having me escorted by about a hundred of his best troops. They'll not be in uniform, of course. Juárez's forces are too close for that, and uniformed troops would invite an attack.''

She stood close to him, her perfume drawing him even closer. It was all he could do to keep from pulling her to him and kissing her. Instead, he took her hand from his arm and lifted it to his lips. He looked at her straight on. ''Joan Boniol, one of these days I'll want much more than this.''

She held his look, and a little wide-eyed, said, ''When that day comes, Tom, I'll be waiting.''

He nodded and went to his horse, liking her even more. She hadn't blushed, or lowered her lids coyly over her eyes. She'd given him an honest straightforward answer.

Riding through town, the stench of garbage and raw human waste caused him to hold his breath. Then, crossing the bridge, he took a hard look at its structure, and in his mind thought it solidly built of good strong timbers, easily strong enough to drive the heavy coach across. That eased his concern a bit as to whether the Frenchies would drive it up- or down-stream and try to ford the river.

JOAN WATCHED FALLON UNTIL HE ROUNDED A CORNER and disappeared from sight. She didn't deny her attraction to him: Big, strong, and as handsome as any man she'd seen, too, he was a gentleman, and just under the surface she thought she detected he could be a very dangerous man if need be. She shrugged, and smiled to herself. A man who wasn't dangerous would be a bore.

She thought about him a moment longer. His build, his voice, his eyes, all seemed to tug at the wispy strings of memory. Perhaps it was his voice. She shrugged that off. Of course his voice would stir any woman's heart. It was deep and soft. She'd been hearing it in her mind ever since Nita's party. She smiled to herself. That was why it was so familiar. She attributed the memory of his eyes to when she met him at the party also.

She looked at her watch hanging by a black ribbon from her neck. Almost seven o'clock. M'sieur Bienville would be here soon. He'd have dinner with her.

Bienville, a handsome man, had left no doubt he looked on her as more than an accomplice in Maximilian's cause, but as long as there was a man like Tom Fallon around, the thought of Bienville didn't muster even a slight increase in heart rate. Nor did the sight of the Frenchman make her breath catch in her throat. She had thought, until she met Fallon, Bienville might be the man for her. Now, she was glad she'd not encouraged him.

THE SUAVE FRENCHMAN ARRIVED PROMPTLY AT SEVEN. Joan waited a socially acceptable time before announcing dinner, then, after being seated, she came right to the point. "When am I leaving, Henri, my sources tell me Juárez is drawing close. I need to be well away from here when he arrives."

He frowned. "The closest I can estimate right now, it'll be another week. The bullion is scheduled to arrive from New Orleans in about three days; that'll be Saturday. Then, I calculate another three days to put the coach back together. Plan to leave Wednesday or Thursday."

She looked up from her salad. "Henri, is there no chance my country will confiscate the gold?"

He shook his head. "Don't think so. The freight wagons bringing it are loaded with goods for the general store and saloons in Franklin. When the provisions are unloaded, we'll take the wagons to the stable and transfer the bullion to our coach. The freight wagons, like in our coach, are built to store the bullion under a false bottom. Too, the same troops escorting the freight wagons will also escort us to Ciudad de Mejico. They all wear rough frontier garb now, as they will when into Mejico. After we enter friendly territory they'll change to uniforms."

Not daring to look directly at him, she asked, "Us? Did you say 'us', Henri?"

He smiled and placed his hand over hers. "Yes, Joan. I've decided to go with you. We'll be able to visit for days on end. I've waited for an excuse like this to leave my duties up here, and give you my full attention."

She forced a smile, not sure she could fend him off for "days on end," and even more sure now he was not for her. He was too suave, phoney, a stuffed-shirt politician like others she'd met.

She said, "Of course, Henri, the chance to visit will be delightful." She pulled her hand from under his while trying not to be rude, but also to make it apparent she wanted nothing like that from him.

The remainder of the evening was cordial enough, but throughout she made it apparent she wanted nothing more than friendship from him.

When he'd gone, she poured herself a brandy and settled into her chair to read. After sitting there for more than a half hour, staring at the page and not reading a line, she put the book aside. Her thoughts had skipped from Bienville, to Fallon, and for the first time she questioned whether she was being disloyal to the United States.

No question about it. She loved her country, but way back somewhere France had been the birthplace of her forebears. Did she owe them anything? Was she hurting the U.S. by helping France? Was she really helping France, or was she helping the Austrian, Maximilian? She pondered those problems until she was more mixed up than when she started. Besides, she'd gotten into this when her country was divided by a brutal civil war.

The War Between the States had changed her, and it had changed her life. Her thoughts carried her back to the day her father died. Her mother had died while birthing her.

The war, though still in its infancy, changed her father and the way of life to which he was accustomed. His heart failed him and left his young daughter to make decisions that caused her to grow up quickly.

She studied the war effort as objectively as she could, and saw no possibility of the South, an agricultural region, winning against the North, an industrial base.

She recognized slavery was no more than a rallying point for the North. The real reason was States Rights, and freight rates from north to south and vice versa. With that in mind, she sold the lands of her large plantation parcel by parcel, taking only gold for each bit she sold until she knew whatever happened she could go wherever she wished, and live as a lady. But, with each parcel of the home she'd grown up on, it was as though she'd cut off a part of her body. She hardened her mind to what she did, what she must do to survive.

While still in her teens, she had dressed the wounds of dying soldiers, she had shot men on two occasions when they threatened to violate her, she had gone hungry when supplies ran low. She sipped her brandy, rolled it around in her mouth, and wondered how much the things she'd done had hardened her. In her mind she thought what she'd gained from her experiences was strength. She'd fight for the things she thought right. She knew she could face up to any adversity and survive, and still the sight of a hungry child, a sick man or woman, brought tears she couldn't hold back. Too the thought of Tom Fallon made mush of her insides. She frowned into her drink. No. She denied she had hardened.

FROM JOAN'S CASA FALLON WENT DIRECTLY TO THE OUT-skirts of Franklin and stood at the corner of the building from which he'd watched Joan and Bienville. He stood there over an hour and could see no indication of activity at the stable before he turned toward the hotel. He'd come back on the morrow and see if the first crew had finished their job.

The next morning dawned sunny, hot and muggy. After breakfast Fallon again went to the building and sat leaning against the wall, hat pulled low on his forehead. Every few minutes, so as not make it obvious, he turned his head and studied the stable.

The day wore on, and the middle of the afternoon someone walked to his side and stood. Fallon looked up at the man he recognized as the boss of the crew he saw altering the coach.

"Somethin' interest you out there, cowboy?"

Angry bile boiled into Fallon's throat. He had it in mind to knock the man's feet from under him and ask what the hell business it was of his, but he choked back his anger, and said, "Sure is, mister, them wide-open spaces out yonder got a strong pull on me now I'm almost broke. Why?"

The stranger stared down at Fallon a moment, frowning, then apparently decided not to push it further. "Jest wonderin'. Figured if there was somethin' out there worth lookin' at, I'd like to see it too."

Fallon grinned. "Worth lookin' at, an' figurin' to leave this here town depends on how empty your pockets are. I still got a little money so figure I'll stick around a while."

"You lookin' for work?"

Fallon slanted him a look. "Doin' what?"

"I'm goin' in business buildin' houses around here. Figure Franklin's gonna grow . . ."

Fallon was shaking his head before the man finished. "No, mister. I don't know nothin' 'bout buildin' houses. You got a job workin' cows I'd take you up on it in a minute. Thanks anyway."

The man shrugged and walked away.

When the builder left, Fallon glanced about for another place to watch the stable. He hadn't realized he would attract attention sitting there in the sun. He stayed until sweat trickled between his shoulders, from under his hat band and down his face.

He'd found what he came for. There was no activity at the stable, so the teardown crew must be through with their part of the job, but he had to find a place from which to watch. The gold could arrive anytime, and he knew they'd not let a wagon, or however they transported it, park where anyone could get curious. The means of transport would be driven into the stable where it would be off-loaded into the coach behind closed doors.

He stood and walked around the building. The side toward the stable had two windows, as did the opposite side. No one had entered the building or left it. Was it abandoned?

# CHAPTER

# 10

How was he to get in the place? If he broke in, somebody might see him and come to investigate. He thought on that a few seconds, then decided to try the door; it might not even be locked.

Rather than try the front door, out where anyone on the street could see him, he walked to the middle of town, cut between a store and a saloon, walked along the back of the buildings until he came to the one he wanted, pushed on the back door—and it swung open. Fallon grinned sheepishly to himself.

The next day, and the next, he sat at the window of the empty building. Each day after breakfast, he had the girl in the cafe fix him a couple of sandwiches, and back at the empty building, after rubbing a spot on the dirty window to see through, he sat, occasionally dozing, but never taking his eyes off the stable for more than a few seconds.

Saturday, mid-afternoon, a man walked leisurely to the stable, looked to his backtrail, and ducked inside. A few minutes later another repeated the act, then another and another, until Fallon counted ten men who had entered, and none had come out. They each carried a bedroll. His blood raced a little faster. It shouldn't be long until the gold arrived. He frowned. Wouldn't he feel foolish if there was no gold. He had nothing that truly pointed to why the coach had been stripped, but he had that gut feel he always had when he was right.

Fallon watched until night closed in and he couldn't see even the outline of the barn in the valvety darkness. Then he went to the cafe, and was almost through eating when Valdez came in and sat at a table between him and the door. By this late hour, eight-thirty, the cafe was nearly empty.

Fallon finished dinner, had a slice of apple pie and another cup of coffee, packed his pipe, made a show of searching his pockets for a match, shook his head, stood, and on the way out stopped at Valdez's table. "Borrow a match, *señor? Por favor?*" Then under his breath said, "Be ready, *amigo,* ten men went in the stable and they're still there." He accepted the match Valdez held out. After lighting his pipe, he nodded, and still in a whisper said, "I'll be in your room when you get there," then louder, *"Gracias, señor."*

Back at the hotel, he slipped his Bowie knife between the door and the frame, pushed, and went in. He sat in the dark about thirty minutes, until Valdez came in, closed the curtains, and put fire to the lamp.

Fallon grinned. "Looks like it's comin' onto fun time, *amigo,* but it's gonna take both of us to be sure when the wagons go to the stable." He sat on the side of Valdez's bed. "Way I got it figured, they'll bring freight wagons in an' unload goods at one of the stores here in town, then leave town and go to the barn at night. Or, they'll go straight to the stable after dark and drive into the door facing away from town."

"What do you wish me to do, Tomas?"

Fallon pushed his hat to the back of his head, frowned, and stared at the wall a moment, then nodded. "Yeah, I think that'll work."

He faced Valdez. "Once they get the wagon, or whatever they're haulin' the stuff in, in the barn, it's gonna

take two or three days to switch its load to the coach an'
put it back in shape for a lady to travel in.

"I was gonna say for you to watch for wagons what
looked too heavy, but that ain't gonna do much good.
They still gotta get it inside the barn, so I'll go out in the
chaparral an' watch the back side of the stable. Soon's I
see any sort of vehicle go in, I'll come tell you, then you
hightail it to Juárez.

"It'll be three or four days after that till I show up at
the holdup site. Gonna wait till I'm sure they're on the
way outta El Paso del Norte 'fore I come to the site. Have
our men stay hidden. And *no* drinkin'. Make sure their
camp is away from prying eyes. I'll be there ahead of the
coach. We'll have time to get in position before it gets
that far."

He stood and said, "Soon's I see the wagon safely in
the stable, I'm gonna buy me the suit of a resplendent
*caballero* an' visit a li'l ole copper-haired girl across the
river. She cain't go anywhere till that vehicle gets fixed
for travelin', an' I'm purely gettin' itchy to see 'er again."
He hitched his gunbelt to a more comfortable position and
stepped to the door. He opened it a crack and made sure
no one was in the hall before he left.

He'd been in the chaparral from daylight until an hour
or so past high noon when the rattle of trace chains, and
grinding and bumping of wheels, drew his attention to the
northeast.

Four freight wagons lumbered over the rough trail at
least a couple of hundred yards from him. A hundred, or
perhaps a few more, armed men escorted the caravan. Fallon eyed them, studied each wagon, and decided the third
freighter in line was the one carrying the payload. It rode
heavy, didn't bounce as much, and its wheels sank farther
into the trail's mud.

When the wagons came abreast the stable, the wagon
he'd been betting on broke free of the others and headed
toward the now open door of the barn. As soon as it was
inside, it closed immediately.

Fallon went to Valdez's room. "Time to go to work. The wagon's in the barn." Then, making sure the hall was empty, he opened the door and said over his shoulder, "*Bueno suerte, amigo.*"

Valdez smiled. "Good luck to you also. Against a hundred soldiers, we're going to need it."

Fallon left Valdez and crossed the river to buy a ready-made suit, much like the one he'd worn to his mother's party. After going to the hotel to clean up and get dressed, he headed back across the river to Joan's *casa*.

When he was only a few houses from where she lived, Fallon saw the door to her house open. He ducked around the corner of the house he was walking in front of. The big-nosed Frenchman, Charles Lebeau, stepped from Joan's doorway, looked back, and said, "Thursday, *mam'selle*. Be ready."

Fallon felt a surge of satisfaction. Lebeau must be talking about the day the French would leave with the shipment. He waited until the Frenchman walked down the street, glad now he'd chosen to walk. He would never have gotten his line-backed dun out of sight.

At his knock, Joan answered the door.

He stood, hat in hand, looking apologetically at her. "Looks like I don't ever show proper bringin' up." He shrugged. "Without askin' if it's all right I just come bargin' in."

She stepped aside, holding the door wide. "Come in, Tom. You can come 'barging in,' as you put it, anytime you wish."

"I was hopin' you hadn't already left for Ciudad de Mejico."

"No, my plans changed a bit. I'm leaving Thursday."

Fallon felt a rush of elation. Her words verified his assumption that the Frenchman had been referring to the shipment when he left. He swept her petite frame with a glance. "Just cain't figure it out, *señorita,* how in such a small body you manage to package all that beauty."

She curtsied and smiled prettily. "Why, thank you,

Tom. Even though it's only to your eyes, it's nice of you to say. Come in. I thought you would have gone back to Falcon Nest by now.''

He shook his head. ''Goin' back in the mornin'. Would've left this mornin' but had to see you again 'fore you left.'' He looked into her eyes. ''Fact is, if I didn't have a bunch of things to do for Pa, I thought about ridin' down there to see you.''

At his words, he thought he saw her catch her breath, and he hoped it was at the thought of seeing him again sooner than it would take her to get back home, not the fact that she wouldn't welcome anyone interfering with the job she had in front of her.

They visited awhile, and when he stood to leave, she stood also. They'd been sitting next to each other on a large couch, close enough to make Fallon uncomfortable trying to fight off the desire to pull her to him. When they stood, she was even closer. He stopped fighting.

He stared into her eyes a long moment and, his voice husky, said, ''Joan, we ain't known each other long, but for now let's make believe this is after your trip an' we've been acquainted for over a month.''

Her face tilted up to him, her lips moist and slightly parted, her breath shallow, and almost in a whisper, she said, ''Why, Tom?''

Not breaking their gaze, he pulled her to him. ''Because, little one, I'm going to kiss you.''

She tilted her head a little more to receive his lips. It was the kind of kiss Fallon had dreamed about, not a hurried, proper first kiss, but one where her body promised all it had to offer. Then, breathless, she stepped back, her words tremulous, and, with a sort of forced laugh, said, ''From that kiss I'll have to make believe my trip lasted six months.'' She put her hand on his chest. ''But, Tom, the truth is, it's been only a few days since we met. Let's don't spoil everything by rushing into something infinitely sweeter than I ever thought it could be. And the way we're both feeling right now, we could, you know.''

He stared into her eyes, hoping his tenderness showed through. "I know, little one." He stepped back, putting another foot or two between them. "I promise you, spoiling something I've waited a lifetime to find is something I won't do." He touched her cheek with the back of his fingers and left.

Back at his hotel, he checked Valdez's room and found he'd gone. In his own room, Fallon stretched out on the bed, put his hands behind his head, and stared at the ceiling. A pang of guilt stabbed him for the way he was fooling Joan. But then, she wasn't playing it altogether straight with him either. The one thing he knew to be real was the man-woman feelings they were discovering.

As his eyes got heavy, the line-backed dun popped into his head. He couldn't ride him. He needed his black horse. Thinking on it a moment, he knew he had time to ride to Las Cruces and get him—but too much might happen here. He'd have to try finding a black horse to rent. His thoughts became more muddled. His eyes closed. Sleep took him.

Fallon's eyes snapped open. Even though it was still the middle of the night, he was rested. And, while asleep, he'd solved his problem. He'd ride to Las Cruces for his horse and other things he might need.

He swung his legs off the side of the bed and reached for his weapons. The Henry rifle claimed his attention first. He cleaned and loaded it. Then he checked his Colt revolver, loaded the spare cylinders, honed his knives, and stood. The trail to Las Cruces was infested with Mescalero.

He didn't wait for daylight. At the stable he saddled the dun and headed out.

During the afternoon and night the ground had dried, and now it was dusty. He set his course by the North Star. The gray light of dawn put him four hours from Franklin.

Yucca loomed ghostly in the half-light, and large clumps of prickly-pear cactus, looking black in the darkness, resembled boulders. He prayed to stay clear of Spanish Dagger; they could cripple a horse, and were hard to see.

When he neared Falcon Nest, he circled it, not wanting to have to explain to his folks why he must leave again. It lay behind him by mid-morning. He rode with more caution. He searched every inch of terrain for Indian sign. Another hour and he crossed single-file pony tracks headed west. He studied them several minutes and figured they'd been made early the evening before. Apache, he thought, and if he was right, they'd be coming back this way. The thought had not cleared his mind when yells and shots broke the stillness.

They were to his left, toward the river. Four Mescalero. A glance ahead and to his right showed no boulders, no buffalo wallows, nothing to hide in. He dug heels into the dun's sides and ran, but could only hope to hold his distance for a short while.

Frantically, he searched for a dry wash, any kind of break in the level ground in which to find partial cover. Then, about a hundred yards ahead, he saw the sandy bed of a long, dry stream.

Hell-bent, Fallon goaded the dun faster. Then—anger swelled his throat, bitter bile flowed from under his tongue. He'd never done anything to those Indians, but by damn, he was about to.

Without thinking, he abruptly pulled his horse to a rearing stop, yanked him around on his hind legs, and headed straight into the mouth of the savage's fire.

He pulled trigger as fast as he could jack shells into his Henry. One rider threw up his hands and fell off the rump of his pony. Another dropped his weapon, grabbed his shoulder, and kneed his horse to the side.

The distance between Fallon and the Indians narrowed. Fallon pulled his Colt, felt a jolt and burning in his side, and shot the one to his right in the face.

He passed them and again wheeled the dun, but the remaining Mescalero had the same idea. Their horses collided.

Fallon didn't have time to change cylinders in his

six-shooter. He dropped it, dived for the warrior, grabbed him by the shoulders, and dragged him off his pony. They hit the ground, Fallon on top. The Indian's breath exploded from him.

He rolled from under Fallon, gained his feet, and pulled his knife.

Fallon lurched to the side, grabbed for his Bowie, and came to his knees. The warrior, in a flying leap, swung his knife at Fallon's chest. Fallon ducked and twisted in time to feel the knife catch his shirt, and take away the side of it. The Mescalero sailed across his back.

Fallon came to his feet. The Indian did the same. They faced each other. The odds now even, they circled, eyes glued to each other, each man looking for an advantage.

The Apache stepped toward Fallon, swung his knife—and missed, leaving Fallon an opening. He sliced with the Bowie, and he missed. They faced off again, circling, wary, knives weaving from side to side. Abruptly, Fallon stepped toward the Indian and sliced; he felt his blade tug at the warrior's side and stepped back—in time to feel the Mescalero's blade burn a streak across his stomach. He backed off, feeling a warm, moist flow at his waist. He'd taken a slug somewhere in his side and now he was cut. He had to end this soon—or the Apache would.

Fallon looked into the savage's eyes. The Indian's gaze dropped for only a moment, but long enough to see the blood he'd brought. A glint of victory flashed in the Mescalero's flat, black eyes. He stepped forward, swung his blade, and gave Fallon the opening he'd hoped for. He moved inside the Apache's arm and thrust his blade into the Indian's gut an inch or so above his baggy britches.

The black eyes lost their glint of victory. They widened, then squinted, and a low moan escaped the Mescalero's lips. He dropped his knife and became a dead weight, with only Fallon's blade keeping him erect.

Fallon looked into the now-dead eyes and jerked his blade free of the Indian's stomach. Only then did the insane anger ebb from him. He bent, wiped his knife on the Mescalero's britches, and sheathed it.

A glance showed him that the Indian ponies had high-tailed it out of sight. The dun stood quietly about twenty-five yards from him. Three Indians lay on the ground. None would ever ride again. He searched for the one he'd wounded, pushing his own hurts to the back of his mind. After a bit, he gave up. It was then he looked at the hole in his side.

The bullet had gone all the way through, and blood oozed from the holes, front and back, in a slow but steady stream. The cut across his stomach was no more than a scratch. He stuffed his bandanna inside his shirt to try and staunch the flow from the bullet wound, then searched the area for his revolver. He found it, and blew the dust off, replaced the empty cylinder with a full one. He located his rifle and shoved it in the saddle scabbard, then toed the stirrup and headed for Las Cruces.

The sun had painted the wispy clouds to the west shades of orange when he rode through the back doorway of Sanchez's livery stable. Groggy from loss of blood, he looked through pain-filled eyes for his friend. Instead of Roberto, one of his hired hands came to help Fallon from his saddle.

He stared down at the man, shook his head, and said in precise, evenly spaced words, "I'll take care of myself. Tell *Señor Sanchez* I must see him. Do it now."

The man left the stable at a dead run.

Fallon moved in careful, studied actions to prevent his wound bleeding again. He eased himself from the saddle and walked back to Sanchez's office. He let himself in and sank to a cot, then stretched out and relaxed. He closed his eyes and let pain have its way.

# CHAPTER

# 11

HE MUST HAVE SLEPT, FOR WHEN HE OPENED HIS EYES Sanchez stood at his side. "What happened, *amigo*?"

Fallon grimaced. "Mescalero jumped me. Need you to dress this wound, pack some of my stuff—one suit of dress clothes, jeans, shirts, shavin' gear—you know the kind of stuff I mean, an' saddle my black horse. Gotta get back to Franklin tomorrow."

"Fallon, you're in no shape to ride. Tell me what you need done and I'll do it."

He shook his head. "There's enough there for both of us. I want you to go back with me. Tell Carmella not to worry, and we'll see 'er in a few days."

Sanchez peeled Fallon's shirt back from the hole in his side, stared at it a moment, then looked him in the eye. "You need a doctor."

Fallon nodded. "All right, but bring 'im here. He can put some salve on it and dress it—that's all. I'm ridin' tomorrow."

Sanchez left, muttering to himself about somebody being a proud, stubborn fool. Fallon grinned through his pain, and closed his eyes to wait for the doctor.

He must have dozed, for it seemed but a minute until

Sanchez returned leading a tall, thin, weatherbeaten old man.

The sawbones leaned over Fallon, inspected the wound, and looked over his shoulder at Sanchez. "How'd this happen?"

Sanchez's one word said it all: "Mescalero."

The doctor grunted and went to work, cleaning and bandaging Fallon's side. When finished, he straightened, and looked at Sanchez. "Keep 'im quiet four or five days, feed 'im light foods, and he should do fine."

"Better tell him that, Doc. He says he's ridin' tomorrow."

The doctor looked at Fallon. "You ride, you'll open that wound and start bleedin' again. I'll come back in the mornin' and put fresh dressin's on it."

"Don't trouble yourself, Doc. I'll be gone."

The doctor shook his head. "Then I've done all I can for you. The coyotes'll be gnawing your bones by sundown tomorrow." He again shook his head and left.

Sanchez stood at Fallon's side. "Whatever it is you must do, *amigo,* let me do it for you. You know I can handle it."

Fallon shook his head. "You gonna have enough to keep you busy. I cut this job out for myself, an' I'll do it."

Sanchez stared at his friend a moment. He knew from experience that to argue the issue would be in vain, knew that once Fallon made up his mind to something he wouldn't budge an inch.

He wondered what it was that was so important; perhaps another gold shipment? He shook his head. If gold was involved, it must be much more than the usual amount. Then, of course, he knew about the proposed attempt on Juárez's life. Maybe the Frenchies were bringing in more assassins. He pondered for a while longer what was so important it would require both of them, then gave it up.

He'd better tell Carmella he was going to be gone a few days, and what had happened to Fallon; he also had to put together some things for them both. He looked down at Fallon. "Be back after a while. I'll put the stuff we need in our saddlebags, an' I'll tell Carmella we're leavin'."

As soon as he walked through the door of his *casa*, he said, "Tomas is down at the livery. Got a hole in his side. Mescaleros did it. He and I leave for Franklin again in the mornin'."

Carmella opened her mouth as though to say something. He held up his hand. "Save your breath, my wife. No, he's not in any shape to ride, but you know him. He's made up his mind, so help me get his and my trail gear together. We'll wait till mornin' to package some food."

Carmella picked up a shawl and started for the door. "Where you goin'?" he asked.

She glanced at him. "I'm going to the livery and see if there's anything I can do for Tomas."

Sanchez shook his head. "We don't need to draw attention to the fact we got a wounded man in there, an' you goin' traipsing down there when you haven't visited my stable once in ten years will sure as hell draw attention to it. Stay here and help me get ready."

Carmella put her hands on her hips as though to argue, then obviously saw the sense in what her husband had said. Her hands dropped to her sides. Her face softened. "Has he said what you're to do, my husband?"

"No, he's hurting too much for that. He'll tell me on the way to Franklin. And knowing Tomas, he'll make sure my task is the least dangerous by far." He frowned. "I only wish there was some way I could take some of the danger from him."

Carmella went about methodically placing weapons, clothing, and ammunition on the table. She looked up from her work. "Has Tomas ever given a hint why he does this for our people? Before he went off to war, he didn't seem concerned about Maximilian."

Roberto shook his head. "He's never said, and I've never asked. Someday he may tell us, but I think that now is not the time." He grinned. "Besides that, Maximilian

didn't take over in Mexico until 1863.'' He stepped toward the door. ''I'll go back to him now. There may be
some way I can ease his hurts, and we'll need to take him
supper.''

Carmella nodded. ''I'll send one of the hands with
something.''

THE NEXT AFTERNOON, STILL A FEW MILES FROM FRANK-
lin, Fallon kept his one hand pushed hard against his side
trying to prevent bleeding, and his other hand holding the
reins, leading his line-backed dun. He breathed in shallow
gasps to ease the pain while explaining to Sanchez that
he wanted him to follow Francois Berne like a shadow.
''Make certain, if he contacts anyone, to find out the name
of that person, or if he buys explosives, or special weapons, to determine what they are. We don't want to be
caught short, *amigo*. Juárez will greet his people, and he'll
be out in the open for all to see, including the assassin.

''I'll see the gold gets into his hands before he rides
into town.''

''But, Tomas, why don't we just kill the man before he
has a chance to do *El Presidente* harm?''

Fallon shook his head. ''Won't do any good. They'd
get someone else to do it, and we wouldn't know who he
was, or where he figured to kill 'im. This way we can
stay ahead of 'im—I hope.''

Sanchez drew rein. ''Suppose Juárez has already gotten
to El Paso del Norte.''

Fallon pulled his horse to a stop. ''Good thought, but
I've had one of his men with me the last few days, and
I've asked *El Presidente* to hold up on entering town till
Valdez gets back to him with the coach.'' A twinge of
pain stabbed him and he flinched. '' 'Nother thing, Juárez
said he must be in El Paso by August fifth. I figure we
got that much time.''

Sanchez sat, frowning. ''You ever figure there might
be someone in town who'll know that animal you ride?
He sure as hell ain't one a man forgets once he sees 'im.''

''Yeah. Been thinkin' 'bout that.'' Another shot of pain

caused him to grimace. "You know anybody close to Franklin, or El Paso del Norte, with a good comfortable stable where you could put 'im for a couple of days—a place where I could get him within an hour?"

"Carmella's sister and her husband have a *rancho* just south of El Paso; you know where it is. You've been there. Your horse'll be safe, and it would take only a short ride for you to get him."

Fallon frowned, calculating the time and distance he'd have to travel once the gold coach moved out of Franklin. With its load, the coach would be slow, but he'd have to reclaim his black horse and ride back to El Paso in time to make certain the coach was on the route he figured, then he'd have to get out to where Valdez had the men hidden to get them positioned for the ambush. He nodded. He could do it.

"Roberto, we'll wait outside of town until after dark. I'll change horses then, and you take this horse to your sister-in-law's *hacienda*. Try to avoid anyone seeing him. By now, I believe there are few who haven't had this black and the bandit described in detail. There are many who would recognize him. When the time is ready, I'll get 'im."

"You'll be in the hotel when I get back?"

"No. Reckon I'll stay in the livery. You stay in the hotel where you can watch Berne. I'm gonna crawl back in that pile of hay an' see if the pain in my side'll ease off a little."

Soon after dark, the two friends rode into Franklin. Sanchez headed for the bridge, leading Fallon's black horse. Fallon rode toward the livery, then changed his mind and stopped at a saloon. He thought to get a bottle of whiskey, good whiskey, to sterilize his wound. Anything less and he might add poison to the raw flesh. He had to get well enough to ride in two days—maybe less.

Before pushing through the batwing doors, Fallon thumbed the thong off the hammer of his Colt. He didn't expect trouble, but that kind of caution kept a man alive. Inside the doorway, he stepped to the side and scanned the room. The area was crowded, men dancing with the saloon girls, some gambling, and all drinking.

Fallon made his way to the bar and made room for himself at the end where his view of all in the area was good. He looked at the man who had moved aside making room for him to stand—and looked into the eyes of *Capitan* Phillipe Escobar.

A chill raced down his spine. He nodded. *"Gracias, señor."*

The Mexican smiled slightly. *"De nada, señor."* He studied Fallon a moment, frowning. "Have we met?" He held out his hand and introduced himself, leaving off the "Captain."

Fallon shrugged, feeling his scalp tingle and his back muscles tighten. "It is possible, Ca—uh, sir. I was born an' raised only a few miles from here." Then, thinking Escobar had noticed his slip, he added, "Reckon I almost called you Captain. You have the bearing of a military man, as I myself was until the Yankees whipped us."

"You were an officer?"

"A major when the war ended."

They talked awhile longer, Fallon making sure to stay away from discussing the war going on to their south. Escobar admitted to having, in the past, been an officer under Maximilian.

Fallon signaled the bartender. "Reach under the bar and bring out a bottle of your best Kentucky bourbon. I'll take it home with me." As soon as the bottle was in front of him, he paid, nodded to Escobar, and left.

In the stable, while dressing his wound, he thought of the Mexican. He had no doubt the officer would command the troops that would escort Joan and the coach south. He hoped he didn't have to kill the man; he liked him, and under different circumstances, they might become friends.

His wound taken care of, and before going to sleep, he asked the stable boy, Chico, to grain feed the dun and give him a good rubdown. Then he climbed to the hayloft, spread his bedroll, and went to sleep.

•   •   •

THE NEXT MORNING HE FELT WORSE; HE WAS COLD, clammy, and he sweated profusely. Infection had set in. He had a fever, and needed a doctor. To give in to his wound was out of the question. He had too much to do. Too much depended on him.

He left the stable and went in search of a sawbones. After he had walked half the length of the street, a cowboy pointed to an outside stairway. "Right at the top o' that there stair. He's usually in his office."

Fallon thanked the puncher and walked to the bottom of the stair. From where he stood, each step looked a mile high. He lifted a leg and pulled himself to the first step, then looked to the next one and lifted the other leg. After what seemed a month, he reached the landing at the top and pushed on the door. It opened to his touch.

A man about Fallon's age looked up from a desk. "Something I can do for you, sir?"

Fallon nodded. "Mescalero put a hole in my side a couple days ago. Figure it's festerin' 'cause I got a pretty good fever."

The doc stood and led Fallon to a bunk built against the wall. "Lie down and let me take a look at it."

Fallon stretched out on the bunk after pulling his shirt from his jeans. The doctor, whose name was Bennett, bent over Fallon, studied the wound a moment, then, probably talking to himself, mused, "Mighty red around the edges. No puss though." He looked into Fallon's eyes. "You're right. That hole looks pretty angry. What I'm gonna do is going to hurt like the devil. Gonna push in some ointment, only name it goes by is Black Ointment." He shook his head. "All that's beside the point. The stuff is good. I'm gonna push some of it slam through to the other side, and I want you to drink some of this tea, it's made from scrapings from the inside of willow bark. It'll lower your fever. Wish I had something to put you to sleep, but I don't, so bite down on this towel while I work on you."

The thought of the doc touching his side, let alone pushing something through the bullet hole, caused Fallon to break out in a cold sweat and tighten every muscle in his body. He unbuckled his gunbelt and handed it to Bennett. "You better put this out of my reach. I might be tempted to use it if you get to hurtin' me a whole bunch."

"No worry about that, Mr. Fallon. You'll probably pass out before you decide to shoot me." He grimaced. "But no point in tempting you." He went to the other side of the room and placed the gunbelt on his desk.

Fallon took the towel and clamped his teeth tight into it. Bennett wrapped a piece of cloth around a rod, dipped it in a jar of the black salve, which looked like axel grease to Fallon, and bent over the wound. The rod hadn't gone far into his side when the room swam, the doctor's face slithered off to the side, a dark fog rose between them, and Fallon fell into a bottomless void.

He came out of the pit of darkness the same way he'd entered it. He struggled to bring Bennett's face into focus. "You through, Doc?"

Bennett nodded. "Almost. Gonna pack some of this salve into you, front and back, then bandage it. Want you to lie still and sleep for a day or two."

Fallon calculated the time he had before heading for the holdup site. He nodded, and stood. His head swam, almost causing him to black out again. He held the edge of the bed a moment until the fog cleared, then took the jar of willow tea Bennett held out, paid him, and left.

The remainder of the afternoon, and all that night, Fallon slept in his blankets on top of piles of hay, waking occasionally to drink some of the tea the doctor had given him, then going back to sleep.

Not long after sundown the next night, he awoke to find himself drenched in sweat, but no longer chilled. His fever had broken. He felt better. He slept again. When he again wakened, it was four o'clock Thursday morning.

He stood, being careful not to make sudden moves. He was sore, but the gut-wrenching pain was gone.

A check of his watch and Fallon figured to get his black horse and wait on the outskirts of El Paso del Norte until he saw the coach, then to hightail it for the holdup site. He frowned. The coach might get a late start and he'd have to sit there in the desert's heat until it lumbered out of town. His side pained him, and he felt weak. He didn't think he could stand it. He'd wait here in Franklin until certain it was on its way.

Fallon took station close to the bridge, thinking the heavily laden coach would not try to ford the river and, he hoped, the bridge would not cave under its load.

About ten o'clock the vehicle rounded the corner of the building from which he'd watched the stable. From here it would have to pick up Joan Boniol before heading out of El Paso del Norte. Fallon stood, toed the stirrup, and headed for Carmella's sister's ranch.

Two hours later, riding his black horse, he searched for signs of the coach passing along the river trail to Piedras Negras and found no deep-rutted wheel tracks. He hadn't thought he would, but had to cover every option.

The next trail he looked at was the one leading to Saltillo; it was the one where he thought he'd find what he looked for. He was right. He would have known the deep-rutted tracks in the dark. He had stationed Juárez's troops in the right place. He kneed the black in their direction.

Valdez greeted him when he rode into camp on his black horse. A bandanna covered Fallon's face, now a familiar sight among the Juáristas. He shook his friend Valdez's hand, motioned the troops around him, and, still sitting his saddle, said, "*Hombres,* there are two things I want you to make certain of. First, do not fire into the coach. Second, the Maximilian forces will not turn the coach over to us; they'll fight like the demons of hell, so show no mercy. Stay behind your cover and empty every saddle unless they throw down their weapons and hold their hands high in the air. Only then will we take prisoners." He swept them with a hard-eyed look. "Savvy?" At their nods, he turned to Valdez.

"*Amigo,* today I wish you to speak for me." A sharp pain stabbed his side and he pressed his hand against it.

Valdez frowned. "You are hurt, my friend. What is the matter?"

Fallon pulled a breath into his lungs, pulled it past the

pain, then looked at Valdez. "*De nada, señor;* I took a bullet in my side. Mescalero." He pulled his friend to the side. "Back to what I was going to ask. I want you to do all the talking. The one in the coach may recognize my voice. I'll not take that chance. I'll show myself only briefly after we have the coach in our possession. Then, I'm riding to Franklin if I can make it. But the important thing is, I want them to know this is the doing of the *Bandido Caballero*. It may take their minds off the assassination of *El Presidente*." Fallon then gave his attention to the troops. "Men, make certain your weapons have a full magazine and a load in the chamber. Take cover, and do not fire until they do. I doubt it, but they may drop their rifles and surrender."

Valdez stood beside Fallon. "*Compadre,* I'm sticking to you like a jealous wife. Maximilian's bunch takes you out of action and they'll hurt Juárez more than the loss of any other man. Don't take any chances." He took Fallon's arm and pulled him toward a large boulder. "Come, I have a safe place for you."

Fallon grinned behind his bandanna. "That include ricochets, my friend?"

# CHAPTER
# 12

VALDEZ RAISED HIS EYEBROWS. "*SEÑOR*, I CAN TAKE care of you only so far. Perhaps we should cover you with rocks, but then we do that only to protect the dead from coyotes."

"Don't reckon I'm ready for that." Fallon's response was dry and didn't reflect the way his guts churned, and the tight feel of his scalp. He despised the need for the orders he'd given Juárez's men. During the War Between the States, he'd given such orders on several occasions. Being the weaker of two fighting forces made it necessary. But necessity didn't wipe the bitter taste from his mouth. Show no mercy was a phrase he hated regardless of the circumstances.

Then he looked at the ragtag bunch of fighting men, who only wanted freedom to live their lives under a government they chose. His resolve hardened.

Sitting behind his boulder, sweat soaking his shirt, his side itching like dozens of ants biting him, he thought of the girl in the coach. Why was she doing this? Why was he doing it? He knew the answer for the latter, but could think of no reason Joan would support the Maximilian regime as she did. If she still spoke to him when she found out he was the bandit, he thought he'd try to get answers to that question. Then, at the back of his awareness, the crack of a whip, the rattle of trace chains, and the grinding of wheels broke into his thoughts. He had gripped the lever of his rifle, ready to jack a shell into the magazine, when he remembered he'd ordered every man to do that earlier so as not to alert the coach's escort of their presence.

Whispers ran the length of the hidden troops; many made the sign of the cross. Fallon waved for them to stay down. Then, judging the vehicle's location by its sound, he hugged the ground until he thought the coach to be abreast of where he lay. He looked at Valdez and nodded.

Simultaneous with his nod, Valdez yelled, "*Alto.* Throw down your weapons and we'll not hurt you."

Without exception, Maximilian's troops swung their rifle muzzles toward the rocks and opened fire. Fallon's men lagged behind them by less than a second. The sharp crack of rifle fire, the stench of powder smoke, and the sight of men falling from their horses filled Fallon's ears, nose, and eyes. The angry whine of bullets creased the boulders surrounding him and his men, and then the staccato firing of a Gatling gun rent the air.

Fallon's gaze swept the field of fire, then locked on the top of the coach in which Joan rode. He'd be the one to break his own order. He centered his sights on the man kneeling atop the vehicle and moving the big gun in a deadly arc of bullets. Fallon's shot knocked the machine-gunner from the weapon. He fell to the ground. The man feeding the belt of bullets to the gun took his place. Fallon's second shot hit that man dead center between his eyes. At the same time, Fallon felt his left leg go numb. Ignoring the second hit he'd taken in only a few days, he moved his sights to another of Maximilian's men. Before he could squeeze the trigger, the remaining men around the coach threw down their rifles and grabbed a handful of air high above their heads—except for two men who took cover under the vehicle, and another two who grabbed horses and headed back toward El Paso del Norte.

Fallon yelled to let them go; no sense in useless killing. He worried Joan might have recognized his voice, but then along with that thought he guessed a yell would not sound the same as his normal voice.

Valdez called for the men to stay behind the boulders, then calmly stepped into the open and fired as fast as he could pull trigger at the two men under the coach. Their guns went silent.

A deafening quiet settled on the area. Only the cry of an eagle soaring high above the deadly scene broke the stillness. The eagle would be replaced by vultures in only a matter of hours. The action had lasted less than a minute. Then Valdez surprised Fallon.

In a deep east Texas drawl, he said, "Ma'am, if'n you'll step to the ground, I'd like to take a look inside that contraption you been ridin' in."

Fallon held his breath, waiting to see if she was hurt. A stray bullet could have hit her, or in the excitement of battle one of his men might have taken a shot at the side of the black monster hauling the treasure.

The door swung open and she stepped down. As far as Fallon could see from his perch behind the rock, she didn't have a scratch.

He sighed, then took a bandanna from one of the troops and tied it tightly around his leg. Not much of a wound, he thought, but it would be sore as hell for a few days. His eyes had not left Joan's face while he worked on his leg. He felt rather than saw his men stand and move from behind their shelter.

Joan looked at them with contempt. "How is it when there is likely to be a real fight, *Bandido Caballero* doesn't take part? Is he scared?"

Angry, hot blood rushed to Fallon's head. Finished staunching the flow of blood from his leg, he pulled himself to his feet and opened his mouth to bark back at her. Before he could make a fool of himself, Valdez cut in. "Why, ma'am, if you'll only look, you'll see he's been here with us all the time. He ain't talkin' 'cause he's got a couple bullet holes in him, an' he's hurtin' a mite too bad to unclamp his teeth.''

Looking at the blood-drenched jeans above Fallon's knee, and the blood-soaked shirt at his side, Joan gasped. A pang of fear swelled her throat. Why she felt this way she couldn't answer. She only knew that this bandit pulled on her emotions as much as did Fallon. She wondered that she could have such strong feelings for two men, one of them her enemy.

She stared at his face, wishing he'd uncover it, wishing she could see his eyes, but his hat, pulled low on his forehead, prevented her look from penetrating the shadow it cast. The bandanna hid the rest.

Before she could ponder the puzzle further, Valdez looked inside the vehicle, nodded, and took her elbow to help her step to its deck. Then with his head poked through the window, he said, ''Ma'am, you gonna be the guest of the President of Mexico for a few days. Reckon you gonna be treated like a lady. Ain't nobody gonna bother you, so behave yourself.''

He glanced at the Gatling gun poised on the roof of the coach. ''*El Presidente's* gonna be so proud to get that there gun he'll prob'ly treat you good as he would Carlota.''

''Her title is Empress. Address her as such,'' Joan said, though she couldn't imagine why it made a difference to her what the man called Maximilian's wife. She felt he mocked her, and she thought behind his phoney Texas accent he was probably a Mexican of good birth.

Valdez grinned at her. ''Ain't my empress, ma'am, so reckon she's gonna remain just plain Carlota to me.''

She stared at him a moment, wishing her look could shoot poison at him. She held his gaze a moment longer, then leaned back and ignored him—but her thoughts returned to the tall bandit of whom she'd gotten only a glimpse. Even though he was her enemy, she still hoped he wasn't wounded badly.

Valdez moved from her to the men. He returned to his native Spanish, ''*Amigos,* take care of our wounded—

theirs, too. Gather the guns. Put them on top of the coach, along with all cartridge belts. Tie the prisoners. Round up their horses. We go back to our *presidente. Vamanos.*''

Fallon watched a moment, long enough to know Valdez was in full command, then went to his horse and toed the stirrup. Despite his leg, now beginning to shoot agony down his thigh and calf, he pulled himself into the saddle. He rode to the side of the coach for a last glance at Joan, then reined the black toward Carmella's cousin's *rancho.*

He stabled his black horse, switched saddles to his line-back dun, and headed for Franklin. As soon as he got there, he went to Dr. Bennett's office. Bennett looked at his leg and then pinned him with a look. ''Mr. Fallon, if I had only a couple more patients like you, I could retire in four or five years.'' From the doctor's office Fallon went to Sanchez's room.

Sanchez looked at Fallon's bloodstained jeans and shirt, then shifted his eyes to look into those of his friend. ''Don't need to ask if the coach escort put up a fight. Was it bad?''

Fallon shook his head. ''Not as bad as it could've been. We didn't lose a man, but had about ten who caught rock slivers, and a couple of ricochets creased a man or two. What was even better, we didn't have to kill all of Maximilian's men. When they had 'bout fifteen men on the ground, the rest surrendered.'' He looked at the wash-stand. ''You got any whiskey in here?'' He sighed. ''It's been a long day.''

Sanchez went to his saddlebags, pulled out a bottle, and poured Fallon about three fingers in a water glass. After he handed it to him, he eyed his friend. ''Want to know what happened here about an hour ago?''

''If it's important. Otherwise, I'm gonna drink this drink an' maybe another the same size, then I'm headin' for the stable an' see if I cain't give this pore beat-up body of mine a rest. Don't tell me Francois Berne's already makin' trouble for Juárez.''

''I wish it was Juárez on the end of this trouble.'' Sanchez shook his head. ''*Amigo,* about an hour ago, I was sittin' in the cafe drinkin' a cup of coffee when two riders rode in hell for leather, their horses caked with sweat. They reined in at the hitchrack in front of French head-quarters and, not even waiting to tie their horses, ran into the building. Didn't take time to finish my coffee. I tossed a coin on the table and hightailed it across the street to see what was goin' on . . .''

"Damn it, Roberto, get to the point.''

Sanchez grinned. "Ain't in any hurry, partner. You're not either, so settle down. Don't want anybody seein' you shot up an' bleedin' like you are. They might tie two and two together and figure out you're the bandit who's been raising so much hell across the border.''

"Sanchez, just what the hell are you babbling about? Make sense, *hombre*. Why they gonna see I been hurt an' figure I'm the bandit?''

Smug-like, Sanchez looked at Fallon. "Those riders who come in were your old friend Phillipe Escobar, and Berne. Before the holdup, I heard Bienville tell his people he was going to Mexico City. He must have changed his mind and sent Berne instead. Anyway, the two of them must have hightailed it while the fight was goin' on. Es-cobar told the Frenchies they'd lost the gold, that you were responsible, and volunteered to lead a posse, or even the whole Maximilian army, across Mexican soil, or American soil, to hunt you down.''

Sanchez poured them each a drink and shook his head. "Tomas, the Frenchies called off killing Juárez until you're dead. They figure you're a bigger enemy than *El Presidente*. And, if they see you, or anybody else show up here shot all to hell, they might figure you're the one they look for.''

Fallon stared into his drink a moment. He had to have clothes and they were in his saddlebags at the stable. He also had to give his wounds a chance to heal. He could go home, but canceled that idea as soon as the thought entered his mind. Being shot would upset his mother and, more importantly, from the ranch he couldn't watch Berne. Finding the *Bandido Caballero* might remain num-

ber one on the Frenchies' list only until they simmered
down from their most recent loss.

He frowned, and wondered how much gold was in the
coach—if it was gold. And he had to admit to himself the
only thing he had to make him suspect it was gold was
the obvious weight of the coach, and the fact they had
used the same ruse as before. They'd used Joan.

He wished now Valdez had had his face covered during
the holdup so he could come back across the border and
give him a report, but the slim Spaniard wouldn't dare
take that chance. Too many people had seen him. And
Fallon didn't even consider going back to Juárez's camp
himself as long as Joan was there.

Suddenly, Fallon realized he'd been staring into his
drink for long minutes. He looked at Sanchez. "Roberto,
I want you to bring my saddlebags to me. They're in the
livery stable. I'm gonna stay here until we get a better
idea what the French're gonna do. In the meanwhile I
want you to keep a close watch over them and Escobar.

"I figure if they still want me as bad after three or four
days as they say they do now, they gonna keep me at the
top of their list. Juárez'll be safe until they corral me.
Soon's we know what's more important to them—me or
Juárez—I'm gonna get my black horse an' go back to the
holdup site if it's me they want the most.

"I figure Escobar's gonna want a big hunk of the game
of 'look for the gentleman bandit.' If he does, he'll get
the same Yaqui scout to track me he used before, figurin'
the Indian'll remember my horse's tracks."

Sanchez frowned. "What you figuring to do, Tomas,
make a target of yourself?"

"Hope not, but I figure to lead those folks on a mighty
long desert chase. I know the water holes as well as that
Yaqui does, an' most of them hold only enough water for
one or two men and a horse."

THREE DAYS PASSED, DAYS DURING WHICH SANCHEZ
stayed glued to every move Escobar made, and at the end
of the third day he told Fallon the Frenchmen and Escobar

were more determined than before to catch him. "Fact is," Sanchez said and grinned, "Francois Berne insists on going with Escobar to track you down, says he wants to get you in his rifle sights, says he wants to be the one to kill you. They're heading out in the morning.

"First, though, the Spaniard is going to get the Yaqui scout and a company of riflemen. Not until then will they head for the holdup site. You better hope your horse's tracks are still fresh enough to read."

"Reckon they will be. Ain't had no wind or rain to erase 'em since the holdup."

Fallon frowned slightly. Things were working out exactly to his liking. He'd been sitting on the floor listening to Sanchez. He stood, moving slowly past the stiffness in his healing flesh, until he came erect and flexed his muscles. He lifted his left leg high a couple of times to test its strength, then looked at his friend. "They leave in the morning. I leave now. I want to lay down a good set of tracks for the Yaqui to follow."

Sanchez looked at him, a worried frown creasing his brow. "You able to take this on, *amigo*? Why don't you let me do it? It'll be the same if I ride your black horse for them to follow."

Fallon shook his head. "There are several reasons it won't be the same. First, I know that desert as well as most Indians. You don't. Second, this is my bronc to bust. I took it on an' I ain't shovin' it off on nobody else's shoulders." He picked up his saddlebags, which Roberto had brought from the stable a couple days before, put them on the bed, and slanted a look at Sanchez. "Gonna make sure I got enough rifle and revolver shells to fight a war, then I'm gonna clean and check my weapons, then I'm goin' to the livery, get that dun horse, an' head for Carmella's cousin's *rancho*. I'll need to take my canteen and yours, and I have an extra one hangin' from my saddle." He slung his saddlebags across his shoulders, picked up his rifle, and before going out the door, said, "Stay close to Bienville and Lebeau. If they change plans, you gonna have to take care of Juárez. *Comprende, amigo?*"

Sanchez heaved an exaggerated sigh of relief. "Damn, and here I was thinking you were gonna hog all the fun for yourself." He slapped Fallon on the shoulder. "Don't worry, my friend. I have this end of it right here." He held out a closed fist.

Fallon stared his friend in the eye a moment, checked the hallway, and slipped toward the back stairs.

THREE HOURS LATER, HAVING PICKED UP HIS BLACK horse, and after riding to the edge of El Paso del Norte to lose the black's tracks in the town traffic, and from there to the holdup site, he stood among the same boulders from which they'd launched the attack on the coach's escort. A glance at the Big Dipper told him it was after midnight. Hungry and tired, he fried a couple strips of bacon, boiled coffee, and made do with that. Then he rolled into his blankets and slept.

Daylight saw him at the top of a hill to the southwest, where he had a good view of the trail and boulders below. Figuring he'd have a long hot wait, he loosened the cinches to give the black breathing room, checked his canteens to be sure he hadn't used more water than he should have, then sat back to watch the road from Saltillo.

The sun climbed toward noon. Sweat trickled from his back, his chest, his face, and dried almost as soon as his shirt soaked it up. Twice, he stood and sponged out the black's mouth. By two o'clock, when he had begun to wonder where Escobar had to go to get troops, he saw a thin dust cloud approaching the rocks. From where he sat against the hillside, the men and horses, in double file, looked like ants crawling along the ribbon of road below.

A glance at the barren mountains over which he intended to lead those who hunted him brought a smile to the corners of Fallon's mouth. "Reckon I'm gonna find out how good an Injun I am," he muttered, more to break the boredom than to hear his own voice.

Escobar and his men rode in among the boulders and milled about for a while, then a solitary figure rode to the side, followed by two others. Fallon guessed one to be the Yaqui, and the two who followed would be Escobar and Berne. Almost simultaneously, the thin column fell in behind, and they headed in his direction.

He mounted and rode toward the same sump marked by the finger of granite he'd tried to reach when looking for Juárez. This time his horse was strong, and he had water for both him and the black if the sump was dry. He made no effort to hide his tracks.

From every vantage point, he stopped to ensure he kept a safe distance ahead. The sun sent fiery streaks into the wispy clouds to the west before he reached the sump. He refilled his canteens and drank his fill, then let the black drink until less than a cup of water remained in the granite depression. He thought to scoop the water out onto the sand, hesitated, then left it where it was. The Yaqui would be ahead of the column, and would find the water and drink, leaving nothing for the troops.

Fallon, still weak from loss of blood and unhealed wounds, slumped in his saddle. He wanted to stop and make camp, but he had learned that lesson well the last time Escobar and the Yaqui tracked him. He rode on into the night, heading for the mountains.

Soon the yucca and cactus gave way to stunted cedar, and still climbing, he came onto a stand of piñon pines, then a small stand of Ponderosas, and still he rode. There had been a small trickle of water from a spring close to the Ponderosa pines, but not enough for even two men with no horses.

The rising sun found him high in the mountains, deep canyons breaking off in every direction. Tired though he was, and holding himself in the saddle by gripping his saddle horn, he knew he must be more wary than before.

Now he had to be watchful for Apache. They had a stronghold here in these mountains somewhere. He stopped making his trail obvious, and made an effort to leave no tracks, to leave the soldiers confused and cost them time. He had to find a place to hide until he could rest and give his weakened body a chance to strengthen.

The mouth of a canyon opened before him; its bedrock

floor was smooth from some ancient water flow. Fallon turned into it, the sound of his horse's hooves ringing loud on the hard surface and then, in ever diminishing strength, echoing off the steep walls. Talus gathered close to the base of the canyon's sides from years of flaking off the granite surfaces stretched high above him, cutting off almost all light even though it was the middle of the morning.

The split from some long ago crack in the earth's surface narrowed even more. Staring ahead it seemed the walls joined, giving no way out but the way he'd come—and Escobar might await him back there at the entrance.

About to turn back, he thought to give himself another chance, although a slight chance it was. He'd ride to the end of the narrow fissure and see if there was a way he might climb out.

He rode to the end, and the walls reared as steeply above him as they had at any point. He dismounted and, leading the black onto the talus slope, searched every inch of the rugged surfaces, hoping for some ancient animal trail, anything that might give his horse footing. Nothing.

He turned back, thinking that the entrance might be where he'd die, thinking that there he would meet Escobar. He had not moved ten feet from the dead end when a fold in the wall's surface on the right drew his eye.

# CHAPTER

# 13

$F$ALLON STARED AT THE CREASE A MOMENT AND moved to continue out of the canyon; then he stopped and looked closer. Barely wide enough to permit passage of a horse, the slight opening cut into the wall's surface for about twenty feet, then seemed to end.

Fallon stared at the blank wall for a moment, then looked back the way he'd come. "Worth a chance," he muttered. "Ain't gonna take but a minute."

Skittish, the black pulled back on the reins. "Come on, boy. Ain't gonna get you in no place that'll hurt you. Come on now." He pulled on the reins, and at his urging the black took one tentative step, then another, while Fallon led the tired horse into the black maw of the opening.

What had looked like a sheer wall that sealed off the fold at its end made a sharp turn, folded back on itself—and widened. His horse looked straight ahead, ears peaked. Fallon pulled his rifle from its scabbard, fearful of a bear or mountain lion. He searched the narrow opening ahead, and then what he could see of the granite walls pushing in on him, but he continued to pull on the reins, even though the black now followed willingly.

Abruptly, the floor of the opening tilted to a steep

climb. Fallon's heart beat faster. Maybe he'd found a trail
to take him out of the box canyon.

He estimated they'd come three or four hundred yards
into the crease on almost level ground. Now the going got
hard. Several times the black's hooves slipped on the hard
surface. Fallon's left leg cramped, tired, tried to give out
on him. "Gonna get us outta here, old horse," he said.
As if understanding, his horse bunched his muscles and
tried harder. The narrow trail got even steeper.

On hands and knees, and pulling on his horse's reins,
Fallon inched up the granite incline. After maybe an hour
of gut-wrenching pain, near to exhaustion, jeans worn
through to his bleeding knees, Fallon felt the trail level
off. Head hanging, staring at the smooth granite surface
under him, he felt a surge of energy that made him raise
his head.

The trail not only leveled, it opened onto a mountain
park of perhaps sixty acres, enclosed on all sides by walls
of about a hundred feet. Grass, lush, standing fetlock-
deep, spread out from a clear, small lake of about four or
five acres in the middle of the bowl. Stands of aspen dotted the park. Flowers—red, blue, and yellow, of a kind
Fallon had never seen—bloomed in patches everywhere
he looked.

Still on hands and knees, he stared, his look not leaving
the lake for a long moment: water, wood, an overhang in
the cliffs for shelter. He closed his eyes tightly, then
opened them wide. What he looked upon was not a dream,
it was real.

Strength returned to him, brought him to his feet. He
didn't have to drag his Morgan horse now. It was him
who was dragged when the black headed for water.

At the lake's edge, Fallon fell on his stomach and drank
until he could hold no more. His horse drank, stood a few
minutes, and again buried his nose in the cold water.

Fallon hunkered by the lake and studied his surroundings. Deer droppings, still shiny, stood in the path running
to the water's edge. He'd have fresh meat.

Deadfall among the aspen promised as much firewood

as he'd need for a long time. A long time? The thought brought his mind to the cliffs about him. Was there a way out? If there wasn't, he could still retrace his steps and leave the way he'd entered—but Escobar and Berne might await him at the canyon's entrance.

He didn't think they could follow him through the rift he'd followed to get here. He didn't think they could find it. And still feeling the weakness he'd brought on himself by riding too soon, he decided to take what time he needed to heal, and to get strong again. He'd search for the way deer came into the park after resting a bit. He lay a few feet from the water and slept.

COLD AWAKENED HIM TO A VELVET BLACK SKY DOTTED with stars hanging barely beyond his fingertips, or so it looked. He stripped his horse, feeling guilty for not having done it sooner, and spread his bedroll. He'd sleep until morning then look at this place he'd found.

The sun, throwing lances of fire into the eastern heavens, awakened him further. He stood, stretched, and found himself feeling stronger. He picked up his rifle and walked to the overhang he'd seen the afternoon before.

He was not the first person to visit this place of the tarn. Ashes, ancient by their look, nested close to the back wall of the overhang. The size of the ash bed indicated that many had used it, in some long ago time. He figured the ashes to be old by the shavings of talus that had fallen from the roof of the cave onto the ashes, for a cave it was, despite being a shallow one.

He gathered wood from a deadfall, stacked it close against the wall, and built a fire to push back the cold of this high country. Then he brought his bedroll and saddlebags to what would be home until he again became strong.

He shot a deer that evening when several of them came to the lake to drink before bedding down. At his shot, all the deer but the one he dropped ran. A glance about the park showed not a sign of them—and they had not left by the way he came in. He knew now for sure that there was a way out, but he'd wait to find it.

MILES FROM FALLON, STILL ON THE DESERT FLOOR,
Berne, Escobar, and his troops dragged on. The Yaqui had
found only enough water for one man, or two at the most,
and none for the horses. All canteens were empty. Berne
rode alongside Escobar. "*M'sieur,* we must turn back.
The horses are almost dead, and we're not much better."

Escobar gave him a look that showed no respect. "*Señor,* when we left El Paso del Norte, we had full canteens.
We have come far, and now we have no water. There is
but one man here who could get back alive."

Berne looked him in the eye. "The Yaqui?"

Escobar nodded. "We are in his hands. If he can't find
a spring, a sump, anything with water in it soon . . ." He
raised his eyebrows and shrugged.

Berne's cold facade cracked. "Why the hell did you let
him bring us out here like this without some assurance he
knew where the water was?"

"*Señor,* I'll remind you, he has taken us to two places
which held water. They were dry. The *bandido* drank his
fill, watered his horse, and rode on, probably laughing at
us, knowing what troubles he left us."

Berne clenched his fists, his face purpled. "All I want
is to get him in my rifle sights. I'll shoot him to pieces—a
little at a time."

Escobar's laugh came out raspy. "From the way he's
outsmarted us thus far, you'd better hope we *don't* catch
him."

The Frenchman stared at Escobar. "What the hell is the
matter with you? You sound as though you admire him."

Escobar pushed his hat back, mopped his brow, and
stared at Berne a moment. "*Señor,* I admire a fighting
man, and one with brains even more. This man we track
is as good as any I've ever seen. He's outsmarted us at
every turn." He waved his hand vaguely toward where
the Yaqui should be. "The *bandido* has confused the Indian, and I'll tell you right now, I've never yet seen that
Yaqui baffled by anyone." He nodded. "Admire him? I
would say I respect him, and yeah, I admire him even if

we don't come out of this alive—and right now, I'd say we stand a pretty good chance of that." He smiled, hoping that through the dust and dirt on his face the Frenchman could read his disgust. "Also, *señor,* I'll remind you, you were the one who insisted on coming along. You wanted to be the one to kill the *bandido.* I came because it was my duty as a soldier to do so." Escobar broke his gaze from the Frenchman and looked to the head of his weary column of troops. He kneed his horse toward them.

Before dark, still fighting the desert's heat, Escobar called for a halt and made a dry camp. His men were tired, thirsty, and hungry. The only things they had to eat were jerky and hardtack. There wasn't a man among them who could muster saliva enough to soften his food and swallow.

Long before the sun sank behind the mountains, the Yaqui rode into camp and went directly to Escobar. The Spaniard knew before the Indian hunkered before him that his tracker brought only bad news, but he had to ask. "Water, the *bandido*—any good chance of finding either?"

"*Nada. Pequeño agua. Bandido—no.*"

Berne, at Escobar's shoulder, asked, "What did he say?"

Escobar shook his head. "He found only a little water, nothing of the *bandido.* He drank the water."

Berne's face purpled. "Why that worthless bast—"

"Don't say it, Frenchman." Escobar's words cut between them like shards of ice. "If any of us deserves to drink, it's the Indian. He's covered more miles, put in harder days, and if we're to get out of this, he'll be the one to find the way. Leave him alone." He looked at the Indian. "Bed down. Go again in the morning."

The Yaqui disappeared from the soldiers' campsite. Escobar spread his groundsheet and blanket, and stretched out on top of them. He lay there, his eyes wide, staring at the sky until long after the stars winked on, one by one. What was he doing here serving an Austrian who wanted his own empire, but was really furthering Napoleon's

quest for a foothold in North America? He'd served Maximilian's armies over two years. Most of that time he'd
not been paid, and the last three months he'd not drawn
a peso.

Mexico was his and his family's country, had been for
generations. He owed the French nothing, so why was he
here?

His only answer was that he was a soldier, and a soldier
did what he was ordered to do. He gnawed at the problem
long into the night. This was the first time he'd questioned
himself, and looked into his true feelings. Finally, he decided to give it a lot more thought, but it would have to
wait until after he crawled into his blankets each night.
He shivered, pulled his blanket over him, and went to
sleep—thirsty and hungry.

Desert night chill had not left the land when he awoke
the next morning. A look at his men brought a lump to
his throat. There would be nothing to eat or drink this day
unless the Yaqui found water. A glance at the barren
mountains ahead did not promise anything better than the
days behind. "Lead your horses, men. We'll ride only
when we can't walk."

Two days later, the Indian found a small seep from
which every man had a couple swallows of water, and the
horses even less, then he found the canyon Fallon had
entered. He reported to Escobar. "*Bandido* go in here.
Not tell if he come out. Rock hard, show only scrapings
where horse walk."

The Spaniard looked into the maw of the canyon,
searched its steep walls, and asked, "Water?"

"Not know. Not go to end."

Escobar squinted and tried to see to the end of the opening, tried to see if it was a box canyon. He shook his
head. They'd have to go as far as they could to determine
that, and even then they wouldn't know if the *bandido*
was still there somewhere.

He and Berne walked deep into the canyon's depths.
When the wall closed in on all sides except the way they'd
entered, Escobar searched its slopes for sign of a trail

leading out, and found none. He looked at Berne. "I see no way he could have gotten up these walls. We'll go out and see if the Indian can find his trail. But, if we don't find water soon, we won't be tracking anything."

Berne jerked his horse around by the reins and headed toward the entrance. The Yaqui left more slowly. He searched the walls, looked at each crevice, but after a while he followed the others.

FALLON SPENT THE DAYS SLEEPING AND EXPLORING HIS mountain park. At some ancient time the park had been a bowl sealed all around by steep cliffs. It had trapped snow and rain, then frozen, and each year the ice packed, until it filled the bowl. Almost like the annual rings on a tree, Fallon could see the scour marks on the cliff where the bowl had added more ice.

Then as the earth warmed, the ice pack melted slowly. With the upthrusts of the earth's crust, the walls split. One of those cracks formed the deep fissure through which he'd entered the bowl, and it had provided the outlet for much of the water, leaving only the small lake that now gave him life.

A week passed. Fallon's wounds healed and his strength returned. He sat by a fire at the back of his cave and looked out at the beautiful place he'd found. He hated to leave this paradise, which had provided the only peace he'd known for over five years. But leave he must.

There was a war going on in which he was playing a major role. The little Zapotec needed him, and Fallon admitted to himself that his own needs centered on the girl with the copper-colored hair.

While exploring his park, he'd purposely avoided looking for an exit other than the one through which he'd come. Now he had to find out if he had to go out by Escobar and his troops, or if there was another way. He hadn't a doubt that the Spaniard would not give up. He was too good a soldier. If he and his party hadn't died of thirst, they'd be waiting for him.

Fallon tossed a twig into the fire, hoping Escobar had

found only misery—not death. He found it strange that he had any feelings for the Spaniard, but he'd liked the man, even when Escobar and his Mexican troops were trying to kill him. He shrugged. Hell, a good soldier did what he had to do.

He glanced from his fire to the cliffs. It was time to find a way out other than the one through which he'd entered—if there was one. He stood, looked at his rifle, and picked it up. He'd seen cougar tracks as well as bear tracks by the lake.

Fallon skirted the talus at the base of the cliffs, but searched every inch of the sheer walls for fissures, figuring that regardless of what he found, he'd probably end up following the animal tracks out. "Sure do hope there's more'n one way out, an' that the bear and big cat took one separate from the deer" he muttered to himself. The sound of his voice comforted him, gave him a sense of pushing back the aloneness, which to his mind was different from lonely.

Fallon was more than halfway around the park's perimeter when he came upon the animal tracks. He got down on his hands and knees and studied them, and knew then that any hope the bear and cougar had taken a different trail was like wishing a green bronc wouldn't buck.

He looked toward the west. The sun had already sunk below the bowl's rim. He'd wait until morning, wait until he saw the animals drink and leave before finding his way down the fissure. He wondered why the animals would leave such a place when there was plenty of water, tender grass, and shelter from the winds that blew in this high country. Fallon pondered that question awhile, then decided they must leave for a place equally good, or better.

He thought to shoot another deer and dry its meat, but decided against it. He had plenty to do him on the way back. A glance at his Morgan horse showed the big black to be sleek as a fatted calf.

Upon his return to his cave, he built a fire and cooked his evening meal. A glance at his provisions told him he'd better find someplace to get coffee and flour soon, and estimating where he was, he knew that wasn't likely. He figured these mountains were far west of Las Cruces.

That night it rained. Sheets of water fell, speared by jagged lightning bolts that exploded against the steep cliffs and lighted the park brighter than the sun. It was a fearsome thing to watch—the power unleashed on his tiny world. But Fallon huddled out of the rain, wrapped in his blankets against the wall of his cave, his fire casting its light on the granite surface, which threw its warmth back on him.

Before banking his fire for the night, he stared into its shimmering golden light, and saw the face of the girl with the copper-colored hair. How had she taken the robbery, and being held captive by Juárez? Was she any closer to figuring out who her nemesis, the bandit, was? Once she found out, would she ever forgive him?

THAT SAME NIGHT, JOAN SAT STARING INTO THE FIRE outside the tent Juárez had provided for her. She glanced at the tent the small Zapotec occupied. He wasn't at all what she had imagined; he was a gentleman by any standard, and his intelligence compared favorably with any person she'd met. Yet there was no doubt he had some connection with the bandit who seemed to know her every move. Her breath caught in her throat at the thought of the tall man she at once hated and liked. Why did she feel the flash of warmth when her thoughts centered on him? She pondered that question a bit then shrugged. Her thoughts went to Tom Fallon.

Before she let her daydreaming take her back to the last moments they'd spent together, a voice at her shoulder said, "*Señorita, El Presidente* invites you to share a brandy with him. Will you come with me?"

Her first impulse was to refuse. It was as though he'd ordered her to come to his tent. She sighed, knowing the poor harried little man would do no such thing. He'd shown her only courtesy, caring, and protectiveness during the days she'd spent in his camp. She smiled and stood.

The sentry held the tent flap aside while she entered. Juárez stood by a chair he held for her. It was the only chair Joan had seen in the camp. "*Señor Presidente, gracias,* but I'll sit on the ground; I'll not take your chair."

He smiled, much as her own father used to smile at her. "Very well, we'll both sit on the ground."

He asked the orderly to bring glasses, and poured a liberal amount of brandy into each. He held his snifter with both hands to warm its contents, then raised his glass to toast her. "Your health, *señorita.*"

They sat quietly a few moments, then Juárez looked at her. "*Señorita,* you will only be my guest another day or two. I must be in El Paso del Norte by the fifth of August."

Joan locked gazes with him. "What will you do with me then, *señor*?

His eyes widened with surprise. "Why, I'll escort you to your own front door and you'll be shed of me."

It was her turn to feel surprise. "But, sir, your men caught me in the act of supporting Maximilian. I thought I was your prisoner."

He chuckled. "I hope, *señorita,* I've not made you feel like a prisoner. I had to keep you with me for security reasons, and too, I had to keep the coach as my only means of transporting such a large amount of gold. That being true, I had no way of sending you to El Paso in the comfort befitting a lady."

Joan sipped her brandy and studied this man of small physical stature who was a giant among all men. Why she said it she didn't know, but she then said, "*Señor Juárez,* I sincerely hope that will not be the last I see of you."

Juárez stared into his glass a moment, then looked into her eyes. "No, my dear, when state business permits, I'd like to count on having you dine with me."

Joan again surprised herself. "*Señor Presidente,* I can't think of anything I'd like more." Abruptly she frowned, wondering whether to ask the question to which she most wanted an answer. She shrugged mentally—why not? "Sir, for the longest time, I thought the *Bandido Caba-*

*llero* was just that, nothing more than an outlaw preying on treasure Maximilian needed desperately. Now I know he works for you. Is he an American, Mexican, or perhaps simply an enemy of Napoleon, and why is he doing it?''

Juárez laughed and shook his head. ''I can't answer your questions. I'm not sure I would even if I knew the answers. All I do know for certain is that he is just what you called him—a gentleman. And another thing is, he is by far the most dangerous man I've ever known, but as long as he is your friend I know of nothing you'd have to fear.''

Joan placed her hand on the ground at her side and leaned on it. ''Tell me about him. I don't know why it's important to me, but somehow it is. He's tall, that's obvious. Is he handsome? Is he truly as gentle and chivalrous as he seems? Why does he give to you all the gold he's taken? If he's not quite well off, I would think he'd keep some for himself.''

Juárez nodded. ''Yes, I believe most women would call him *very* handsome, and yes, I believe he is gentle and chivalrous with certain people. And it's only a guess, but I don't think he needs money. At any rate, I somehow don't think money is very important to him.'' He drank the rest of his drink and smiled. ''Now, young lady, I'm going to run you off so an old man can get some sleep. You go dream about a handsome bandit whom you've alternately hated and admired.'' He hesitated a moment, then asked, ''Perhaps you'll breakfast with me?''

Joan stood. ''Yes, *Señor Presidente,* I'll breakfast with you. *Buenas noches.* Sit still, my tent is only a step or two.''

Back in her tent, Joan's thoughts lingered on Juárez, the bandit, and her own sentiments. Then, she thought of Tom Fallon. She knew what his lips on hers did to her. Just the thought of them turned her warm all over. His direct gaze did as much to cause her heart to quicken as his lips did. The thought of him, and of the gentleman bandit, and the desire to know them much better, muddled her thoughts even more. Why, in such a short time, had she met two men who turned her emotions into a confused mass of questions and desires? Before going to bed, she wished she could have them both in the same room at the same time, and make a sensible comparison—but that in itself wasn't very sensible. Was it?

She lay there long into the night, wondering about Fallon, convinced she'd met him in the past. But why, if she'd met him, had she forgotten the when and where of their encounter? She thought of many men in the past, men in whom she'd not been one whit interested, and she could remember the time and place and occasion of their meeting. No—if she'd met Tom Fallon, she was certain she'd remember every detail of it. Wanting so desperately to get to sleep, she tossed and turned until exhausted. Finally, she closed her eyes and slept the sleep of the dead.

# CHAPTER

# 14

Fallon made breakfast and prepared to leave the park. He stood, stretched, flexed his muscles, and picked up his saddle. The ease with which it came to his shoulder told him his strength was where it had been before he was shot. His satisfied grunt said it even better. After saddling his horse, he checked the ties on his bedroll, jacked a shell into the magazine of his Henry, and, carrying his rifle, headed toward the fissure.

Upon entering the narrow opening, the black pulled back on the reins. Walking ahead of his horse, Fallon urged him to follow, knowing the smell of big cat and bear must be strong in the confines of the narrow, cliff-enclosed trail.

His neck muscles tight, his stomach muscles pulled against his gut, he studied every shelf, every crease along the walls. Fallon thought the bear would have gone on to wherever this trail exited, but the cat might easily have eaten and now be stretched out on one of the ledges.

Still only about fifteen minutes into the crevice, he moved forward a few feet at a time before stopping and again searching the cliffs. As he was about to take another step, the smooth line of a shelf to his right caused him to plant his foot and squint at an upward curve along its plane. The lines of the break in the shelf swelled upward, and a tawny body took shape against the dark surface.

The cat stood, then crouched. Fallon's hope that the cat would turn and run, as they frequently did, evaporated. A shot behind the shoulder was not likely with the animal high and in front of him. He had to try a head shot, and hope he didn't miss. A bad shot and the cat would be on him.

He thought to fire, then run backward to try and get beyond the lion's spring, but shook his head. He decided to fire and, as soon as the animal left the ground, run toward it, hoping the monster would overshoot its mark.

Still in its crouch, belly almost touching the ground, the mountain lion's muscles rippled along its shoulders, claws dug into the rock surface—and he left the ground.

In one smooth, fluid motion, Fallon's rifle came to his shoulder and spit flame. The sound of the shot rang back and forth against the cliff walls. He launched himself toward where the big animal had crouched above him and jacked another shell into the magazine. He threw himself flat, rolled, and fired straight up into the lion's belly when it passed over him. Fallon pushed himself to his knees and again worked the lever of the Henry.

Squatted there, ready to fire again, smelling the acrid stench of gunsmoke and his own fear, he stared at the lion stretched full length on the granite path.

Still alive, the animal blinked hate-filled eyes at him. The big cat tried to snarl, but emitted only a mild growl, shivered, and lay still.

Fallon squatted there a moment letting the tremors along his backbone subside. He wiped cold sweat from his brow and took a deep breath. A look across the dead animal's body searched for his horse, hoping he'd not been hurt. The black was nowhere in sight. He must have bolted back toward the park, the only way he could have gone without running under the lion.

The sound of his shots still rang in Fallon's ears in the close confines of the fissure, and he worried a moment

that Escobar and his party had heard them. Then he
shrugged. Even if the sound of his shots had escaped the
fissure, along with their echo, it would have been almost
impossible to determine the direction from which they'd
come. He pulled his Bowie knife and approached the cat
with care. He walked around it and pricked its rear quarter
with his knife's point. The animal didn't stir.

He skinned the big animal, cut prime parts into small
hunks, wrapped the meat in the skin, and headed back the
way he'd come. He'd eaten cougar twice before and found
it to be as good, perhaps better, than the meat of any other
animal.

When he caught his horse, the black shied from him
and the smell of blood. A look around the park, and a
glance at his watch, and Fallon decided that, rather than
spend another night here, he would head out. There was
only an outside chance Escobar, or his Yaqui, had heard
the shots, and even a longer shot that they could tell from
which direction they came, but he'd not take even that
small chance.

On the second attempt to travel the cliff-shrouded trail,
Fallon used as much care as he had his first try. Two hours
later, he walked out onto a high mesa, and as he'd
thought, the grass was lush, and a small stream wended
its way toward some unknown path of escape to lower
ground. He toed the stirrup and climbed aboard the black.

Without the slightest notion where he was, he reined
his horse toward the north, wanting to get back to his own
country. The black stepped daintily through the tall grass
and acres of mountain flowers. Sundown found him
alongside a stream, still high above the world. He'd seen
no sign that anyone had ever traveled this high country
before. A few mountains stood watch over the tableland,
and Fallon was sure that when he reached the edge of this
beautiful, lonely place, he would find more peaks below
where he rode.

There was plenty of game—antelope, deer, and sign of
smaller animals—but he didn't bother them. He'd not kill
needlessly.

He made camp, hoping on the morrow he'd find a trail to lower ground. He hunched close to his fire, shivered, and pulled his blankets around his shoulders. He'd not brought a sheepskin with him. The idea he might need one had never entered his mind until he headed for the mountains. But now some of that desert heat would be welcome.

Lying by the fire after he'd eaten, he wondered where those hunting him might be. By his count, Juárez should be preparing to enter El Paso del Norte in a few days, and he needed to be there before the Zapotec, find Francois Berne if he wasn't still in the mountains looking for the bandit, and stop whatever assassination plan the Frenchman had come up with. He thought, too, about the girl with the copper-colored hair. He tried to think how such a petite, beautiful woman had encircled his heart so easily. He'd known many women, but never one he thought to spend his life with. He wondered if there was a way he could keep his banditry from her. He wondered why she had shown such strong support for Maximilian. "Aw hell," he grunted and pushed down into his blankets.

THE NEXT MORNING, FALLON HAD AN HOUR OF RIDING behind him when the sun crept above the mesa's edge. He still headed north, for there lay his homeland.

About three o'clock, he circled a large boulder and looked out across the world. Several thousand feet below lay the desert floor, and off fifteen or so miles, rugged escarpments stood on end, painting the horizon with cliffs streaked orange, red, gold, and black. The desert floor broke into white flats and dark shadow. Judging by the deep black shadows, there were ravines down there to test man and horse.

He studied the land's slope until he thought he saw a way to the bottom, then his gaze swept the desert, looking for, but hoping not to see, a dust cloud, hoping if he did it would not be Escobar. Finally, satisfied he had this stretch of world to himself, Fallon kneed the black onto the slope. It was now only mid-afternoon, and he figured by sundown he could get far toward those painted cliffs. His canteens were full. He still had cougar meat, but no coffee and flour.

Sundown found him only four or five miles from the escarpments. He camped there that night, and the next day rode into a small Mexican town called Agua Prieta. He smiled to himself. He knew where he was, and the border was only a few miles to his north. Once in the New Mexico Territory, he'd ride on to Lordsburg, a rough town, but one he'd be happy to see. Tonight, he'd stay in Agua Prieta.

Covered with alkali dust, Fallon and his horse rode down a street bordered on each side with crude one-room adobe shacks. Sitting in front of each were men and women, none of whom raised a friendly hand in greeting. He considered riding on through, but changed his mind. He wanted a drink—tequila, mescal, or whatever they had. It would take something that strong to cut the dust from his throat.

Almost out of town, he spotted a *cantina,* if such it could be called. Four horses were tied to the hitchrail. He looped the reins tiredly over the rail, hitched his handgun to a comfortable position along his thigh, thumbed the thong off the hammer, and went through the opening that served for the doorway. Dirt floors, no doors, no windows—only gaping holes in the walls that served as such—but it did have a slab of rough-cut wood acting as a bar.

"Tequila, *señor*?"

"*Sí, señor.* You wan someting to eat?" The fat Mexican behind the bar spoke English.

Fallon answered him in fluent Spanish. "Tequila first," he said, then hesitated. "Two tequilas first, then food."

At the other end of what served as a bar, one of the four men, a tall, swarthy, very dark man Fallon guessed to be the owner of one of the horses in front, asked, "You are Mexican, *señor*?"

Fallon shook his head. "Nope, *Americano*."

The man next to the one who had questioned Fallon—
short, thin, with a scar running from hairline to chin—
said, "We don't drink with *gringos* in here."

Anger swelled the muscles in Fallon's throat. He tried
to keep his feelings from showing, but he knew his eyes
were an icy green. He'd been told they got that way when
he was angry. He turned them on the man, dropped the
Spanish, and spoke Texan. "Ain't nobody asked you to
drink with me. Till I do, keep your damned stinkin' mouth
shut."

A wolfish leer covered the thin one's face, and in an
almost catlike purr, he said, "Ah, *gringo,* I theenk you
'ave make a beeg mistake. Nobody talks to Pedro Morales
that way."

Fallon never used the term "greaser," but the Mexican
had used the derogatory term "*gringo*," so he retaliated.
"Only one mistake been made since I walked in here,
greaser, an' you the one who made it. You ain't big 'nuff
to whip me, so pull that gun you're wearin, try usin' your
knife—or run, an' I'm talkin' 'bout right now."

Morales's hand flashed to his side. His six-shooter almost cleared leather before Fallon made a move toward
his gun. His first shot dusted the thin man over his shirt
pocket, knocking him back a couple of steps. Fallon ad-
justed his aim and thumbed off another shot. His second
shot pushed the button at the top of Morales's shirt into
his chest. The Mexican stared at Fallon a moment. His
mouth worked, tried to say something, then his legs
folded. He fell forward onto his face.

Fallon moved the barrel of his handgun only a fraction
to point at the other three. "I come in here for a drink an
somethin' to eat. Still figure on it. You want to join yore
friend in hell, pull iron."

They stood there wide-eyed, staring at him, then the
tall swarthy man who had first spoken to Fallon said, "*Señor,* I have never seen a *pistola* appear so fast. He brought
the trouble to you; we have no fight with you. Have your
drink, eat your meal, and leave. There will be more trou-

ble over this as soon as his two brothers hear what you have done.''

Fallon edged up to the bar. In a blur, he removed the cylinder from his Colt, slipped a full one in its place, calmly punched out the spent shells, reloaded, and dropped the cylinder into his pocket. ''Pour my drink, Bartender, then get me something to eat.''

The fat Mexican put a glass on the bar, and his hand shook so hard the bottle he held to its lip played a tattoo. ''*Señor,* I be ver happy to get you some food, but if I were you, I'd take this bottle and get gone. Morales has friends hereabouts.'' He knocked the cork back into the bottle neck, handed the bottle to Fallon, and turned toward the back of the bar. ''I'll wrap you some of these tortillas and a hunk of cabrito you can eat as you ride.''

Fallon knocked back his drink, tossed a cartwheel on the bar, picked up the bottle and package of food, and backed toward the door. ''*Gracias, señor.* You have treated me well.''

On the way out of town, his horse in a flat-out run, Fallon noticed that despite the heat, all of the town's citizens had disappeared into their *jacals.* He rode as though heading for Nogales, and held that course for almost an hour, then reined toward Lordsburg. After another half hour of hard riding, he pulled his horse in and sat listening. The black was breathing hard enough that Fallon had trouble hearing. He was tempted to ground-rein the horse and move off into the desert a ways to hear better, but if something scared the black and made him run, Fallon knew he'd be as good as dead afoot here in the desert. He toed the stirrup, rode on, and ate in the saddle.

About four o'clock he looked for a place to make camp. It would soon be daylight. He'd have a dry camp, but wanted one he could defend. The wan, sickly moon trying to push its light through thin clouds gave him little help, but his eyes, now accustomed to the dark, searched every hill, every stand of cactus for a likely place, but found nothing to suit him. A hot, brassy sun found him still pushing the black horse farther north.

Now he again rode in mountains, only they were barren and rocky; even the cactus had disappeared. A mountain to his right showed signs of vegetation. Splotches of dark green high on its shoulders were probably juniper, but higher still there was more green; Fallon figured that to be pines. He shook his canteen. From its heft and the splash in it he figured it was still half-full, and the two tied to the pommel had not been opened. He reined his horse toward the mountain he figured to have trees on it. It would be cooler there, and the likelihood of water better.

While climbing, he wondered at his talent to get out of one scrape and into another. Now he had not only Escobar to worry about, but the Morales brothers as well. He muddled that thought around a bit, then shrugged. "What the hell," he said aloud. "Cain't live forever. By rights I shoulda bought the farm the day I left that Yankee prison." He chuckled and urged the black on up the mountain.

STILL DEEP IN THE SIERRA MADRE OCCIDENTAL, ESCOBAR walked upstream from his horse, dropped to his knees, bathed his face, and took only a few swallows of water. If that sat well on his stomach, he'd drink more. The Yaqui stood at his side, as did Francois Berne. The Frenchman stood there only a second, then turned and ran from the stream, stopped, bent, retched, and emptied his stomach of the water he'd gulped in huge swallows.

Escobar looked at him and shook his head. "*Señor,* I told you, it is always best to drink only a little when you've gone so long without." He leaned over the water and drank a few more swallows, then looked up at the Yaqui. "What do you think, *amigo,* shall we still search for the *bandido*?"

The Indian stared down the long expanse of arid peaks, shrugged, and spread his hands at his side. "*Señor,* I weel hunt for heem as long as you say, but I theenk he ees somewhere making the big laugh at us. We weel not catch heem, *señor.*"

Berne cut in, "I want that man *dead*. He has made fools of us. He took gold the Emperor needs desperately and has led us almost to our deaths. *I* want him."

Escobar's face muscles tightened. He tried not to show the anger and contempt he felt toward the Frenchman, then he thought, To hell with him. Being a good soldier for the Austrian puppet went only so far. He'd almost killed a company of good soldiers, and he'd not jeopardize them further. He stared into the Frenchman's eyes. "*Señor,* you want him dead, you find him. We're a week from home. A week of deadly thirst, down to starvation rations, and our horses worn to skin and bone, leaves me with the thought I don't give a damn what you do. I'm taking my men and heading for home."

"Y-y-you're disobeying orders?" Berne stammered, his face flushed, veins standing out. He slobbered. "I'll put you before a firing squad when we get back." His voice rose, came out little short of a screech. "I'm gonna see that bandit and you both dead."

Escobar looked at him a long moment, then worked up a mouthful of saliva and spit at the Frenchman's feet. He looked at the Yaqui. "Show us the way out of these mountains, *amigo.* You've done your job well. *Gracias.*" He again looked at Berne. "You can stay here, or follow us. I don't give a damn which."

"Leave the Indian with me."

Escobar shook his head. "The Yaqui stays with me."

Berne, still looking like a bomb about to explode, took a deep breath. "You leave me no choice, Captain. I will go with you, but prepare for a court-martial when we get to Franklin."

Escobar raised his eyebrows. Do as you like, *señor.*" He turned to his men. "We stay here tonight, *hombres.* Drink and rest. Tomorrow we head for home." A cheer from the parched throats rose around him.

He drank again, then rationed a small amount of grain for his horse and spread his blankets. His thoughts went back to the holdup. When they'd tried to find tracks left by the coach the next day, the *bandido's* forces and wind had swept the desert floor of any sign. Then, taunting them, the *bandido* had shown himself and led them into the jaws of hell, leaving tracks even Berne could have followed. With a company of men like the bandit, Escobar figured he'd charge hell with a teaspoonful of water.

Then his thoughts turned to Maximilian. There were rumors many Mexican imperialists were defecting to the Republic. In the past, there were those who had defected to Maximilian, redefected to Juárez, and again defected to the Emperor. Escobar shook his head. Maximilian, or Juárez, would be a fool to depend on people with that degree of loyalty. One defection, he could understand, but those whose loyalties depended on the tide of battle were not to be trusted. Then he pondered his coming court-martial until he fell asleep.

FALLON RODE DOWN THE DUSTY STREET OF LORDSBURG, and even though it was mid-morning, miners jammed the street, laughing, shouting, drinking, and brawling. These were the ones who'd worked all night in the silver mines. Others were underground scraping out the gray rock that held the ore, and in the end the whorehouses, saloons, and gamblers would rake in the sweat-stained dollars.

He passed several saloons, and at each resisted the urge to stop for a drink. He wanted a bath, shave, and clean clothes more than anything, then he'd have a drink. He'd had a good night's sleep and was not ready to crawl between his blankets again.

A narrow two-story building showed itself on his right: a hotel. He hitched his horse, pulled his Henry from the scabbard, and went to the desk.

The desk clerk, pale, mid-twenties, asked, "Need a room? Got two left, or you can share a room with most any in here."

Fallon studied the man a moment. "First off, I ain't sharin' a room with nobody. Second, when did you change the straw in them mattresses an' wash the covering? Third, I want wash water brought to my room so I can bathe."

The clerk stared back. "You sorta particular, ain't ya? I'll answer your questions, though. First, you don't have to share a room with nobody long's you pay a dollar a day. Second, I got a room just had the bedding washed and fresh straw stuffed into it this mornin'. Third, you haul your own bathwater."

Fallon's lips quivered at the corners, then he laughed. "Reckon you just rented a room. Gimme the key, a bucket, an' tell me where the well is. Then have a boy take my horse to the livery, rub him down, and grain feed him."

Two hours later, clean from the skin out and shaved, Fallon went down the street to the nearest saloon. He knocked back two drinks, then saw an empty seat at a poker table against the back wall. He held his glass out to the bartender. "Fill it. Think I'll take that vacant seat back yonder at that poker table."

The chair was against the wall at the back of the table. After making sure the players would let him in the game, Fallon sat facing the door. He wondered if the Morales brothers had been able to trail him this far—and wondered, if they had, would he be able to take them both on. Few men he knew of were fast enough, and accurate enough, to fight two men at once, and if Morales's brothers were as salty as Pedro had been, he'd have his hands full. He didn't want to kill again, but he knew nothing short of a miracle could prevent it.

Fallon played conservatively, won enough pots to stay about even, and kept a look at the saloon doors. About midnight, he closed his eyes to slits, widened them, and squinted toward the door again.

They're good, very good, he thought. Figured it'd take 'em at least until tomorrow night to find me. He looked at the players. "There's gonna be shootin' right here at this table in a few seconds. You men grab your chips, move over against the side walls, an' come back when the smoke clears. I'll be here," he said and then to himself he added, "I hope."

Fallon edged closer to the table, pulled his Colt, and held it out of sight below the tabletop.

They had to be the Morales brothers; they looked like Pedro and had the same build and arrogant look about them.

Inside the batwing doors, they split, one taking each side of the doorway. Fallon watched their eyes travel to each person in the room, then move to another. Then they homed in on the side tables, until their searching looks came to where he sat. Fallon thumbed back the hammer of his .44.

# CHAPTER

# 15

THEY WALKED TOWARD HIS TABLE, EYES NEVER LEAV-
ing his, and stopped about eight feet in front of him. The
only difference between these two and Pedro was that the
brother to Fallon's right had a sleepy eye. His left eyelid
drooped, almost closing off sight. He was the one who
spoke. "We 'ave beezness weeth you, *señor.*"

Fallon took a deep breath, smelling the saloon's stale
alcohol and sweat from dirty bodies. He studied the brothers a moment. He didn't want to kill them, but knew the
shoot-out was as good as inevitable. Of course *he* might
be the one killed. "You're brothers to the man I killed in
Agua Prieta. He brought it to me, *señors*. I did not want
a fight. All I wanted was a drink, something to eat, and
then to ride on. He didn't see it that way."

The one standing next to Droopy Eye raised one eyebrow. "Ees bad, *hombre*. We onerstan' you must fight,
but he was our brother, you keeled heem. You must die.
Eet ees a matter of honor."

Fallon nodded. "I, too, understand, *vaquero*. You have
this to do, so turn loose your wolf."

They both slapped leather at the same time, and each
dived to the side, one to Fallon's left and one to his right.

With his left hand Fallon pushed the table over, and his six-shooter bucked twice before he felt a burn along his leg. He thumbed off two more shots, one right, one left. A great cloud of smoke billowed between him and the brothers, and the smell of gunsmoke stung his nostrils— but no more shots came from their direction. Fallon moved to the side, trying to see under the blanket of smoke.

The brother with the sleepy eye lay on his back, one eye staring into the smoke-shrouded room, the droopy eye closed forever. The other brother, still alive, looked at Fallon. "You do not want to keel us, but we make you do eet." He closed his eyes, trembled, sighed, and went limp.

"What the hell was that all about?" The question came from a gaunt, hollow-chested man, who looked as though he might have lung fever. He wore a star over his left pocket.

Fallon, his eyes smarting from the powder smoke, blinked and looked again at the two men he'd killed. "Marshal, whatever my words are, they won't justify killin' two men. Their honor, revenge for a third brother, who died because he hated Americans, caused these two to track me to your town. You saw what happened."

The marshal signaled to four men standing with the onlookers. "Take these two and have the coroner fix 'em for burial soon's I go through their pockets, see who I need to write about them bein' dead. If they ain't got enough money on 'em to pay for boxin' 'em and diggin' the hole, the town'll have to pay for it."

Fallon thought he could pay for burying them, then changed his mind. Whether he chipped in on the funeral wouldn't make any difference; they'd get the same kind of box and the same hole regardless. He looked at the marshal. "You got any charges against me?"

The lawman only shook his head.

Fallon set the table back on its legs and motioned the players who'd been sitting with him. "Reckon we can get the game goin' again."

Two of the men, miners to judge by their dress, shook their heads and said in unison. "We quit. You done took the fun outta playin'." The other four took their places at the table.

Fallon played about even until he thought he might get some sleep. He pushed the sight of the two brothers far back in his mind, but try as he might, the sight and thought of them would come back to haunt him in the dark lonely night hours.

Back at the hotel he turned in. Tomorrow he'd head for Las Cruces, then to the ranch and pick up help, then to Franklin to find out if Berne and Escobar still hunted him.

He lay there long into the night, wondering at the wispy thread by which life clung to this earth. The last few years of his life had demanded he take the lives of others. If he had acted in any way other than as he had been forced to, he'd be the one dead. Now that he'd met Joan, if things worked out, he'd have a lot to live for. He thought then he might hang up his guns, and in the same thought he knew better. As long as there were Apache, or lawless men wearing guns, he must also.

Early, as soon as the general store opened, Fallon bought provisions and headed east. He uttered a dry, humorless chuckle. Now all would be smooth sailing—except for a few thousand Mescalero. With luck he wouldn't cross Apache tracks.

While riding, Fallon wondered if Juárez had jumped the gun and gone to El Paso ahead of time, then decided *El Presidente* wouldn't move until he had to, and that was the fifth of August. Then he wondered whether Joan had been sent in ahead of the president's party. Again he decided Juárez would keep her with him for her own safety.

Anxious to get back to Franklin, Fallon rode late. Well after sundown, far ahead of him, a faint orange pinpoint of light flickered, weakened, and flared. Damned fools, he thought. Unless they were a large party, they had set up a beacon with which to lead the Apache to them. He urged the black a little faster.

When still a quarter of a mile away, the silhouettes of

prairie schooners stood stark and dark against the large fire in the middle of the circle. Riding closer, Fallon counted fourteen wagons, maybe enough to defend the group against a small Apache war party. He hailed the camp, and at their invitaion rode in.

Gathered about the fire, Fallon counted twenty men, four of them old men, two of them probably about sixteen, and the rest, he assumed, the husbands of the tired, middle-aged women, old before their time. There was a whole passel of kids he didn't bother to count.

"Climb down and set, stranger. You're ridin' mighty late, ain't yuh?"

Fallon eyed the man, apparently the wagon boss. "Yeah, ridin' late, an' maybe lucky for you I am."

"How's that? Don't see nothin' you can do fer us." The man poured a cup of coffee and handed it to Fallon.

"Sir, know it ain't none o' my business," Fallon glanced at the fire, "but if I was you, I'd douse that fire down to nothin' but embers. You're in the middle of Mescalero country."

The man stood a little straighter. His face stiffened. "You right, mister, it ain't none o' your business. We ain't seen a Injun since we left St. Louis. Ever'body keeps tryin' to scare us with them stories, but we been makin' out mighty fine without nobody's help."

Fallon nodded. "You're right. Reckon I shoulda kept my mouth shut." He handed back the coffee cup, still almost full. "Reckon I'll ride on." He reached for his horse's bridle, hesitated, and again pinned the wagon boss with a hard look.

"Mister, I don't give a damn what happens to you, but these women and children deserve better. The Apache don't usually attack at night, but they can locate you by your fire, an' when they're ready they'll hit you so sudden you won't have a chance. Now I done told you, an' I'm leavin'. I'll camp out where I won't be a victim of your stupidity." He toed the stirrup and rode from their camp surrounded by total silence.

He'd not ridden a half mile when he reined in and

looked back. The fire still begged an attack. He raised his eyebrows, shook his head, and looked for a place to make camp.

Minding his own advice, he made a dry, fireless camp, chewed a piece of jerky and a hard biscuit, and, lying with his head on his saddle, worried about the families less than a mile away. They had a fool for a wagon master—but it wasn't their fault. Finally, figuring he'd done all he could to save them from folly, he turned on his side and slept.

The next morning, a rosy cast in the eastern sky announced the coming of another scorching day. Fallon pulled the cinches tight against the black's belly, grabbed the saddle horn, and toed the stirrup. He hesitated before pulling himself to the saddle, took his foot from the stirrup and cocked his head to hear better. A faint popping noise sort of like rifle fire broke the silence. He led his horse toward the crest of a knoll, where he removed his hat, flopped to his belly, and peered toward the small wagon train. From where he lay, he counted twenty-two riders circling the wagons. Small puffs of smoke came from the muzzles of rifles fired toward the train. Fallon studied the scene being enacted before him, sighed, toed the stirrup, and headed toward the attack. If they don't get me killed first, he thought, maybe they'll let me pump some sense into that dumb bastard they put in charge.

A quick search of the terrain showed no place to hide— no rocks, no land swell, nothing but creosote bush and yucca. Figuring the Indians would give all their attention to the wagons, Fallon rode hard toward them until within easy rifle range. He pulled his Henry from its scabbard, dismounted on the run, and tugged his horse down beside him.

He landed beside a giant old yucca, its arms spread to the sky. Without hurrying, he drew a bead on the warrior closest to him, squeezed off a shot, and watched him throw up his arms and fall off the side of his pony. In a fluid move his sights centered on another Mescalero. The Indian dropped his rifle and pulled off to the side. Now they knew another rifle had joined the fight. They headed out of rifle range. Fallon counted them again. There were sixteen still astride ponies. Somebody among those folks in the wagons could shoot.

The war party sat there talking it over. Their arms waved, and at least one of them pointed toward where Fallon lay. As soon as they had gotten out of range, he had quit firing. No point in letting them know only one rifle out here had taken sides.

Fallon gauged the distance and figured with a little luck he could still draw blood, but he held his fire. One warrior rode a few feet toward him, shouldered his rifle, and fired. His shot splatted against a yucca several yards from Fallon.

He drew careful aim and squeezed the trigger. One more Apache fell from his horse.

Fallon's stomach churned. He swallowed hot fluids draining from under his tongue. If the remainder of the Apache decided to launch their attack at him, his ma and pa would be minus a son.

The Mescalero leader held up his arm and signaled his men to follow him, and they rode toward the north.

Reckon they figured it wasn't a good day to die. The thought came to Fallon at the same time his gut stopped churning. He waited until the depleted war party disappeared over a rise, then mounted and rode to the wagon train.

Inside the circle of wagons, he didn't wait to be invited to dismount. His head throbbed, and angry blood pushed against his temples. He walked to the man who'd thought he knew it all the night before. "Gonna tell you somethin'. Your stupidity didn't only almost cost your people their lives, it damned near cost me mine—that makes me madder'n hell."

He glanced around. The wagon train's members crowded close to him. "Gonna tell all o' you somethin'. You voted this incompetent know-it-all in as your leader. If you're smart, you'll hold another meeting and elect another wagon master—an' you'll do it 'fore you hitch up for the day. That's all I'm gonna say.''

He had pulled his horse closer to climb aboard and leave when a gaunt, sun-baked man stepped forward. "Mister, I don't blame you for your opinion of us. We treated you poorly last night. Set an' have some breakfast. And if you'd be kind enough to give us some advice 'bout what we should do to be safer, an' tell us 'bout that desert land we gonna be crossin', I'd be almighty grateful.''

Fallon locked gazes with the man, then looked at the women and children drawn close, and felt the anger drain from him. "Be happy to tell you the things I've learned from experience, sir. And, yes, I'd appreciate having breakfast with you. Ain't had a hot cup of coffee since yesterday mornin'.''

While he ate, Fallon told them of the intense heat they could expect west of Lordsburg, of the long stretches of barren desert between towns, of the lawless towns ahead, towns such as Tuscon, Nogales, Tombstone, and others. He told them about what lack of water would do to man and beast. He told them about blowing sand, about rock piled high to form mountains, and he told them about the miles of Apache-laden country.

Finally, he accepted another cup of coffee and sat back, packed his pipe, lighted it, and locked eyes with each of them, including the women and children. "Ain't tryin' to scare y'all none, just tellin' you what you can expect, and hopin' you'll be prepared for it.'' He puffed his pipe a couple of times. "You folks been travelin' together a good while now. You've had a chance to get to know each other real well. Among you there is a man who will listen, a man who can think, a man who will do what is best for all of you. You've all made up your mind who that man is. You'd best put him in charge. And one last bit of advice: When you get to Lordsburg, see the marshal there and get him to recommend a good scout to lead you to California. Without a scout, you're gonna have a hard time makin' it.'' He drank his last swallow of coffee, tossed out the grounds, and stood. "Thanks for the meal and coffee. Don't reckon I'd'a eaten hot food before Las Cruces if y'all hadn't fed me.''

He stepped toward his horse, but the man Fallon had heard called Briley, the same man who'd given him a hard time the night before, stood in his way. ''Mister, you come in here givin' free advice last night, an' today you come back an' try to get me throwed outta my job.'' He spat tobacco juice at Fallon's feet. ''Mister, I'm tellin' you I don't like what you done last night, or what you tried to do today to get me fired.''

Fallon stared at the man a moment. On the surface he appeared to have leadership qualities—a big man, smooth, maybe too smooth, and he was confident—but arrogant. Fallon looked at the blob of tobacco juice not yet dry at his feet, then looked back at the man. ''Briley, the only thing I care about in this train is those women and children. I sure don't care a whit what you like or don't like. Now step outta my way an' I'll be goin'.''

''You ain't goin' nowhere till I take you down a notch or two.''

Fallon studied Briley a moment, then said, ''You best take a good look at me, Briley. I'm bigger'n you by 'bout twenty pounds. I know how to handle guns and knives. That don't leave you much choice as to which way to fight me. You gonna lose whatever you do.''

Without further conversation, Briley lowered his head and ran at Fallon.

Fallon sidestepped and let the mouthy one run by. He didn't want to fight the man, but knew he must, for he'd made him out to be a fool before all of his acquaintances.

Briley whirled and came at Fallon again. Fallon again stepped aside and stuck out his foot. The mouthy one tripped and fell. Before he could gain his feet, Fallon stepped to his side and put his foot on Briley's chest, holding him to the ground. ''Briley, you're feeling compelled to fight me because I hurt your pride. Give it up. You can't win. Some men would learn a lesson from this, but sadly I don't think you've got the sense to be one of them.''

He took his foot off Briley's chest and walked to his horse. Before he could mount, a woman's voice yelled, "Look out, mister, he's gitten' a gun."

Fallon whirled. His six-shooter appeared in his hand as if by magic, but before he could fire, a shot sounded. The man who'd invited him to breakfast, whose name was Brown, stood, pale, smoking rifle in hand, staring at Briley, who clutched a rifle and lay writhing on the ground a few feet in front of him.

Fallon stooped at Briley's side, pulled the rifle out of his grasp, and turned him over. His shoulder bled, and on closer look, Fallon saw he'd only been creased. He held the rifle out. "Who owns this?"

A thin man who looked like a farmer nodded. "Reckon it's mine, Mr. Fallon. I shouldn't'a let him grab it."

Fallon smiled. "That's all right, sir; it could happen to any one of us." He looked at Brown, the man who'd invited him to breakfast. "Thank you, sir. You saved my life."

Brown only nodded, then looked at Briley. "Pack your wagon, hitch up, and get out. We'll not have you in this train another day."

Fallon looked from one to the other of them. "Mr. Brown, if you'll permit me to interfere again? I don't think you've ever shot a man before, less o' course you gonna count Injuns. What I'm gonna suggest is, disarm Briley and let 'im travel as far as Lordsburg with the train. You don't, an' the Apache'll have a whole lot o' fun makin' 'im die real slow-like. I wouldn't wish that on him, an' I don't think you would either."

Without hesitation, Brown turned to a couple of men in the crowd. "Search his wagon for weapons, search him too." He looked at Briley. "It's gonna be like Mr. Fallon said, you travel with us far as Lordsburg—that's all."

Fallon squelched a smile. It looked like these people had found themselves a leader. No one contested his orders; they went about getting ready to hitch up for the day. Briley mouthed meaningless threats at Fallon.

Another glance around the circle of faces and Fallon

nodded, smiled, and said, "You folks'll make it. Good luck." He climbed aboard the black and rode out, tipping his hat to them when he cleared the wagon circle, feeling much better about the survival chances for these folks.

He once again turned his horse toward Las Cruces.

# CHAPTER

# 16

FALLON RODE INTO SANCHEZ'S LIVERY STABLE AFTER dark. He stabled the black, rubbed him down, and fed him. He had finished when Sanchez walked to the stall. "Hey, *amigo,* if I didn't recognize the horse I'd not know the man. Where you been? I can't even see you for the dust covering you."

"Long story, Roberto. After I wash some o' this dirt off in the horse trough, we'll go to your *casa,* I'll tell you some of it, then I gotta head for Franklin." He frowned. "Better go by the ranch first and let Ma and Pa know I'm all right. I sure ain't treatin' them good, but I just can't till this is all over."

Fallon washed the surface dirt off, then went to Sanchez's *casa* and got rid of the rest of it. There, he dug out his buckskins, dressed, ate, slept, and headed out. He took Sanchez with him at Carmella's insistence. She said Roberto could keep him safe. Fallon saved her from having to insist too hard. He'd figured on taking Sanchez with him right along.

A day later he and Sanchez rode into his father's ranch yard. "Roberto, if you'll take care of the horses, I'm gonna see if Two Buffalo is here. I want him with us."

After finding the Mescalero, he headed for the house, knowing he'd once again have to skirt the truth as to why he was gone so much. But this time it was different.

After all the hugging and kissing by his mother, and her greeting Sanchez just as warmly, Fallon's father called him into his study, poured them all a drink, and pinned Tom with a no-nonsense look. "Son, I don't know what you're up to, but now I figure it isn't travelin' round the country raisin' hell.

"An army officer, a Major Sikes, visited us asking for a Colonel Fallon, U.S. Army. He went back to Franklin, said he'd wait for you there." Brad Fallon took a swallow of his bourbon, grimaced, and again gave Tom that straight-on look. "I tried to question 'im, but he wouldn't say much, except his business with you was top secret." He spread his hands at his sides. "Son, why the hell didn't you tell us you were in the Army on secret business?"

Tom looked at Sanchez, frowned, and again looked at his father and mother. "Pa, Ma, you already know more'n you should know, for your own good, as well as mine. When I finish this assignment, I'll tell you what I'm permitted to." He sighed. "Reckon long's you all know this much, and keep quiet, don't even say a word to your closest friends, it's all right. Maybe it'll keep you from worrying. Roberto and Carmella know what I'm doin', so I ask you not to question either of them. You could get them killed."

He finished his drink and reached for the bottle, poured Sanchez and himself another, then grinned at his father. "Shore is good to drink good whiskey I ain't havin' to pay for."

"Tom, I do wish you'd stop saying 'ain't.' "

Fallon laughed, looked at Sanchez, and said, "Yep, I'm home." He took a swallow, and stood. "Ma, Pa, we gotta slope outta here if that major's waitin' in Franklin. Don't know when I'll get home again, but maybe it'll be for good the next time."

•   •   •

IN FRANKLIN, FALLON GOT THEM ROOMS; TWO BUFFALO
stayed at the livery. Fallon then went to the lobby to wait
until he could spot the major. He did not have long to
wait. A crusty old-timer in uniform walked through the
lobby, with a stop at the desk to ask if the stage had
brought mail, then climbed the stairs. Fallon waited only
a second, then followed. At the top of the stairs he peered
around the corner until he saw which room Sikes entered,
then went to the door and knocked.

When Sikes pulled the door open, Fallon asked, "Major Sikes?"

Sikes nodded. "Come in. You'll be Colonel Fallon, I
suppose?"

"Yeah, but I'd just as soon you forgot the Colonel. As
far as I know, you and two others are all who know I
have anything to do with the Army." He went in and sat
on the edge of the bed, leaving the only chair for the
major. "Hear tell you want to see me."

Sikes came right to the point. "I didn't give a damn
about seeing anybody it's taken me a week to find in this
desert. It's General Sheridan, he sent me for you. Said for
me not to come back till I found you." He smiled.
"Reckon he said it strong enough for me to believe him."

"When we gotta leave, an' how much ridin' we gotta
do?"

"We leave soon's you get your bedroll. The general's
'bout two days' ride southeast of here."

"You got provisions, an' ammunition for our weapons?"

Sikes nodded. "I have provisions, but you'll have to
make sure I have the right caliber ammo."

Fallon calculated the time to reach Sheridan and get
back. With hard riding both ways, he could get back before August 5, and that would give him a little time to
find out what had been going on. "Reckon if the general
wants to see me I better go. I'll pick up my bedroll and
rifle; ain't had time to unpack anyway, so I'll be right
with you."

He stopped by Sanchez's room, told him what he had

to do, and told him to see if Escobar and Berne had gotten back in town. "If Berne's back, stick to him like a cocklebur. 'Tween you an' me, an' I mean you, me, an' Two Buffalo, we gotta keep *El Presidente* alive. I'll be back before Juárez enters El Paso del Norte."

They talked a few moments, then Fallon went to find Sikes. He found him at the livery, ready to ride. "Major, you sure are in a hurry to get me outta this town." While talking, Fallon threw his saddle on the black and cinched it down.

"Colonel, when the general says do something, he figures you to get it done yesterday. He doesn't mess around. I been gone long enough now to get a first class butt scrubbin' when I get back. Let's go." He toed the stirrup and rode out ahead of Fallon.

The long-legged black soon passed the major, and Fallon kept him to a hard walk. "Hey, Colonel, I didn't mean we had to wear these horses out in order to get there. Slow down."

Fallon looked across his shoulder at Sikes. "Mister, no matter what the general says, I gotta be in El Paso del Norte by August fifth. Come hell or high water, I'm gonna make it."

"Don't know 'bout the high water, Colonel, but I can promise you, if the general don't see it that way there'll be a whole bunch of hell."

They rode in silence after that exchange. Despite his hurry, Fallon kept up a sharp search of the surrounding terrain. He noticed that Sikes did the same. "Done much Indian fightin', Major?"

Sikes's face hardened. "None. But I fought enough of you Johnny Rebs. Never saw a Reb who couldn't measure up to an Apache in sneakin' through the brush, woods, rocks—you name it. I been a field officer ever since I got in this man's army."

Fallon let a thin smile break the corners of his mouth. "How'd you figure me for an ex-Rebel?"

"The general told me—but that's all he told me. Don't want to know more'n that."

They made a dry, fireless camp that night, and were back on the trail by four o'clock the next morning. Soon after sunup, Fallon spotted four riders ahead. He closed his eyelids to slits and stared toward the four. Heavily armed, they all wore Confederate gray.

Fallon eased his Colt in its holster and looked at the major. "Take your rifle out, and lay it across the pommel. Put a shell in the chamber. Don't make any threatening gestures, but be ready."

Sikes stared only a moment at Fallon, shrugged, and did as he'd been ordered.

Fallon kept his eyes on the approaching four. There were many in the South who figured to continue the war. These riders might be some of them. While they were still a hundred yards or so from him, he drew in a deep breath, blew it out, and relaxed.

The gray-clad riders were all tall, thin, dirty, and unshaven. They rode to within a few yards of Fallon, within easy six-shooter range, before reining in. The one who'd ridden at their head, a dark-haired man with sloping shoulders, looked at the major, then slanted a look at his men. "Well, well, looks like we got a blue belly here." He glanced at Fallon. "An' one o' them rugged bastards dressed like a Injun fighter in them skins 'n all."

Fallon felt the hair at the back of his neck tingle, his stomach muscles tighten. "Mister, we got no fight with you," he said. "The war's over." He casually dropped his hand to his thigh and said, "Cock it, Major." A sharp click followed his words.

The one who'd spoken pursed his lips. "Oooo-eee, the blue belly's done cocked that li'l ole Spencer. He done scared me to death, boys. How 'bout y'all?"

The rider sitting next to him said, "He's got me tremblin', Boss." His words triggered each gray-clad rider to rein to the side. Fallon didn't wait. "Now," he yelled and slapped leather. His .44 slipped into his hand and was throwing lead before the four could get set to bring their guns into action. The major's Spencer cracked a cap and one man slammed backward over the cantle of his saddle.

Fallon thumbed off shots as fast as his thumb could slip the hammer. Horses screamed with fright. Lead whined by Fallon's head—then utter quiet, except for the pound of the rebels' retreating horse's hooves.

The four renegades lay on the ground, two of them obviously dead, with half their brains blown out. The other two lay thrashing on the ground.

Gut-shot, Fallon thought. He dismounted and walked to stand at their side. The two, one of whom had been the leader, were still alive, and had been hit at least twice each. As Fallon had thought, they both had holes in their stomachs. With the toe of his boot, he flipped them over.

Gaping holes where the shots had come out showed through their tattered shirts. He rolled them over again. When he did, the one next to the leader shuddered and died. The man still alive stared at Fallon. "Thirsty, mighty thirsty."

Water would only cause more pain, but Fallon figured the man would be dead before the water reached his stomach anyway. He pulled the cork on his canteen and held it for the man to drink. The renegade leader convulsed once, doubled up, and blew out a rattle-like breath.

Fallon stood a moment looking at the four. He wondered what they'd found back home, after the war, to lead them to this. He had a hunch that, whether the major had been in uniform or not, these men would have attacked them. They seemed like white trash who had always wanted something for nothing. Another look, a shrug, and he reached for his horse's reins.

Fallon looked over his shoulder at the major. "Ain't got time to bury 'em. Go through their pockets and see if there's anybody we can notify. Then let's ride."

It took only a moment for Sikes to search their pockets. Fallon climbed back in the saddle, and before he could knee his horse ahead, the major said, "Colonel, we can't let them lie here without dirt thrown over 'em."

Fallon stared at him. "The hell we can't. I got a job to do. A job a whole lot more important than buryin' these four. I ain't got the time. Stay if you want." He kneed his horse toward the southeast. When he looked back a few minutes later, the major trailed him by only a few yards.

They rode another thirty minutes before either said a word, then Sikes drew alongside. "You're a hard man, Colonel Fallon."

His face feeling stiff as dried leather, Fallon looked between his horse's ears. "Sikes, that damned war has already cost me over four years of my life. Confederate rabble—or Union rabble, don't make no difference—ain't gonna cost me another minute. I'm gonna finish this job I'm on, then I'm goin' home, find me a woman, get married, and grow roots in that west Texas soil slam down to China." He finally turned his head to look at Sikes. "I didn't ask for that fight back there; they brought it to us. They got what they asked for."

"But, Colonel, you didn't wait. We might'a talked 'em out of fightin'. You were right sudden with your gun."

"I'm gonna say this once, Sikes. If we'd tried to talk 'em out of it, we'd be the ones lyin' back yonder. An' I guaran-damn-tee you, they wouldn't have buried us."

Two hours later, they rode between neat rows of pup tents. The major led Fallon to a much larger tent and nodded toward it. "General Phil Sheridan'll be in there."

Fallon looked at the tent. He wondered what kind of man Sheridan was. Would he listen to reason? Would he look down on an ex-Confederate? Had President Johnson told him what Fallon's assignment was? A thousand more questions tumbled around in his head. Finally, he shrugged, stiffened his shoulders, and dismounted.

He saluted the sentry and said, "Colonel Fallon to see the general. He's expecting me."

Sheridan sat behind a small desk leafing through papers. He looked up when Fallon stood before the desk. "Colonel Fallon, I presume."

"Yes, sir. Reporting as ordered."

Sheridan motioned to a camp chair. "Have a seat." His gaze swept Fallon from head to foot. "Looks like you had a hard ride. Join me in a glass of bourbon?"

"Yes, sir. Thank you, sir. The major you sent for me said it'd take two or more days to reach you. We made it in a little less than a day and a half. I needed to get here and get back. All hell's about to break loose over in El Paso del Norte. I need to be there."

Sheridan smiled. "Not so fast, young man. President Johnson has not shared with me what assignment he sent you on, but from his words I judge it was very important, and he also led me to believe you've accomplished it in commendable fashion."

"The job's not over yet, sir. That's why I have to get back to El Paso."

Sheridan took a swallow of his drink. "According to the President, your job's over. I have your backpay with me, and I'm authorized to swear you in as a colonel in whatever unit you choose, then write you orders assigning you to that unit. We'll create a vacancy for your rank." He paused, squinting at Fallon. "Further than that, I cannot go."

Fallon sat there a moment studying the bottom of his glass. If he told the general what his mission had been, would he listen? If he told him, he'd be violating the secrecy President Johnson had sworn him to. Was total success of his assignment what was expected of him, or would Johnson be satisfied with what he'd accomplished? He studied his drink a moment longer, then made up his mind. Regardless what anyone expected of him, and whether in the Army or out, he was going to finish the job.

"General Sheridan, I'm going to violate a trust. You and I are both here for the same reason—stop Maximilian, get him outta Mexico. I'm gonna tell you what I'm charged to do despite the fact only two others know what it is, an' they already told me they'd disavow ever having heard of me if I got caught—but this is important enough to break my word of secrecy. You got time to listen?"

Sheridan nodded. "Go ahead, sir."

Fallon started with his release from the prisoner of war camp. He told him of the robberies of the gold shipments and turning the loot over to Juárez. He told him of the untold richness of the last shipment, the loss of which in his estimation would break the back of Maximilian's hold on his troops. He told him of leading the Mexican captain and his men on a chase through desert and mountains which either lost them their lives, or at the very least stymied the efforts of Francois Berne to assassinate Juárez. He didn't miss any detail of acts for which he'd been responsible. Finally, he sat back and swallowed the rest of his drink. "So you see, General Sheridan, my job's not done. If I quit now, if I let them kill Juárez, Maximilian will have won, if not the war, certainly a major battle."

Sheridan picked up the bottle and refilled Fallon's glass, then lighted a cigar and smoked until a long ash hung off its end. All the while he stared at the top of the tent pole. Finally, he looked at Fallon. "We're both here for the same reason, Colonel, but I can't take a hundred thousand troops into Mexico unless the United States is threatened, and I'll be honest with you, I don't see any way that I, or my troops, can act to save Juárez without creating an act of war."

Fallon leaned forward. "That's the point, General. Right now, there are only three people in the world who can tie my acts to the U.S.—you, President Johnson, and Secretary of State Seward, and I swear I'll not call on any of you for help. I have crossed, and can continue to cross, the border and commit whatever acts I think necessary without casting suspicion on our country." He sat back, a slight smile creasing the corners of his mouth. "Besides all that, General, you cut me loose from the Army an' I'll act on my own to save the little Zapotec's life. I like him. He's a brave, compassionate man, a man dedicated to his Republic of Mexico, and one of the most gentlemanly men I ever met. You don't have to acknowledge me, but I will ask that you keep me informed of things that transpire which could help, or hinder Juárez. I'll see he gets the word."

Fallon pulled his pipe from his pocket and looked questioningly at Sheridan for permission to smoke. The general nodded, and Fallon, sensing he'd won Sheridan over, grinned and said, "Well, doggone it, reckon I can talk Texan again. All that Yankee grammar I been usin's done tired me to a frazzle."

Sheridan didn't laugh, but his whole face looked like he wanted to. His lips quivered at the corners, and his eyes tightened a little. "Was wonderin', Fallon, how long you would keep up that stiff military demeanor. Have another drink?"

"No, thanks, General. I got a long ride in the hot sun. Figure another drink and my brains would fry inside an' out."

Sheridan sat there a long moment, puffing his cigar, sipping his drink, and obviously giving Fallon's words a lot of thought. Finally, he gave him a straight-on look. "Tell you what I think might work. I'll swear you in as my special aide. You can resign your commission anytime you wish if you decide not to stay in the Army. Then, I'll issue you extended furlough papers. I can't tell you what to do while on vacation, and you can see this assignment through to its end. And as you can imagine, I, too, will disavow ever having heard of you.

"As to getting word to you without letting someone else in on our secret—well, that'll take some doing."

"General, if I may make a suggestion, I have a friend you might hire as a scout. You won't have to pay 'im. He's got more land than you could ride over in a week. He'll know where I am most of the time, and can find me if anything of importance comes up. He doesn't know under what authority I've been workin', but he knows what I've been doin'. His name is Roberto Sanchez, one of the old land grant families in the New Mexico Territory."

General Sheridan nodded. "Sounds good. Have him report to me as soon as possible."

"One more thing, sir, I had it from a good source you were gonna start leavin' supplies along the riverbank, an' wouldn't get upset when they disappeared across the river. Is that true?"

Sheridan smiled. ''You had a very good source, but the schedule for that has slipped. It'll be January before I can start leaving 'surplus' material there.''

Another hour, and Fallon had resigned his presidential commission, and been resworn in by Sheridan. The general urged him to stay overnight and rest up a bit, but when Fallon insisted on leaving immediately due to the critical situation evolving in Mexico, Sheridan relented.

Furlough papers in hand, Fallon rode from the encampment.

# CHAPTER

# 17

O N THE WAY BACK TO FRANKLIN, FALLON SKIRTED THE
area where the rebels lay, but the stench, reached him,
borne by a slight breeze. His stomach churned when he
thought of what the bodies would look like after the sun,
coyotes, and vultures had had time to do their damage.

Back in town, sweaty and wanting a bath, he looked
for Sanchez, and found him and the Mescalero in the cafe
drinking coffee. Sanchez told him Berne had not returned,
and that Juárez was still encamped where Fallon had last
seen him. "Two Buffalo scouted the Juárez camp. He
says there's not any indication *El Presidente* expects to
move right away."

Fallon frowned, then nodded. "Good. Now, here's
what I want you to do." He then told Sanchez about General Sheridan's agreement to take him on as a special
scout. "He may be sendin' you back here when he thinks
he has information I need. Gonna have Two Buffalo stay
pretty close to the Juárez camp so he can let me know
what's going on there." He nodded to the lawyer's office
across the street. "I think it's time Brad Fallon's son paid
the Frenchies a social visit—soon's I clean up, of
course."

A couple of hours later, with Sanchez and Two Buffalo on their way, and he himself clean and dressed appropriately, Fallon went to the office of Henri Bienville. Charles Lebeau, Anton Belin, and Bienville sat around a desk playing poker.

"Ah, I see the Emperor's statesmen have little to do, an indication all is well with the war, I hope."

Bienville stood. "Have a seat, *M'sieur* Fallon. To tell you the truth, we aren't getting much information up here. We're thinking of moving our office to Monterrey. Closer to the action, you know."

Fallon swept them with a glance. "I see *M'sieur* Berne is not present. He's not ill, I hope."

Bienville hesitated, then sat back and lighted one of his terrible-smelling French cigars. "No, no, he's on state business. We expect him back any day now. The fact is, he's been gone much longer than I expected."

Hating the smooth diplomatic role he played, Fallon said, "I wouldn't worry; he looks like a man who can take care of himself."

"Would you care to join us in a few hands of poker?"

Fallon thought a moment, then nodded and took a seat at the desk. If they played long enough, one of them might drop a bit of information he could use; however, he'd already learned what he'd hoped to find out. Berne must still be wandering around in the desert somewhere. He packed his pipe and lit it while the first hand was being dealt.

It was soon obvious the poker game was not a good way to pass the time. The Frenchmen had little to do, and didn't take much interest in their cards. They talked more than they played. Fallon listened.

Soon the conversation turned to the gold robbery. Bienville looked at Fallon. "You have heard of the bandit and his men who held up the coach and killed most of the men escorting *Madam* Boniol to Mexico City?"

Fallon frowned. "No, I don't believe I have. Of course I've been out at the ranch most of the time. What happened?"

They told a story Fallon would not have recognized as being part of the robbery in which he'd taken part. The bandit and his men had taken *mam'selle* prisoner; *M'sieur* Berne, who took Bienville's place on the trip, played a heroic roll in trying to save her, but ended up in narrowly escaping with his own life while desperately wounding the bandit leader in the ensuing battle, shooting him once in the side and again in his leg—a battle, according to Bienville, in which the outlaw band killed all but a few of the troops escorting *Mam'selle* Boniol. Bienville leaned forward and, in confidential tones, said, "We might as well acknowledge it, *M'sieur* Berne is on a mission to capture the rogue; and perhaps free *Mam'selle* Boniol. He will return soon with them both. I, myself, might now be dead had not *M'sieur* Berne taken my place on the coach with *Mam'selle* Boniol." The Frenchmen never mentioned the coach being loaded with gold.

Fallon feigned shock at what he'd heard. "I can't imagine what would cause them to attack a coach carrying a poor defenseless woman. There must be some other reason."

His ploy didn't work. The Frenchman, his voice sharp, said, "No. There was no other reason." Then he shut up like a clam.

Fallon played only a few more hands, then excused himself. "I've business to attend here in Franklin. Be here a few days for that matter. I'd like to stop in again if I may."

"Drop by anytime, *m'sieur*. We'd like to see you. Perhaps by then we'll have good news of the lady and Berne."

"I surely hope so, *M'sieur* Bienville." He tipped his hat and left, thankful to get away from the foul smell of the French cigar.

On the way back to his room, Fallon pondered what he'd heard. Then he decided that the only thing worthwhile he'd learned was that Berne was still missing. He smiled to himself. The Frenchman and Escobar must be wishing they'd never heard of the *Bandido Caballero*.

Juárez had told him what building he would take over for his offices and living quarters, and rather than commandeer houses and businesses of the people in which to house his troops, *El Presidente* figured to set up another tent encampment at the edge of town. Fallon thought he would scout Juárez's office area and see how it could be defended.

When he'd come by his home ranch, he'd left the big black horse and selected a rangy bay gelding, a horse he'd ridden before and whose speed and staying power he knew. He saddled the bay and rode across the river to El Paso del Norte.

The two-story stone building in which Juárez would set up government stood in the center of town. Fallon rode around it several times and looked at alleys and narrow streets leading to it, and buildings from which a rifleman could fire and get away quickly. There was one two-story building across the street from the future Juárez headquarters, surrounded by one-story, flat-roofed buildings. He tried to put himself into Berne's place. What would he do? How would he set it up? Would he use more than one assassin, or would he try to do the job alone? A plan began to take shape in Fallon's mind.

Then, even though he knew Joan would not be home, he thought he'd plant the seed that he didn't know about her being taken captive in the holdup. He rode to her house.

At his knock, her lady-servant answered the door. "Is *mam'selle* receiving today?"

"Oh, *m'sieur, mam'selle* is not home. She has not been here for days. I do not know whether she is in Mexico City, or if something awful has happened to her. I hear there was a robbery outside of town, and do not know if it was aimed at her coach, and if so, whether she was harmed."

He frowned. "A robbery? Ah, surely she was not in the robbery I have heard about. I'm sure she must be all right. Please tell her I called when she gets home. I'll call again in a few days." He tipped his hat and left.

• • •

JOAN WAS ALL RIGHT, ALTHOUGH WISHING FOR THE COM-
forts of her own home. Juárez had shown her every courtesy and consideration, but his treatment of her could not
take the place of her servants, her own bath, her wardrobe.
She had taken to long evening walks within the bounds
of the encampment, not only for the exercise, but to give
her time to think, to daydream. She had now finished the
first half of this day's exercise.

She wondered if Tom Fallon missed her. She wanted
to feel his lips on hers again, see if she was only imag-
ining the power of his kisses. Had the stirrings his lips
caused grown in her mind while they were separated?
Then, too, she wondered what it would feel like to have
the wild, dangerous man who had robbed her coach hold
her close. She pictured him as a very handsome Spaniard,
and Juárez's words had done nothing to allay that dream.

Oh, how terrible I have grown, she thought. She admitted to herself how strong the attraction to each man
was, and tried to shake them off. She wondered how she
could let herself turn wanton for two men when no other
had pulled on her heartstrings, or body.

Certainly Tom Fallon was as much man as any woman
could ever hope to have, and his raven hair and green
eyes could hynotize her. "Ruggedly handsome" was the
term she applied to him, but still . . . the bandit . . .

She looked up from her musings and saw that she was
abreast *El Presidente's* tent. Her own father had died
when she was only a toddler. Now she wondered if he
had been as kind and compassionate as the small Zapotec
Indian she had grown so fond of.

She no longer questioned where her loyalty lay. Yes,
she had ties to the French, but they were in the distant
past. Juárez and Mexico were today, now, and she had
grown to know he had the education and intelligence to
govern this land and its people.

She walked past the coach that was the reason for her
being here. It had not been touched. It still sat heavy on
wheels sunk several inches into the sand. She had no idea

how much gold it held, but knew it was an amount that could save Maximilian from losing more troops than he already had. She'd heard his treasury was broke, and his forces had not been paid in months.

She had raised the flap of her tent and bent to enter when Juárez called from in front of his own. "*Señorita* Boniol.*"

Joan dropped the flap and turned toward him. "*Sí, mi presidente?*"

Juárez's eyes widened only a bit, but that slight change in expression showed his surprise at her addressing him as her president.

"Will you join me in a brandy before dinner, *mi hija*? I would be most grateful."

Joan felt a surge of elation; a lump filled her throat. He felt about her as she did him. He had called her his daughter. "*Sí, mi presidente,* your company will be most welcome. I had decided to go to bed without dinner from sheer boredom."

"It will not be but two more days, *mi hija,* then we'll go to El Paso del Norte. There you'll be in your own *casa.*"

She had mixed feelings when Juárez told her they'd break camp. She'd welcome being home again, but was going to miss the tender little man. Joan walked back to his tent and entered while he held the flap for her.

A few minutes later, sitting, holding her brandy snifter, she stared at the old man. She thought she had watched him age in the short while she had known him. "Will you call your wife Margarita back to Mexico after you set up your government, or must she stay in New York?"

Juárez shook his head. "I only wish I could have her with me, but I must wait until it is safe for her. *Señorita,* I miss her and my children terribly, but I must wait."

Joan's eyes moistened. "I don't have anyone of my own, but I can imagine how terrible it must be to be separated from your loved ones."

They sipped their brandy in silence, Joan feeling the loneliness, the void of having no one to call her own. She finished her drink, and before she could set it down, Juárez asked her to stay for dinner. "I'm afraid I'm not very good company tonight, *señorita,* but I don't want to be alone right now. Your company keeps me from getting maudlin."

Joan smiled. "Ah, I must try to be more cheerful, *mi presidente.* You have been very good to me."

They had a pleasant dinner, and then Joan went to her tent and, after sponging her body with cool water, went to bed. Again the thoughts of two handsome men haunted her. She wondered where Tom was, and what he was doing.

Then her thoughts turned to the bandit. She had no doubt but what he had strong ties to Juárez. If not, why had he used the Republic's troops to help rob the gold shipment? And if not, why was the coach sitting outside her tent still loaded with Maximilian's treasure? Then she wondered how the bold outlaw had learned of the shipments. These were questions she dared not ask Juárez; he would only think her trying to get information Maximilian could use.

Her thoughts turned from the two men she couldn't rid her thoughts of to Bienville. She wondered if she had hurt his feelings. She had made it clear she didn't think of him in a romantic way. Perhaps she'd been too blunt. If not, why had he given up his seat on the coach to Berne? By his own words he'd looked forward to being with her on the ride to Mexico City. She frowned into the darkness. She hated to hurt anyone's feelings, and hoped that wasn't the reason he'd given up his place on the trip, though she was glad she'd not had to fend him off for such a long time. Her thoughts again turned to the two men who occupied her every thought, then back to the hard days during the war.

She had seen too many men die horrible deaths, many from wounds suffered on the battlefield, and far too many from crude surgical methods: amputations of legs or arms performed without benefit of sedation, bandages made of torn clothing not yet sterilized, and putrid, runny, unmedicated sores killing men from gangrene. She had worked in the Army hospital, first for the Confederacy, then for the Union. The situation was bad regardless which army occupied the area. She put on a happy face for the soldiers while with them, but went home at night and cried herself to sleep, wishing there was something more she could do for them, wishing she could take some of their pain and suffering into her own body. When the war ended, her only thought was to escape the area that held such horrible memories—and now here she was again in the midst of another war.

She forced her thoughts away from the war and back to the two men who so preoccupied her. She went to sleep with warmth flooding her body.

AFTER CALLING AT JOAN'S *CASA*, FALLON WENT BACK TO Franklin, to the cafe, and ordered steak and eggs. He sat by the window where he could watch the hotel and the shyster's office.

He drank enough coffee to float the steel-clad *Merrimac*, gave up on seeing Berne ride in, and went to bed.

He lay there thinking of Maximilian. The loss of the gold shipments had undoubtedly hurt the Emperor. And in Europe Napoleon was having trouble; Prussia was pushing Austria to the hilt, and Napoleon had his troops spread thin, trying to support the war in Mexico and the Austrian defense. Too, the United States' deployment of one hundred thousand troops to the Mexican border under Phil Sheridan was no secret. Napoleon had to be concerned. He muddled the facts, as he knew them, around for a while, then turned on his side and went to sleep.

The next morning he took up his vigil again. After about his fifth cup of coffee, the cafe owner stopped at his table. "Mr. Fallon, I'll rent that table to you for a nickel, then you won't feel like you gotta drink all the coffee in town." He grinned. "Besides that, it'll be a whole lot easier on your kidneys."

Fallon grimaced. "Reckon I'll take you up on that. I'm 'bout to explode."

Mid-afternoon, his vigil paid off. If he'd ever seen a more dejected, ragtag figure in his life, he couldn't remember when. Berne rode to the hitchrack in front of the lawyer's office and, almost falling, climbed from his horse.

Covered with dust and dirt and many days' growth of beard, and riding a horse whose every rib stood out, Berne was hard to recognize.

Fallon waited until the Frenchman disappeared through the door, then stood and headed that way. He wanted to hear Berne's story.

When he walked through the door, Berne was falling into a chair.

"Pardon me for intruding, *m'sieurs,* but I am as anxious to hear the good news as I know you must be." He looked at Berne. "Is the girl safe? Do you have that renegade locked up in El Paso?" Then he couldn't resist the opportunity to stab the vicious little Frenchman where he knew it would hurt. "You look like he led you on a merry chase, *m'sieur.* Perhaps you killed him when you caught him?"

Berne stood, veins standing out on his forehead. "Fallon, what we did is French business." He dropped his hand to touch the walnut grips of his side gun. "And if you utter one more word about my appearance, I'll blow your damned head off."

Fallon went quiet inside. He'd pushed the Frenchman too far considering what he'd been through. Despite that, blood rushed to Fallon's head, clouding any attempt at reason. He dropped the pretense of being a smooth, well-brought-up gentleman. "Berne, gonna tell you somethin', down here in this Texas country, them kind o' words'll get you dead real sudden. You ever touch your six-shooter again when you're facin' me, be damned sure you mean it—an' use it." Never taking his eyes off Berne, he continued, "Now I'm gonna tell you somethin' else. You don't have official status here, an' if you think your gov'ment's gonna protect you, think again." He backed to the door and went out.

He headed to his room to change into buckskins. City clothes had never felt comfortable on him. He chuckled to himself, figuring that gone forever was any chance Bienville and his bunch would think him a Maximilian sympathizer. He spent maybe a split second regretting his actions, then shrugged and figured to hell with the bunch of them. His prime objective now was to protect Juárez, and tomorrow was August 5.

FALLON GLANCED AT THE SUN: TOO EARLY TO GO TO bed, too late to scout El Paso del Norte, and Berne would probably clean up and sleep the clock around. He headed for the saloon. A couple of drinks, a few hands of poker with men interested in the game, and then he'd go to bed.

He wished he dared be there to greet Joan when Juárez came into town, but that might lead her to figure out he knew where she'd been all the while. Of course, by now she knew the bandit and Juárez were on the same side, but she didn't have reason to know Fallon was the bandit. At least he hoped not.

He played a few hands, lost four in a row, and sat staring at the batwing doors. His mind wasn't on the game, the whiskey was raw, and he wasn't enjoying any of it. When he was about to cash his chips, Two Buffalo pushed through the swinging doors and looked around. Before he could spot Fallon, a bullwhacker, obvious by his dress, ragged frock coat, and rusty, baggy trousers stuffed into the tops of his boots, sitting at one of the front tables, said, "We don't allow no damned Indians in here. Get out."

Fallon pushed his chair back. "Mister, I allow that In-

dian in here. Get back to your drinkin' an' leave 'im
alone.''

The bullwhacker shoved back his chair and stood, his
hand held close to the six-shooter jammed inside his belt.
He turned his attention to Fallon. ''I ain't drinkin' with
no Indian. You want to make somethin' of it?''

Another man sitting at the table said, ''Rowdy, drop it.
That there's Tom Fallon. He's fast, he's accurate, an' he's
meaner'n hell. He'll kill you 'fore you can get that six-
shooter halfway outta yore trousers.''

Rowdy swallowed, gulped, turned a shade paler, and
glanced from Fallon to Two Buffalo. He then cleared his
throat, looked around the room, said, ''Reckon I done
made a mistake,'' and sat down.

Someone at the bar said loud enough for all to hear,
''Yeah, and it coulda been fatal.''

Everyone in the room laughed, breaking the tension.
Fallon walked to the front of the room. ''Come, *amigo*,
I'll get a bottle an' we'll go to my room to drink.''

In his room, Fallon poured them each a glassful and
questioned Two Buffalo. He hadn't learned anything new.
Juárez was going to be in El Paso del Norte the next day.
Then Fallon asked about Joan.

''The woman is good. Don't nobody bother her. She
spend much time with little big chief.''

Fallon hoped Juárez would be closemouthed with her,
then cast that thought aside. *El Presidente* knew she had
been working for the imperialists and wouldn't trust her
as far as he could throw the gold coach.

He took a swallow of his drink and grimaced. It was
just as raw as the one he'd had a couple hours ago. He
grinned. Two hours aging hadn't done a thing for it.
''Two Buffalo, I need you to stay around a couple of days.
May not need you to do nothin', but just in case, stick
close by. I'm gonna stay close enough to Berne I'll feel
like his skin.''

They had another drink, and the Mescalero told Fallon
he'd sleep in the livery. He didn't want a room in the
hotel even though Fallon offered it. He said the rooms

were too small, didn't give him room to breathe.

The next morning, Fallon was at his regular window seat at the cafe when Bienville came in with Berne and the other two Frenchman. Berne cast him a hard-faced look and sat at a back table.

Fallon shifted his holster to a more comfortable position, one with the grips on his six-shooter close to hand, and continued drinking his breakfast coffee. He wouldn't trust the wormy little Frenchman not to shoot him in the back.

While they sat there, a man, not in imperialist uniform, came in, whispered something to Bienville, and Bienville whispered something in return. The man left, climbed back on his horse, and headed for the river bridge.

Fallon would have given his prized saddle to know what Bienville had said. He figured the messenger had told the Frenchman Juárez and his troops were on the move. Then, mentally, he shrugged. Berne was the man he had to watch, and he hadn't had time to set anything up. His glance swept the hot, dusty street, rested on one or two of the people, then moved on. Abruptly, he stopped and brought his look back to a peon standing against the hotel wall. White canvas trousers, a shirt with three-quarter-length floppy sleeves, covered with a serape and a too large sombrero that fell around his ears, did little to camouflage the erect soldierly bearing of the man: Escobar.

Fallon wondered what the soldier was doing here in Franklin. He must know by now that Juárez was in control of El Paso del Norte, which would make his attempt to get back to his own territory more dangerous. He studied the tall Mexican a moment, then decided to walk close enough to Escobar that if the soldier recognized him and wanted to acknowledge it, he would speak. He stood.

Before leaving the cafe, Fallon couldn't resist tossing another barb at Berne. He walked to the Frenchmen's table. "Mornin' gentlemen. Looks like *M'sieur* Berne cleaned up pretty well after chasing one li'l old bandit around Mexico." He shook his head. "Amazing what a bath and a good night's sleep can do for a man."

Berne jumped to his feet, his eyes blazing. "You're going to push me too far, Fallon. I'll kill you someday."

Fallon smiled, feeling his face stiffen and his eyes grow cold. "Anytime, *amigo,* anytime." He spun on his heel and left.

In front of the hotel, he paused long enough to say softly, "*Capitan,* you're in great danger here. Why not go back to your troops while there is time?"

"*Señor* Fallon, I must talk with you, but not here."

Fallon made a show of tightening his belt and said, "Room three. Come up after a few moments."

In his room, not knowing what to expect, Fallon eased his Colt in its holster and waited. Only a moment passed and a light tap sounded at his door. "Come in, *Capitan.* It's unlocked."

As soon as Escobar entered and closed the door, Fallon, still standing, asked, "This a friendly visit?"

Escobar swept his sombrero from his head and smiled. "*Sí.* I come only for advice."

"*Mi amigo,* I am a poor man to give anyone advice. I been taking my own advice a long time, an' I stay in trouble most of the time—but ask. If I can help, I will."

"First, I wish to make a few explanations, then I'll ask."

Escobar pulled the serape from around his shoulders, dropped it on the bed, and held his hands out. "You see the only weapon I have, and the leather thong is pulled over the hammer. I mean you no harm. May I sit?"

Fallon nodded. "Sit." He looked at the almost full bottle left from the night before. "Have a drink?"

The captain shook his head, then changed his mind. "Yes, I think I will." He accepted the glass from Fallon, sipped, and looked at him straight on. "First, the explanation as to why I fight for the imperialists." He again took a swallow of his whiskey. Tears came to his eyes, but he was polite enough not to grimace.

Fallon laughed. "Go ahead, sputter, make a face, whatever suits you. I think it's terrible whiskey, too."

Escobar put the glass on the washstand and smiled. "I've had worse, sir. But now, for the explanation. I come from a very old Spanish family, strongly Catholic, and when Juárez put into his constitution words that proposed separation of church and state, it didn't fit with the privileged class. Most of us went with Maximilian as a result. There are many who have vacillated back and forth—one day for Juárez, the next for Maximilian. I am not one of those, *Señor* Fallon. I started out an imperialist and stayed, but I've had time to think about my country recently, and for the first time I'm going to defect to Juárez, and once I do it, I'll stay loyal to him. Even though he has some hard days ahead, I believe he's the one to govern my country. I want you to help me."

Fallon sat quietly, letting the silence build. He studied Escobar. Finally, he said, "Why, *Capitan,* do you come to me? I am an American."

Escobar frowned, scratched his head, then locked gazes with Fallon. "Mr. Fallon, it took me a while, but I finally put it together. You see, I know who you are."

A chill ran up Fallon's spine. He lowered his eyelids to hide his reaction, but still held his eyes on the Spaniard. He let a slight smile crinkle the corners of his eyes to cover his surprise. "Yes, I am not surprised at that. Many know me around here. I'm the son of a relatively well-off rancher up the river a few miles. What more do you know of me, *señor*?"

They had been speaking English; now Escobar switched to Spanish. "*Señor* Fallon, I think—No, I *know* you would answer to the name *el Bandido Caballero*."

Fallon tensed. "What makes you think that, *Capitan*?"

Escobar raised his eyebrows. "*Señor* Fallon, it was not as troublesome as you might think. During both holdups, which I personally observed from the losing side, I noticed your hair, black as obsidian, and your eyes, green as emeralds. At first I thought you to be of one of the old Spanish families, but after meeting you here in the saloon a few days ago, I changed my mind."

"There are many men with hair and eyes the way you described mine."

Escobar shook his head. "You are too modest, *señor*. Anyway, during the second holdup, the big one, which may have broken Maximilian's back, I also saw that your height, build, and pantherlike walk matched exactly those of the man I met in the saloon." He spread his hands and raised his eyebrows. With a slight smile, his gesture said he knew he was right.

Fallon let a frown touch his forehead. "That is little to go on, Escobar. Too little to accuse a man of such a crime. It would not stand up in a court of law."

Escobar, his throat already seared by the raw drink, tossed down the rest of it. Then he laughed. "*Señor,* I know it would not stand up in court. The Americans would not try you. You have committed no crime on American soil." He cleared his throat. "No crime of which I'm aware. And Juárez has control of the courts in northern Mexico. You certainly would not be prosecuted in a Juárez-controlled court, and as you Americans would say, 'That makes the cheese more binding.' " He again spread his hands, "Besides, I have no reason to turn you in." He smiled. "I doubt I have the gun expertise, or the physical capability to subdue you."

Fallon, his gaze never leaving Escobar's face, said, "All right, let's assume for the moment you've figured it out, how can I help you?"

Escobar reached for Fallon's bottle and poured himself a healthy drink, obviously to bolster his nerve. He took a huge swallow and looked at Fallon. "I want you to introduce me to *Presidente* Juárez, vouch for my loyalty, and try to get him to let me retain my rank, let me serve under him as a *capitan*."

"Hmmm, that's a pretty big order, Escobar. Why should I trust you? For that matter why should *El Presidente* trust you?" He hesitated a moment. "And to complicate it even more, why should Juárez trust me?"

Escobar again switched to English. "Simple, *mi amigo,* you have proven your loyalty. You've turned over a king's ransom in gold to him. He will trust you, and more to the point, I believe you're a good judge of men. Do you trust me?''

Fallon studied the handsome Spaniard for a time that stretched into minutes. Escobar might want to act as an agent for the French, and where better to do so than in the middle of the Juárez encampment? He tossed several questions about in his head, then made up his mind. He nodded. ''All right. To do as you ask, I have to admit to being who some call the Gentleman Bandit, but I'll probably have as much trouble getting in to see Juárez as you would.'' He smiled. ''You see, *El Presidente,* himself, is the only one who has seen my face. I've always approached his camp with my face covered.''

Escobar poured himself another drink, then poured Fallon one. He cast Fallon a silly, drunken grin, his mouth slewed off to the side, and mumbled, ''Gettin' drunk. First time.'' Bleary-eyed, he looked at Fallon. ''Why don't you do like you always have, look the only way his men have seen you, pull your bandanna up on your face, walk in, and turn me in?''

Fallon frowned. Right in the middle of a teeming city, outside the Republic's headquarters, cover his face like a desperado? He didn't know whether it was the two drinks he'd had, but damned if he didn't think it would work. ''We'll do it your way, *amigo.* Maybe it'll get us both killed, but what the hell, a man can't live forever.'' He held out the bottle, now almost empty. ''Have another drink.''

Escobar drank only a couple of swallows, then lay back on Fallon's bed and passed out.

FALLON KEPT THE SPANIARD IN HIS ROOM FOR TWO DAYS, days in which he got to know him pretty well. When he threw the empty bottle out and told the ex-imperialist no more drinking, Escobar looked solemnly at him. ''Fallon, I don't even want to see any more whiskey, or nothing else with alcohol in it. It'll take the rest of my life to feel like a human being again.''

During their talks they'd found how much they had in
common, especially their love for ranching. Escobar had
been a *vaquero* on his father's ranch until military service
interrupted.

Fallon sat cleaning his weapons, looking down the barrel of his .44, and nodded. "Once *Juárez* don't need me
no more, figure I'll ride up to my pa's place, climb into
jeans, an' get on with cowboyin'."

Escobar frowned. "Fallon, why do you speak perfect
Spanish sometimes, and perfect English at others, then
lapse into a language not many but Texans would understand?"

Fallon laughed. "Mostly 'cause I like talkin' Texan,
an' some because it causes my ma to get her dander up."
He chuckled. "Ma just purely don't like me not usin' my
education."

On the second day, Fallon strapped on his gun, stood,
and said, "It's time, *vaquero*. Let's go meet *El Presidente*. You go out the back, and meet me down the street
a ways in case Bienville and his bunch are lookin'." He
watched while Escobar again donned the peon dress. "Escobar, long's you walk like you got a poker up your ass,
people gonna know you're military. Slouch, man, drop
your shoulders, bend a little, and shuffle your feet."

When Fallon walked out the front door, Bienville and
Berne were headed for the cafe; Belin and Lebeau followed about ten feet behind. Fallon waved and received
an acknowledgment from Bienville and the others. Berne
ignored him.

Not far from the bridge, Escobar fell in alongside. Fallon thought he could get his weapons into play faster if
he was afoot, although now the enemy was in Franklin.

They attracted no attention while walking the half mile
to Juárez's headquarters. Still a hundred yards short of the
sentries posted at the door, Fallon pulled his bandanna up
over his nose. When he did, he braced himself, his back
muscles tightened, and he felt the hair on his neck tingle.
He'd not taken ten steps when a shot rang out and someone yelled, *"Bandido, bandido."*

Another shot tugged at Fallon's sleeve. He grabbed Escobar's arm and ducked behind a two-wheeled wagon loaded with brush. He looked back to see if he could spot the shooter. No luck. "This, Escobar, is what I was afraid of. Them people don't know me. They probably think I'm out to harm their beloved president."

He'd drawn his .44, but figured to use it only as a last resort. He didn't want to hurt any of these people. Their actions were exactly as they should have been, and what he'd expected. Another shot rang out.

People scurried out of the way, others joined in the shooting. Abruptly, several soldiers ran into the street. The lead one yelled, "*Alto, alto. Theeze ees El Presidente's bandido.* Heez friend."

The sentry continued to yell his message, grabbing men at random and disarming them. For only a few seconds, pandemonium reigned, then quiet settled in over the dusty street. The smell of gunsmoke, horse droppings, dust, and garbage was the first thing Fallon noticed, mostly because he'd dived to lie on the street. He stood, and looked at Escobar. "You all right?"

The Spaniard grinned. "Scared to death is all. Why didn't you warn me it would be like this?"

Fallon cast him a sour look. "Figured you had 'nuff sense to work that out for yourself. Now, let's see if that sentry will take us in to see Juárez."

# CHAPTER

# 19

THE SOLDIERS WHO HAD RUN INTO THE STREET SUR-
rounded Fallon, pushing Escobar aside. "No, no. He must
go with me. I take him to *El Presidente*," Fallon explained to the sentry.

The man looked from Escobar to Fallon, frowned, then
said, "I have orders to let in no one but you, *Caballero*.
I must not disobey my orders."

Fallon thought a moment, then said, "I will hold my
*pistola* on him while I take him in. All right?"

The sentry looked from Fallon to Escobar, and back,
grinned, and nodded. "*Sí*, you take heem een, but I go
weeth you and I, too, weel keep my *pistola* pointed at
heem."

Fallon drew his .44 and pointed it at Escobar. The sentry escorted them to chairs and stood at their side until
Juárez came from his living quarters and dismissed him.
He turned to Fallon. "Ah, *mi amigo*. It's so good to see
you again. The last little present you sent to me was—
how would you say it? Oh yes, the icing on the cake."
Fallon pulled his bandanna down. Juárez frowned and
glanced at Escobar. "Does this man know you?"

Fallon grinned. "If he didn't, he does now. But to answer you, sir, yes. He figured it out while tracking me across many miles of desert and mountain trail. He is the reason I have come to you." He went on to tell Juárez the entire story, then said, "*El Presidente*, he is a loyal, dedicated man. He's thought about this much, as have I. He thinks the future of Mexico rests on your shoulders— so do I, and I trust him. He wants to serve under you, and I believe you would do him a great disservice, as well as yourself, if you didn't give him a captaincy in your forces."

Juárez studied Escobar a long moment, then turned his attention to Fallon. "You vouch for this man, *señor*?" Fallon nodded. Then, Juárez, used to making quick decisions, looked at Escobar. "Do the imperialists know of your defection?"

The Spaniard frowned. "I don't believe so, *mi presidente*. *Señor* Berne of the French contingency over in Franklin knows I admire *Señor* Fallon, both as a man and as a frontiersman. The fact is, he threatened to have me court-martialed because of it, but no, I don't think any of them would suspect me of defecting."

Juárez shuffled some papers on his desk, picked up a pen, laid it down, then locked gazes with Escobar. "*Señor*, or now I will address you as *Capitan*, would you be willing to go back to them, stay with them, and report to me anything you deem important: gold shipments, troop movements, or information from Napoleon to Maximilian? You realize what I'm asking will be an act of treason in their minds. If they catch you, they'll shoot you."

Escobar sat forward, frowned, and nodded. "I understand, *señor*, but I've given this a lot of careful thought. Too, they might have other plans for me, and *M'sieur* Berne may still carry out his threat to have me court-martialed, but I will do my best."

Juárez stared at his desk a moment, then again locked gazes with Escobar. "One's best is all any man can ask of another, *Capitan*. That's all I ask of you. You do realize that if you are caught, I may not be able to help you?''

"*Sí*, but, *señor*, I can't remember the last time I had much help doing anything. I have a Yaqui I'd like to keep with me. He's loyal to me and no one else.''

Juárez nodded. "I'll take care to make it official, but as of now you're a *capitan* in my army.''

He slanted a sly little glance at Fallon. "*Señor*, I must tell you, there is a *señorita,* who is now home in her own *casa,* who would like very much to see you.''

Fallon squinted his eyes and frowned. "Does she know who I am? I mean, does she know I am the bandit who robbed her more than once? You know she is an imperialist; how is it she has stayed here with your forces in charge?''

Juárez laughed. "Hey, one question at a time, *amigo.* No, she does not know you are the *bandido* who has robbed her. Yes, I know she is, or perhaps was, an imperialist, and she has stayed here because she knows I will allow no harm to come to her.''

"What do you mean, 'or perhaps *was*' an imperialist?''

Juárez stared at him a moment. "I think, during her stay with me, I detected a subtle shift in her attitude as to whether the French were best for her country. I don't think it would take much to put her in our camp.''

Fallon rubbed the back of his head. "Well, what do you know, Joan may become a Juárista. Still, I reckon it would be a good idea to keep anyone except us from knowing I'm the bandit.'' He grinned. "It sure as hell's gonna be better for my health if we do, and too, there might be other gold shipments.''

"*Sí*, it will be as you wish, *amigo,* but I can't believe they will chance losing more gold. I don't think they have it to lose.''

"That assumption is a good one. I hear Napoleon is having a rough time in Europe, and is forced to withhold much support for Maximilian.''

They visited awhile, and before leaving, Fallon told Juárez the arms and equipment he had said would be stacked along the river still would be, but it might be late January before that could happen. "My sources tell me the change in plans is because of tension between my country and the French."

They talked awhile longer, then Fallon left to go back to Franklin. Escobar stayed with Juárez to plan "strategy," as *El Presidente* put it.

Fallon was tempted to go by to see Joan, but dressed as he was, he decided against it. Everything he wore, he'd worn the first time he'd held up her coach. She might be swinging toward Juárez, but Fallon wasn't willing to chance it—yet.

He'd been back at the hotel about three hours when he looked out the window and saw Escobar, now dressed as a *vaquero,* ride to the hitchrail and walk toward the doorway. He left the Yaqui with the horses.

ESCOBAR CHECKED IN, GOT HIMSELF A ROOM, DUMPED his gear, then took a deep breath and decided he might as well see how the Frenchmen received him. He headed for the lawyer's office.

When he walked in, Bienville looked up, nodded, and said he was glad to see him back. He wanted to know if Escobar had had any problems getting through El Paso del Norte with all the Juáristas there. Escobar shook his head. "There was a shooting in the middle of town, which took a lot of their attention. But I couldn't find what it was about. It seems they caught a *bandido* and took him to the *cárcel.*"

Bienville laughed. "Well, we know if they put him in the jail, it wasn't the same one who led you and *M'sieur* Berne on that fruitless chase."

Berne sat there, slumped in his chair, his face red, his jaws knotted. "You bring that worthless Indian with you?"

Escobar looked at him, his eyes slitted, his chest feeling hollow, his breath short. "*M'sieur*, that worthless Indian, as you call him, is the only reason we got back without losing half our men, and you, *m'sieur,* as sorry as you conducted yourself, wouldn't have made it through half the trip without him.''

Berne, obviously choking back his anger at Escobar's words, hissed, ''I'll still see you court-martialed. You had nothing but admiration for that *bandido,* your words almost treasonous.''

A chill in his words, Escobar said, ''I have always admired a man who is good at what he does. That *bandido* out-thought us at every turn, then when he decided he had us so far from civilization it would take us a week to get back, he simply rode off and left us.'' He looked at Bienville. ''He, whoever he is, *M'sieur* Bienville, is *mucho hombre.*''

The French leader smiled, his brow slightly puckered. ''You have the soul of a big man, *m'sieur.* He had you, all of you, on the verge of dying from thirst, yet you admire him. I must say, I would like having a man of your caliber as an enemy.''

Berne had opened his mouth to say something when Fallon walked in. He clamped his jaws tight and glared at the big man. Bienville looked at Fallon and said, ''*M'sieur* Fallon, I want you to meet the *capitan* in charge of the unit which the *Bandido Caballero* led across half of Mexico. *Señor* Fallon, *Capitan* Escobar.''

Escobar looked at Fallon. ''We have already m—''

Fallon cut in. ''Yes, we stood next to each other in the saloon several days ago. Can't say we actually met, but we took a moment to criticize the quality of their whiskey.'' His gaze scanned Escobar from head to toe. ''Looks like you recuperated pretty well from your desert experience.'' He shifted his gaze to Bienville. ''Just wanted to drop by and see how things were going. I hear the petite woman with the copper hair, the one we met out at Pa's ranch, lives in El Paso del Norte. Think I'll call on her.''

Berne sat forward. ''Don't waste your time, *m'sieur.* I have already made up my mind to marry her.''

Fallon raised his eyebrows, and allowed a slight smile to show at the corners of his eyes. ''Have you made her aware of this, Berne, or are you going to blunder about with it like I've heard you did when the *bandido* led you about by the nose?''

Berne jumped to his feet, sputtering. Before he could say anything, Bienville interrupted. ''Sit down, Berne.'' He turned to Fallon. ''*M'sieur* Fallon, I'll have to ask you to stop antagonizing *M'sieur* Berne. You keep him on the verge of apoplexy.''

Fallon apologized to Bienville, then said, ''But I am going to see *Ma'mselle* Boniol. She is a very beautiful woman. Good day, gentlemen.''

He tipped his hat and left, knowing Escobar would alert him if Berne made a move toward the assassination of Juárez.

On the way out, he passed the Yaqui squatted against the wall of the French headquarters. The Indian slitted his eyes against the bright sunlight and studied Fallon's tall form. After he'd gone into the hotel, the Yaqui stood, went to the street, and bent over Fallon's bootprint in the soft dust. He looked at the doorway through which Fallon had disappeared, and said to himself, ''There goes *mucho hombre*. The *señor* will be happy to know I have seen him.''

Fallon dressed with more care than usual, then went to the livery, saddled his bay, and rode across the bridge.

Joan answered the door. ''Tom, I'm so glad to see you. Where in the world have you been?''

''I think the question would rightly be, Where have you been, beautiful woman?''

Joan blushed at the compliment. ''It's a long story. Do you have time to listen?''

He nodded. ''Joan, I'd listen if you were gonna tell me a bedtime story,'' he paused, ''especially if you were going to tell me a bedtime story.'' Her face turned a flaming red, but she ignored his statement and went to the cabinet to pour him a drink. Then she launched into all that had happened to her. Finally, she looked up, her eyes shaded, and said, ''I know our sympathies lie with Maximilian,

Tom, but the *Señor* Juárez was nothing short of being a perfect gentleman. He is so kind. He's a sweet old man, and I like him.''

''Although I'm jealous, sounds like he captured your heart, *ma'mselle*.''

Joan's chin lifted, her jaw set in stubborn lines. ''I reserve the right to like, or dislike, whomever I please, *m'sieur*.''

Fallon laughed. ''Don't go stubborn on me, lady. If ever I meet the president, I might also like him, but that doesn't change my loyalties.''

''Nor mine, Tom, but I do like him very much. He was almost like a father to me.''

They talked awhile, then Fallon told her of the scene in Bienville's office. Her face flushed. ''Why, that arrogant little worm. If he was the last man in the world, I-I-I—''

Fallon laughed. ''Sorta the way I had it figured.''

''Oh? And what kind of man would you have me attracted to?''

With a thoughtful look, he said, tongue in cheek, ''Well now, let's see. Perhaps a man a little over six feet tall, black hair, green eyes, and a perfect gentleman at all times . . .''

Joan laughed. ''Tom, you're about as subtle as a hammer.'' Then her eyes took on a smoky look. ''A perfect gentleman at all times? I really can't think of anything more boring. But stay, have dinner with me, and we'll discuss my kind of man afterward.''

They had dinner, an after-dinner drink, and a delightful few moments when she let him hold her close, but Fallon didn't stray across the line he'd drawn for himself.

He went back to his hotel humming. Let Berne try to horn in on his territory and he'd fix the little Frenchman with five friendly knuckles in his teeth.

He wondered why he disliked the mouthy little Frenchman so much. He mentally made a list. First off, Berne would shoot a man from ambush, that man being Juárez. Second, he had an uncontrollable temper without being man enough to back it up. Third, he was arrogant, thinking he could walk in and marry Joan Boniol without a courtship, and, and, and . . . Reckon that's enough, Fallon figured. The fact was, he just flat didn't like the little bastard. He didn't need a reason.

When he got back to his room, he cleaned and oiled his weapons, even though they were spotless. Then he went to the cafe and had a cup of coffee, although he didn't want one, and from there he went to the saloon and had a drink. He didn't want it either. Back in his room, he shook his head. "Damn, civilian life is just plain boring." His voice in the close confines of his room sounded loud.

He'd no sooner had that thought when Sanchez tapped on his door and slipped in. "Hey, *amigo,* the general sent me with this letter to see you. How're things going here?"

Fallon threw him a sour look. "Ain't nothin' to do. Good mind to ride out toward Mesilla an' see can I round up a few Mescalero to shake up the day."

Sanchez laughed. "Thought you got a gutful of them last time you tangled with 'em." He held out the letter. "Maybe there's something in here to brighten your day."

In Sheridan's own handwriting, Fallon read: "No more gold shipments. Napoleon pinched for money on the Prussian front. Your entire assignment: Keep the Mexican president safe. Maximilian posted fifty-thousand dollar reward for capture of *Bandido Caballero.* I doubt he has the money to pay it, but be careful. Best regards, Sheridan."

Fallon tossed the letter on the bed. "That does it. All I gotta do is keep Juárez safe, an' the little wart who's s'posed to go after 'im ain't makin' a move to do nothin'."

Sanchez raised one eyebrow and, with a slight grin, said, "Tomas, why don't we just go down to the street an' shoot up the town, or we could go to the saloon and tell those in there what the general told me: Maximilian has put up a bunch of money for your capture. Course we'll have to tell 'em you're the *Bandido Caballero.*

Then, too, we could announce it to Juárez's own troops. Probably ninety percent of them would try to get you for that much money.''

''Aw, go to hell. This ain't funny. Here I am wastin' away, doin' nothin, an' you're tryin to be a comedian.''

Sanchez sobered. ''Take it easy, *amigo*. Berne's gonna make a move soon, and when he does, you're gonna be busier'n a *vaquero* with a two-thousand-pound bull on a short rope. Want me to stay here an' help you?''

''Do what? Take a *siesta*? Play mumblety-peg? Watch the sky for rain? No. Reckon you better get back to Sheridan. He might have somethin' that'll stir the pot.''

Sanchez had been gone only a few minutes when Fallon looked out his window and saw Berne come from the Wells Fargo office carrying a wooden box about four feet long and only a few inches wide. Fallon frowned. A box that size could easily contain one of those expensive German rifles he'd seen in New York before the war.

Berne walked toward the hotel, shifted the box to his other hand, and came in the door. If what he carried was government business, he'd probably have taken it to the office. Fallon opened his door a crack, peered into the corridor, and waited until the Frenchman topped the stairs and went to his room.

Berne stayed in his room only long enough to open the box, inspect its goods, and come out—without it.

Fallon went back to the window and watched until Berne went into the French office, then, thinking all of the French contingency would be at work, he slipped down the hall to Berne's room. It took less than a minute to slide his knife between the door and the frame, slip the lock back, and go in.

Laying on the bed was what he expected: a beautifully engraved rifle, .44 caliber. Fallon flipped it on its side to see who made it, and at the same time thought he heard a noise in the corridor. Without looking, he put the weapon back the way he'd found it, went to the door, and peered out to find the hallway empty.

He glanced at the rifle, then cat-footed out the door and

pulled it shut. While his hand was still on Berne's door-knob, Charles Lebeau stepped from his room across the corridor.

"What're you doing in Berne's room?" Lebeau reached for his gun.

Fallon didn't want to hurt this harmless, good-natured Frenchman, but he had no choice. Lebeau had his handgun out and was coming level to point at him. Without thinking, Fallon's hand went to the back of his neck and swept forward, and his throwing knife buried itself hilt-deep in Lebeau's chest. The Frenchman dropped his gun, and with both hands grasped the handle of the knife. His mouth worked to say something, his eyes bulged, a gusher of blood passed his lips, and he fell forward.

"Damn," Fallon muttered, and on silent feet he moved to the Frenchman's side. He turned Lebeau over with his toe, bent, pulled his throwing knife free, and cleaned it on Lebeau's shirt. He stared at the man who but a few moments ago had been full of life. His stomach churned, and he blinked to clear his eyes of unexpected moisture. Why did this have to happen? Why of all the Frenchmen did it have to be this one? Fallon choked down his nausea and studied the body a moment.

His first thought was to get as far away from the hotel as possible before someone discovered the body, but then people would ask why the man had been killed. He'd have to make it look like a robbery.

He went through Lebeau's pockets and left them pulled out of his pants. He unbuckled the Frenchman's trousers and removed the money belt he found around his waist; he emptied its contents into his own pockets, then threw the money belt carelessly across Lebeau's chest.

Fallon glanced in both directions of the hallway, then slipped silently to the back stairs of the hotel. He hoped the desk clerk would not remember seeing him go to his room.

Before opening the door leading to the outside, Fallon tied his Colt to his leg and settled his Bowie knife at the back of his belt. He went down to the street to watch for

Berne. Figuring the Frenchman now had the weapon he intended to use to kill Juárez, Fallon was going to stick to the assassin like a leach.

He leaned against the wall of the general store, and had been there about fifteen minutes when Berne left the office and headed toward the bridge, afoot. Fallon studied him from behind. As far as he could see, the mouthy little assassin had no weapons with him, unless he had a handgun tucked inside his shirt.

He was sure Berne would have slung the rifle from his shoulder if he were bent on killing Juárez now, but he followed. He wanted to see what the small man had in mind.

He tracked Berne, in civilian clothes, to the center of town. He watched him walk to the front of Juárez's headquarters, look at the buildings across the street, carefully step off the distance from the front of one of the stores to the front of the Republic headquarters, nod, then circle to the back of the headquarters building, to Joan's *casa*, not fifty feet from Juárez's living quarters.

Berne leaned against the hitch post in front of Joan's house, and looked back the way he'd come, seeming to study every foot of his path.

Fallon frowned. What was Berne doing? When he'd paced off the distance between buildings in front of Juárez's headquarters, Fallon thought he was probably estimating the rifle range and vantage point from which to fire the fatal shot. But how did Joan's house figure in it?

The Frenchman stood there a moment, looked to each side of the government building, retraced his steps, looked at his watch several times, then walked back to Franklin. Fallon, following him, was certain he'd just watched Berne plan from where he would fire the shot, and his escape route—but where did Joan fit in?

She had helped transport gold to Maximilian, but Fallon could not, would not, believe she'd have anything to do with killing a man. Besides, she'd told him how much she liked the little Zapotec.

In Franklin, Berne walked past the office and went on

to the livery stable. He stayed in there about twenty minutes. From the livery he returned to the French headquarters. Fallon went in to see the liveryman.

He eyed the half-crippled old puncher a moment, then asked, "What that Frenchman want, the one who left here a few minutes ago?"

"Funny you should ask that, Mr. Fallon. I wuz wonderin' the same thing myself. He's got his own hoss, but wanted to rent two more, two of the best horses I got. He rented tack for 'em, too." He scratched his head. "He wants 'em saddled an' ready by ten o'clock in the mornin'."

Fallon studied his boot toe a moment, pulled a cartwheel from his pocket, and handed it to the old-timer. "Thanks. When he comes for the horses, don't say anythin' 'bout me askin'." He took another cartwheel from his pocket and handed it to the old man.

"What's this here for?"

"I want my bay horse ready to go when Berne's are. Put 'im in a stall outta sight. I'll come for him soon after Berne leaves."

He sighed. This might all be over before long.

He walked slowly back to his hotel, hoping that by now someone had found Lebeau and removed his body. Hoping that someday the killing would stop.

When he climbed the stairs to his room, only halfway up voices sounded, several voices. Topping the stairs, he had to step around two men carrying the Frenchman, and came face-to-face with the marshal. "How long you been gone from the hotel, Fallon?"

"Don't know, couple hours maybe. Why? What happened?"

The marshal stared at him a moment. "Somebody killed one of the Frenchies, knifed him. Looks like a robbery, money belt empty, pockets turned wrong side out."

Fallon glanced at Lebeau's corpse, then back at the lawman. "What you askin' me 'bout 'im for? I ain't in need of money, an' I sure as hell ain't a crook. You sayin' you figure I had somethin' to do with this killin', Marshal?"

"Aw hell, Tom, you're the last man I'd ever figure to rob a man. Just thought if you were here you mighta seen somethin'."

Fallon let the fire go from his eyes and slanted the marshal a crooked grin. "Naw, I ain't seen nothin'. Reckon I took offense without cause. Sorry, Jess. Reckon I'm still ridin' a hair trigger since the war. Gotta get over that."

Minter nodded, stared into Fallon's eyes, and said, "Yeah, Tom, reckon you better work on that. Ain't many know you like I do, an' you're not makin' any friends the way you been actin' since you come home. Apology accepted."

He tipped his hat and Fallon turned toward his room, letting a slow breath escape his lungs. He figured he'd lie down, catch a nap before supper, then check his gear for what might turn into a long, hard ride.

# CHAPTER

# 20

In his room, Fallon changed his mind about the *siesta*. He checked his weapons, made certain he put his moccasins and buckskins in his bedroll, then went by the desk and told the clerk he'd be gone a few days and not to rent his room to anyone.

From the hotel, he went to the general store and bought provisions for a week. He made these preparations hoping he wouldn't need them, but if he didn't get Berne when he attempted the assassination, he figured to track him to hell if he had to. And hell it might be, because the liveryman had told him Berne had asked for three canteens full of water to be hung from each saddle horn of the horses he'd take out of there.

"He's either figurin' on a long desert ride an' got horses enough to change often, or he's rememberin' them long days I led 'im through," Fallon said to himself. Now he had to wait. The next few hours were going to crawl.

Later that afternoon he watched Berne head for the bridge, but didn't follow. The Frenchman carried no weapons and rode no horse. Fallon figured the mouthy little man was not bent on his deadly errand without his

weapons and a quick means of escape, so he went to the
stable to stay close to the horses.

FALLON SHOULD HAVE FOLLOWED THE FRENCHMAN.
Berne was still in the process of laying the groundwork
for his killing. In El Paso del Norte he went directly to a
saloon only a block from where he would shoot the *presidente*.

With a glass of wine in front of him, he stood at the
bar and studied those who entered. Finally, he saw a man
who fit his plans push through the doors. His clothes were
ragged but clean, and he was close to the same build as
Berne. The man walked to the bar and told the bartender
he'd take the trash out for a *cervesa*. The bartender took
him up on it.

While the little Mexican drank his beer, Berne edged
over next to him, and when the peon's glass neared
empty, Berne ordered him another.

"*Gracias, señor, gracias*. To what do I owe this favor?"

Berne looked at him a moment, wondering if he could
trust him to do as he asked, then decided he had to trust
someone. He said, "*De nada, señor*. I was wondering, do
you have a horse?"

The Mexican shook his head. "No, *señor*. Only the
very rich have horses. Someday, if I work very hard, I,
too, may have my own *caballo*."

"If I tell you I'll give you a horse for doing something
for me, would you do it?"

The peon drew away a short distance, maybe two feet
from Berne. "*Señor*, I am poor, but I will not steal, and
I will not kill—even for a horse."

Berne shook his head. "No. It is nothing like that. I
ask you to do nothing dishonest, or in any way against
the law. The horse I will give you will be saddled and
ready to ride. All I ask is, when you see me give you a
wave, climb on him and ride like the wind. I'll also give
you ownership papers for the horse, papers that will sat-
isfy the law." He moved closer to the Mexican and in a

lower voice told him where he was to be and what time, and in addition to the horse he gave him a few pesos.

Satisfied he'd done all he could to ensure his escape, Berne went back across the bridge and went to bed.

THE NEXT MORNING, FALLON SAT AT HIS USUAL TABLE IN the cafe. He could watch the hotel and the lawyer's office from there. Figuring this might be the last meal he didn't have to cook for himself in quite a while, he ordered a half dozen eggs and the biggest steak they had, along with grits, gravy, and biscuits.

He was through eating when Bienville came in with Berne. Fallon stayed, and once again drank more coffee than he wanted. Finally, seeing that the two Frenchmen had only a few more mouthfuls of food on their plates, Fallon swallowed the last of his coffee and headed for the livery. He went in the hotel, walked straight through to the back and out, and behind the rear of stores to the livery.

As soon as he entered the stable, the liveryman pointed to a stall. Fallon went in and crouched at the side of the saddled and ready-to-ride bay.

Another twenty minutes and Berne came in, his new rifle slung from his shoulder. Through a crack between the boards in the stall, Fallon watched while Berne slid the rifle into the saddle scabbard, tightened the cinches, toed the stirrup, and rode out.

Fallon waited a few moments, then followed.

The Frenchman crossed the bridge, and instead of going to the back of the building across from the front of Juárez's headquarters, he went to the front of Joan's house and hitched two of the horses there. He took the canteen from the horse he rode and hung it along with the others, from the two horses he'd tied to the post.

A lump came to Fallon's throat. He hadn't wanted to believe it, but from what he'd just seen, it seemed certain that Joan was part of the Frenchman's assination plans, and even worse, it looked like she was going to go with Berne.

He felt like he'd been kicked in the stomach. It was then he admitted to himself he was in love with her, wanted to marry her, had intended taking her to the ranch and having a big fiesta and wedding. He wanted to work the cows and come home at the end of the day and have her love him. He glared at the Frenchman's back.

He didn't know how the French had gotten their hooks into Joan, but he thought it had to be something bad. He swallowed, hard. She couldn't be doing this to him, to Juárez. She'd shown too much caring for the little Zapotec, and her lips on Fallon's, her body pressed against his, promised too much for him to have read it wrong. But if she was going of her own free will, he'd cut it short; he'd make damned sure she watched Berne die.

Berne rode the horse with the rifle, but no canteens, down the side of the government building to an alley across from it. Fallon chose the next alley from Berne's, and went toward the rear of the stores. He peered around the corner until he saw the Frenchman hand the reins of his horse to a slightly built Mexican, say something to him, dig in his pocket for what Fallon assumed was money, then climb to the roof of the one-story building.

Fallon hitched his horse at the rear of the two-story building next to it and climbed to its roof.

It went through his mind that he couldn't wait for Berne to fire at Juárez. It would be too late then to do *El Presidente* any good. But he had to wait for Berne to bring his rifle to a firing position, to give him the benefit of any doubt—then he'd blow the little bastard to Kingdom Come.

He took up a position to the rear and above where Berne lay on the roof, and studied the layout. Firing down was always tricky, easy to misjudge and fire over the target. He glanced to the rear of each building. If he missed, Berne would be able to reach the ground much quicker than he, and would be able to get to his horse far ahead of him. Fallon shrugged, not caring how far the Frenchman got ahead of him. He'd catch him and make him pay.

The sun beat down mercilessly. The tin roof threw heat

back at him like an oven. Soon his shirt had soaked up all the sweat it could hold. Perspiration ran in rivulets down the side of his face, down his neck, under his arms. His jeans, soaked by now, stuck to him. He wished for one of his canteens.

His face hardened. If he was hot—so was the Frenchman. The thought brought satisfaction and a degree of pleasure. If he could watch the little worm cook to death, he'd take his chances of surviving. Then it occurred to him that Juárez might not come out of his headquarters at all on this day. He wondered if Berne could stand the heat for that long, and decided that the Frenchman, poisoned with hate, would stay there to his death.

He pushed his hat off his forehead, mopped sweat, pulled his hat back low on his brow, and moved a few inches for a more comfortable position, then quickly moved to cover the same spot he'd lain in. It felt like the hot metal had boiled the sweat in his jeans.

The sun sank lower, a red ball in the sky, until only half of it showed above the mountains. The roof cooled a bit, but the air remained hot and dry. Fallon was again mopping his brow, when from a relaxed, prone position, Berne got to his knees, and using the facade of the store for a rest, settled his rifle into firing position.

Not prepared for such action this late in the day, Fallon hurried. He snapped his long gun to his shoulder, centered his sights between Berne's shoulders, and snapped off a shot. His and Berne's shot sounded as one, but he'd fired too soon. The Frenchman rolled to the side, fired a shot at Fallon's position on the roof, rolled to his feet, and ran for the back edge of the roof. Fallon jacked another shell into his Henry, squeezed the trigger—and it misfired.

Before he could get another shell in the chamber, Berne slid over the side of the store. By the time Fallon reached where he could see, the slight form of the Frenchman streaked away on the horse he'd had the Mexican hold for him. Fallon cleared his rifle and fired. The range was too great. The rider never swerved to indicate that the shot had been close. Fallon slid to the roof of the first floor, then dropped to the ground.

He stared after the fast disappearing horse and rider, his jaws knotted, eyes slitted. "I'll get you, you French bastard. I'll get you whether you hit *El Presidente* or not." His voice came out rock hard, harsh.

By then, men had come from the street and surrounded him, all pointing rifles or revolvers at him. Fallon kept pointing toward the rider, trying to tell them they had the wrong man. They didn't listen.

Some were for dragging him to the river and hanging him to one of the cottonwoods. Others wanted to shoot him to buzzard bait where he stood. The soldiers took command.

The sergeant in charge said, "No. We are lawful people. We'll take him to *El Presidente,* let him pronounce sentence, then we'll stand him against a wall and shoot him."

Fallon sighed, yet every muscle was taut and he had trouble swallowing. He was back where he'd started. He might as well have faced the firing squad the Yankees planned for him. Then the soldier's words sank in. "Take him to *El Presidente*," he'd said.

While the soldiers dragged him toward the street, he asked the sergeant, "You said you'd take me to Juárez. Did the shot not hit him?"

"*Americano* dog, shut up." Then the sergeant looked at him with a victorious smile. "No, dog, you hit the wrong person. You killed one of the *señor's capitans.* Perhaps you thought it was him. The man you shot was of small stature, as is the *presidente.*"

Even with the trouble he was in, Fallon still felt a sense of relief. Juárez lived.

They dragged him through the heavy wooden doors of the headquarters building, to the desk at which Juárez sat. *El Presidente* looked from the soldiers to Fallon, disbelief in his eyes. "I cannot believe you'd do this to me, Señor Fallon. What is your explanation?"

"You're going to listen to my story, even though your

men have already decided I am the one who tried to kill you?''

"*Señor,* you have done too much for my cause for me to believe such of you. There must be a reasonable story behind it. Let's hear it.''

"*Señor Presidente,* I told you a few weeks ago there was a plot to kill you. The Frenchman Berne cooked it up.'' Fallon then told Juárez the whole thing, including Berne stashing two horses in front of the *Señorita* Boniol's *casa* and taking a single horse to the back of the store, where he climbed to the roof of the building. "*Amigo,* if your men will go to the two-story building and the single-story building, they'll find spent rifle shells on the roofs. My shells are on the two-story roof. They're rim fire; the shells the Frenchman used will be on the one-story roof. His are center fire. Don't believe me until your men have checked out my story.''

All the while Fallon talked, Juárez's face softened. "*Amigo,* I believe you, but I want my men to also know you are innocent. I will send them to do as you say.''

While the troops went to check out Fallon's story, Juárez sat twiddling a pen in his fingers, obviously in deep thought. Less than twenty minutes later, the sergeant brought the shells to him. He inspected them, then handed them back to the sergeant, a smile breaking the hard lines of his face. "The *Señor Fallon* is innocent of the charge you've brought against him.'' He cleared his throat. "Sergeant, I also have a strong reason to believe him. Let him go.''

Fallon looked at Juárez, then to the soldier. "Sergeant, I have long been *El Presidente's* friend. You have seen me in your camp several times, and always I brought badly needed gold to the Republic. Sergeant, I am the one you call the *Bandido Caballero.* I would not harm your *presidente,* and my friend.''

The soldier looked at Fallon, studied him from head to toe, then turned his eyes on Juárez. "Is true, *Mi Presidente?*''

Juárez smiled. "Is true. Now, leave me with him until

we can see why the Frenchman had three horses and only used one, although I think I know the reason.''

When the soldiers had returned Fallon's weapons and left the room, Juárez asked, "*Amigo,* did you see Berne mount the horse in the store's rear and ride off?"

Fallon shook his head. "*Señor,* if I had been that close, I could have shot him. No, *señor,* he was already a considerable distance away when I got to the edge of the roof.''

Juárez's face hardened. "Fallon, we've all been duped. I'll bet you that last coach full of gold you brought me the two horses in front of the *Señorita* Boniol's *casa* are gone. They're the ones he used for escape. He probably hired some *vaquero* to take the horse behind the store, thinking we'd do just as we did. At the very least it bought him time.''

Fallon's face felt like old weathered leather. "*Mi Presidente,* a lifetime won't be enough for him. I studied the hoof prints of each of those three horses while they were in the livery. I'll track 'im to hell if I have to.'' He stared hard at Juárez. "But, *señor,* when I catch 'im, he won't be comin' back to you, an' when I get back, the first thing I'm gonna do is run them other Frenchmen off American soil, then you can take care of 'em.'' He looked toward the door, then to Juárez. "Am I free to leave, *señor?*"

Juárez only nodded, then, his voice soft, he said, "*Vaya con Dios, mi amigo.*"

While Fallon walked toward where he'd seen Berne tie the other two horses, and thought of Juárez's words, he shook his head. God would not escort him on the mission he'd set for himself.

As soon as he rounded the corner of the headquarters building, he saw Joan's maid standing on the steps wringing her hands and crying.

"What's the matter, *señorita?*" he asked.

"Oh, *Señor* Fallon, he has taken her, *Señor* Berne has taken her.''

Fallon frowned. "What you mean, he took her? Didn't she go freely, of her own accord?"

The maid burst into heart-wrenching sobs. "Oh no, *señor*. The Frenchman broke through the front door, grabbed her arm and told her she was to go with him. She fought like a tiger, but he pulled her outside, threw her on one of the *caballos*, tied her hands to the saddle horn, and leading her horse, rode off at a dead run. He deed not even give her time to pack extra clothing. She is such a little thing; don't let him hurt her."

After questioning her as to the direction Berne took, Fallon realized his horse was still tied behind the stores. "Go inside and stop crying; I'll get your mistress back. It might take a while, but I'll bring her back." He ran toward the other street.

After collecting his horse, Fallon again looked for the hoof prints of Berne's horses. The angry knot in his throat, caused by his thoughts that Joan was part of the conspiracy to assassinate Juárez, had disappeared. But he was not entirely satisfied that the whole scene at Joan's *casa* wasn't a cooked-up deal.

To save time, he planned to check first the direction the maid had said Berne took. Outside of town, he picked up the trail of the two horses, headed straight south. The Frenchman would either go to Saltillo or Monterrey. The maid had not lied to him. His feelings toward Joan softened.

The sun had disappeared behind the peaks of the Sierra Madre more than a half hour before. In the soft twilight, Fallon had time only to confirm Berne's direction before night set in. He made a dry camp in a pile of boulders.

The next morning, Fallon made a fire from the twigs of a creosote bush, cooked breakfast, and sat drinking coffee until the sun sent spears of light from behind great dark clouds to the east, and painted their edges with silver.

Fallon looked at the clouds, worry creasing his brow. A hard rain would wash out tracks, and with all the possible destinations Berne might have in mind, Fallon needed tracks.

He saddled and got on the trail. Every so often he cast glances to the east. The clouds seemed to be hovering close to the horizon. He prayed they were, prayed rain, or wind, would hold off until he could determine Berne's main travel direction.

An hour later, he stopped, stepped from his horse, and on hands and knees studied the horses' tracks. They had changed to a northwesterly course. "Damn." He gazed off to the west, hoping Berne was not fool enough to try and take the same trail Fallon had led Escobar's troops on through the desert.

The Frenchman wasn't smart enough, or wily enough, to make that journey without a guide. If Berne thought where he headed was better than the *Jornado del Muerto,* he was about to learn what a real journey of death was.

Fallon stayed on the tracks, occasionally casting a glance to his rear, hoping the clouds stayed in back of him.

At first, thin lacy stringers moved out ahead of the dark mass, then thickened. About midday, the Frenchman's tracks bent toward the north. Fallon again stopped to think. It looked like Berne was headed back to North America, back toward the Rio Grande. Where was he thinking to take Joan? He couldn't take her to any town. People in the west wouldn't stand for a woman being mistreated.

Fallon was certain the Frenchman wouldn't stay in the desert after his experience with Escobar and the Yaqui. He'd head for the mountains, maybe up into the Sacramentos, or the Capitans, but either place, although beautiful, with plenty of game and water, would put the Frenchman and Joan right in the middle of Mescalero country.

Fallon wanted to climb on the bay and ride belly-to-the-ground to try to catch them, but that would be stupid. It would be easy to miss a turn they might make, and he'd kill his horse. Fallon's gut churned, his breath shortened. Surely, the Frenchman wasn't dumb enough to go into Indian country. But maybe he didn't know the dangers of the Apache lands, maybe he didn't know where he headed *was* Mescalero Apache territory.

Fallon crossed the Rio Grande, and had followed Berne's and Joan's trail about two miles when the rain came, at first a few large drops, then a white curtain that engulfed him—rain so heavy it seemed that if he opened his mouth to breathe, he'd drown. He climbed off his horse, put his slicker on, and spread it to cover his saddle. A wet saddle would rub his rear end raw in short order.

The downpour lasted about an hour, slackened to light drops, then stopped. These high desert storms usually covered a small area; Fallon hoped this one had been like that. He glanced where the tracks had been, only to see no sign that anyone had ever passed this way.

He mounted and rode over a mile before he gained the edge of the summer storm. Even while riding, he studied the ground where the rain had been hardest. Back on dry ground, there were no horse's tracks. He reined the bay toward the mountains, riding along the edge of where the rain had slackened. His course took him in a semicircle, until, almost back at the river, he crossed tracks. He slid from his horse and studied them. They were those of Berne's horses. The storm had cost him a couple of hours.

Back in the saddle he followed the sign Berne's horses left. It curved around rock formations, down to, and across, small mountain streams, and turned up again toward the dark green of trees in the distance. Ultimately, the course was higher.

Fallon found ashes of a small fire where Berne had stopped for breakfast, or perhaps his nooning. Fallon didn't know how far they were ahead of him. He climbed down and felt the ground around the ashes—cold. They were several hours ahead of him. He stopped long enough to scoop dirt over the now dead fire. There might be a few live coals in it, enough to start a forest fire.

Back on their trail the ground began to take on truly mountainous characteristics—rocky, and mostly climbing. At times he covered a couple of hundred yards without seeing a track. Occasionally he'd see where a horse had slipped, scarring the rock upon which it walked, and, even

# CHAPTER

# 21

SEVERAL HOURS AHEAD OF FALLON, BERNE REINED IN alongside a rushing mountain stream. Joan, saddle sore, tired, and dirty, looked at him, hoping nothing but pure venom showed in her gaze. "*M'sieur,* I assume you're now feeling safe since the rain behind washed out our tracks, but let me tell you, Tom Fallon is not one to quit. He'll catch you, and when he does you'll—"

Berne cut her off. "Tom Fallon. You think that big, uncouth cowboy can find us? Let me tell you something, *ma'mselle.* He's dumb. When he finds us, if he finds us, it'll be too late to help you. I offered to marry you, what more could you ask? But, no. You threw that lout's name in my face." The veins stood out on his forehead and his face flushed. "I tell you now, I hope he does find us. I'll show you how a Frenchman takes care of his enemies."

Joan stared at him, then at her wrists, securely tied to the pommel. She felt sick inside. If only her hands were free and she had a gun. She had no idea how long it would take Fallon to hear what had happened, but she was certain he would take up the trail if their kiss had meant as much to him as to her.

The Frenchman sat there, smirking. Joan wanted to cut

his heart out, but was thankful that, so far, his fear of what lay behind had forced him into riding late, and early in the saddle the next morning. The pace he set tired them both such that he'd not shown the urge to harm her, although she'd caught him looking at her with the oily sheen over his eyes she'd learned to fear—a look greasy, nasty, and full of desire. If he dared touch her, she decided she'd kill herself before going to Tom a damaged piece of goods, but first she'd find a way to kill the French vermin.

Then, for some reason, her thoughts went to the *Bandido Caballero*. He, too, might take up the chase. Why her thoughts turned to him she didn't know, except it seemed he would not allow this to happen to a woman. She had heard how he'd led Berne and Maximilian's troops on a chase that was talked about around every Juárez campfire. She heard the term '*mucho hombre*' applied to him more often now than *Bandido Caballero*.

Berne dismounted, walked to the side of her horse, untied her wrists, dragged her from the saddle, and pushed her to the base of a sapling about four inches in diameter. He pulled her arms behind it and again tied her.

Joan thought to change her approach, seem to give up, be sweet to him, and maybe he'd untie her. Then all she could hope for would be a chance to grab a gun or knife. The thought of being sweet to the wormy little Frenchman made her want to throw up. She'd find another way.

With the tree supporting her, she tried to find a comfortable way to hold her arms, then gave it up. Her wrists had been rubbed raw by the harsh pigging strings he'd used to tie her, and because she was not used to riding astride, the inside of her thighs burned like fire. She'd wished a hundred times for a sidesaddle on their ride from El Paso del Norte.

Berne cooked supper, and untied her long enough for her to eat. When she was finished, Joan stabbed him with a look. "I have personal needs I must take care of. Will you allow me to go into the forest for a few minutes alone?"

Berne glanced from her to the woods. A hot, greasy look came to his eyes again. "*Non, ma'mselle.* I will accompany you, and I'll not turn my back. I want to watch."

Joan froze inside. For the first time fear got a stranglehold on her. It crept up her body, paralyzing her. She'd never been looked at by a man when anything but fully dressed. She'd never been touched by any man, and had wanted only one, maybe two, to do so, but that had never happened because, somehow, she knew the two men she thought of would never treat a woman with anything but courtesy, kindness, and respect.

She stared at Berne a moment. She had held her needs too long now. She'd heard a person could become poisoned and die if they didn't succumb to nature's call— but maybe death would be better than what she feared Berne had in mind.

Finally, she said, "All right, you slime, watch."

They stepped a few yards from camp, Berne untied her wrists, and, feeling the blood rush to her face, she whimpered like a hurt animal, whimpered with anger and embarrassment, but she did what she had to.

While trying to keep him from seeing the most intimate part of her body, she felt a smooth, fist-sized, rock under her hand. Hope took the place of embarrassment. She gripped the stone, and made as though to turn toward him, hoping his filthy prying mind, and lust, would draw him nearer.

He did as she'd thought. He bent, his eyes apparently trying to penetrate the darkness. She waited, and when she thought he was close enough she raised herself to her toes and propelled her petite body straight at him. She swung the rock with every ounce of her strength at his head. He sidestepped, and swung his right fist to her cheek. Lights exploded inside her skull, then swam in alternate dark and light circles, blinding her, making her feel as though she were going to pass out. She squeezed her eyes shut tight and tried to push the dizziness back, tried to keep from blacking out. She fell.

"Not fast enough, *ma'mselle*." He grabbed her by the hair and dragged her back to the tree, where he retied her.

He stood there, and his eyes traveled from the swell of her breasts to her feet. The oily sheen came back to his eyes. Saliva drooled from the corners of his mouth. He bent over her, gripped the front of her bodice in his hands, and jerked downward, tearing her dress and bodice, exposing her breasts. He grabbed her undergarments, and tore them from her. She lay there, nude, feeling his greasy eyes devour her body, watching saliva flow down his chin, hearing his breath come in short, rasping pants.

Her first instinct was to cover her breasts with her arms, but they were tied behind her. An all-consuming, unreasoning, maniacal anger burned her face and her body, and she felt her eyes turn to ice. "Look. Look, you animal. You're the only man to ever see me. Someday Tom Fallon will be the only *living* man to have looked upon my body, no matter what you do to me. He'll cut your heart out, and I'll watch him do it, but first I'm gonna take that big knife he wears, and when I get through with you, you'll no longer be a man."

Berne, ignoring her words, shifted from one foot to the other. He gripped his belt, loosened it, and unbuttoned his trousers. Joan's eyes shifted from the Frenchman to three silent forms gliding from the trees. She gasped. Even though she'd heard horror stories about what they did to women, she welcomed the sight because whatever they did to her, Berne would get treatment as bad or worse. The Apache would save her from one fate, but what they could deal out might be worse.

Berne must have seen them at the same time. He turned a terrified face toward them, pulled his trousers up, and ran. The Indians glanced from the Frenchman to Joan, and didn't hesitate; they let him run, and gave all of their attention to the white woman.

FALLON COOKED SUPPER, ATE, AND SAT BY HIS SMALL smokeless fire drinking coffee and smoking his pipe. This-end-of-the-day respite he usually enjoyed was not the same. He couldn't relax. His pipe went out. He lighted it. He tossed out the cup of cold coffee, and poured a hot one. He picked up a stick to throw on the fire, and stopped. What was the matter with him?

He walked a few feet from camp, then went back and rolled his bedroll. Maybe he was a damned fool, but he felt something telling him, even though night had set in, to keep after Berne.

To try to track him in the dark would be futile, but if he let his horse have its head, let him pick the way, then in the morning he could ride a circling search until he again found their tracks.

The bay picked his way daintily through the trees. The occasional shift of his weight to rest against the saddle's cantle told Fallon they still climbed. He grunted his satisfaction, figuring that as long as they climbed, he was on the right track.

Long after midnight, his horse slightly shifted his route, went downhill, crossed a small stream, and again climbed.

Any other time, Fallon would have savored the clean, fresh smell of pine, the utter quiet, the being alone, but now he couldn't get Joan out of his thoughts. Had the wringing of hands and the flow of tears by her maid all been an act to throw him off? Had Joan gone with Berne voluntarily, or had he really forced her? If the Frenchman had taken her by force, what was he doing with her now? That thought brought blood to Fallon's head, and an angry suffocating swell to his throat.

He rode another hour, sometimes dozing, then snapping to full wakefulness. One of the times when he came awake, and opened his eyes wide to shake off sleep, he thought he saw a pinpoint of light through the trees far ahead.

The thought that what he had seen might be a fire brought him fully awake, and after he'd ridden another fifteen minutes or so, he knew he'd been right. A fire flickered and danced through the trees, a fire too large and in too open a space for any but a fool in this Mescalero country. The Apache was not supposed to fight at night, but Fallon could almost hear their thoughts: two people, one a woman; what chance was there that the two could kill them, the mighty Mescalero, and cause their spirits to wander in the afterworld, lost forever? Chances were they'd attack.

Fallon rode back to the stream and, already wearing buckskins, loosened his bedroll and put on moccasins. Then he slipped the Henry from its scabbard, tethered his horse, and on ghostly feet slipped silently through the timber.

Careful to place his feet where he wouldn't break a twig or kick a rock, he closed on the fire. When he was fifty feet or so from the blaze, he dropped to his stomach. He'd done this so many times when scouting Union camps during the war that it came as second nature. He slithered toward the fire. Every few feet he stopped and tested the air for horse smell, then moved another few feet. If he crawled up on Berne's horses and startled them, they might alert the Frenchman.

Now that he could see the camp clearly, he was only ten or fewer feet from its periphery. He studied the ground each side of the fire, looking hard at the spread bedding. Nothing. Neither Berne nor Joan was in sight. He lay there a minute, then heard something sounding as though it were being dragged. Berne came into camp tugging a struggling, stumbling Joan behind.

Fallon lay there a moment. He wanted to fire at Berne, but he was fearful of hitting Joan. He heard her spit her hate at the Frenchman. He heard her tell him Fallon would be the only *living* man to ever look on her body. His throat tightened. She was his woman. She wanted to be his woman. He put his hands down to push to his knees, then stopped and again sank to his stomach. Three Apache moved like shadows into the firelight. Berne had not seen them. He stood in front of Joan, letting his eyes sweep her petite body from head to toe while he frantically tried to rid himself of his trousers. Then, for some reason, he glanced over his shoulder, took one terrified look at the silent Mescalero, pulled the front of his trousers together—and ran.

Fallon's first impulse was to go after Berne, hate and anger burned in him that strong. He glanced after the retreating Frenchman, then turned his attention to the Apache, who gave Berne only a glance, then obviously couldn't resist looking at the white woman, naked, tied to the tree in front of them.

They jabbered in low guttural voices, often pointing at Joan, then at themselves. Fallon couldn't understand what they said, but guessed they were arguing about whom the girl belonged to.

Finally, having reached a decision, the three of them approached her. Fallon didn't wait.

He rose to his knees and, bringing the Henry to bear on the nearest warrior squeezed the trigger. The Indian was already in the spirit world when he squeezed off his second shot and sent that Apache on his long dark journey. The last of the three pulled his tomahawk from his breeches and looked wildly about for something to fight, but Fallon's buckskins blended with the underbrush. The warrior spun on his toes and ran.

Fallon took careful aim and fired. This one, he wanted only to wound, to stop from running. A plan, now only sketchy, formed in his mind. The Indian lay on the ground, writhing, clutching his leg.

Fallon walked into the firelight, picked up the coffeepot, still over half-full, and doused the fire down to only a small flickering blaze.

Wanting to save Joan further embarrassment, Fallon averted his eyes. He went to the Apache. In sign language he told the warrior he'd let him go back to The People if in one week he, or others, would come back to this spot; then he signed what he'd agree to do in return. He dropped his hands to his sides and waited for the Indian to sign back.

The Mescalero stared at him through hate-filled eyes, hesitated, then finally signed back, "It will be as you say. Fix my leg and I will go."

Fallon had been careful to give the Indian only a flesh wound. He tied it with his bandanna, took the warrior's weapons, and let him go. He watched until the Mescalero disappeared into the trees, hoping the Indian would keep his word. Not until then did he look toward Joan. He gathered up one of Berne's blankets and spread it over her nakedness. She said not a word until he covered her, then in a voice so calm he wondered if he'd heard her, she said, "Thank you, Tom. I wondered when you'd come."

He pulled his Bowie knife from its sheath and cut her loose from the tree, then freed her legs. "Got here soon's I could, woman. You know, you got a real talent for being in the wrong places at the right time." At his words, fire sparked in her eyes. She swallowed her anger.

"Get me something to put on. As you saw, I have nothing much on under this blanket. Berne gave me no time to take extra clothes. Look in his things. I'll dress in something of his until I can find better."

While he went through Berne's clothes, he looked across his shoulder at her. He considered mentioning that he'd heard what she said to the Frenchman, and taking her in his arms to comfort her. Then he put that thought aside. After the brutal, animal-like way she'd been treated, she deserved to be courted, made to feel again she was someone special. That would have to wait until they were back in El Paso del Norte.

Even in this dim light Fallon would have sworn he could see her blush. For the first time she must have thought how she looked to him, sprawled out, tied hand and foot, stark naked. "Don't worry 'bout it, *ma'mselle*. I didn't look at you, an' in this dim light I couldn't've seen nothin' anyway. Berne's the only man who's seen you, an' he ain't gonna live long enough to think on it."

She pulled the blanket up around her shoulders, her hands opening and closing on its edge, crumpling it in wads. She stared up at the tree limbs directly overhead, then turned her eyes on him, showing no embarrassment. When she spoke, she hesitated, faltered, but showed no hysteria, only a deadly calm which worried him. He would have felt better if she'd showed emotion of some kind. "Tom, I want you to kill him. I never wanted anything as much as I want that. You will track him down and kill him, won't you, Tom?"

While he picked up things strewn about the camp, including the beautiful foreign-made rifle of Berne's, he answered her. "Joan Boniol, that there's a question you didn't have to ask. I figure you know the answer. There's a small settlement somewhere here in these mountains. It's close by. A few people are beginnin' to call it Ruidosa. I'm gonna take you there, put you on the stage to Franklin, an' then I'm gonna hunt that Frenchman down. You don't want to know what I'm gonna do to him. After I take care of him, I'm gonna come callin'—if you'll see me."

Still in a deadly calm voice, she said, "Tom Fallon, you've never had reason to believe you'd be anything but welcome at *mi casa*." Then for the first time her voice showed feeling. "As a matter of fact, Mr. Fallon, if you don't come calling, I'm going to come looking." She hesitated a moment. "That is if you still want to see me after that animal tore my clothes off and looked at me—all over."

Fallon went to her and looked into her eyes. "Joan, in less'n a week, there won't be a livin' man who can say he ever saw you any way but fully dressed. I promise you that." He hedged on that statement. He'd seen her beautifully nude body, but wanted to save her the embarrassment of knowing he had.

She gave a little jerk to her head. "That's what I thought you'd say, but I want to come with you, see you put an end to him."

Fallon studied her a moment. "No. What I'm figurin' to do would be too dangerous for you. Tell you 'bout it later."

She opened her mouth as though to argue, then clamped it shut.

Fallon gathered Berne's handgun, horses, and camp

# CHAPTER

# 22

BACK IN FALLON'S CAMP, HE SPREAD BEDDING FOR them both, putting Joan on the opposite side of the fire from him. He felt her staring at him. "What's botherin' you, girl? You ain't said a word, but you're sure enough thinkin' 'em."

"Just wondering, Tom. What were you signing to that Indian, and why'd you let him go?"

Fallon wondered whether to tell her what he had in mind, and decided he wouldn't. He was going to carry out his plan regardless what she said, and he didn't want to argue with her as to whether she could go with him.

He pulled his blanket around his shoulders and said, "Go to sleep, woman. We got travelin' to do come daylight. I'll tell you 'bout it someday."

Two days later, they rode into the small settlement: two saloons, a blacksmith shop, and the livery stable on one side of the dusty, rocky street; and a general mercantile store, cafe, and hotel across from them. The Overland Stage office had space on the lower floor of the hotel.

Fallon got them each a room, then they went directly to the general store. "I got money, Joan. Buy everythin' you need—from the skin out." He thought a moment, then added, "You better get two outfits so's you'll have a change 'tween here an home, if you get a chance to change. While you're doin' that, I'm gonna see when the stage'll be in."

Her face set in stubborn lines. "You're not taking me with you, are you?" Her chin lifted and she looked at him straight on. "Well, I'm going."

Not breaking his gaze, Fallon pushed his hat off his forehead. "Nope, you ain't. You might's well get used to doin' what I say,'cause out here I'm the boss."

She stared a moment longer, then her gaze fell. Her voice soft, she said, "What you're going to do is dangerous, isn't it? And it has something to do with that Indian you made all the sign language to, doesn't it? You're trying to protect me."

She looked so vulnerable Fallon almost relented, but the danger of his plan, if it didn't work, would put her in more jeopardy than if he had left her with Berne. "Yes, I'm tryin' to protect you; I care for you, that's why I followed you all this way. And yes, it has somethin' to do with that Apache, and yes it's dangerous. You ain't goin'."

She looked up at him, her eyes wide and fearful. "Tom, I'll do as you say if you'll promise me to be careful— extra careful. That vicious little man would shoot you in the back if he got the chance."

He grasped her shoulders. "Little one, get it in that pretty little head of yours: I'm always careful. I do things could get a man killed, every man does, anythin' from topping off a raw bronc to snagging a two-thousand-pound steer on the end of my rope, but whatever it is— I'm always careful."

Fallon left her in the store and went to the Overland Stage office. The agent told him the next arrival headed for Las Cruces and points east would be in on Friday. This was Wednesday. He bought one ticket, then went out to the boardwalk, studied the town's layout, and wondered if Berne knew of this town. He was alone out there in the wilderness, without weapons or a horse. Even if he were lucky, his chances of making it this far were slim.

Fallon figured at first the Frenchman would want only to put distance between himself and the Apache; after that he'd worry about a safe haven. Without Joan to tell people what he'd done, Berne was free to go into any town. He'd figure the Apache had taken care of her. At best, he should not reach this settlement until Saturday.

Wanting to give Joan time to buy the things women put on under their dresses, Fallon went to the nearest saloon for a drink. There were but six men drinking and playing cards at the far side of the room. He went to the bar and stood with his back to the wall at its end. He ordered a straight whiskey, knocked it back, ordered another, and studied the big Irishman behind the bar. He wanted to ask the bartender to let him know if a man of Berne's description came into town, but decided against it. He'd watch for the Frenchman himself.

BERNE, SOBBING WITH FEAR, LOOKED OVER HIS SHOULder at his campfire growing dim in the distance. Two shots rang out, sounding close together. He dived behind a large ponderosa pine, every muscle tensed against the flesh-tearing jar of a bullet. Then a single shot. The shots didn't come close, didn't even clip twigs from the nearby trees. The Indians must be firing wildly, hoping to hit him.

His stomach churned; fear shoved a hard knot into his throat, choking him. He cried in great gulping sobs. When daylight came, the savages would track him. The night was his only ally. Even though he had no idea in which direction he ran, he had to get as far from the Apache as possible before they picked up his trail. Right now distance, distance was the thing.

His breath came in gasps, but he ran on, sucking for air to his tortured lungs. Brush scratched his face, his hands. He stumbled going down an embankment, fell into the icy waters of a small stream, scrambled to his feet, and ran on. Finally, he could run no farther. He crawled under a deadfall, pulled dead branches to cover himself, then lay on the moist earth, sucking air into lungs that had forgotten what a deep breath meant.

For the first time, his thoughts went back to the horrible nightmare in his camp. The Boniol woman lay there, naked, stripped by his own hand. The savages must even now be enjoying what was rightfully his, what he'd taken such chances to obtain for himself. Anger pushed his fear aside. If she'd married him when he'd told her to, this wouldn't have happened to her. She deserved whatever the Indians did to her. It was her fault. Lust embedded itself in his anger. Even the thought of the Indians ravishing and mutilating her body aroused him.

He lay still until he could breathe normally. The chill waters of the snowmelt stream and the mountain air turned him into a shivering, trembling hulk. His teeth chattered so hard he thought they'd chip. He couldn't stay here; he had to keep moving, to get away, and to warm his frigid body. He pushed the pine boughs aside, crawled into the open, and, now with a degree of sanity, walked.

Daylight found him miles from his camp—he hoped. He got his bearings from the sun and headed west, roughly in the direction of the settlement of which he'd heard.

He'd lost his weapons and his horses. He made the sign of the cross and thanked the Lord he'd not had time to shed his trousers before the savages came. His money was in his pockets.

Boots were not made for walking. By dusk Berne's feet were one huge blister. He tried walking on his heels. It didn't help. His clothes stank from sweat, caused by fear and the labor of his efforts. Dirt covered his face, clothes, and every exposed part of his body. When it became too dark to see where he walked, he crawled under some brush and slept. He had lost his matches and had no fire. Before sleep took him, he thought of the way many of these uncouth Americans made fires without matches, with flint and steel, but then it occurred to him that he wouldn't know how to use those tools even if he had them.

Two days later, soon after noon, a slim column of smoke in front of Berne threaded its way into the heavens. He studied it a moment, hoping he'd found a small town, hoping it wasn't an Apache village. He turned his raw and bleeding feet toward it, slipping from tree to tree, wishing to see cabins, white people, stores. He had no fear of entering town. The Boniol woman was the only one who could tell others of his stealing her, and by now she was dead—or worse—at the hands of the Apache.

An hour later, he paused at the top of a rise and looked down on the town. Whimpering like a small, hurt pup, he ran on his bloodied feet down the hill. He made mewling sounds deep in his throat, much like a hurt animal, as he staggered down the middle of the one street. He ran until someone jumped from the boardwalk and tackled him. A deep, kindly voice soothed him. "Whoa now, fella. Take it easy. What's happened to you?"

Berne, half out of his mind with joy at having reached civilization, and still insane with fear, babbled his story to the small crowd that gathered around him, a story true except for the part Joan Boniol played in it.

THE TALL, HARD-FACED MAN STANDING IN SUNSHINE IN front of the saloon smiled with satisfaction. Berne had found his trip into town painful, almost deadly, just as Fallon had hoped. A couple of townsmen picked up the Frenchman and carried him to the doctor's office—well, not a doctor exactly; he was the town's horse doctor, and his office occupied a room built onto the side of the livery. "Fix him up good, folks," Fallon muttered. "I want 'im in good shape when I take 'im outta here." He felt a cold, wintry smile break the hard planes of his face.

When the men disappeared through the door with Berne, Fallon stepped from the boardwalk and went to the livery, where he checked the three horses. When he and Joan rode in, he'd left orders for them to be grain fed, rubbed down, and kept in good shape. When he left here, he'd be traveling long and fast. The tack for each horse rested on the stall walls.

After making certain the horses were in good shape, he returned to his place in front of the saloon; it was one of the warmest places in town.

He hadn't brought a coat with him when he left Franklin. He'd gone through Berne's clothing after rescuing Joan, found the small Frenchman's coat, and put it on Joan. Small as she was, it was a good fit. It would keep her warm until he could buy another. She'd worn it when she boarded the stage.

Fallon shivered. He figured to hell with freezing and went across the street to the general store to buy himself a sheepskin. While trying the coat on, he hoped Berne froze, or caught pneumonia, when he took him out of here. After paying for the sheepskin, he went out and again stood on the boardwalk.

The same two men who had taken Berne to be cared for came out of the doctor's office and helped him across the street to the hotel. Fallon figured the shape the Frenchman was in he'd sleep the clock around—if Fallon allowed him to do so. He waited until the two men came from the hostelry, then went back to the store and bought trail provisions. Coffee, jerky, flour, bacon, pipe tobacco, and other things he'd learned a man might need, from having to do without on other trips. He bought only enough for himself. He took his purchases to the livery and stashed them in his saddlebags.

That night he went to the saloon and played poker until midnight, then checked the stack of cartwheels in front of him, figured his luck was running, and decided to play a few more hands. When he raked the silver dollars into his hat, he asked the bartender for double eagles in their place. The cartwheels weighed a ton. He was a couple of hundred dollars winner. One of the players glanced up, grinned, and said, "Ain't gonna give me a chance to get my money back?"

Fallon looked him in the eye, wondering if this was trouble. "Partner, I learned a long time ago to quit when I'm ahead. 'Sides, the money I seen in this game, there's plenty to go around."

The man nodded. "Good luck, cowboy. I ain't never had that much sense."

Fallon went from the saloon to the hotel. No one was at the desk. This made it easier for him to do what he planned without leaving anyone behind who would remember him asking about Berne's room. A note by the register said, "You want a room after ten o'clock, take a key off the wall, sign the register, and pay in the morning." Fallon grinned, thinking the clerk had a lot of confidence believing those who came in here would know how to read. He twisted the register around so he could read it. He checked names and room numbers of the guests. Berne slept in room three.

Moving like a shadow, Fallon went to his room and got his rifle. He took a few pigging strings from his bedroll, tied his bedding, tucked five or six of the ties in his belt, then went to room three.

His Bowie knife slipped the lock on the door. Inside the room, he carefully placed his gear on the floor, walked to the side of the bed, and put his hand over Berne's mouth. The Frenchman came awake as though from a nightmare, only to find the real nightmare standing at his bedside. He squirmed against Fallon's steel grip like a fishing worm on a hook. He stared through horror-filled eyes at the tall figure standing over him.

Fallon pressed Berne's head against the bed until, with one hand, he pulled his bandanna from his neck and gagged him. Then he tied the Frenchman's hands, shouldered his bedroll, slung his rifle over the same shoulder, and jerked Berne to his feet. "Gonna walk you outta the back door of this hotel, Frenchie, an' you better walk quiet or I'll slit your gullet like a stuck pig. *Comprende?*"

Berne nodded, his eyes wide, dripping fear.

Fallon opened the door a crack and peered out. The passageway stood empty. He pushed the terrified man toward the rear door. At the same time, a door between him and the back opened. A man stepped out. "Hey, whatcha doin' to that man? He's sick."

"Keep quiet, stranger, an' you won't get hurt. This man

caused my woman to get killed. Gonna take care of him like he oughta be cared for.'' His voice hardened. "Now, get the hell outta my way.''

The stranger showed no fear. He studied Fallon a moment, then looked at Berne, who was shaking his head frantically. Then, apparently accepting Fallon's words, the stranger nodded and stepped back into his room.

Fallon pushed the Frenchman toward the door.

It took only a few moments to reach the livery. Fallon pushed Berne to the back of the stall and saddled one of the horses. He lifted the little man to the horse, tied his feet to the stirrups, and then saddled his own bay. He'd lead the third horse.

When he left the stable, only the lanterns painting the windows of the two saloons a golden hue showed signs of life in the small town.

The forest soon swallowed him and his French baggage. He wended his way through the trees until gray, turning lighter by the minute, brightened the darkness to the east.

Fallon searched for a place to build a fire and cook breakfast, a place where his fire could only be seen a few feet away. Even then the smoke smell might be detected by roving Apache.

He found a place under the bank of a stream, a place where smoke would dissipate through the branches of overhanging boughs, and where the small blaze of his fire was sheltered on one side by a bend in the stream, and on the other by a rock outcropping from the stream's bank. The fire would likely not be seen.

He dumped Berne from the saddle and looked at him. "You see how I picked this site to do my cookin'?'' He shook his head. "Nope, don't reckon you're smart enough to realize what I did, an' ain't gonna do no good to teach you. You gonna be dead 'fore you get a chance to use that teachin'.''

"What're you going to do with me, Fallon? I've done you no harm. You told that man back there I killed *Ma'mselle* Boniol. I didn't do it. The Apache killed her.

I defended her as much as I could, and when they toma-hawked her, I saw she was dead and I ran. Wouldn't have done any good for me to stay there and get killed, too.''

Fallon went about preparing breakfast, savoring the smell of frying bacon and boiling coffee. When he'd fin-ished cooking, and sat eating the fruits of his labor, he swallowed and looked at Berne. ''Not that way at all. You ran soon's you seen them Indians.'' Then he told the Frenchman he'd seen the whole thing.

''Well, why didn't you save her if you saw so much? You didn't have the guts to tangle with those Mescalero any more than I did.''

Fallon stood, went to the stream, and cleaned his cook-ing and eating gear. Berne watched him, licked his lips, and asked, ''Fallon, I've not eaten in three or four days. Aren't you going to allow me even a few bites?''

''Don't believe in wastin' food, Berne. I feed you, it'd be a waste. Ain't gonna make you any difference in a day or two whether you ever ate or not.'' He came back to the fire with a coffeepot full of water and doused the fire. ''Gonna tell you somethin', Frenchie. I did keep the Apache from killing her. She's on her way back to Frank-lin right this minute. I killed two of them Indians, but I saved one of them. He promised to go back to his camp and bring others. They're gonna show you how an Apache treats a coward.''

''What do you mean, they're going to show me?''

Fallon grinned. ''Berne, I like surprises. It wouldn't be much fun if I told you everything, now would it? I want you to be surprised, but I'll tell you this much: I'm gonna strip you, tie you spread-eagled to the same tree you tied Señorita Boniol to, then I'm gonna wait out yonder in the woods till I see them Apache find you. I want you to think on the things they'll do to you, an' whatever you think of ain't gonna come close to what they'll have in mind. That's all I'm gonna tell you.''

Berne fought his bonds a moment while staring at Fal-lon. ''You can't do this. You're worse than those savages.

If I get away, I'm going to the authorities. They'll hang you.''

"Aw hell, Frenchie, I'm gonna save you that trouble. Gonna tell 'em myself.''

Berne opened his mouth and yelled as loud as his throat could stand.

Fallon went to him and crammed his bandanna in the Frenchman's mouth. "You yell, an' the Apache will come down on us sooner'n I figure. Fact is, you might even get me hurt. I wouldn't like that. Now, shut the hell up.''

He kept Berne gagged for two more days, days during which Fallon took it slow and easy. He was in no hurry to get back to the site where the Indians attacked Berne's camp, although he wanted to get there before they did.

The afternoon of the third day, Fallon tethered the horses in a deep ravine, one where there was water in a shallow stream at its bottom, and tender grass on the shoulders of the bank. Satisfied the horses were as safe as he could make them, he pushed Berne ahead of him toward the spot where he'd found Joan. He kept the Frenchman gagged. The Indians might already be at the campsite.

When they were within a hundred yards from the site, he tied Berne to a tree, checked the bonds on his hands and feet, tightened the gag, and left.

He drifted quiet as smoke from tree to tree, and when he was within a few yards of the camp, he dropped to his belly and snaked his way closer. Within spitting distance, he lay behind a pile of brush and, hardly daring to breathe, searched the surrounding forest. Every tree, rock, tuft of scrub brush, slight swell in the ground, came under his eyes. His ears were atuned to sounds that might be foreign to the area. Birds continued to sing; a lone marmot whistled somewhere in the rocks. He glanced at the sky. An eagle soared on a vagrant lifting of air high above, and the sun sat only an hour from sinking behind the western peaks.

Fallon figured the Apache would wait now until the coming of a new day, but he lay there, quiet, not moving, until full dark settled on the land. Only then did he wriggle back a few yards, then snake his way another fifty or so yards before he stood and made his way to where he'd tied Berne.

He couldn't see the Frenchman's eyes, but could feel them on him. Both hate and terror were in those looks. Fallon softened. He could take Berne back to Juárez, let him face a firing squad, or take him back across the border and turn him loose in the desert, or, or . . .

Then he thought of Joan, tied spread-eagled, naked for that French filth to look at, and he thought of the hundreds of soldiers, good men, he'd seen maimed or blown to bits. To think that slime tied to the tree breathed the same air those men had, turned his stomach to a hard, cold knot.

The Apache would skin Berne, stake him out on an ant bed, pour honey over his body, and let the ants do the rest—while they watched. Or, they might do it the way he'd seen them kill a man one other time. They might dismember him, one joint at a time, taking care to keep him alive and in as much pain as possible until he died from loss of blood.

Fallon sat on a log and pondered whether to take the Frenchman to the site now, in the dark, stake him to the ground, and leave him for the Indians to find, or wait and chance they wouldn't be there at sunrise. If he waited until sunrise, he would jeopardize his own life. He shook his head—no point in taking that chance. He decided to do it in the dark. He stood, ready to drag Berne to the campsite, then stopped, shook his head, and muttered, "Can't do it. Ain't no savage—yet."

# CHAPTER

# 23

F ALLON STOOD LOOKING AT BERNE, THEN CUT HIM loose from the tree and jerked him to his feet.

"W-where you taking me, what're you going to do?"

"Walk real quiet-like, an' shut the hell up. It might save your worthless hide—for a while."

He pushed the Frenchman toward the tethered horses. Berne stepped on limbs, broke them, and stumbled heavy-footed over rocks, all making noise Fallon could have sworn would bring the whole Apache nation down on them. "You wantta get outta here alive, Frenchie, you better try walkin' soft. The Apache hear you, I'm gonna do to you what you did to Miss Boniol, leave you for them to entertain themselves with. Oughtta do it anyway— fire a shot, leave you, get the horses, an' go."

"Y-y-you mean you're not leaving me for them?"

Fallon shook his head. "Gettin' soft, I reckon. Figure to take you to Juárez, let him legally decide what to do with you. Figure it'll be a firin' squad."

"Aw, m'sieur, let me go. Juárez has already sworn to kill every imperialist he captures, except those ignorant Mexicans. He'll take them back into the fold."

Fallon laughed deep in his throat. "Let you go? You're

dreamin'. I'd kill you right here, slow-like, before I'd do that. Get movin'.''

At the horses, Fallon again tied Berne in the saddle, and then led them down the mountain. He made sure all the canteens were filled before they got to the desert floor. ''Berne, you see me fillin' these canteens? This water's mostly for me an' the horses. Gonna give you barely enough to keep you alive till I turn you over to Juárez, then it ain't gonna make any difference whether you have water or not. Fact is, with all the holes that firin' squad puts in you, it'd leak out faster'n we could pour it in.''

Berne eyed Fallon a moment. ''Fallon, you're a worse savage than those you were going to turn me over to. You're torturing me with words.''

''That's exactly what I figure to do. Figure to drive you to the brink of insanity, then of course I'll back off awhile. Want you to know what's happenin' to you.''

They rode the rest of the night, ever on a descending course. When light began to push darkness back farther under trees and into crevices, Fallon stopped at a mountain freshet to cook breakfast, again choosing the site with care.

He opened a tin of beans, put coffee on to boil, and bacon to fry. When he had a good bit of grease in the frying pan, he mixed flour and water and fried some bread. The aroma wafting across the site made his mouth water. He looked at Berne. ''Ain't had nothin' to eat in some little time, have you, Frenchie?'' After helping himself to bacon, bread, coffee, and beans out of the can, he again slanted Berne a hard look. ''Gonna do you the same with food as I am with water—just enough to keep you alive. Don't want you too healthy when Juárez gets you.''

After watering the horses and topping off the canteens, Fallon again led them on an ever descending course toward the dry land of the rattler and sagebrush below.

AT THE SAME TIME FALLON FLOORED OUT ON THE DESERT, Joan stepped from the stagecoach in front of the Falcon Nest *hacienda*. She'd asked the driver to swing his coach the two miles off the trail to take her to her friends' home.

Nita Fallon rushed out to take her in her arms. "Oh, what a wonderful surprise. Come in, come in, my dear. What in the world are you doing this far from civilization?"

Joan glanced at the sun sitting at high noon, then looked Nita in the eye. "It's a long story. I'll tell you soon enough, but first please invite me in out of this hot sun."

"How awful of me. Yes, do come in." Nita looked at the driver. "Bring her luggage in, sir."

The driver squinted against the bright sunlight to look at the *Señora* Fallon. "Ma'am, she ain't got none. Just what she's carryin' in that there bag. I spect she's been through some sort o' bad happenin'."

Nita studied the driver a moment. "Where did she board your stage, sir?"

"Little mountain town just now bein' called Ruidosa, two, maybe three, days back of me. A big man, most would call 'im handsome, stuffed 'er on the stage an' told me to keep 'er there till I got at least far as Las Cruces. I kept the horses movin', ain't stopped for nuthin'. They's been a right smart o' 'Pache trouble out that way."

Nita nodded. "You and your passengers come in. I'll have the cook feed you—or stay overnight if you will."

"Ain't got time. Already late, thanks anyway." He cracked his whip above the horse's backs and drove off.

Nita put her arms around Joan and ushered her into the huge, cool living area. Joan fell into the nearest chair, leaned back, and closed her eyes. The last thing she heard before falling into an exhausted sleep was Nita telling the servants to prepare a room and bathwater for her.

Joan opened her eyes, and looked toward the large front doors. Long shadows lay across the ranch yard, and the smell of spicy food cooking told her she'd slept the afternoon away. She stirred and looked across the room. Nita sat sipping a glass of something that looked deliciously cool. She turned her eyes on Joan.

"Awake, my dear? Your room's ready if you'd like to tidy up a bit before supper, or, if you will, join me in a drink. I've been sitting here eaten up with curiosity as to what's happened to you.''

Joan stretched, covered her mouth, and yawned. ''Yes, I'll have a drink, and yes, I'll tell you the horrible things that have happened with me, but I'd like Brad to hear it, too.''

Nita sent one of the servants for her husband, and another to fix a drink for Joan. Finally, the three of them sitting close in the big room, Nita said, ''Joan, if you don't tell us what's happened to you pretty soon, I think I'll wring your pretty neck.''

Joan nodded and told the whole story, beginning with Berne's kidnapping of her. When she'd finished, she swept them both with a questioning look. ''How well do you know your son? I know you sent him off to an Eastern school to take some of the burrs off his hide, but I'm here to tell you that schooling didn't take; maybe the war had something to do with that.

''I've seen him in the environment which, I believe, is the one most suited to him. He can be as gentle as a fawn, and as savage as any Indian ever born. It depends on the circumstances. Your son, my friends, is one helluva man. I've met only one other who might be able to walk in his shoes. The way things are now, I'll probably not get the chance to see them both in the same room and make my comparison, but for my own peace of mind I'd surely like to.''

Nita sat staring, obviously studying her, and thinking of the reasons she'd given Tom such glowing praise. Finally, she tipped her glass up, drained it, and again turned her eyes on Joan. ''Sounds as though you're more than a little in love with my son, but not quite sure you could be faithful to him if the other man showed up.''

Joan felt blood rush to her face. ''Nita, Brad, I suppose I'm only now beginning to admit to myself that I do love Tom, but let me assure you, if he ever courts me and asks me to marry him, I intend to tell him how mixed up my feelings are. He's given me reason to think he cares for me, but I'm not certain how deeply.'' She sighed. ''I suppose I'll just have to wait and see how things develop. But I wanted to tell you before he says anything to you. I wouldn't want to marry him unless the two of you think you could accept me into your family.''

Still staring at her, Nita smiled. ''Joan Boniol, you're an honest woman, and my dear friend. If Tom decides you're the one for him, I assure you I'll welcome you with an open heart.'' She glanced at Brad, eyebrows raised. He took the hint.

''Well, gosh ding it, reckon this is the first time I ever heard of the woman asking for permission to be courted. But, yes, I cain't think of anyone I'd rather see that hell-raisin' boy marry.'' He cocked an eyebrow at her, a slight smile breaking the corners of his mouth. ''You're the one who should be worried, Joan. I don't believe you realize what you're lettin' yourself in for. He's hard headed, stubborn as an old mule, and hot tempered.''

''I know all that, Brad. And,'' she grinned, ''it would be a case of the pot calling the kettle black.'' She settled back in her chair. ''I think we could survive each other.'' She drank the last of her drink and stood. ''Now, I think I'll tidy up before dinner.''

FALLON AND BERNE CAME DOWN ONTO THE DESERT about midmorning. Ever since sunup, rising heat had brought sweat to Fallon's skin, and by the time he bottomed out into the sagebrush and creosote bush, his shirt refused to soak up more perspiration. He pulled his hat low on his forehead and led them toward the Rio Grande.

About three o'clock five horsemen showed through the ghostlike heat waves shimmering across the white hilly surface. Fallon urged the horses into a dry wash and, after taking Berne from the saddle, pulled the horses to the ground. ''You keep your mouth shut, Frenchie, an' you'll prob'ly still be wearin' your hair come sundown. We got company—an' they ain't white men.''

''Cut me loose and give me a rifle.''

Fallon smiled. ''No way. If I have to fight, I'll do it

alone. If I lose, I'll be dead, an' you'll be tied up nice an' tight for them.''

He raked his hat from his head, crawled up the bank, and peered toward the riders. He could tell from the way they sat their horses they were Indians, but he wasn't sure whether they were Apache or Comanche. If they were Comanche, they were way off their usual range. But after studying them a few minutes, he figured that's who they were. They sat their ponies like they were part of them. No Apache could ride like those Plains Indians, but Apache or Comanche, it didn't make any difference—one Indian was as bad as another if they got ahold of you.

His mouth dry, and the muscles between his shoulders one large center of pain, Fallon kept his eyes on the lead rider.

They rode so as to cross Fallon's route about two hundred yards ahead. When they got closer, he saw that they were probably a hunting party. They wore no paint and were too small a group. The lack of war paint didn't make him feel better. A lone white man, far from help, would be good sport.

Abruptly, they turned toward where he and Berne lay. Fallon cursed, wondering what had caused them to change course. He brought his rifle into firing position. He wanted to jack a shell into the chamber, but didn't. The noise would alert them of danger. There was a small chance they wouldn't see him. He breathed short hurried breaths, tasting the raw, sour taste of fear deep in his throat.

The leader raised his hand for them to halt, then stared toward where Fallon lay. Fallon didn't wait. He jacked a shell into the chamber, centered his sights on the one who was apparently the leader, and fired. He moved his sights to another in one fluid motion, and dropped him from his pony. Now the remaining three rode straight at him, yelling like the savages they were. He knocked another warrior backward off his horse.

When they were within fifty yards of him, the two remaining warriors pulled arrows from their quivers, nocked them, and lofted them toward where he lay. They sent

arrows his way as fast as he could jack shells into his
Henry and fire. At first, they fired toward the sound of his
rifle. Then they were close enough to see his head and
shoulders. Two of their feathered missiles sank into the
ground at his side—another buried itself in his thigh.
Every nerve in his body screamed when the arrow went
through his leg. Fallon ground his teeth against the pain,
swung his rifle to center on one of the remaining two
warriors, fired, and knocked him to the side off his pony.

The last Comanche pulled his knife while he swung
from his pony's back. Fallon dropped his rifle and reached
for his revolver. It came to hand in as quick a draw as
he'd ever made. He thumbed two shots into the Indian's
body, rolled to the side, and fired again.

The Comanche buried his blade in the sand at Fallon's
side. Blood spurted from two holes in the Indian's chest,
and a hole in his stomach seeped just enough blood to
stain his loincloth. He stared at Fallon and his mouth
worked as though to say something. Then, with a slow
drool of blood down his chin, he lay back, pulled his
knees up to his stomach, straightened, and died.

Fallon looked at the warrior long enough to make certain he was dead, then glanced at those he'd shot out in
front of him. None of them had moved since leaving his
horse. Fallon struggled to sit. He holstered his Colt, then
pulled his Bowie and slit his trouser leg to the crotch.
Pain shot through his leg into his lower stomach. He
wanted to retch, to get rid of the breakfast he'd enjoyed
so much. He swallowed, twice. He had to get the arrow
from his leg. His fingers searched behind his thigh and
found about half of the arrow's feathered end sticking out.

He studied the arrow and his leg a moment. He'd have
to break the shaft between his leg and the fletch, grip the
shaft in front of his thigh, close to the point, and pull it
through. The thought caused his stomach to roll, and
every muscle in his body to tighten. But there was no
other way.

"Cut me loose. I'll help you, Fallon."

Fallon glanced at him. "Yeah, Frenchie, I'll bet you'd

help me. You'd send me on a fast trip to hell. No, you treacherous bastard, you gonna stay tied, an' you better hope I don't get so sick I don't know where I am 'cause then you gonna die tied up, unable to get water or food. Don't know which'll be worse, starvin' or thirst. You better hope you don't have to find out.''

He again looked at the arrow. He struggled to his feet and went to his saddlebags. He'd wondered when he bought provisions in the small mountain settlement why he bought a bottle of whiskey; now he knew. He took the bottle, pulled the cork, and turned it up, taking three large swallows. Then he again sat, and poured a small amount of whiskey on each side of his leg. He waited a few minutes for the alcohol to numb him a bit, then reached for the arrow.

He broke it as close to his thigh as he could, then grasped the shaft in the front of his leg and pulled. The arrow didn't budge. Dark circles swam in front of his eyes—and grew larger. He fought off passing out. Berne might roll to where he lay, get his Bowie, and cut himself free. If that happened, Fallon knew he was a dead man.

When his head cleared, he took another healthy swallow of the raw whiskey, and with both hands grasped the shaft in back of the arrowhead, and jerked straight up. All the demons of hell danced in his chest, before his eyes, up and down his spine—but the shaft pulled free of his leg.

Sweat drenched him, sweat that had nothing to do with desert heat. His breath came in short gasps, as though he'd run a mile. Lying waiting for his quivering muscles to relax, bracing against the agonizing pain shooting up his thigh, Fallon took another swallow of whiskey. It began to taste like good bourbon. Through his pain, with part of a grimace, he grinned. He was close to getting drunk.

A glance at the sun told him it was nearing four o'clock. He'd not stopped for a nooning, thinking to make as many miles as possible on this first day out of the mountains. The Indians had changed that thinking. He needed to eat, and rest. Strips torn from one of his shirts bound his wound. No blood showed through the bandages. He frowned, looked at the bodies of the dead Comanche, and decided despite the pain to move on until dark. It wouldn't take long for the carcasses to bloat and start stinking. Too, if he sat for a while, his leg would stiffen, the pain would get more intense, and he might take on a fever.

He got Berne back in the saddle and they rode on.

That night, Fallon stopped early. His leg throbbed and he felt warm. Fever. His leg must be festering.

He fixed supper, then sliced two pieces of bacon and tied them to his wound, one on each side. His mother used to use fat bacon on his cuts when he was growing up, said it drew the poison from them. He hoped if it ever worked, that it would this time. Again, he let Berne go without food, but this time it was because he didn't want to get too close to the little Frenchman, and he didn't want to untie his hands for him to eat.

Before bedding down, Fallon took the chance and tied the Frenchman to a large old yucca, then he walked into the desert a short way and spread his blankets.

He slept in short naps, waking every time he rolled onto his leg, or scraped it against the ground. Each time he wakened, it took a while for him to get back to sleep.

Morning saw him feeling drug out, tired, as though he'd done a day's work. He didn't want to make the effort to prepare breakfast, but he needed his strength.

After eating, he felt better. His leg hurt, but he wasn't feverish. His mother's remedy worked. He scrubbed breakfast dishes out with sand, packed them and Berne onto a horse, and headed toward El Paso del Norte.

While riding, Fallon planned what he must do before severing himself from the task he'd taken as a personal objective. Once in Juárez's hands, Berne would not be a further problem, but Bienville and his crew remained, and despite his liking for the gentlemanly Frenchman, Bienville was as guilty as Berne in the attempt on Juárez's life. He'd sanctioned it. Fallon figured he'd have to give this problem a little more thought.

Then there was Joan—beautiful, desirable, petite Joan—

an imperialist. How would she react when she learned he was the *Bandido Caballero*? She was more than fond of him, that had been obvious from the start, but could he overcome her loyalty to the Maximilian cause? Would she forgive him for his part in the robberies? He shrugged mentally. Why borrow trouble? He'd take on that problem when the time came.

That night, he rode to a sump, one in which he planned to refill the canteens. A crazy quilt of cracked, dried mud covered the bottom. It had been long since it held water. A glance at the canteens, at least two of them empty, caused Fallon to try to swallow the dry, scratchy feel in his throat. Except for a swallow once or twice a day for him and Berne, the horses would get the rest.

Despite the lack of water, Fallon made camp, cooked his meal, and gave Berne a few bites of what he had left. "Don't want to fatten you up too much, Frenchie. It'd be a waste, what with you facin' a firin' squad in a couple o' days."

The next two days Fallon spooned water and victuals to the Frenchman. Noon of the third day he rode into El Paso del Norte, tired, filthy, unshaven, and in more pain than he imagined a man could withstand.

While approaching the front of the Republic's headquarters, he pulled a dirty rag over his face, only because that was the way Juárez's men would know him, and stepped from his horse. He dragged Berne from his saddle, trembling and staring wide-eyed at the sentries. Fallon dumped him on the ground and looked at the pair of guards. "Tell *El Presidente* the *Bandido Caballero* wishes to see him." He glanced at Berne. "And drag that garbage in at the same time."

The sentries came to rigid attention and saluted. "*Sí, señor.* Wait here *un momento.*" The sentry to Fallon's right disappeared through the doorway.

Only a moment passed before he came back out. "Come, *señor, El Presidente* will see you now."

Fallon limped to stand in front of Juárez's desk. "*Mi*

*Presidente,* I bring you a gift. Not gold this time, but the man who attempted to kill you.''

Juárez, disregarding what Fallon told him, stared at his friend, then his eyes went to the tattered, bloody trousers leg. *"Madre de Dios, mi amigo,* what in the name of heaven has happened to you? You're hurting.'' He pulled his own chair to the front of the desk. ''Here, sit down.'' He looked up at an orderly. ''Tequila, bread, food, and find my doctor.''

*"De nada, Señor Presidente.* I've ridden over a hundred kilometers like this. If I may, while I eat, and the doctor ministers to my wound, I'll tell you all that's happened.''

The doctor came, as did a waiter with food. Fallon started at the attempted assassination and told Juárez the entire story. When he'd finished, he frowned. ''I must call on the *Señorita* Boniol after I scrub about two tons of this dirt off me. I need to see if she got home safely.''

''Rest your worries. I had dinner with her last night, in her own *casa.* And, *señor,* I believe her only worry now is that you are safe.'' He pursed his lips, his eyes twinkling. ''I believe I detected a somewhat more than friendly interest there. Might there be a budding romance?''

Fallon laughed. ''You Mexicans would find romance between two yucca plants if you didn't have humans to worry about. But, well, yeah. If I can make it happen, and she forgives me for being the *bandido,* there might be romance in the offing.''

''Does she know you are the *bandido*? If she doesn't, I'll tell her for you, and try to smooth over your lawless acts. I believe she is my friend and will trust me.''

''No, *señor.* That is something I must tell her myself.'' He looked at Berne still lying on the floor in front of Juárez's desk. ''I assume, *señor,* you'll take care of this human garbage. I don't want him put in front of a firing squad that'll get it over in a matter of seconds; I want him to die slow—a little at a time. If so, I'll go to my hotel, bathe, and sleep forever.''

Juárez pinned him with a look Fallon hoped never to see if he was the subject under discussion. "*Señor* Fallon, that is the safest assumption you'll ever make. Go, get your rest, and by the time you waken, *M'sieur* Berne will no longer be with us."

"*Señor Presidente,* there are a few things I must take care of first, to bring this entire *bandido* episode to an end, but in a few days I'd like to call on you again and tell you the rest of the story."

"There is more?"

Fallon grinned. "Not yet, *señor,* but there will be. I'll tell you about it then." He stood. "With your permission, *Señor Presidente*?"

"*Sí. Vaya con Dios, mi amigo.*"

Fallon smiled. If God hadn't been with him the entire last few years, he wouldn't be here. He nodded his good-bye and left.

# CHAPTER

24

IN FRANKLIN, FALLON WENT DIRECTLY TO THE LIVERY, left the horses, and asked the liveryman if he'd seen Two Buffalo.

"Yeah, that mean damn Indian's up in the loft sleepin'. All he does is sleep, drink, an' raise hell."

Fallon knew better. Two Buffalo might put on an act of drinking, but when he'd been left with a job to do for his friend Tom Fallon, that was his only concern until it got done.

After telling the liveryman to rub the horses down and grain feed them, he climbed toward the haymow. Before topping the ladder, he looked down at the old cowboy. "Them horses had a rough few days; treat 'em right."

When he stuck his head into the loft, he saw that Two Buffalo sat leaning against a hay bale. "Smell you soon's you walk into stable, Fallon. Knowed it wuz you by your stink. Mebbe you take bath soon?"

"Never mind the humor, Great Warrior, I got somethin' for you to do."

"You call me 'Great Warrior' means you ain't gonna let me have no fun. You gonna make enemies dead, not let me help. Give me squaw work."

"Never mind givin' me all that garbage, Two Buffalo. I need you to get Sanchez soon's you can, an' both o' you get back to me *rapido*."

The old Indian stood, picked up his rifle, and gave Fallon a sour look. "Go now. Come back. Make enemies dead."

Fallon went from the livery to the hotel, and in the lobby, he told the clerk at the desk to bring up a washtub, warm water, and one bar of lye soap.

"All due respect, Mr. Fallon, don't look like one tub of water and one bar of soap's gonna do the job." He grinned when he said it.

"Son, got only enough time to use up that much soap an' water 'fore I fall into bed an' sleep till I get tired of it."

While waiting for the clerk to bring water, he cleaned and oiled his weapons, and reloaded them. He stood his rifle in the corner and his revolver on the bed stand. Then he cut strips from a clean shirt to use as bandages.

After his bath, he glanced out the window, thinking to go to the cafe, but decided against eating. Dark had set in. He locked the door and tilted a chair against it, then fell into bed.

When he awakened, the sun had not yet risen. He looked at his watch—four o'clock, an hour before the cafe opened. He pondered how to go about the next phase of his plan. He had no doubt but that he intended to get rid of Bienville and his crowd, one way or another. But he couldn't walk into their office and cut down on them. Regardless of the Frenchies' political loyalties, the U.S. law would take a dim view of killing them unless it was self-defense, and he couldn't think of a way to make it appear so. He finally settled on the only sensible option he had. He'd have to wait for Sanchez and Two Buffalo. In the meanwhile, he'd eat, then renew acquaintances with the French.

A few minutes before five, he stood, dressed, buckled on his handgun, and left his room. After eating, he headed back to the hotel to wait for Sanchez and Two Buffalo.

On the boardwalk, he reached for the door. Before he could take hold of the knob, the door opened and Bienville came out. Fallon made a show of looking at his watch, then grinned at the likable bureaucrat. "Damn, *m'sieur,* I didn't know you Frenchmen ever got up 'fore the sun. Must be big business."

"I'm expecting one of my men to return at any moment with good news. Thought I'd see if his horse is in the livery." He nodded and, while pushing past Fallon, said, "Drop in anytime, *m'sieur,* and visit. We're not very busy these days."

Fallon watched Bienville walk toward the livery. He frowned. The Frenchman would find Berne's horse and wonder why he'd not checked in after failing in his assassination attempt. Too, Bienville might wonder why Fallon always seemed to show up after fate dealt Maximilian a deadly blow. He shrugged and went to his room.

Before opening his door, he went to Escobar's room and tapped lightly. Only a moment and it opened. The Spaniard pulled the door wide and motioned with his head for Fallon to enter. After closing and locking the door, he clapped Fallon on the back. "Good to see you, *amigo.* Where have you been?"

Fallon told him all that had transpired, including Berne's fate. "He'll face a firing squad by noon, but our task now is to get Bienville and his men outta the U.S."

"Why not pull a gun on them and march 'em across the border to Juárez?"

Fallon frowned, then nodded. "Yeah, I could do it that way, but, *amigo,* I've been responsible for too much killing. I want only to get him outta my country. Besides, he has only one man left, Anton Belin I believe his name is."

Escobar shook his head. "Don't bet on it, Fallon. Bienville can snap his fingers and have twenty men at his side in an instant."

"You sure?"

"Believe it, *señor.* There are many here, some from your war, who would side with him. If you have plans for staying alive, get him out of your country, quietly and secretly."

Fallon mulled Escobar's words over a moment. "*Capitan,* I'll do as you say. Soon, prob'ly by this afternoon, there'll be two more men to help. I want you to report back to Juárez. Ain't no way I'm gonna ask you to stick your neck out farther than you have."

Escobar smiled. "Remember, *señor,* Mexico is my country. What you do is for Mexico. I'm with you." He rolled a cigarette, lighted it, and said through a cloud of smoke, "I have a friend in town who I'm certain will join us also."

"Can you trust him, Escobar?"

The slim Mexican nodded. "I'd trust Juan Valdez with my life, *señor.*"

Fallon grinned. "I didn't know Valdez was within a hundred miles. He's here, huh?"

"You know Valdez? How?"

Escobar's smoking made Fallon want to smoke. He packed and lighted his pipe, then pinned the Spaniard with a look. "You remember the first time I held up your coach? You followed two men from the holdup site, then they split. You followed me—that's when I put a bullet in your shoulder—and the man who got away without a fight, that was Valdez." He nodded. "Yeah, I know 'im."

Fallon spent a few more minutes explaining his plan to Escobar, then said, "Find Valdez, and get him here to your room, along with a good rifle. Sanchez an' Two Buffalo will be back today, so in the morning you and Valdez go to the French office as usual. I'll drop in for a visit about ten o'clock. We'll take Bienville and Belin then."

"So you're going to do it in broad daylight?"

"Figure that might be the safest way. Don't think no one's gonna believe we'd do somethin' like that in the middle of the day. Besides, I figure the men who'd side with Bienville will be sleepin' off last night's drunk. I'll have the liveryman saddle our horses, and put a pack saddle on an extra one, about nine o'clock."

Late that afternoon, Sanchez and Two Buffalo showed

up. Fallon told them of the plans. Two Buffalo responded with only a few words. "Now have fun. Somebody chase, make dead."

Knowing the old Indian as well as he did his own father, Fallon could only shake his head. Two Buffalo was not joking.

The next morning, Fallon stayed busy. By eight o'clock, he'd been to the livery and the general store, bought provisions and extra ammunition, and made sure a bedroll was behind each saddle, and rifles in the scabbards, then gone to his room to wait.

Shortly before ten, he stood, sucked in a deep breath, trying to relax his nerves, and headed for the lawyer's office. Valdez and Escobar should already be there; Sanchez and Two Buffalo were with the horses. Taking Bienville and Belin should be easy; keeping them was another story.

Fallon stepped into the office of the French contingent. Bienville, Belin, Escobar, and Valdez were the only ones there. Fallon swept the room in a glance, and eyed Bienville. "Where's Berne, my favorite word target, sleepin' late?"

The tall Frenchman cleared his throat. "He has not yet returned from his mission. I expect him at any moment."

Fallon let a hard grin surface. "Forget him, *m'sieur*. Berne faced a firing squad yesterday." In a smooth motion, he drew his Colt. "If you don't want the same fate, keep very quiet and follow me." He waved his revolver at Belin. "You, too, *m'sieur*. We're gonna take a little trip."

Bienville glanced at each of them, stood, squared his shoulders, then looked directly at Escobar, his eyes cold as an arctic wind. "I should have listened to Berne when he wanted you court-martialed. You're a traitor, *m'sieur*."

Escobar slowly shook his head. "No. I finally realized what was best for my country, *señor,* and I couldn't see an Austrian—or Frenchman—in charge of its future." His voice hardened. "Now, come quietly and you'll not be hurt."

Valdez and Escobar had drawn their weapons when Fallon drew his. He shook his head. "No. Holster your weapons. No need to draw undue attention." He nudged the Frenchmen toward the back door. "Move out."

Fallon's two allies fell in on either side of Bienville and Belin; Fallon brought up the rear. He, too, holstered his Colt. The walk to the livery went without incident.

If any of the five had looked up when they got there and loaded the two Frenchmen on, tied them to their saddles, they would have seen a burly, unshaven man, in articles of Union uniform, take in the scene below with more than normal curiosity. They left the livery at a fast trot.

Bienville, his face hard, set in concrete, stared straight ahead. After about an hour, he looked at Fallon. "What do you intend doing with us, and what business is it of yours what we do in the United States?"

"Gonna get you off American soil first, then I'll make up my mind what to do with you." He hesitated, frowned, and looked at Valdez. "*Amigo,* I got a feelin' I'm gonna need your rifle before this day is done, but there's somethin' more important. Want you to go back to Franklin, hire some men to help you, then clean out and box everything in the French office. Got someone I want to send it to; someone who'll know how to analyze it."

"You sure, *señor*? I also have a feeling my rifle is going to be very valuable to you."

Fallon's leg was hurting; he didn't want more fighting, more killing, but he knew before he got Bienville into Mexico it was a safe bet there would be shooting. He smiled tiredly at the handsome Spaniard. "Juan, if I didn't think what I'm asking of you to be more important than what we're doing, I guarantee I'd keep you with me. Now, circle down toward the river going back and be very careful to avoid any group of horsemen. I figure even now we have men chasin' us."

Bienville, his face red with anger, interrupted. "You touch anything in that office, it'll be a violation of French sovereignty."

This was the first time Fallon had seen him lose his temper. He shook his head. "Tsk, tsk, *m'sieur*. Who is violating that? If in fact you have any claim to sovereign rights, there are no U.S. representatives involved; only a lone cowboy. And I might add, *m'sieur,* that cowboy can be very hard to catch. If your henchman Berne were here, he could vouch for that. Fact is, ask *Señor* Escobar, he can tell you."

The Frenchman stared at Fallon, his jaw slack. "You are the *Bandido Caballero*?"

Fallon shook his head. "No more, *m'sieur,* but long enough for the gold shipments intended for Maximilian to end up in Juárez's coffers." He shrugged. "Now, no more gold—no more *bandido*. I have served *El Presidente* honorably."

Valdez cut in. "And I'll add 'with distinction' to those words, *amigo*."

"Thank you, *señor*. Now, if you'll hightail it back to Franklin, and do what I ask, before we get in a real shoot-out, I'd appreciate it."

Valdez held up his hand in farewell and urged his horse toward the Rio Grande.

Fallon looked over his shoulder toward Franklin. A dust cloud boiled above the brow of a distant hill. "Check your rifles, *amigos;* we must find a place we can defend, our four against," he studied the cloud, "I'd guess maybe fifteen or more men."

With a last, longing look toward the disappearing Valdez, wishing he had been able to keep him and his rifle, Fallon kicked his horse into a run.

A hill loomed ahead. It looked like a pile of boulders, stacked as though some giant hand had picked up a few dozen at a time and dropped them at random on top of one another; huge slabs leaned against others, and smaller boulders piled against those. Fallon waved his arm in that direction.

"Stay close together for the first volley, then spread to keep them guessin' how many we are."

Two Buffalo rode alongside, grinning. "Have fun now—make dead?"

Fallon, although not feeling like it, returned the old warrior's grin. "Yeah, you savage bastard, make all dead."

Two Buffalo opened his mouth and gave a war cry that curdled Fallon's blood.

At the rocks, they dragged their horses into the most sheltered part of the piled-up boulders, pulled the Frenchmen from their horses, and tied them together, back to back.

"Don't fire till you got a sure shot, men. They ain't got the protection we have, so empty every saddle you can during the first minutes. I figure they gonna withdraw after that. If they lose enough at first, they might go home."

Sanchez mumbled, "Don't bet on it, Tomas. Depends on how much they gonna get paid for this shindig."

The dust cloud drew closer, then at the top of a land swell, horses materialized out of the dust. Fallon waited until the attackers were within two hundred yards before he drew a fine bead on the lead rider, took a deep breath, held it a moment, let it out, and squeezed the trigger. The man fell over his horse's rump. By then, Fallon's friends were firing. Three more fell from their horses. In the sound of shots Two Buffalo let out his not-of-this-world war cry again, and shouted, "Make dead, make dead."

Fallon put his sights on another rider—and dropped him. Two more men hit the ground at the same time, then three riders tried to pull their ponies to the side but fell from the saddle, pulling their horses down with them. The riders behind piled into the downed horses. More ponies fell, screaming their fright, some of them hurt badly. Their riders, those who were able, got to their feet and ran. The first charge ended.

"Hold your fire, men," Fallon shouted. He didn't want to kill needlessly. Two Buffalo continued throwing lead at the attackers, yelling like the Apache he was. Fallon scrambled over a boulder to get to him, and pushed the barrel of his rifle skyward. "Hold it. They're runnin'."

Two Buffalo looked at him, his eyes wild. "Much fun. Make dead." He pulled his rifle down to aim. "Get more."

Fallon swept his arm against the rifle, again knocking the barrel up. "No more shootin'. They've had enough—for now."

Two Buffalo looked from Fallon to the retreating riders. His shoulders drooped. He looked like a spanked child. "No fun. Make *all* dead."

The attackers withdrew out of rifle range. There were five who still sat their horses. Fallon counted the bodies at the base of his rock fortress; eight lay stretched out, not moving, and three crawled toward the small group of horsemen. He let them go.

He turned his attention to his men. Roberto Sanchez had a sprinkling of bloody spots on his right sleeve. "*De nada, amigo,* rock fragments."

Fallon knew Two Buffalo was all right, but he didn't see Escobar. Only a few moments' search among the boulders brought him to a great slab tilted toward the hill. Escobar lay at its base holding each hand against a blood-soaked hole—one in his side and one high in his right shoulder. His face twisted in pain. He looked at Fallon bending over him. "Shoulder'll heal; don't know about the one in my side. Take a look."

Fallon ripped the Mexican's shirt to bare the two holes. He looked for bubbles in the blood still oozing from the wounds, and found none. Then he checked Escobar's mouth and lips. No blood. He sighed with relief. "Don't look like either one nicked your lungs, but we gotta get you to a doctor."

The Mexican shook his head. "Don't. Too chancey. Bienville's men'll be back with help. Bandage me and leave me here. I'll keep 'em off you. Give you a chance to put distance behind you."

Fallon shook his head. "No way, *amigo.* I'd turn Two Buffalo loose on Bienville and his cohort 'fore I'd do that." He looked over his shoulder. "Sanchez, dress Escobar's wounds. I'll check Bienville and Belin.''

The tall Frenchman looked up at him when he approached. "They'll be back, Fallon. My men don't give up easily.'' Bienville showed no fear, only a resolve to get even. Belin, on the other hand, stared at him with fear-and pain-filled eyes.

"I'm hit, *m'sieur*.''

It took Fallon only a few seconds to determine Belin had no more than a crease along his shoulder. "You'll live. I've seen worse rope burns than what you got.'' He stood, checked the horses, then went to Sanchez, and in little above a whisper, said, "Roberto, take Escobar to the general. He'll have doctors. We'll see Bienville's taken care of.''

"Hell, Fallon, that'll leave only you and Two Buffalo. Bienville's men come back with reinforcements and there's no way you can hold 'em off.''

"Don't intend to try. Gonna run like hell.'' He glanced out at the field of battle. " 'Fore you leave, take your pony and round up six of those horses runnin' loose out there; their owners ain't gonna need 'em. Give each of us an extra mount. Can Escobar ride?''

"*Sí, señor,* I'll ride if you can get me on a horse.''

Less than a half hour later, Fallon watched Sanchez and Escobar on their way. The way the Mexican sat the saddle caused Fallon to shudder and hurt for him. Then he and Two Buffalo got the Frenchmen on horses and set out at a pace that would have killed a horse if they'd had but one apiece, but that was what he'd counted on. Any pursuit Bienville's men gave, he figured them for only one horse each. He said a silent prayer he was right.

They skirted several small settlements on the American side of the river. Fallon had them change horses every hour. Finally, the sun sinking low on the horizon, he looked for a campsite they could defend. The best he found was the riverbank.

In some distant past the Rio Grande had carved deep into the desert floor, leaving an escarpment of about fifty feet on the U.S. side, about a quarter mile from the river's edge. Fallon thought to cross the river and defend from the Mexican bank if he had to, but put the thought aside. He wanted to get far from any settlement, Mexican or American, and if he stayed on the U.S. side and needed anything, he was more apt to find it. But he hedged his bet. He rode to the river and found a place they could ford with some safety—if they had to.

He spread the Frenchmen's bedding within the circle of firelight, then he and Two Buffalo went away from the fire, into the dark, to spread their blankets. Bienville's men might not have returned to Franklin for support. They might have figured to follow and wait for a better chance, a less defensible spot in which Fallon might camp.

He went to where the old Indian lay. "Keep your ears open, Great Warrior, might have another chance to 'make dead.' Figure they'll come from the desert, afoot." He knew Two Buffalo would hear anything a good watchdog could. He went to his blankets, closed his eyes, and instantly slept.

It seemed he'd no more than closed his eyes when he felt a light touch on his shoulder. "They come, *señor*."

Fallon put his hat on, pushed his feet into his boots, belted his holster, and picked up his rifle. Then he stopped all movement, his ears attuned to the quiet of the desert. A slight scraping sound reached his ears. Cloth against brush. Another sound, a different kind of scraping. Someone slithered toward the camp. He didn't move. The next sound told him Two Buffalo had gone to work. A thud, a moan. Knife, Fallon thought.

As still as one of the rocks that lay around, Fallon listened for the scrape of material on brush again, then a dark shape, less than two feet from him, crawled toward the fire. He pulled his Bowie, lunged toward the shadowy bulk of the man, and thrust straight out. The handle twisted in his hand. The blade had hit bone. When it twisted, it slipped to the side and went in to the hilt. The man groaned loud enough to alert the others they were expected.

Fallon pulled his knife free and, as silent as a vagrant

breeze, moved a few feet to the side and again squatted, not moving a muscle. He'd been in this kind of situation before; the first man to move would likely be the next corpse.

Silence followed, the only sound that of a slight sighing wind caressing the desert plants in passing. Even the night animals stopped scurrying about, as though helping him listen.

An hour passed. Fallon waited. Then came a muted crack, probably a dried twig from a creosote bush. A man crawled to pass between Fallon and the fire. He never made it. Fallon's arm lifted, and his hand reached to the back of his shirt collar and swept forward. His throwing knife buried itself high in the intruder's side. The attacker uttered a guttural, growling noise and stood, his hand trying desperately to reach the knife under his armpit. He stumbled toward the fire and fell at its edge.

Another sound came, that of running feet, running away from where Fallon had stopped after throwing his knife; then the loud scream of a man in agony cut short by two thumps sounding like two hard knife thrusts to a man's body. Two Buffalo had had more fun.

Fallon figured the danger was over, but he held his position another hour before standing and calling the old Indian to the fire.

# CHAPTER

# 25

WHEN TWO BUFFALO WALKED TO THE FIRE, FALLON pinned him with a gaze. "How many?"

The old Indian grinned and held up three fingers. Fallon nodded. Five men, and there hadn't been a single gunshot. That accounted for all of those he'd seen withdraw from the rocky hillside. They hadn't had time to go to Franklin, get reinforcements, and come this far. Now he could take time to fix breakfast before heading out.

He glanced at Bienville, who sat up, yawned, stretched, and grumbled, "Never get used to you savage Americans getting up before daylight. You going to build a fire so we can have a hot breakfast?"

Fallon smiled. "No reason why not. Reckon we got 'bout as much time as we need."

Bienville frowned. Fallon figured he must wonder why the change in attitude. Why weren't they going to saddle up and get going with the possibility of more men on their trail?

After breakfast, they rode well into the morning, and every few minutes the Frenchman twisted to look behind, obviously wondering why his men weren't close on Fallon's tail.

After several hours of this, Fallon gave Bienville a hard-eyed stare. "You can relax, *m'sieur;* they won't be coming. While you slept, they called on us. Two Buffalo an' I took care of them."

"You joke, Fallon. I heard not one shot after I went to my blankets."

Fallon nodded. "Knives do their work right quiet, *m'sieur.* Bank on it, they won't be coming. You're through."

Bienville slumped, looked again to their backtrail, then gave Fallon an icy stare. "You will not get away with this, *m'sieur.* I'm going to report this whole affair to my government."

Fallon let his lips crinkle at the corners. "Report and be damned, Bienville. I don't give a damn 'bout you, or your gov'ment."

They rode all that day and much of the next. Then, well away from either an American or Mexican settlement, Fallon led them across the Rio Grande, and another two days into the desert. He stopped, had Two Buffalo cut the feet of the two Frenchmen loose from the stirrups, drag them from their saddles, and cut their hands loose.

Fallon leaned, his arms crossed on the saddle horn. "Gonna tell you somethin', Bienville. Ain't gonna kill you or your henchman. Gonna set you free—no horse, no weapons, no lucifers, but I am gonna leave you a couple canteens of water. Any town along here might hold Juáristas, or imperialists. You take your chances. The one thing you can bet your French ass on is, if I find you anywhere along the Rio Grande, in any town, I won't be so generous the next time. I'll give you the same treatment I gave those men the other night." He grinned. "Or, I might let Two Buffalo entertain himself with you. Now, go."

The old Indian had been listening. At Fallon's words he cast Bienville a satanic grin. "Make dead, much dead."

Bienville stared at Fallon, long and hard. "You're sending us to our death. We can't survive with only two canteens of water, no weapons, no matches, and nothing to eat.''

"Better hope you can, Bienville. This's your only chance.'' He nodded to the south. "Somewhere out yonder is Monterrey, Saltillo, or perhaps some other town where you might find others who believe as you do. I'm betting you won't make it.''

He watched the two until they were lost in the maze of ocotillo, yucca, prickly pear, and greasewood. "*Vamanos,* Great Warrior, let's go home.''

On the way to Franklin, Fallon led them a couple of miles around the rocky hill where they'd had their fight. A great mass of vultures circled over the area, and Fallon held his breath, thinking he could smell the rotting bodies from where he rode. His only consolation? They had asked for what they got.

Another day and they rode into Franklin. Fallon stabled the horses, told Two Buffalo the fun was over, no more "make dead,'' and told him to go back to the ranch. From the livery, Fallon went directly to what had been Bienville's office.

Juan Valdez and three men were putting the last of the French papers in boxes. He looked up when Fallon walked in, and with a solemn look said, "Knew you were on your way in, *señor.* The wind is from that direction. Thought it might be you when you were a couple miles out.''

Fallon raised his eyebrows. "That bad?''

Valdez threw him a crooked grin. "Damned near, but how'd it go? You lose anybody?''

"Don't know. Escobar took a bad one in the side, an' one in the shoulder. If Sanchez got 'im to the doctor 'fore he bled to death, he'll make it.''

Valdez stared at the floor a moment and, barely above a whisper, said, "I hope so, *amigo;* he is a very good friend.''

Fallon nodded. "My friend, too. Let's hope he makes it.'' He looked at the stack of boxes. "Gonna rent a freight wagon, take these boxes to a man who'll know how to look at 'em.''

While Fallon negotiated for a wagon, Sanchez ducked his head through the livery doors, stepped from his horse, and nodded. "Escobar'll be all right. I stayed with 'im till the doc said he was outta the woods. Gonna be in that field hospital awhile, but the sawbones says, barring infection, he'll make it.''

Fallon sighed. "Best news I heard in some time. Valdez'll be glad to hear it, too.'' He went to a bale of hay and sat, then he told Sanchez what had happened since he left the rocky hill with Escobar. When he finished, he gave his friend a tired grin. "Reckon you can go home to Carmella, Roberto, we done our job. I figure the little Zapotec can handle things on his own now.''

"Tomas, if *mi esposa* misses me as much as I do her, I reckon we're gonna have us a right nice honeymoon— again.''

Fallon laughed. "Sanchez, seems to me you two been havin' one long honeymoon ever since you married. Now, I gotta get a bunch of boxes delivered to General Sheridan. When I get back, I figure to go courtin'.''

Sanchez rubbed the palms of his hands on his jeans, then looked at Fallon. "You're serious about that little woman, aren't you?''

"Roberto, I never seen a woman I cared for before. Yeah, I'm serious. Don't know how she feels 'bout me, though. Reckon I ain't gonna find out till I try.''

Deadpan, Sanchez stared at him. "Tomas, you know your mama gonna give you hell for sayin' 'ain't.' ''

Fallon didn't take time to rest, bathe, or eat. He took the wagon to Valdez, packed it, and headed out.

TWO DAYS LATER, FALLON PULLED THE EIGHT-HORSE team to a halt in front of Sheridan's headquarters tent. He returned the sentry's salute and went in. "Don't get too

close, General. I figure you mighta smelled me comin'
from a mile out.''

"Fallon, from what Captain Escobar tells me, you've
done one helluva job. Sit down. Tell me about it.''

Fallon brought the general up to date on his activities,
then grinned. "General, for some time now I ain't known
whether I was in the Army or actin' on my own. Anyway,
if I'm in, I want out, if I ain't in, leave it be.''

Sheridan frowned, stared toward the tent opening, and
looked at Fallon. "Hate to hear you say that, boy. I need
men like you. I have a vacancy for you here in my command; it's yours if you'll take it.''

"No, General, thanks anyway, but I'm just a cowboy.
That's all I want to be. I'm tired of mandatory killin',
war, not seein' my folks, no wife to come home to. An'
the worst of it is, I'm not buildin' anything for the future—now that I have a future.'' He shook his head.
"That's it, sir. I want out.''

"So be it.'' Sheridan nodded toward the wagon outside.
"What you bring me?''

"Everything Bienville had in his office. Figured you'd
have somebody who'd make sense of it. Tell me where
you want it an' I'll drive the wagon there, get it unloaded,
and head back to Franklin.

"I mentioned I didn't have a wife to go home to? Well,
I'm gonna try to change that situation.'' He stood. "With
your permission, sir, I'd like to visit Captain Escobar, tell
'im what happened after he left.''

General Sheridan stood, shook Fallon's hand, wished
him well, and said he'd have his orderly take him to see
the captain. "When you get through, I'll have your backpay and discharge papers. Pick 'em up on the way out.''

Two hours later—no rest, no bath, no food—Fallon
headed back to town despite Sheridan's urging him to stay
and take care of all three. He was a free man, free to
control his life as he saw fit—and that didn't include any
fighting, unless it was forced on him.

When Fallon went through the lobby, he told the same

kid who had been at the desk before, "Bathwater, lye soap, an' towels."

The kid shook his head. "Seems like that's all you ever say to me, Mr. Fallon. Cain't say as how you don't need 'em, though. I'll have 'em to your room soon's I can heat some water."

Fallon had stepped toward the stairs when the young man stopped him. "Sir, got this letter for you. Looks sorta important."

Fallon recognized Juárez's handwriting on the envelope, and the melted wax on the flap had the president's seal stamped in it. He tore it open.

In *El Presidente's* own handwriting, Juárez invited him to an informal dinner with him and a few close friends. The invitation was for Saturday night—two days from then. The note also said Joan Boniol would be there. If the invitation had been for this same night, tired as he was, Fallon would have gone.

The next two days, Fallon spent sleeping, eating, and thinking of Joan, wondering what she would do when he told her he was the bandit who'd held up her coach several times. Even if she changed her political beliefs, and joined the Juáristas, would she forgive him putting her life in jeopardy? Would she forgive him for sending her home when he went after Berne? Would she forgive him, even though he couldn't help it, for looking on her naked body when Berne had her staked to the ground? His breath shortened thinking of the way she'd looked—dirty, scared, embarrassed, but to his mind the most beautiful, desirable woman he'd ever seen.

Maybe he could get Juárez to talk to her, but with that thought his face hardened. Hell, he'd always forked his own broncs; he'd continue to do so. Besides, he wasn't ashamed of what he'd done; fact was, he felt a great sense of pride.

Late Saturday afternoon, rested, clean, and dressed as a *caballero,* Fallon hesitated to wear his gun, studied on it a moment, then decided to strap it on. He could take it off at the door of Juárez's headquarters. About to go out the door, he again stopped and went to his saddlebags, dug to the bottom, and took from them the small revolver he'd taken from Joan Boniol's reticule the first time he stopped her coach. That day seemed like a lifetime ago.

He stuck the weapon inside his shirt, wondering why he did so, then smiled to himself. Anyone watching would think he'd prepared for a gunfight instead of a state dinner.

At the bridge, Fallon nodded with approval. Juárez had posted riflemen there to protect against imperialists trying to enter El Paso del Norte from the American side.

The guards at the bridge had no reason to recognize him, dressed as he was. He showed the invitation with Juárez's seal on the flap and they waved him on.

At the door to the headquarters building, he went through the same routine. Juárez met him at the door.

"Ah, *mi amigo,* you are early, as I hoped you would be. Tell me about the *importante* business you had when you last left me; business so important you couldn't stay in El Paso del Norte long enough to call on the *señorita.*"

Fallon raised his eyebrows. "Well, figure you haven't time to listen to a long, drawn-out story, so I'll make it short. In the future you won't be worried with Bienville and his crowd. Didn't kill 'em, but if they don't die where I left 'em, reckon they gonna be gone a long time. That important enough?"

"I knew it had to be something like that, Fallon." Juárez changed the subject. "Does the *señorita* still not know you are the *bandido* who caused her so much trouble?"

Fallon shook his head. "As far as I know, she has no idea I'm anything more than a rancher's son from upriver. I'm surprised, though, she hasn't put it together. Some of the things I did sort of dovetailed with those of the bandit."

They had a drink before the other guests began to arrive. The first to arrive were brothers, Generals Porfirio and Felix Diaz. Others high in Juárez's government also came in, by twos and threes. Soon there were more than a hundred people milling about, talking, drinking.

Looking at them, Fallon wondered what Juárez would call a large party, if this was "small and informal." It was then Joan came in, escorted by one of Juárez's aides. Her gaze flicked back and forth across the room, passed him, and returned to rest on his face. Her expression hardened, her chin tilted, and without a nod, a smile, or acknowledgment of any kind, she looked the other way.

Fallon felt blood rush to his face. So that's the way it's going to be. Well, damned if he was going to let it end this way. He excused himself to the person he was talking with and headed across the room. When he managed to thread his way through the throng, she was no longer there. Where had she gone? He searched for her until dinner was announced. One of Juárez's aides escorted him to the raised dais, and seated him next to *El Presidente*.

Fallon looked at the officer. "You sure about this? There are generals here, top generals, any one of whom should sit next to the president, rather than me."

The officer smiled. "*Sí, señor, El Presidente* himself ordered it. Be seated *por favor*."

Seated, looking out over the crowd, searching for Joan, Fallon was hardly aware of the others being seated at the head table, until a faint, but unmistakable, scent reached his nostrils. Joan's perfume. He twisted to look next to him.

She sat there, and stared out at the people being seated at the tables, her face set in stubborn lines.

"Don't know what I've done to deserve this, *Señorita* Boniol, but whatever it is, I apologize."

She looked at him, her blue eyes cold as a winter morning. "*Señor* Fallon, you came through this town when you turned *M'sieur* Berne over to the president. That was well over a week ago.

*Señor* Juárez had your invitation to this dinner delivered to the hotel in Franklin. You were that close, yet you weren't interested enough to come see me. Well, *señor,* if you were no more interested than that, I can hardly see why I should show you anything more than I would a casual acquaintance.''

"Joan, after dinner will you give me only a few minutes? I assure you I can explain everything, and you'll think my reasons are good ones. I swear on my mother's grave.''

"Your mother is very much alive. She's not yet in her grave, but with a son like you I don't doubt she soon will be. No. I can't think of a thing you could say that would excuse your behavior.''

Through dinner they sat there as though a wall separated them. Every so often he slanted a glance at her from the corners of his eyes. At first his sense of loss tightened his chest, a knot formed in his throat, then blood mounted in his head, angry blood. Soon anger replaced any emotion he'd originally felt. If he'd felt any sense of neglect or wrongdoing, he would have admitted it, but he'd done only what duty and his sense of right made him do. Joan Boniol was a proud, stubborn, unreasonable female. He didn't need that.

When all had finished eating, Juárez stood and tapped his spoon on his wine goblet. "*Señors, señoras, señoritas,* and honored guests.'' He seemed to look at each of the people at the tables. "I have called this dinner to honor a man who some of you already know, though some have not had that pleasure. This man has done so many things for me I'll not enumerate them here, but suffice it to say, he single-handedly saved my life; and perhaps more, he has done as much as any officer here to save the Republic. He is not only a staunch ally, but, *mis amigas y amigos,* he is my friend, one I love as a son. He did not know this dinner was in his honor, so I'm certain he has no prepared speech. I now want all of you to welcome *Señor* Tomas Fallon.''

Fallon's mind had been wandering. Through his anger he wondered what he could do to thaw Joan, to make her listen to him. He didn't hear any of Juárez's introduction. Joan, for the first time, acknowledged that he sat there. She nudged him, and said under her breath, "*El Presi-*

*dente* just introduced you as the honored guest of this affair. Show your manners—if you have any.''

Fallon snapped out of his funk, glanced at those seated in front of him, and grinned, trying not to show his embarrassment. He stood amid a round of applause, wondered what this was all about, then decided that blunt honesty might serve him here as it had in the past. He acknowledged the guests, then looked at Juárez. "*Señor Presidente,* I apologize. Reckon I figured yours was going to be just another dry, long-winded, after-dinner political speech. I wasn't listening.''

Total quiet settled over the crowd. Juárez was the first to laugh, then one among the guests couldn't hold it in and laughed uproariously. That broke the ice; the entire audience laughed.

Juárez sobered, looked at Fallon with an amused smile, and said, "*Señor* Fallon, this dinner is in your honor. I told our guests you saved my life, and I want to take this opportunity to thank you, if words can thank another for such a deed.''

Fallon, still embarrassed, shrugged. "*De nada, Señor Presidente,* I just happened to be in the right place at the right time, but I'll assure you, *señor,* I would do the same thing a hundred more times to keep the Republic in your hands. I do thank you for this honor. I-I had no idea this was all for me.'' Applause again thundered against the walls.

Juárez picked up a long wooden box from the floor at his side. "I had one of our silversmiths plate and engrave this as a token of my sincere thanks to a great friend.'' He handed the box to Fallon.

He lifted the hinged lid. A Winchester .44 rifle, model 1866, rested inside. It was engraved to read: "To Tomas Fallon from one who loves you like a son. Your friend, Benito Juárez.''

Fallon read the inscription to the guests, although he had a problem getting words past the lump in his throat, and seeing through the moisture clouding his eyes. He took out his handkerchief, wiped his eyes and nose, and looked at Juárez. *"Mi Presidente, muchas gracias ..."* He choked, could not finish, reached out and pulled Juárez to his chest. And only for Juárez's ears, he whispered, "Friends forever. If you ever again need me, I'll be there." Applause again thundered against the walls.

The remainder of the evening Fallon stayed clear of Joan. She'd made it obvious she wanted nothing to do with him. More effort on his part to explain would only make matters worse.

After all the handshaking and congratulations, he went back to his hotel determined to think of something to make her listen. Then angry blood again pushed aside his thoughts of trying to mend things between them. And then his anger mellowed and he again thought of the petite copper-haired woman he'd spent so many nights wishing to be at his side. He swallowed the hard knot in his throat. He'd get her attention one way or another.

# CHAPTER

# 26

IN HIS ROOM, FALLON POURED A GLASS OF THE RAW whiskey, poured it back in the bottle, thought to go to the saloon and play poker, and cast that aside as a sorry idea. In his frame of mind, he'd lose. Finally, he unbuckled his gunbelt, hung it over the bedpost, and sat on the edge of the bed.

Damned stubborn woman sat there all night and gave him the silent treatment. What was there about women that made them think silence ever solved anything—unless she just plain didn't give a damn about him? He'd seen his mother treat his father the same way, and in the end Pa apologized, although Fallon would have bet his prized saddle his father didn't know half the time for what he was asking forgiveness. Maybe he'd be better off to forget the whole thing—stay single. No. He was damned if he'd let her get off that easy.

Finally, he stood, undressed, and put Joan's little revolver on the bed stand. Before snuffing the lamp, he lay there staring at the ceiling. When he reached to turn the lantern down, his eyes rested on her handgun. He withdrew his hand from the lamp and stared at the small weapon. He thought a minute, shrugged, and mumbled,

"Worth a chance. If it don't work, things ain't gonna be any worse than they are now." He turned, trimmed the wick, and went to sleep.

THE NEXT MORNING, FALLON WENT TO THE LIVERY AND arranged to rent a horse. Joan had seen his big bay and would know it from a block away. While at the stable, he rubbed the bay down, gave him a bucket of corn, and made sure the liveryman took good care of him.

Then, for the first time, he wished he was back east, where there were flower shops. Women liked flowers. But wishing to buy a bouquet in Franklin was like wishing for the pot at the end of the rainbow. Instead, he searched for a gift through everything the general mercantile store had in stock. No luck. Then he thought of a house he'd passed in El Paso del Norte. Someone in that house had planted flowers; he'd seen them through the wrought iron fence—roses, bougainvillea, honeysuckle, ferns, black-eyed susans, and others he didn't know the names of. Maybe that someone would sell him a fistful. With that in mind he went back to his room, took pen and paper, and began to write.

It was a brief note, but somewhere Fallon had heard brevity was stronger than wordiness. "Dear *Señorita* Boniol: It is my wish to return something of yours which I've had for quite a while. I thought to keep it, for it is the only possession of yours I'm likely to ever have, but after careful consideration I knew that would be not quite honest, and despite rumors to the contrary, I am an honest and honorable man.

"I beg of you to receive me at seven o'clock tonight. You will be safe in my presence." He signed it, "Sincerely, The *Bandido*." He hired a messenger to deliver the message to Joan.

While at the store, he'd bought a new bandanna, and when he dressed to go across the river, he took care to dress exactly as he had when preparing for his holdups of the coach. Then, he wrapped and boxed Joan's revolver, tied a bow around the box, and went from the hotel.

In El Paso del Norte, he tied his horse at the hitchrack in front of the *casa* with the flowers. At his knock, a servant answered the door. "Will you tell the *señora* a *caballero* bent on an honorable mission wishes to speak with her?" He spoke Spanish.

The maid studied him a moment, and although he was clean, she cast a disdainful look at his jeans and work shirt. "*Caballeros* do not call on ladies dressed as you are, *señor*."

Fallon's voice hardened. "I did not ask your opinion of my dress, woman. Tell your mistress I, Señor Tomas Fallon, am here."

The mousey little maid scurried away. In a moment, a kindly gray-haired woman came to the door. "Yes, *señor*?"

Affairs of the heart were irresistible to the warm-blooded Spanish, so Fallon explained to the woman that he was bent on winning his lady's heart and, in the absence of a flower shop, hoped she might soften her heart enough to sell him a small bouquet of fresh blooms from her garden.

She glanced at the wrapped box he held. Her face softened. "No, *señor,* I will not sell you my flowers," she smiled, "but for so wonderful a cause, I myself will cut you a bouquet. Come."

Fallon followed her into the garden, where she cut flowers until he had to ask her to stop. "You're sure, *señor*? For so handsome a *caballero* I will cut many more."

He smiled. "*Señora, muchas gracias,* but I assure you, you have already exceeded any generosity I might have hoped for." He held out his hand for the flowers. She walked past him. "Come, I'll wrap them in moist moss; to keep them fresh, you see."

Before he left, the lady exacted a promise he would stop and visit at some other time, and let her know how his lady responded to his courtship.

On his ride over, he had decided not to go to Joan as

the *bandido;* he'd go as Tom Fallon and she could like it or not.

Only a few houses from that of the flower lady, he stopped in front of Joan's *casa.* He knocked, waited a moment, and knocked again. Joan's maid answered his knock. "Tell the *señorita,* Tomas Fallon wishes to see her, *por favor.*"

In a moment the maid was back. "The *señorita* asked me to tell you she doesn't desire to see you, *señor.* Besides, she has another guest who'll be calling at seven."

"You tell the *señorita* I'll sit here on her doorstep if she doesn't let me in. Tell her I'll tell her other guest I was here first, and will fight him for her favor."

This time, Joan came to the door. "Can't you accept no for an answer, *señor*? I do not wish to see you."

"All right, I'll just sit here until you relent." He pulled his watch from his pocket and checked the time. "It is twenty minutes of seven, twenty minutes until your guest arrives. Let me in and I'll leave peaceably when he arrives. If you don't, I'll sit here and cause a scene."

Fallon couldn't believe blue eyes could shoot such a cold flame. Her look scorched him. "If you were a gentleman, you'd leave. The person coming to see me is a gentleman, a very dangerous gentleman. As disgusting as you are, I don't wish to see you harmed. Come in, but for only ten minutes—that's all."

She refused the flowers he tried to hand her, but the maid took them and put them in water. Standing in the middle of the floor, Joan stared at him. "All right, what is it you want?"

"Like I said in my note, I have something of yours I wish to return."

"You, you wrote that note and signed it the bandit? How despicable. You even lie to gain your way."

Fallon's face stiffened, felt like dry paper. "Ma'am, ain't nobody ever called me a liar." He thrust the box at her. "Here. I said I had something of yours, and here it is. I'll let myself out. Good night, and good-bye."

She pulled her hand from the box as though from a hot

stove. "Whatever it is, *señor,* keep it. If you have touched it, I'm sure it is no longer of worth to me."

Fallon gripped the box in his right hand, spun, lifted the latch, stepped outside, and pulled the door toward him. He looked through a red haze. This time he made no effort to push his anger aside. He toed the stirrup and kicked his rented horse into an all-out run.

When he crossed the bridge back into Franklin, Juárez's guards stepped in front of his horse to try to stop him, but apparently thought better of it when he didn't slow the rented mustang. They jumped to the side, then tried to bring their rifles to bear on him, but he was past and in the middle of the throng of people in Franklin's only street. They would not shoot a man on American soil.

THE MOMENT THE DOOR SLAMMED BEHIND FALLON, JOAN ran to stop him. What was she doing? She'd let her stubborn pride stand between her and the man she loved. She pushed the door open, words already formed on her tongue to call him back, to apologize. She was only in time to see him toe the stirrup and ride full-tilt toward Franklin.

Fear tightened her chest, threatened to push a sob past the lump in her throat. Now she'd done it. She'd refused to let him explain, and she admitted to herself he'd tried, hard, twice to get her to listen. She'd refused his flowers and gift, and then topped it all by calling him a liar, something Tom Fallon would not excuse.

She watched him until he was out of sight, her shoulders slumped, tears misting her eyes, tears of anger toward herself. She went back inside, closed the door behind her, walked to the center of the room, and stood, trying to think. What was she to do now? What could she do to make Tom know she cared? He was the only man she'd ever given her lips, the only man—well, almost the only man, who caused a warmth in her body, and a swelling in her heart. What did she know about the other man, the *bandido;* she only knew that his very presence during the holdups excited her as only Tom had before him. Regardless of how this turned out, she was going to find Tom and tell him of her feelings—and ask forgiveness.

After a great while, Joan realized she stood in the center of the room, staring at the wall, her maid standing to the side wringing her hands. "Is there something I can help you with, *señorita*? I 'ave never seen you so troubled by a man before. He is the one you love, is he not, *señorita*?"

"Yes, Teresa, and now I've done a very foolish thing. I may have lost him." She straightened her shoulders, knots forming at the back of her jaws, her tears dried. "But, I'll tell you something, *mi amiga,* I'll not let him go without a fight. Find me a trustworthy messenger. I'll write a note while you're doing that—then help me pack. Pack yourself a bag, too. I want you with me."

WHILE JOAN WAS BUSY PACKING, ACROSS THE RIVER from her, Fallon checked his weapons, rolled his bedroll, and stuffed his good clothing, along with the wooden box that held Joan's small handgun, into a pair of saddlebags.

The bitter taste of the scene with Joan sitting in the back of his throat would not leave him. He went to the livery for his bay horse, and then headed toward the ranch.

Not more than a mile outside of Franklin, he pulled his horse down to an easy walk. No point in killing a good horse just because his anger still burned like a lump of white-hot coal within his chest.

He'd ridden out of town without giving thought to provisions. He'd do without supper, ride straight through to the ranch, and be there in time for breakfast.

Sometime during his ride he decided to get his black horse and head into the hills. He was in no frame of mind to explain his hurt, his anger, and his frustration to his folks.

About three o'clock, still dark, he rode to the stable and swapped horses. He had only tossed his saddle across the back of the black when Two Buffalo spoke from the darkness. "Ride late. Got trouble? Me help. More kill, more fun."

Fallon had to chuckle at his bloodthirsty friend's words,

even though he knew the old Apache was not more than half joking. Two Buffalo had had as much to do with bringing him to manhood as had his mother and father. "No, old friend, this problem won't call for any killin'. It's one I'll have to solve on my own.

"Help me round up some provisions. I figure to spend a few days in the hills. Maybe the Everywhere Spirit will show me the way."

"Good thinkin', Tomas. Everywhere Spirit know everything."

Three hours later, the sun at his back pushing his shadow ahead of him, Fallon reined in in front of Indian Jake's trading post, a *jacal* with no doors or windows to fill the holes in the adobe walls. Jake's only claim to it being a trading post was the rotgut whiskey he handed across the barrel he called a bar, and the few rusted-out rifles he stocked to trade to the Mescalero.

When Fallon stepped into the small room, he and three other customers were the only ones there besides Jake. Fallon swept the three with a glance, didn't recognize them, and told Jake to give him a glass of tequila.

Jake, a Comanche breed, poured tequila in a water glass and handed the drink across the barrel to Fallon, who held out his left hand to take the glass, at the same time flicking the thong off the hammer of his revolver. Jake slanted him an oily smile. "Why you do that, Fallon, ain't nobody here gonna try you?"

Keeping his eyes on the three men, without looking at the breed, Fallon said, "Notice one thing, Jake, I'm still alive. Know why? I'm careful."

While talking to the breed, Fallon studied the others in the room. The looks of all were centered on Fallon's black horse just outside the gaping doorway. "Something wrong with my horse, *amigos*?"

As one their eyes turned to Fallon. The tall, thin, dirty one on their right shook his head. "Naw, mister, Sam here wuz jest sayin' as how he never seen such a animal here on the border. Me, Johnny Breen, put my stamp on them words." Fallon's glance moved from Breen to Sam.

"Gonna tell you somethin', Sam, they ain't no other animal like 'im nowhere on the border, an' you can tell that fat pig next to you, whatever his name is, to get whatever thoughts he has about my horse outta his mind. Ain't one of you, or all three, good enough to take 'im from me—so don't try."

The fat one had opened his mouth to say something when Breen put his hand on his arm and shook his head. The fat one's mouth clamped shut.

Fallon wondered why they seemed so reluctant to start something with the odds all in their favor. He shrugged, tossed his drink down, and walked out.

By high noon he was deep into the mountains, the black doggedly putting the flat lands behind. By mid-afternoon the hairs at the base of Fallon's skull prickled, feeling as though they stood out from his neck. The sensation stayed with him despite frequent glances to the rear. He looked for a slight dust cloud, movement—anything that might indicate someone followed, but there was no sign anyone was within a hundred miles.

The feeling wouldn't leave, and by sundown the muscles in his back, tense all afternoon, felt as though they were tied in hard knots. He had lived too long with death as his saddlemate to ignore these feelings. He looked for a campsite he could defend. A night and a day in the saddle was too much for horse or rider.

The trail he followed wound its way up the side of the mountain, most of the time only wide enough for one horse, occasionally opening to the width of two, and sometimes three, horses.

Twice, Fallon passed shelves with clusters of pines, but checked the approach to each and didn't like what he saw. He would have fair cover, but so would those tracking him.

Night set in, velvety dark, a crisp coolness to the air promising a cold that begged for a large fire, but Fallon would have no fire. He would not lead his trackers with so telltale a sign. He looked to the stars, which seemed just beyond his fingertips. Then, he felt rather than saw the kind of place he looked for. The trail widened into a small park with little cover on the approach. A cluster of dark deeper than the night surrounding him stood in the center. Trees. Aspen probably.

He headed for them, and led his horse deep into the tangled, clustered, spindly trunks. After tethering the black in the middle of the copse, Fallon worked his way back through, gathered armfuls of dry twigs which lay about on the ground, and scattered them around his campsite. If anyone tried to sneak up on him, he felt certain they'd ultimately step on one of the branches, break it, and alert him.

It wasn't until he spread his blankets that the long hours in the saddle, the nerve-tearing events of the scene with Joan, and the tension of the afternoon, knowing he was trailed, took an abrupt hold on his body, numbing his senses, turning his muscles to lead. He was so tired he dared not lie down. He'd sleep too soundly, and those following him would make his rest an everlasting one.

He spread his blankets, bunched brush under it, so as to look in the dark like he lay there, put his saddle at the head, pulled his rifle, and for some reason dropped Joan's small revolver in his coat pocket, then melted deeper into the thick growth of trees.

He sank down to rest his back against a pair of saplings, got as comfortable as the rocky ground and slim tree trunks would permit, and settled back to wait. He'd have traded a white buffalo robe for a cup of hot coffee—if he'd had a white robe.

By his best guess he sat there about three hours listening to the wind rustle the aspen leaves overhead, the movement of night animals, and straining his ears to separate usual night sounds from the slight noise an intruder would make.

Another half hour, eyelids drooping almost closed, and he came fully awake. His chest muscles tightened; the leaders in the back of his neck strained as though they would pull apart. Somewhere in the brush to his right a twig had snapped, not a loud noise, but as though a carefully placed foot had caused it to break just before being pushed into the ground. Then a hoarse whisper.

"Dammit, Fatty, step soft. You want to wake the dead?"

"Aw hell, Breen, that *hombre* ain't in these trees. He ain't got no reason to figure we're after 'im."

"Maybe not, but walk soft."

From their whispers, Fallon placed two of the three, but where was Sam? Fallon couldn't figure why three men would trail him just to steal a horse. Yeah, the black was a tremendous animal, but to chance getting killed for a horse didn't make sense. Then Sam's whisper intruded on his thoughts.

"He's in here somewhere. I found his horse." Sam's words came from off to the side of where the other two had been talking.

"Damn the horse. We want *him*. That *hombre*'s worth more money than all of us together will ever make." This time it was Breen's hoarse whisper.

"Yeah, but we gotta git 'im down into Mexico an' deliver 'im to Maximilian. That's gonna take some doin', an' that there man ain't no pansy we're about to tackle," Fatty whispered.

"You wantta back out? Get goin'. Me an' Sam'll take care o' him. We'll only have to split two ways."

"Aw now, I wuzn't meanin' nothin' like that, Breen. Let's see if we cain't find 'im, but we better stick together. Don't figure one gun's gonna put 'im down."

"Well, let's find 'im. If we stay together, we ain't likely to shoot each other. Let's go."

They moved off into the tangle of trees, making an occasional slight noise that allowed Fallon to keep track of their movements. His only break so far was that they'd decided to stay together. He didn't cotton to the idea of trying to defend himself from three directions. He figured they'd soon find his blankets, for they were moving that direction. He was right.

Fallon gave them a chance to move away from him a short way, then eased to his feet. He drifted silent as smoke toward where he'd spread his blankets, hoping they would give him some sort of warning when they found them. He wanted to be close but not right in their middle when they found the blankets.

Night vision helped some—but they had the same advantage. Then he got the break he needed. Breen's whisper, barely audible, said, "There—his blankets. Try not to kill 'im; we don't need to take a stinkin' corpse to Maximilian."

Three dark shapes dived to land on the blankets, clubbing at them with handguns. Fallon stepped into the small clearing.

"Hold it right there. Stay where you are, roll to your backs, and I won't have to kill you." With his last word, Fallon slipped to the side a few feet.

They did as he told them, only they opened fire as soon as they could bring their guns level. Fallon fired three fast shots, moved again to his right, and triggered the last three shots in his handgun. He slipped the hammer from under his thumb again, only to realize it fell on fired cartridges. He holstered his handgun, switched his rifle to his right hand, and moved farther into the dense growth.

In the dark he'd seen two of the vague shapes stretch full length and groan. Those two, by his thinking, wouldn't bother him. He thought he'd put two shots into each of the three, but couldn't be sure. "Damn you, Fallon, you laid a trap for us an' we walked into it." It was Breen's voice.

Fallon didn't answer. He stood there carrying a rifle with an empty chamber, and he wasn't about to give away his position by jacking a shell into it.

Breen gave a pain-filled chuckle. "Yore hammer's ridin' on empty, Fallon. I still got a six-shooter what ain't been fired. You try reloadin', I'll hear you, then you die." With his last word he fired twice, blindly. Fallon leaned his rifle against a tree, slipped his Bowie knife from its sheath, and circled the area, trying to get on the outlaw's blind side. When he figured he was at the bounty hunter's back, hoping his attention would be in the opposite direction, he slipped toward the spot where his saddle lay. His only chance was to get close enough to locate the outlaw, dive onto him, swing the Bowie—and hope for a lucky thrust.

He heard a groan, pulled up short, and felt a heavy bump against his left hand. He frowned and grasped his pocket. Joan's revolver. He'd forgotten he'd slipped it into his coat pocket, more to keep from losing it than from any idea he'd ever need it. He had checked it several times in the past and knew it carried shells in all six cylinders. He took it from his pocket, wishing for a .44, but this small-caliber gun might do the trick—if he got lucky. He stuck his Bowie in his belt and shifted the revolver to his right hand.

He eased himself to the ground, groped for a rock, a stick—anything that came to hand. His fingers found a stone. He picked it up and tossed it with his left hand. It landed in the brush on the opposite side of the clearing from him. Breen triggered two shots, the muzzle flashes looking almost as one.

As soon as the rock left his hand, Fallon ran toward his blankets, firing, using the flashes from the outlaw's gun to gauge where he should be. He dropped Joan's handgun and pulled his Bowie. Breen fired again. This time Fallon didn't luck out.

A blinding flash of light exploded behind his eyes. Blindly, he swung the Bowie and felt it bite into flesh. Then the deep void trying to claim him sucked him into its depths.

# CHAPTER

## 27

FALLON STIRRED, STIFLED A GROAN, AND OPENED HIS eyelids a slit. A bright red haze clouded his vision. He lay there a moment, trying to will the pounding, pulsing drums in his head to stop, trying to recall what had happened.

The scene of the night before slowly took shape in his mind, right up to the moment Breen triggered the shot that put him out. He wondered why Breen hadn't finished the job, then figured that his head wound must have bled such that Breen thought him dead. But the three outlaws had it in mind to collect the bounty Maximilian had put on him, so why hadn't Breen slung him across a saddle and headed for Mexico? All the money would now be his.

Those questions slopped around in his aching head awhile, until finally Fallon gave it up. He strained his eyelids to open eyes so he could see. This time, a small bit of daylight showed through the red. Without moving his head, he moved his eyes so as to see as much of the campsite as lying still would permit.

He lay across Sam's stiff, cold body, and by shifting his eyes only a bit, he saw Fatty a couple of feet from him, spread-eagled, sightless eyes staring at the leaves overhead. When he'd searched everything within his restricted vision, he'd seen only the two bodies.

He lay there, afraid to move, afraid to show he still lived, in case Breen sat close by with a gun pointed at him. He broke into a sweat, and his muscles tensed against the shock of the bullet he expected the outlaw to fire into him. Finally, he figured to hell with it, die now, or die a few minutes from now—what difference did it make.

He lifted his head only a bit, then afraid he'd black out again, he let it fall back to the earth. Pain lanced through from side to side behind his eyes. It felt like someone had shoved an ice pick into his skull and wriggled it around. He lay there a few moments, or a few hours—he knew not which—until he again opened his eyes. The day didn't appear to have waned much since he first tried to see.

He gritted his teeth, and again forced his eyes open, knowing Breen could put another bullet in him at any moment. He moved his head.

The slim outlaw sat against a small sapling, a satanic grin stretched over his broken and rotted teeth. His right hand holding his handgun rested on one knee, his left lay lax on the ground at his side. Fallon braced himself for the feel of a slug tearing into his body. His scalp tightened against his throbbing head, then he noticed the outlaw's eyes. A fly buzzed around Breen's head and landed on one of his staring eyeballs. Breen didn't blink. He had died like that, waiting to put another shot into Fallon, but wanting him to know it was coming.

Fallon lay there a few moments. His tensed muscles relaxed; a bit of the pain in his head subsided. Finally, he moved to free himself from Sam's body, rolled to his knees and then to his feet.

He stood there, swaying as a huge tree would before being toppled to the ground. When his head stopped swimming, Fallon looked at his shot-up blankets, discarded the idea of making a bedroll, and slowly, painfully gathered his gear. He was hungry, but he wouldn't have a fire and food here among this carnage.

He checked Breen's wounds, wanting to know what

had killed him. He found two .44 holes and three small .25-caliber holes. Joan's little gun had been the difference. He gathered his rifle, Joan's handgun, and his holey blankets, then saddled his horse, took what provisions the three bounty hunters had, and rode on up the mountain.

This time he looked for a campsite he could defend, but one he figured to spend a couple of days in while he gave his head a chance to heal, and so he could ponder what to do about Joan. He knew one thing for damn sure. If he had to hog-tie her, she was going to listen to his side of the story.

Before he found the kind of site he looked for, the sky over the western peaks showed every shade of pastel color he'd ever seen. He set up camp, boiled coffee—and went to sleep with only two swallows gone from his first cup.

JOAN'S CARRIAGE ROLLED THROUGH THE GATEWAY OF Falcon Nest. She cast looks in every direction, hoping to see Tom, but he was nowhere in the ranch yard. When she stopped at the steps of the veranda, Nita stood waiting for her.

She ran down the steps, arms outstretched. ''Joan, what in the world is wrong? Your note sounded so urgent—as though the world would end if you didn't leave immediately to come see me. Have your driver bring your luggage in, then tell me what's wrong.''

A few minutes later, her luggage stowed in her room, the driver settled in the bunkhouse, and her maid in a room of her own, Joan told Nita what had happened between her and Tom. She also told of the state dinner held in Tom's honor by Juárez, although she admitted she had not the slightest idea why Juárez had honored Tom. Then she told Nita the way she'd treated her son that night. She gave her hostess a straight-on look. ''Nita, I've been as big a fool as any woman could be, and I've found that is saying a mouthful. I love your son. I'm not going to give him up without a fight. All I want is to be able to look him in the eye and tell him how I feel—and to apologize for being such a hard-headed, stubborn fool.''

Nita rang a small silver bell sitting on the table at her side and asked the maid to bring drinks and sandwiches. She frowned, obviously thinking of what Joan had told her, then looked directly into her eyes. "Joan, if there were any way to do this without admitting you were wrong, I'd say do it that way, but I can't see an alternative."

"Nita, I don't want to play any female games with him. In the first place, he's too smart to swallow them. In the second place, it's not my way. I'll look at him straight in the eye and tell him what a double-ace fool I've been, and that I love him. I hope you and Brad don't disapprove of me, but regardless, I'm going to let him know my feelings."

Nita chuckled. "I assure you, Brad and I have talked many times since you and Tom met, and each of those times we've worried that you two would not realize you were made for each other. Why, that marriage will make the War Between the States seem like a small skirmish. Now, what do we do?"

Joan glanced about the room. "I suppose the only thing we can do is wait for Tomas to come in from whatever task Brad set him to doing this morning, and let me face him."

"But Tom hasn't returned from Franklin. I've not seen him for several days." Nita frowned and spread her hands, palms up. "I don't know where he might be. It has been seldom since he returned from the war that I've known where he was, or what he was doing." Abruptly her face brightened. "But don't worry, my dear, he'll show up sooner or later, and when he does, we'll leave you with him long enough to wring his neck if you wish. It might take something like that to get his attention." She smiled. "I think he's finally met his match." The maid brought their drinks and sandwiches, and they sat in silence for a few moments. After a bit, Nita said, "You get settled in, and no matter how long before he gets here, stay and we'll visit. It'll be nice to have another woman around the house."

• • •

JOAN HAD BEEN AT FALCON NEST ALMOST A WEEK BE-
fore Fallon felt up to the ride back to the ranch. His scalp
wound had scabbed over, but his headache persisted. After
washing his face and hands in a cold mountain stream, he
decided he'd try to make it home. The continuing headache told him he'd had a pretty bad concussion, so he
determined to ride slowly and give himself a chance to
heal inside as well as out. He packed his gear and headed
down the mountain.

Two days later he rode the black through the rear entrance of the stable, stripped the gear from him, rubbed
him down, and gave him a bucket of corn. Then he went
to the *hacienda*'s rear door and entered the kitchen. He
poured himself a water glass full of bourbon from the
bottle his father kept in the kitchen, and walked tiredly
into the front room. The first person he saw was Joan,
sitting next to his mother on the large davenport.

He pulled up short, stared at her a moment, turned, and
went back into the kitchen. She followed him.

"Tom, please don't treat me this way."

"Why not, *señorita*? It is the way you said you wanted
it the last time I saw you. I figure to accommodate a lady
any way I can." He tossed down about half of his drink,
spun, and went out the door, headed for the bunkhouse.
There, in a man's world, he knew how he'd be treated.
Her footsteps followed him down the veranda steps into
the yard. He ignored her.

Finally he heard her turn back toward the house. He
went on to the bunkhouse, and seated outside in the shade
was Two Buffalo.

The old Indian's gaze raked him from head to foot, then
centered on the scabbed-over wound along the side of
Fallon's head. "You tell me no more fight. You go find
fight, get hurt. You want all fun, Two Buffalo have
none."

"I didn't figure to have trouble, old friend." He looked
at the half-full glass of whiskey he'd taken from the

kitchen. "Come on in. I'll split this drink with you and tell you what happened."

Inside, seated on a bunk, Fallon told Two Buffalo, and part of the crew who had gathered around, what had happened. He didn't tell them why the three men who had died on the mountain wanted him.

"Not happen, you take me with you."

They talked of Fallon's most recent fight, and others the crew had been in, until the cook yelled that grub was ready and he'd throw it out if they didn't come.

Tom, with anger and hurt clouding all other feelings, didn't realize how hungry he was until he sat at the long table with the men he understood most. They ate in silence and, when they were through, washed their mess gear and went outside to smoke. It was there Joan found him.

She walked to stand in front of the row of men squatted against the wall. "Gentlemen, if you'll excuse me, I must talk with Mr. Fallon." She looked him in the eye. "Will you come listen to me, sir, or must I talk here in front of the men?"

Fallon felt blood rush to his face. Angry and embarrassed, he wouldn't let the men hear the words he knew might be said between him and Joan. He unfolded his tall frame from against the wall, stood, and walked to her.

Before he could say anything, words gushed from Joan. "Oh, Tom, you have every right to be angry. The way I treated you, then topped it off with calling you a liar. I can't blame you if you never speak to me again, but I want you to know how very sorry I am that I didn't give you a chance to talk." She'd been looking him in the eye; now she dropped her gaze. "Tom, I'm just a hard-headed, stubborn witch. I know what you must think of me, but please don't. Please try to understand how hurt I was that you didn't come see me as soon as you could."

Fallon stared at her a moment, feeling the anger, and some of the hurt, drain from him. "Gonna tell you somethin', little girl, I ain't apologizin' for bein' angry. I want you to know you can push me just so far." Then remem-

bering she didn't know he was the bandit, he said, "An'
I'll tell you somethin' else; we got a bigger problem
'tween us than me not comin' to see you. I hope it won't
make a difference,'cause if you'll say yes, I figure to make
you my wife."

"Y-you are proposing?"

" 'Fore we get into that, you better hear what I got to
say. Don't think I could stand bein' disappointed again."
Then, realizing they stood in the middle of the ranch yard,
the setting sun casting long shadows from them, he took
her arm. "Come. I got somethin' to show you."

Joan held back. "It looks like we have a lot of talking
to do, but first, let me say that if that was a proposal, I
couldn't accept without telling you something, something
that might change your mind about wanting me."

"Woman, it'd have to be mighty bad to change the way
I feel 'bout you—but go ahead, tell me."

Still standing in the yard, she locked gazes with him.
Her chin lifted, and that stubborn, determined look came
to her face again. "All right, Tom Fallon, I woulda told
you anyway, and now is as good a time as any. You have
to know I have a very strong attraction to another man, a
man I've only met a few times, a man whose face I've
never seen, and I'm afraid if he were standing here right
now I'm not sure which of the two of you I would choose
if given my choice."

Tom's face hardened to feel like dry, crinkly paper.
"You mean to say I'm competing with a man you've
never met—formally, I mean?"

"That's true. I can't explain it, Tom, it makes no sense,
but every time I've been in his presence I've been pulled
toward him as strongly as I've been to you. I've felt so
guilty, but I couldn't help it, and I couldn't come to you
as a bride without you knowing about those feelings I
have for another man."

"Well, I'll be forever damned. Here I am competing
with a ghost." He took a deep breath. "Anyway it might
not make any difference. Once you see what I'm about to
show you, you gonna know what kind of man I am." He

again took her elbow and steered her toward the stable. "After I show you what's in the stable, I'm gonna tell you why I was so long in coming to see you—an' by damn, you're gonna listen or I'll take you over my knee."

Joan bristled like a porcupine, her chin came up, her eyes turned icy—then her shoulders sagged. She nodded. "I'll listen."

Fallon walked her to the back stall, where his saddle-bags hung over a partition. He reached into one, moved his hand about, shook his head, then reached in the other and pulled out her small revolver. He held it out to her. "This I believe is yours."

"Wh-why that looks like my *pistola*. The one the *bandido* took from my reticule. How did you get it, Tom?"

He didn't answer, but swung the stall door open wide so she could see the black horse within. "That's where our next disagreement comes in. Knowin' how strong you feel about the Maximilian government, you gonna hate me, even though you and Juárez seem to be good friends. I am the one who took your gun from your reticule."

Joan looked from her revolver to the horse, then, her eyes narrowed, she studied him—his eyes, his hair, his face, his build—then her look went back to the horse. "Why didn't I see it all along? Everything about the two of you is the same, and to top it off, the same attraction to him as I have for you—the *Bandido Caballero*."

"You mean the bandit was my competition? But Juárez is my friend, the one I did it all for." Blood rushed to his face. He pushed his hat to the back of his head. "Well, not exactly all for him; some of it was for a very nice friend back in Washington, D.C., and some for my country. You being a die-hard imperialist, I figured you'd be mad enough to spit."

Joan, a slight smile at the corners of her lips, said, "First off, ladies don't spit; second, I'm sure you've heard it's a woman's prerogative to change her mind; and third, I love that little Zapotec. He's been like a father to me ever since you so callously turned me over to his troops after your last robbery."

Fallon couldn't believe what he was hearing. But he still had to explain why he had not come to see how she was when he got back with Berne. "Joan, when I came through El Paso del Norte, and left Berne with *El Presidente,* I still had loose ends to tie together. I had to get Bienville and his crowd off American soil, and I had a friend, loyal to Juárez and me, who was sorely wounded in an Army hospital about a day's ride from Franklin. I went to check on him. I had to know in order to tell Juárez how he was. When I got back, Juárez's invitation to dinner arrived at my room, and in it he said you'd be there. I saw you as soon as I could." He stood back and studied her face. "Now you heard it all, you understand? You still mad at me?"

"Mad at you, Tom? I've never been mad at you. I was hurt, and since you'd seen me," she blushed, "well you know, without any clothes back there in the mountains, I-I thought you were so disappointed in what you saw that you didn't want me anymore."

"Didn't just want your body, woman, I wanted the whole of you, wanted to take you 'fore a parson, or priest, or whatever'll make us a man and wife, and get us married forever and ever."

"That's the second time you've brushed the subject of marrying me, Tom. I'm not going to wait for a third time before saying yes—you might change your mind."

She tried to say more, to tell him yes she'd marry him, but his lips kept getting in the way.

# JACK BALLAS ABOUT JACK BALLAS

I GREW UP IN A COUNTRY TOWN, PLAYED HIGH SCHOOL football, track and baseball, and was always around cattle, horses, woods, hunting, fishing, and the like. My love of the West started early in life.

About age eight, I read Arthurian novels, and then, to my mind, moved in a natural progression to Westerns. In those days one could buy a Western magazine for a dime. Those magazines were called pulp, but they had good stories.

The knights of old, knights of King Arthur's round table, had the same values as did the cowboy. Chivalry was not just a word to either of them—it was a way of life. They treated women with courtesy and respect, a trait my mother instilled in me from infancy, and to this day I believe women should be treated that way. That belief is reflected in all my books.

My desire to write started in high school, but for me high school wasn't enough. I went out into a world of no jobs, poor pay, and a deep depression. In early 1940 I realized war was imminent, and having been taught by both my father and mother that my country came second only to God and family, I went into the Navy. I still carried the dream of one day writing, but was ill equipped to do so, both from experience and education.

It was on an aircraft carrier in the Pacific during World War II that I learned about violence. I earned eleven battle stars while on that carrier, the USS *Bunker Hill*.

I learned about love from my mother, a strong woman, who showered her four children with all the caring and guidance a family could want. But I still wanted to write; not just to write, but to write Westerns.

While serving in a squadron in Japan, I learned of two professional writing professors at the University of Oklahoma who, it was said, could teach a tree stump to write. I figured I qualified. After retiring from the Navy, following twenty-two years' service, I attended O/U, and earned my degree in journalism, but didn't want to work for a newspaper. I went into industry and retired from there after eighteen years, after progressing into upper-middle management.

I take every opportunity to travel and explore the West. I study its towns, its people, its history, its vegetation, and its terrain.

The beauty of the West is in every direction, whether it's the badlands, or the sun setting across a desert or turning miles of waving short grass into a field of gold. The faint perfume of pines or spruce carried on the breeze is more stimulating than any made in Paris. Wildflowers painting a mountain meadow with their blanket of color, shimmering sunlight on a lake, or the sight and sound of streams falling down a mountainside, chuckling and whispering to the rocks and boulders as they pass by—all of these tie me tighter to the breast of my first love: the West.

Or visiting an Indian reservation, studying its people, and the way they live, or looking across miles of prairie to see snowcapped peaks in the distance, or coming upon a herd of buffalo, antelope, or deer—these are the things I see in the West. These are the things that tighten my heartstrings to the land and its people. When I write of a place, you can lay odds I've been there.

The men and women in my books are bigger than life.

It is said by many that the Wild West was a myth. Not so. In my opinion, any man or woman who would leave a comfortable home, a good job, load his or her family into a Conestoga wagon, and head into an unknown wilderness populated by savages and wild animals was a hero. Some of these people were good, some bad, and it was that mix that made the West what it was—a land embracing peoples of rollicking, lusty, sometimes brutal behavior, but a land to captivate the imagination of all mankind. Even today, the Western lands are not for the timid. The West is my land, its people my people. I wish to write of nothing else.

# ELLEN RECKNOR

## LEAVING MISSOURI

The story of a spirited young woman who shot a husband, travelled to Europe, befriended Frank James and Queen Victoria, and married a Duke. The amazing life story of Chrysanthemum "Clutie Mae" Chestnut, and one of the most memorable historical novels in years.

__0-425-15575-7/$5.99

# ME AND THE BOYS

Armed with a map showing where a fortune in gold is buried, Gini Kincaid sets out on an adventure across the West that will turn her from a girl of sixteen into a woman of legend. With a Bowie-sharp mind and a sweet taste for arson, she is possessed of a mouth that gets her in all manner of trouble, including becoming the target of a manhunt unlike anything seen in the Old West.

__0-515-11698-X/$5.99

AN EPIC NOVEL OF AMERICA IN THE MAKING

# CRIPPLE CREEK

●

They came from all across America, many of them recent
immigrants—all of them in pursuit of the same dream. They
came with their mining tools sharpened and their hopes
high. Working hard all day in the dangerous mines, they
were fired by thoughts of a brighter future. They left their
homes and families to find a land of opportunity of their
very own. Many paid a high price for following their
dreams. They found only hardship in the depths of the
mines—and greed and deception in the hearts of others.
But for a lucky few, the golden dream became a
sparkling reality...

●

## Douglas Hirt
__0-425-15850-0/$5.99